Praise for *Girl in the Moonlight*

"*Girl in the Moonlight*, Dubow's second novel after *Indiscretion*, is a sleek, brisk, Gatsby-esque tale. . . . It is beautiful and sad, hypnotic and tragic, and compulsive reading to the party's end when the cocktails run dry, and the 'good life' exposes its shimmering, self-absorbed flaws. But what an elegant and ebullient journey!"

—*Providence Journal*

"Seduces readers with a tantalizing, salacious tale. . . . Almost every page here is watermarked with love, lust, wealth, creativity, betrayal or heartbreak."

—*USA Today*

"*Girl in the Moonlight* is the story of one man's obsession with a woman who drifts in and out of his life. . . . Dubow cleverly pulls the readers into the affair and lets them feel Wylie's frustrations. . . . If you are a romantic, you will devour every page of this book. . . . You might not admire Cesca and her choices but you will remember her long after the pages of her story have ended."

—*Huffington Post*

"An enchanting tale dabbling in love, obsession, relationships, and beauty. . . . The perfect book to devour beachside."

—*Hamptons* magazine

"Dubow offers a heady, intoxicating tale. . . . A story of the most interesting people you will ever know, told with style and verve."

—*Kirkus Reviews*

"*Girl in the Moonlight* is an infinitely nuanced novel that is unpredictable in the best possible way."

—*Cape Codder*

"An evocative and maddening tale of obsession. . . . Beautifully descriptive. . . . Questions about whether a person can change, or if we are all doomed to repeat the same mistakes time and time again, will be swirling through readers' minds." —*Publishers Weekly*

"From Paris to Barcelona to New York, *Girl in the Moonlight* takes the reader on a whirlwind journey. . . . The story does not offer one big climax, but instead small explosions throughout, keeping the reader guessing from chapter to chapter. Dubow's second novel is a passionate story that explores the capacity of love—and its unyielding ability to control us."

—*BookPage*

"A page turner for avid readers of romantic novels."

—*Library Journal*

"Inspired. . . . [Dubow] evokes a mystical atmosphere around Cesca's mesmerizing power. . . . Wylie and Cesca see tempestuous years pass in struggling to define the magnetism they feel for one another, and readers will be spellbound by the process."

—Shelf Awareness

"This page-turner about a man's no-holds-barred obsession with a mysterious, seductive woman doesn't disappoint, and that's thanks in no small part to Charles Dubow's beautifully constructed prose, which we first fell in love with while reading his previous novel, *Indiscretion*. Equally enticing, this newly drummed up story of love, lust, and betrayal centers around the devious Cesca Bonet, who ensnares Wylie Rose into a heart-wrenching affair."

—Instyle.com

"Compelling. . . . From the very first page his sometimes spare, Hemingway-like prose invites the reader to settle in for an engaging tale."

—Joan Baum, WSHU, Public Radio Group

Praise for *Indiscretion* by Charles Dubow

"An homage to Gatsby—right down to its Nick Carraway-ish narrator—this is a suspenseful, diverting debut."

—*People*

"A lesson about extra-marital lust. . . . A riveting read."

—Daily Beast

"Smart, sensuous . . . delicious."

—*O, The Oprah Magazine*

"Dubow creates four richly drawn characters as fully formed, flesh-and-blood men and women. . . . His first work is a bright beacon."

—Bookreporter.com

ALSO BY CHARLES DUBOW

Indiscretion

GIRL IN THE MOONLIGHT

GIRL IN THE MOONLIGHT

CHARLES DUBOW

wm

WILLIAM MORROW
An Imprint of HarperCollins*Publishers*

GIRL IN THE MOONLIGHT. Copyright © 2015 by Charles Dubow. All rights reserved. Printed in the United States of America. No part of this book may be used or reproduced in any manner whatsoever without written permission except in the case of brief quotations embodied in critical articles and reviews. For information address HarperCollins Publishers, 195 Broadway, New York, NY 10007.

HarperCollins books may be purchased for educational, business, or sales promotional use. For information please e-mail the Special Markets Department at SPsales@harpercollins.com.

A hardcover edition of this book was published in 2015 by William Morrow, an imprint of HarperCollins Publishers.

FIRST WILLIAM MORROW PAPERBACK EDITION PUBLISHED 2016.

Designed by Jamie Lynn Kerner

Library of Congress Cataloging-in-Publication Data has been applied for.

ISBN 978-0-06-235833-2

16 17 18 19 20   OV/RRD   10 9 8 7 6 5 4 3 2 1

To the memory of loved ones I miss every day

To the Sirens first shalt thou come,
who beguile all men whosoever comes to
them. Whoso in ignorance draws near to
them and hears the Sirens' voice, he
nevermore returns . . .

—HOMER, *THE ODYSSEY*

GIRL IN THE MOONLIGHT

PROLOGUE

THE DIRT ROAD TO THE HOUSE HAD BEEN PAVED AND SHORT-ened. What was once in my childhood dense woods had been over the years sold to developers. Large, modern houses now sprawled over the lots until there was only a thin barrier of trees separating one from the next. I had camped out in these woods. Built forts, startled deer. That was before the area became fashionable and the land alone worth millions.

Our house was one of the oldest on the pond, built when the area was a separate summer colony and a round-trip by horse or wagon to the village of East Hampton would consume a whole morning or afternoon. That was long before my parents bought, in the early 1960s, back when my father was just starting out. A weekend house was more than he could afford on his law-yer's salary, but they had fallen in love with it, with its charm, its seclusion, and its views, and economized in other ways to make the mortgage. For the first few years there was almost no furniture. The house would echo with emptiness. It was a giant playground for me. I could ride my tricycle from room to room without worrying about hitting anything. Fortunately, the previous owners had left behind a few things, including a butcher-block dining table and bright yellow straight-back chairs, so my parents could at least have the occasional dinner party.

It was a beautiful old house. A traditional saltbox built on a massive scale, its shingles brown with age. In the back was a wide, screened porch that faced west toward the sunset over the pond, the scene of many pleasant evenings. Old wicker furniture. My father, clutching a glassful of bourbon, at his mellowest.

Now my father is dead, and the house is being sold. There were taxes. Also, it needed a new roof, central heating, a proper foundation. The costs would have been prohibitive. In the end it was easier to sell. The buyer had promised he wouldn't tear it down. The house had architectural significance, after all. This would be my last chance to see it.

I stopped the car by the brick path to the front door and stepped out. It was a cold November morning, and the drive out from Manhattan had taken only two hours. The grass was covered with damp leaves. No one was around to rake them up anymore. In the past we would have been getting ready for another Thanksgiving here. Fully extended, the dining room table could seat twenty, and most years it did. But that table was gone now, sold at auction, like so much of the other furniture.

This was not the first house that had vanished from my life. There had been an old family place in Maine, my parents' apartment in New York that went after the divorce, my grandparents' horse farm in Virginia—now all gone—but this house had been the one constant. It had been my home. I had spent every summer of my life here. Thanksgivings, Christmases. Had grown up within its walls, made the passage from boy to man. Had played touch football on the lawn, gotten drunk for the first time, made love, slammed doors in anger, slept uncountable nights.

A large, empty metal Dumpster sat ominously in the front yard. I walked past it down the slight decline to the rear of the house, crossing the wide back lawn and out to the large, brackish pond that stretched all the way to the ocean. At night, when everyone was in bed and the house was quiet, it was possible to hear the faint roar of the waves. I stepped carefully onto the old dock that extended over the bulrushes, the planks creaking beneath my feet. In certain spots the wood had already rotted away.

I always came here first. To the pond. The beauty of the view. The purity of it. The familiarity. Even now, years later, I can conjure it effortlessly. It would stay with me forever. The seamless melding of water to trees to sky.

In the distance a family of swans bobbed ornamentally on the slate gray water. The wind was raw. We sailed here from May to September, or even later, but the little boat, like so much else, had been sold.

I walked back up the hill around the other side of the house to where, under the rhododendron, I fished for the hidden key that was always hung on a nail. Unlocking the heavy oak front door, I pushed it open and stepped into the barren and dark front hall. The house was cold, the air slightly musty. There were a few last things left for me to sort through, to keep—or not. The rest would be thrown out. It was up to me. The kitchen counter had a cold cardboard coffee cup that must have been left by one of the contractors. It was next to an old, unplugged toaster and a final heating bill. The refrigerator stood open and dark, its shelves barren. The water had been turned off. There is nothing emptier than an empty house.

I wandered through the wainscoted dining room, the sitting room, and the downstairs bedrooms, opening closets and finding nothing except scattered mouse droppings. The second and third floors were just as barren. The books from the shelves that once lined the hallway had all been boxed up and dispersed. In my old room, a metal bed frame leaned against the wall. In the closet, there was a box of old tiles and several bare wire hangers on the rod. Nothing remained in my parents' former room. I could see in the worn carpet the indentations of where my father's chair had sat for decades. Disconnected phone jacks. A broken window shade.

My ultimate destination was the attic, where deeply recessed closets had been built under the roof for storage. I had been given one of these as a place to store my old belongings, things of sentimental value that could not fit in my New York apartment. Boxes from school and college. A few pieces of furniture. Suitcases of old clothes. A battered camp trunk full of letters and photographs. Bank statements from accounts long closed. An old paint box full of crumpled tubes of cadmium yellow, cobalt blue, and burnt sienna. A small bundle of brushes, held together by a rubber band, their handles smudged with long-dried color but their bristles still soft.

I carried the boxes and bags to the middle of the floor, creating two piles: what I would keep and what I would throw out. In one box, old comic books that would have been worth some money if I had taken care of them. In another, books of military history, which had been my prepubescent passion—along with painting model soldiers—and for which I saved up my allowance to buy in a tiny shop, long since closed, on Madison Avenue near the Seventy-Ninth Street bus stop. I flipped through one of them, recognizing the colorful plates of Napoleonic soldiers, the bearskins, the braids, that I once spent hours poring over. Still other boxes contained old cassettes, photographs, memories from schools and summer camps. Most of it would go in the Dumpster.

I had saved the rolls of canvases until last. At one time, I had been fond of some of them, even proud. Now, as I unrolled them, they struck me as obvious and unoriginal. There were some embarrassing Rose Period imitations. A few with intimations of Corot and even Hopper. Others aimed for Velázquez but failed. These I quickly moved to the discard pile.

In another roll were several portraits. These were better, less pretentious and more straightforward. There was nothing wrong exactly with my work. I had always been able to draw well. I could deftly capture the shape of an eye, the curve of a lip. But there was something lacking too. The special animation that turns lines on a page or brushstrokes on canvas into something magical. I had the skill but not the talent. That distinction is everything.

On top there were a few self-portraits revealing my younger self. It was a face I was still surprised not to see in the mirror every morning. The thick hair, the lean cheeks. It is the other way around now. There was one of my father, looking impatient at having to sit still for so long. A few nudes from class. Then came the ones that I wanted most to see. The first, Aurelio, with his long poet's face and dark eyes. I couldn't stop myself from noticing the imperfections in my brushwork, the faults in perspective, wishing I had the chance to do it again, to make it better. Not only had it been too long since I had held a brush but that golden moment in time had passed, never to be recaptured or reclaimed.

I looked at the portrait for several minutes, remembering when I had painted it. How old would he have been? Nineteen? Twenty? I had been even younger. The years slipped by. Whole lifetimes had been lived since then. The hum of summer outside his studio. The strong sunshine and the salt smell of Long Island Sound. I had taken my time while he, the better painter, struggled to relax, unaccustomed to being on the other side of the brush. "Let me draw you next," he had said, laughing. His teeth white with health and youth. A cigarette burning on the table next to where he sat.

I placed Aurelio's portrait to the other side, sure that I would keep it. There was only one painting left, the most important. I unrolled it, feeling the warmth of recognition. It was a full-length portrait of a recumbent woman, naked, beautiful, lit as if by moonlight.

Cesca.

Like her younger brother, she was dark, but where he was angular, almost ascetic, she was soft, sensual. Her eyes simultaneously playful and carnal. Both siblings possessed an otherworldly beauty, as though they were composed of a rare element, one not found on earth, something that usually burned up as it hit the atmosphere, and that, because of its rarity, made it even more precious.

The painting stirred many emotions in me, not the least envy. Because, unlike the other portraits, I hadn't painted this one. Aurelio had, a long time ago. But now it was mine. It was my most treasured, and dangerous, possession. Cesca had given it to me.

It had been years since I had last seen it. And now I was no less struck than when I had first beheld it. The perfect brushstrokes, the play of color and light. The quizzical smile that was both an invitation and a warning. It should have been hanging in a museum instead of hidden away in an attic.

Some women might have been embarrassed to see themselves depicted so lushly naked, but not Cesca. Her gaze was bold, unashamed. She was an artist's daughter, after all; had been posing since she was a baby. There had been depictions of her in her father's hand at various stages of life all over their house. Cesca as an infant in her mother's arms. Cesca as a skinny child. An oil of her on the verge of womanhood. Charcoals of her laughing, serious. The penumbra of her hair framing her face. Always her beauty staggering. For an artist to have such a daughter would have been a miracle of fortune.

"These are only the ones that Mare chooses to display," she told me once, referring to her mother. She pronounced it "MAH-ruh." It was the Catalan word for "mother." Her father was Pare. "There are hundreds more somewhere."

But I didn't have hundreds more. These canvases in the attic, like the last coins of a once-rich man, were all that remained. After them, there would be nothing. Nothing that tied me to a time and a place when I was a different person—younger, more idealistic, hungrier for love.

Life is filled with what-ifs, the roads not taken, the doors left unopened, the lovers left behind. Like Borges's forking paths, the choices are infinite. There is no map, no instruction manual. When we are very young the choices are made for us. This school, those friends. The world then is small, limited, and comparatively safe. That is how it should be. As we age, the opportunities multiply, but so do the dangers. Early stars burn out. Fortunes reverse. Many young men and women I had known, full of promise, fell by the wayside, victim to drugs, but also to indulgence, idleness, lack of direction, greed, arrogance. Not all though. Some went on to great success. Became CEOs, heads of foundations, Oscar winners, professors, even painters. Some merely rich. An old college friend of mine is now foreign minister of his country.

The tragedies are what stay with me. Did I have a knack for attracting the melancholy, the unfulfilled? The suicides, the defectives, the weak of will? One of the smartest, most talented youths I ever knew was a particular idol of mine when I was a teenager. I remember his speed on the football field, laughing as his powerful legs increased the distance between himself and his pursuers. Also, his brilliance. His eloquence. His blond good looks. He could have been anything. Unknown to me at the time his parents were undergoing a bitter divorce, the reverberations of which were shattering. He was kicked out of one school and then another. All his promise crashing to earth. There were drugs too. Cocaine. We lost touch. Today he is a yoga instructor on an ashram in Oregon.

I had made many choices, some good, most not, that had led me to this attic, weighing my past and bidding farewell to a house I loved but could not save. The years peeled away, and in my mind I was once again a teenager. Tall and slender. But even then nothing was simple. What if I had chosen differently? Would I be here at this moment? There are the dreams our parents have for us, and then there is the life we create for ourselves. It is impossible to know. The secret, they say, is not to regret— but that, I have found, is impossible. The most one can hope for is to forget. Memory, though, is a poor servant; it bursts in on you when you least expect it.

I didn't need anything physical to remind me of Cesca though. I find myself thinking about her every day, passing by a certain street corner where we once walked, hearing a song on the radio, imagining her face in the crowd, the figure that had just turned the corner. At night she is often in my dreams, always just out of reach, across a table, laughing, climbing a stair, disappearing into the next room, or on the verge of love, until something causes me to wake up unconsummated, aware of her continued absence in my life even if her memory was still with me every day.

I remember when I first met her. It changed my life.

1

IT HAD BEEN IN SUMMER. I WAS A CHILD OF TEN. WE HAD driven over in our old Ford station wagon. This was when my father was young, just starting out. Before the money, but he had the confidence that one day he would be rich. He would have been one of Bonaparte's lucky generals. Nothing had ever stopped him. My mother and I were going along with him when he went to play tennis with his old friend Roger Baum, whose family owned a large compound in Amagansett, complete with a clay court.

There I met four children, brothers and sisters. Their looks were dark, exotic. The eldest was Francesca, who was called Cesca, followed by Aurelio. They were both older than I; she by two years, he by one. Then the twins, Cosmo and Carmen, who were about my age.

At first I shyly stayed with my mother. She would have been in her early thirties then. Her long dark hair tied back by a bright kerchief, wearing the large oval sunglasses in fashion at that time. She was a great beauty, a daughter of the aristocracy. Her fingers long and elegant. In her voice a whisper of honeysuckle. She was christened Barbara but everyone called her Babes. Her maiden name was Wylie, which carried great weight in certain parts of Virginia, and which she had insisted on making my first name. My last name is Rose, which was shortened from something else when my father's parents emigrated from Russia. Against all odds—class, income, temperament—my father had won her. She was his great prize.

Who else would have been there? Roger's girl of the moment probably. His sister Kitty, who was the mother of the four siblings. Her married name was Bonet. A few others, but I can't remember. On the table bottles of Miller High Life. Gin and tonics. Everyone smoked. The rest of us watched Roger and my father, both in white. They were in the prime of life, competitive as only old friends can be. When they served there were loud grunts of effort, and mild oaths when a point was lost. The racquets were wooden, carried in presses. Roger had been playing his whole life, but my father was the more aggressive.

"Wylie, darling. Go and play with the other children," my mother said to me. They had already disappeared. I did as I was told, my steps slowing the farther I got from her, my courage ebbing. I did not make friends easily. My life had been a protected one. One spent reading. The majority of my adventures were fantasies dreamed up from the comfort of a couch. My mother was a great reader too. Nothing made her happier than curling up with a book. I had just started wearing glasses. When I played baseball, I was invariably sent to the outfield, where I could do the least harm.

I could hear the laughter of the Bonet children. They moved like a unit, a wolf pack. I was of no interest to them. With four, they had no need of other playmates. They lived in what they called the Playhouse, but it was a real house, one of several on the property. Their grandfather, Roger's father, I had been told, was enormously rich.

When I went inside I saw a kitchen. Stairs to a second floor. On the shelves unfamiliar toys and puzzles. Cartoon books in a foreign language. There was no television. I dared not touch anything. Outside, Aurelio, the taller of the boys, tried to be friendly. He explained the game to me.

"You have to climb up that rope, see? Then jump from the branch onto the roof. The trick is not to fall."

Nothing like it would have been invented now; the risks are too great. Parents were more accepting of fate in those days, less fearful and litigious. The children less coddled. Already I had heard about the son of one of my father's friends, only a year older than I, who had drowned in a sailing accident because he wasn't wearing a life jacket. Such calamities were accepted. One pushed on. These were people of the generation that remembered the war, knew fathers and brothers and husbands who never came home.

I watched as one of the girls, skinny as an acrobat, swarmed up the rope. She used only her hands, like a pirate. Then the leap and a smile. It was obviously dangerous. That was the thrill.

"Want to try?" she asked.

I nodded. There was no alternative but shame. I was a goose among swans, the unwelcome guest. I clutched the thick, knotted rope. Pushed up my glasses. I was never good at climbing. Four pairs of dark eyes watched me, suddenly aware. Waiting. It was an initiation of sorts. If I passed this test, there would be another, and another. It was a club I would never be allowed to join, but that had not yet been made clear to me, and I was too young and trusting to know otherwise. I tried to hoist myself up. It was impossible. I lacked the upper-body strength. I had no brothers or sisters, no one to compete against. One of the children laughed, but I pretended not to notice.

I tried again, and this time actually got a purchase on one of the thick knots and was able to reach up quickly with my other hand for the next knot. Jumping up, I closed my feet around the base of the rope. And then I hauled. The branch was barely ten feet off the ground, but it seemed as high as heaven, and as unattainable. Slowly, difficultly, I inched up the rope, nearly falling once or twice, my heart pounding, on the verge of tears, my soft palms burning, the insides of my knees raw. I dared not look down.

"Good, now grab the branch with one hand," said Aurelio. He had thick, longish black hair. The lean build of a soccer player. Kindly eyes. He was already my hero. I did as he instructed, feeling the rough bark under my hand. "Now the other," he said. "And swing yourself up." I did that too, badly scraping my arms and inner thighs, hugging the branch with my bare pink legs and hands. "Now stand up and walk toward the roof."

But I couldn't. I froze, unable to advance or retreat. I would never get down unless I fell.

"It's easy," called one of the girls. It was Cesca, the eldest. Like her siblings, she was dark-haired and barefoot. Fearless. Tanned, coltish legs, her knees covered in scabs. Dried calamine lotion on her ankle. It was easy to see they spent the summer outdoors. Like cats, they only came inside when it rained.

I stared at her. Even at that age everything about her seemed authentic. She was almost a teenager. On her slender frame her breasts just beginning to bud. It was clear she would be a great beauty. Already her parents' friends noticed it.

That was not how I saw her. To me, at that moment, she was already perfect, blinding. "Just grab one of the branches above you," she said. I looked up and saw a slender one above me in the canopy of green leaves. I reached for it. It was surprisingly resilient. Tentatively, I slid my feet down the limb toward the roof, the limb unsteady under my weight. I was doing it for her. I wanted to impress her with my bravery. Nothing else was important. But what seemed like a negligible distance from the ground now yawned before me. "You can do it!" she yelled. One of the children whistled. More laughter. I leapt.

Except, of course, I couldn't do it. I had misjudged the distance. Or did I have second thoughts at the last minute? I can't remember. It is all a blur. In any event, I fell to the earth, luckily missing the paving stones and only breaking my left arm. My howls of pain were unmanly, but I was no longer trying to show off for anyone. My mother appeared first, hysterical, which made me cry even louder. The men, who had finished playing tennis and were now sitting on the deck drinking beer, came next. My father picked me up, his shirt wet with perspiration, his forearms slick. "It's okay, champ," he said, as he placed me in the backseat of our station wagon next to my mother for the long drive to Southampton Hospital.

2

YEARS PASSED BEFORE I SAW CESCA OR ANY OF THE BONET children again. But that didn't mean I didn't think about them— and that my attention wasn't drawn to hearing about them.

Throughout my early adolescence, I dreamed of seeing Cesca again, eager to redeem myself. It was not Aurelio, Cosmo, or Carmen I wanted to impress. It was only Cesca. As I grew, I carried her image before me. I had no idea what she was really like, so I made her up in my head. She was not only the most beautiful girl in the world but the kindest, bravest, and smartest too. Everything I did, I did in the hope that she would find me worthy. When I did well on a test, when I scored a touchdown, I told myself it was for her. One day I hoped to make her love me. I don't know why I fixated on her, but I did. No one else had ever inspired these feelings in me. It was the purest kind of love, of course. That of a knight for his lady. It was the kind of love I read about. That was all I knew.

On the sporadic occasions when I heard my father men-tioning that he had dined with Roger or had been at a cocktail party where he had seen Cesca or one of the other children, I squirmed a little with remembered embarrassment. It wasn't just that I had fallen from the tree. It was more than that. That afternoon was my first inkling that there was more to the world than it appeared. Like the glimpse of a secret garden through a crack in the door, I discovered something I hadn't known was missing. Where colors were brighter, tastes stronger, feelings deeper. And once I recognized it, I wanted it, missed it—and was unsure I would ever find my way back to it. It was a land of Cockaigne, the hidden kingdom.

Such a moment is unequal, though. Like passing a beautiful woman in the street who doesn't register you: It is of no importance to her but might have changed your life forever. I was sure that Cesca and the others had forgotten me, or, if they did remember me, it was only as the kid who fell and broke his arm. Though I had met and already discarded details about numerous playmates and children of my parents' friends over my short life, I recalled all four of the Bonet children vividly. And in my dreams and youthful fantasizing, it was always Cesca's face that returned to me.

I admit that I invented scenarios, some absurd, that put us together. She would be drowning, and I would save her. Or maybe it was a fire. It didn't matter. In all my fantasies, I played the romantic lead, she the grateful maiden. But I was to be frustrated in my hopes of showing my bravery. I envied Tom Sawyer the chance to rescue Becky Thatcher, Perseus's winning of Andromeda.

Whenever my father casually suggested I accompany him to the Bonet house when he went to play tennis with Roger—by now I had learned to play—I eagerly grasped the opportunity, hoping each time that I would enter their world and Cesca would see me. But no matter what, I always seemed to be one or two steps behind.

Invariably Cesca was never there when I was. She and her siblings had already left by the time I arrived; gone to the beach, a party, or somewhere else that, I felt sure, was much more glamorous and fun. Even so, I was convinced that, in her wake, there were little bits of light, like the disappearing tail of a comet. Wherever she went was brightest, everywhere else dull by comparison.

Sometimes she hadn't been there at all. Every summer the Bonet children would spend a month in Spain with their father. They were a family to whom passports, other languages, knowledge of the world—all of which was unimaginable to me—were commonplace.

Disappointed, I would stay at the tennis court and play a few sets of doubles if a fourth was needed. Or I would sit there with a Coke or an iced tea, feeling like a passenger who had missed a connecting flight.

When no one was watching I would wander through the house, looking at photographs, piecing together my own version of history. Cesca aged five on a pony. Another one of her a few years later in a bathing suit, laughing in a translucent Caribbean surf. Aurelio on skis. The whole family with the Eiffel Tower in the background. On a sailboat, slightly older. I looked at all the photographs, but it was over Cesca's image that I lingered longest.

I couldn't bring myself to go upstairs where their rooms were, however. That would have been a violation, I knew. And what if I were caught? It would have been unpardonable. So, like a zoologist in the field, I contented myself with studying my subjects' natural habitat, inspecting empty nests and broken grass, while I waited for them to show up. I began to feel that I knew them even if they didn't know anything about me. And, of course, most of what I thought I knew turned out to be wrong.

What I did know was that they, like me, lived in the city and came out to Long Island on weekends and the summer. I had heard of their school, but it was not where I went. It was a school where, unlike mine, the boys didn't have to wear jackets and ties. They could wear pretty much anything they wanted. The girls too. This was an undreamed-of freedom. They lived in Greenwich Village. At that time, I had never been south of Fifty-Seventh Street. Downtown in those days was a different continent, exotic as Africa.

The New York of my childhood was almost feudal in character; neighborhoods were like fiefdoms, duchies. There was little exchange between them and often open hostilities. Even the language changed. When people ask me today where I am from, they often don't believe me, expecting all true New Yorkers to speak like the Dead End Kids. They aren't aware that my part of town also has a distinctive accent. The Upper East Side, where I lived, was the castle on the hill. For those defectors like Kitty, the Village was a rejection, a thumbing of the nose. A way to *épater le bourgeois*.

As with many bohemians, family money was funding the rebellion. Roger and Kitty's father, a self-made millionaire, had, in the time-honored fashion, fought his way from a tenement apartment on Eldridge Street to a town house off Park Avenue. Like many rich men who had been born poor, he spoiled his children, determined to give them everything that had been denied him. Servants, cars, piano lessons, and private schools. Trips abroad in the years before and after World War II. The *Queen Mary*. Claridge's, the Ritz. During the war it was Palm Beach, Yellowstone, and the Super Chief to Los Angeles. Roger, the only son, had gone to Harvard, where he met my father. Generous trust funds allowed Roger and Kitty to live as they liked and to marry whom they liked.

Roger, a ladies' man, married several times but never had a family of his own. Kitty married the painter Ugo Bonet. There was a younger sister, Dot, who never married.

Ugo was Spanish—or, to be more precise, Catalan. He and Kitty met at a party in Greenwich Village in the 1950s, when the Village was the center of the art world. Much more I learned later, when I no longer had to snoop. When it was all offered to me.

I didn't know Ugo then, of course, but I was told that, when he was young, he was very handsome. His children, who all greatly resembled him, adored him. He was effortlessly masculine in the way of Latin men. Tall and dark, coarse black hair. Rugged hands like a fisherman's. Cesca had the same hands; strong, capable. He was older than Kitty. After the war, he had lived in Paris. It was said that Peggy Guggenheim had fallen in love with him, offering to pay his way to New York. When Kitty met him, he had no money, which had never been a concern for him. He had always been able to find a woman who could give him a place to stay, something to eat. For a few days or a few months. It didn't matter to him.

When Kitty became pregnant, she insisted he marry her. His response was to disappear, only to be found several weeks later in Brooklyn by detectives hired by Kitty's father. They presented him with an ultimatum and he accepted the less unpleasant option. There were advantages to having a rich wife, after all. They were married in City Hall and then went to India on honeymoon. Several months after they returned, laden with Benares brass, Mughal miniatures, and rugs from the Kashmir, Cesca was born. She once said to me that the reason she found it so hard to settle down was that her mother traveled so much while she was pregnant with her.

Kitty's father bought them a town house on Perry Street and installed a studio for Ugo on the top floor. The other three children followed in rapid succession. But Ugo was not a man to be tied down. A brief trip he took home to Spain extended into nearly a year, the money Kitty kept sending him for his return passage inevitably being used to prolong his stay. When he returned, his children barely knew him. The first thing he did was paint them. The painting still hangs over their mantel. I have seen it many times. Kitty, a resentful Madonna with the twins in her arms, surrounded by the other two children, beautiful as angels.

His wanderings became a pattern. Ugo would disappear and reappear without warning, leaving an unfinished canvas on the easel. A cigarette burning by the sink where he washed his brushes. The phone would ring, and people—gallery owners, surprised women—would complain that they had an appointment with him, and he never showed. Europe, South America, New Mexico. Kitty knew it would do no good to hide his passport. Deny him money. He would find a way. Once, he worked his way to Morocco on a tramp steamer.

She endured his absences, daubed at the paintings she tried to make, opened her home to artists and writers, critics and choreographers. There were parties, lectures, buffet suppers. The rooms blue with smoke. Sometimes the sweet smell of marijuana. It was a time when everyone drank to excess. Bins full of empty bottles were hauled out to the curb the next morning by the maid. A critic for the *Voice* once fell down a flight of stairs, and to everyone's amazement got right up and staggered away into the night. It was obvious to most people that Kitty was not a great painter, but everyone agreed on her charm. She was sexy, long-legged, and busty. Her laugh was irresistible. As was her hospitality. She took lovers. Some of them Ugo's friends. Her children helped pour the drinks and clean the ashtrays. It was a better education than anything they could learn in school.

To the children their father was a wizard, a djinn who could fly over mountains. He would send them letters, lavishly illustrated, from his journeys. Poems in many languages. Packages wrapped in brown paper and clustered with exotic stamps would arrive from time to time, filled with strange candy, costumes, enormous seashells, or, once, the complete skeleton of a fruit bat. He could perform magic tricks, pulling cards or coins out of ears. He tore dollar bills into pieces and made them whole again. Read the children's futures in coffee stains, promising them all long, happy lives and prophesying fame and fortune. When he was home, they knew to leave him alone while he worked. The door to his studio was closed. But when he emerged, he took them for long, rambling walks down to the docks, where he would converse with sailors and stevedores in one of the languages he spoke. They were never sure how many. Was it four or five? Did dialects count?

They would sit quietly by his side while he drank with friends in bars or visited other painters' ateliers. The afternoon sunlight slanting through the window. The children doodling on napkins, talking quietly among themselves. Their bond unbreakable. Everywhere they went it was obvious that people were happy to see him. And because they were his children, people were happy to see them too.

Occasionally, he would take Kitty's car and drive them out of the city even though he didn't possess a license. To the beach, to the markets along Arthur Avenue, to find baby goat to roast in the backyard, to fish for striped bass along the Hudson. Some days it would get too late, and they wound up spending the night, sleeping in the car if they didn't have enough money for a hotel. He was a terrible driver. The kind who gesticulated with his hands and looked at his passengers to make a point or tell a story. Everyone agreed it was a miracle he never killed himself or anyone else. Once he forgot to put gas in the car, and they all had to return to the city in the back of a milk truck.

Ugo was also a cook. Kitty, like many rich girls, was not good in the kitchen, nor did she care about food. An old black woman named Mamie came in every day to clean and cook for the children. Fried chicken, stew, spaghetti, lamb chops. When Mamie wasn't there, Kitty would burn TV dinners for the children. But their father created marvelous meals. Traditional fish stew, of course, but also whole cod with raisins and pine nuts, *fricandó*, a kind of pizza called *coques*, loin of pork that melted in the mouth, tuna *escabèche*. Telling them the names for the food first in English, then in Spanish, and last in Catalan, so it would stay with them. "This is *esqueixada de bacallà*, this is *escudella*." While drinking wine, he would sing and tell jokes. He taught the children how to chop garlic, how to tell when snails were cooked, how to look at a fish's eye to know if it was fresh. He had deals with the butcher, the fishmonger, the grocer, the liquor store owner. He would trade drawings for food and drink, flirt with the waitresses and the shopkeepers' wives. Kitty would press money on him, but he would only pocket it, preferring to barter. So many fish for a drawing of such a size, so many bottles of wine for a painting. It was an inexact but virtuous math.

Unsurprisingly, the marriage didn't last. Kitty and Ugo were divorced in the early 1970s, although life carried on much as it had before given Ugo's long absences. They remained friends. He would still return to his wife's houses, still cook for his children, even occasionally still make love to his now ex-wife, assuming her latest boyfriend didn't object too strenuously, and he would still depart without warning.

BEFORE THE DIVORCE, EVERY SUMMER FOR FIVE OR SIX years when the children were very young they would all accompany Ugo back home to Catalonia, to the village on the Ebro where he had been born and where he still had much family. There he would be welcomed like a returning celebrity, bringing presents of duty-free whisky and American cigarettes bought with Kitty's money. Donkeys and chickens wandered in the yard, where lunch was eaten outside underneath an arbor, the scent of lemon trees perfumed the air. The tables were rough, wooden. Cesca and Carmen, as girls, helped to cook and serve while the men sat and joked and played *botifarra*, Kitty insisting on sitting with them.

There were always picnics, expeditions to the ruins of a nearby castle sacked during the Peninsular War, and fishing trips for mackerel and bonito. Later, they would spend a few days in Barcelona. A visit to a favorite restaurant, where one of Ugo's paintings hung on the wall. A tour of the galleries. Gaudí's Sagrada Familia. Drinks along the Ramblas. Once, a bullfight, but never again because it made Aurelio throw up, and Kitty forbade it. Late nights with the children in tow, Carmen asleep on Cesca's lap in a nightclub while their parents danced.

Ugo knew people everywhere. Once he led them up in the hills above Nice to visit friends who owned a restaurant in Saint Paul-de-Vence where another of his paintings hung next to a Léger. Trips to Paris, where they would stay with other friends of his who lived in the Marais. Another time they visited London, where he took them to the Tate to look at the Turners. Many trips to the Prado, the Louvre, the Uffizi. They all agreed Spanish painters were the best, followed by the Italians. Miró, also a Catalan, was the greatest of them all.

Every winter Kitty took the children skiing in Gstaad while Ugo, who did not ski and had no interest in learning, remained in the house on Perry Street to paint. He continued to use the studio even after the marriage was over. It was a relationship that may have puzzled other people in a similar situation, but there was very little that was conventional about any of their lives. They enjoyed the kind of freedom that only the very rich, very creative, or very selfish can ever know.

3

AFTER THE DIVORCE UGO CONTINUED TO TAKE HIS CHIL-
dren on trips, but, as they were growing older, he took only one at
a time. Cesca went first because she was the eldest. She was fifteen
but looked older, ripe for experience. She had an irresistible face,
a rock against which ships would be dashed, drowning all who
came too close.

Ugo took her to the Costa Brava. It was summer. They stayed
for a month with a woman he knew who had a villa overlooking
the bay in Cadaqués. The woman was one of his many lovers.
Cesca could hear them behind the door, where they often slept
in past noon.

She was free to wander about the town. Exploring Cap de
Creus and its rock pools, walking to the lighthouse, watching
the hippies who congregated along the waterfront. She wanted
to meet Dalí at his home in Port Lligat, but he was never there.
Every morning she fetched the bread and in the evening wine
from the local shops, often eating alone. After breakfast she
took her scooter to the beach and spread her towel out over the

smooth white pebbles and lay in her bikini in the sun. Her skin became the color of caramel, darker. In her bag she carried a bottle of water, money, a copy of Rodoreda's *The Time of the Doves*, and a pack of cigarettes.

Staring out at the water, she became aware of a group of local teenagers, a little older than she, that she had seen before. She sat there and lit a cigarette—she had recently started smoking—and tried not to notice them, pretending to read. Their presence, their camaraderie, underscored her solitude. Like all teenagers, she craved the reassuring company of her peers, was afraid of being singled out or laughed at. She missed her brothers and sister. With them she never felt lonely. She wondered where they were. Did they miss her too? She worried about Aurelio. He was allergic to bees. Sometimes he would invite complete strangers back to the house for dinner. Last year a young man had come home from the beach with Aurelio and ended up stealing a string of Kitty's pearls.

There were other concerns. Would Cosmo be nice to Carmen? Who was looking after them, without her there? In Amagansett they ran wild. Her mother would never be able to keep up with them. It was Cesca who made them breakfast most mornings or cooked pasta with butter and Kraft Parmesan cheese for lunch. What if Aurelio attempted to hitchhike to Montauk again? He had tried last summer. He was thirteen then. They had all taken the Volvo and gone searching for him, but he had only gotten as far as Hither Hills State Park. They found him walking by the side of the road, thumb trailing. Instead of punishing him, their mother kept on driving until they reached the lighthouse, now a state park, the farthest point east in the United States. Aurelio loved it, loved that the next landfall was Ireland, somewhere so far he couldn't even see it but somehow knowing it was there. Then Kitty took them for hamburgers at the park's cafeteria. There was a commotion at the cash register because she only had hundred-dollar bills. There was no reason Aurelio wouldn't try again.

Cesca had never been away from them for this long before. She heard laughter and looked over at the other teenagers. One of them had a transistor radio. They were playing in the surf. At school in New York she was popular and had many friends. Already there were parties, boys. She had been kissed. The older brother of one of her friends, home from college, had put his hand under her shirt. Down her pants. But that was as far as she would let him go.

She surveyed her knees, her legs, her trim stomach, where her thighs joined her body, at the scraps of material covering her breasts, her loins, thinking how flimsy they seemed, how little effort would be required to push them aside, to defile her; it would be like defending yourself with tissue paper.

One of the boys came up to her.

"Who are you?" he asked in Spanish. "I thought I knew all the pretty girls who lived around here."

She had seen him before. He was the one she would have picked. Bold. Tall, dark-haired, calf-eyed. Seventeen, maybe eighteen. A thin gold chain around his neck, a broad, taut chest.

"I am from America. We are staying there," she replied with a smile, pointing up in the direction of the villa where her father and his mistress Teresa lay in bed. Her Spanish was as perfect as her Catalan, and she even knew some of the local dialect.

He raised his eyebrows, impressed. "From where in America?"

"New York City."

"Ah. You must be very rich."

"My father is Catalan. From Amposta."

"I know it. I like here better."

"I wouldn't know," she replied. "I have not been here long enough."

"What do you think of it?"

"It is very beautiful."

"But not as big as New York, eh? Maybe one day I will go there." He smiled. "Maybe you will invite me?"

She smiled back. "Why would I do that? I don't know you."

"But I would like to know you."

"I don't think so. Anyway, I have to get home now. My father will be waiting."

He nodded his head. "I understand. Maybe I will see you again?"

"Maybe."

"Maybe you will let me show you around? I know some special places. Places tourists don't know about."

"Maybe."

"Say yes. Come tomorrow. At eleven. I will take you on my scooter."

She said nothing but could already feel his hands on her. Having dinner with her father and Teresa that night, she could think of nothing but the boy. Every time she convinced herself that she would not go she changed her mind.

"How was your day?" asked her father, dipping his bread in the soup. The hair on his head and deeply tanned chest was shot with gray. He was still handsome but no longer as thin as he had once been.

"Fine."

"Did you do anything?"

"Not really. I went to the beach as usual."

"I am sorry there are no friends here for you. Have you met anyone?"

"No."

He nodded. "Are you having a bad time? I am sorry if I have not been able to see more of you. Maybe tomorrow we'll go for a drive, mmh? Go up into the hills. Teresa, what do you say? Shall we make a picnic of it?"

"Yes, of course," answered Teresa. "I know just the spot." She was a handsome blonde in her forties with a voluptuous figure.

"Excellent! What do you say, *nuvi*?" he asked, using the pet name he had always called Cesca, the Catalan for sweetheart.

Cesca stared down at her plate, resigned, her stomach sinking. It would be easier this way, taking the decision out of her hands. It was fate, a sign. God did not want her to see the boy tomorrow. This made her want to go all the more. She knew if the boy appeared at the door at that moment, she would run away with him, become his slave.

"Yes, fine, Pare," she said.

She hated the thought of sitting in the back of the car like a child while she watched Teresa in the front with her father, laughing at his jokes. The thought that she would never see the boy again. Standing up, she reached for her father's bowl and stacked it in hers. Then Teresa's. Her father was already smoking. Teresa had given him a gold lighter. A Dunhill engraved with his initials. Her first husband had lost millions to her in the divorce. Cesca walked into the kitchen and washed the bowls and utensils in the sink and placed them in the drying rack by the window. It was dark. The stars shone, their light reflected in the sea.

"We're going out," called her father. In Cadaqués the night didn't start until after ten o'clock. There were discotheques and bars crammed with wealthy visitors from Barcelona who owned homes nearby. French and British tourists taking advantage of the exchange rate. There were few Americans. Teresa liked to dance. They would be home around four and stay in bed past noon.

Outside, the car door slammed, and Cesca heard the crunch of tires on the driveway. She finished cleaning up and then went back out to the terrace overlooking the bay and lit a cigarette. Most nights she would just get in bed and read until she fell asleep. But not tonight. There was some wine left, and she filled a glass and drank it. The bottle was empty so she opened up another. She did not drink often. She had friends who did, boys who would sneak vodka into parties. Some of the kids also smoked pot. She had tried it a few times and liked it. Tonight she needed to get a little drunk and try to forget the boy. She poured first one glass of wine and then another. The ends of cigarettes piled up in the ashtray. For the first time she was glad her brothers or sister were not there. They would have told her she was being silly and that was not what she wanted to hear.

There was only one thing to do. Tipsy now but feeling sure of herself, she went up to her room and changed, slipping off her jeans and T-shirt and putting on a halter top and short skirt. It was an outfit she had been saving for a special occasion. She added some mascara to her eyes and a swipe of red lipstick. A few dabs of the Shalimar she had stolen from her mother before leaving. More wine, more courage. She looked at herself in the mirror, liking what she saw. The long legs, the bare shoulders and midriff, the lift of her breasts. It was the person she wanted to be. Someone older, more experienced. Herself in five years.

She grabbed money and cigarettes and threw them in her bag, then ran down to her scooter. There was no stopping now. No time for second thoughts. The lights of the town were twinkling ahead as she negotiated her way down the hill and through the narrow back streets until she came to the waterfront. On the beach there were overturned fishing boats, their nets drying in the night air. There were a number of brightly lit cafés along the quay with plastic chairs and tables spilling out over the paving stones. Every café was crowded. Umbrellas were emblazoned with logos: Anis del Toro. Heineken. Carlsberg. The languages of Catalonia, Spain, Germany, Britain. Busy waiters in white shirts and black pants. This was the high season. In a few months the same streets would be nearly empty.

Cesca parked her scooter and walked by several cafés, the sea to her back. Men started whistling at her. Women usually did not travel alone at night. It was important to keep moving. *What was she doing?* she asked herself, her nerve deserting her now. What would she do if she saw him? It was unlikely he would even be here. There were dozens of cafés all over the town, assuming he was even out. He might even be with another girl. He and his friends would all laugh at her. She would look like a fool. The only thing to do was go back to the villa before it was too late.

But that's not what happened. The boy was there. As if by magic, he was standing in the square with friends, illuminated by the light from a café. He was wearing tight black pants and a reddish shirt. He was laughing, taller than the others, slim-hipped like a dancer. Even better-looking than she remembered. But she couldn't bring herself to move. If he looked in her direction, he would see her, but he did not. Like an actor with stage fright, she stepped out of the light.

A hand grabbed her from behind. "Where you going, cutie?" asked a voice. She could smell garlic and wine and body odor. She turned and saw a crude-looking middle-aged man with a mustache and thick hair leering at her. His hand was now on her breast.

"Leave me alone!" she screamed in English, knocking the man's hands away. She ran out of the shadows toward the boy and his friends. There was no other choice.

The boy saw her.

"You! What are you doing here?" he asked.

"That man," she said, pointing, finding her Spanish again. The man had followed her.

"Pau," said the boy, laughing. "The girl is with me."

The man grinned, showing dirty teeth. "Then the *puteta* should have said so. She better watch her cute little ass."

When the man was gone, the boy said to her, "He's right, you know. It's not a good idea for a pretty girl to wander around at night by herself. What are you doing here, anyway?"

She could not look him in the eye. "I was coming to find you. I had to tell you something."

"Tell me something? What?"

"That I wouldn't be able to meet you tomorrow. My father surprised me with plans for a picnic. I didn't want you to think I didn't want to come."

He nodded his head. His friends had melted away. "Come with me," he said. "I want to show you something."

He led her to his scooter and helped her on. He stepped on and kicked it to life. She clasped her hands over his hard, flat belly. In silence, they drove out of town, along the coast. She rested his cheek against his shoulder blade, feeling the thin layer of muscle, smelling him, the mixture of sweat and scent.

"This is where I was going to bring you tomorrow," he said when they stopped. It was a little cove, quiet, moonlit. The beach was sand and not the usual pebbles. "We don't want the tourists to know about it."

He smiled at her, white teeth visible even in the darkness. It was a nice smile, she decided. She hadn't been wrong. It was time. Something she had been waiting for all her life but hadn't realized until now. She stood still while he embraced her, pressing his lips to hers. It felt good to her. He was confident, a little rough. His breath tasted faintly of peppermint and tobacco.

It was obvious she was not his first. She grabbed his arms, encouraging him. She could feel him hardening, and for a moment it frightened her, but in a good way, like the way she felt before diving off from a high board or skiing down a black diamond run. It was the precipice, the line in the sand. The Greeks had a word for it: *kairos*, the supreme moment.

He lowered her onto the ground and slipped off her underwear. She willed him on, saying nothing, closing her eyes, kissing him, waiting for the unexpected, the unknown, hoping it would not be painful, would not disappoint, gasping silently when he entered her, and then relaxing.

He was neither fast nor slow. He was liquid. Strong. The stars above his head became a blur, and she felt the turning of the world, the motion of the planets. She ignored the bite of the grit and pebbles beneath her back and held him tighter, trying to inflict on him the same pain. And when he sped up, she joined him, matching him thrust for thrust until they both collapsed, crying out into the night.

Days of love followed. The boy's name was Andreu. He was entering university in the fall to study pharmacy. She could not keep her hands off him. It was a physical need; she craved him. His touch, his smell, the way the black hairs curled down from his navel. They did it everywhere. At night against a wall in one of Cadaqués's narrow *rastells*. In the water. In the bathroom of the café his parents owned and where he worked as a waiter.

She did not tell him how old she was. It would not have mattered. But she lied to enhance herself. She was also entering college. Oh yes, where? Harvard, of course. The most famous. His friends welcomed her. She was exotic to them, glamorous. They admired her blue jeans. *"Explica'ns sobre Nova York."* Tell us about New York, they would ask. Were the buildings really that tall? Was everyone rich? Had she met many movie stars? She had met Paul Newman once at a film opening with her mother. He was shorter than she had imagined. Yes, his eyes were incredible.

She invited Andreu to the villa. Her father welcomed him. He had an artist's indifference. The boy was nervous at first but then relaxed. After dinner, when Ugo and Teresa went out, Cesca took Andreu upstairs to her room. It was their first time on a bed. The first time they had been completely naked in the light together. The whiteness of her skin where it had been covered by her bathing suit. His tongue between her legs. Everything slowed down. She could inspect every inch of his body. There was no fear of being caught. The world did not exist beyond the door. There was a thin scar on his thigh she had never seen before. The beauty of him. She took him in her mouth. It was the first time for that too.

She had aged years in the few days since he had first possessed her. That night, Andreu slept in her bed. In the morning, Ugo did not chase him out of the house with a shotgun, as Andreu's own father would have done if he had found a boy in bed with Andreu's sister. Instead he made him coffee, and the two chatted about FC Barcelona.

On the day she was to leave, Cesca told her father that she wanted to stay. "Oh," he replied, "and what will you do for money? Where will you live? And what about school?"

"I will live with Andreu. I don't need to go to school."

Ugo laughed and kissed his daughter. "You are still so young, *nuvi*. I won't stop you from staying, but I wouldn't recommend it. And have you discussed this with Andreu?"

"Yes." She blushed. They had talked about the future like children—in bed, where the most impossible dreams are made—as though it were something far away. "He thinks it is crazy," she said.

"Ah, well. In that case, he is no fool."

"I don't care. I love him and he loves me," she said.

She had imagined them living together in a small flat in Barcelona. The walls painted white. She would do the washing, cook him dinners, help him with his studies. In the evenings they would make love.

"Has he said so?"

She stared at her father for a moment, the loser of a hopeless argument. Love was an ocean, too vast to cross.

"No," she confessed in a small voice.

"No, I didn't think so. Do me a favor, *nuvi*. Go back to New York. If you still feel this way about the boy in a year then you can come back. But the heart of a young girl is not only deeply impressionable, it is also incredibly adaptable. I know you want love, and you will have it," he said. "With any luck you will fall in love many times before you decide to settle on one man, if you ever do."

She stood, her eyes filled with tears, but said nothing. "Thank you, Pare," she said.

He was very proud of her. She had strengths unimaginable to him. When he went to knock on her door to tell her the car was waiting, she was packed and ready.

"Have you said good-bye to him?" her father asked.

She shook her head.

"Do you want to?"

Again she shook her head. "If I do, I'll cry."

He took her hand gently. "Come," he said. "We can drive by the café. He is working today, no? We have time."

The car took them to the café. He was there, carrying a tray. There was a table of pretty girls. He was flirting with them. Already a single man again.

"Do you want to get out?" her father asked.

"No."

"Come here, *nuvi*," he said, reaching his arm out for her. "You have much to learn still, you who have already learned so much."

Back in her room in New York several days later, she was

relieved when her period came. The blood on her underwear reassured her. Around Christmastime she wrote to Andreu at the restaurant. It was a dishonest letter. There was no Harvard. None of what she wrote was true.

A letter came back a month later. She had never seen his handwriting before. Large cursive letters spelling ESTADO UNIDOS below her name and address. The flimsy blue envelope covered in stamps. In it he wrote that he was well and working hard at his studies. Would she be back next year? He joked that maybe he would still come to New York.

She never wrote back. By then she was dating other boys, a senior at Dalton whose father was a prominent art dealer in Manhattan. A premed student at Yale who drove down to see her on weekends. A guitarist in a rock band. Already she was sneaking into nightclubs. Older men were buying her drinks. She had the beauty and confidence of someone more sophisticated. She slept with whom she chose. Her doctor had put her on the pill. In March her mother took her skiing in Gstaad for her sixteenth birthday. Cosmo and Carmen came too. Aurelio was sick and had to stay home with a hired nurse.

The next summer, instead of returning to Cadaqués, she went to Los Angeles to work for the father of a friend who was a film producer. She even had a screen test. There is a copy. I have seen it. The camera adored her. If she had wanted, she could have been a film star. She could have been anything.

4

IT WAS NOT UNTIL CESCA WAS EIGHTEEN AND I WAS SIXTEEN that I finally saw her again. The occasion was a big party for her grandfather Izzy's eightieth birthday. It was to be at the compound. It was the middle of July, and I was home from my second year at boarding school, a lonely place in New Hampshire that my mother's father and grandfather had also attended. I had now grown. Lost the baby fat. Become tall. The jamb in our kitchen a record of my rapid evolution. Stand still, my mother would say, holding a ruler over my head.

It was my secret hope that Cesca would be at the party. Ever since my father had informed me that I was invited—family members were welcome—it was all I thought about. If she would be anywhere that night, I reasoned, it would be there. After all, it was her grandfather's birthday, a milestone event. What could be more important than that?

But I had been disappointed in the past. It was possible she might not be there. A previous commitment, something unavoidable. Maybe even an unforeseen delay? There was a storm over the ocean, the flight was canceled. It was impossible to anticipate such an eventuality.

And if she were there, then what? What would I say? What would I do? I was not only younger than she was but also a stranger. It had been six years since I had seen her. And what would I say to her if I even got the chance? Good evening, you probably don't remember me but I've had a crush on you ever since I fell out of your tree years ago.

I had a job that summer, my first, working as a carpenter's assistant, helping to build houses for new millionaires on former potato fields in Sagaponack. My father had insisted on it. He had worked during the summers and believed it would be good for me too. To teach me a strong work ethic, the value of exchanging labor for money. He didn't want me to be like many of my friends, who spent their summers at the beach or playing tennis at the club.

Work started at six every morning, fueled by hot coffee and rolls slathered with peanut butter and butter from the deli near the train station, its parking lot filled with idling pickup trucks. Quitting time was three. I was living in an old barn on our property that had been converted into a pool house. After work I would come home and go for a long run or a swim, cook dinner for myself, and most nights be asleep by nine.

In the weeks leading up to the party I had thought of little else. Some days I believed it would be better if I didn't go to the party at all. Other days I knew I had to be brave, to seize the moment regardless of the outcome. A faint heart never won the fair maid, my mother had always told me. And of course I had no real idea what Cesca was like. I had only a memory and my imagination.

But there was also much truth in my conception. Through my father I had heard vague reports about Cesca over the years.

He was plainly impressed by her, the way he would be by the child of a friend who was a star quarterback or a valedictorian. He would shake his head and laugh about seeing her play tennis or the cluster of boys hanging around the house, each one hoping he'd be the one she chose. He'd never seen anything like it, my father said admiringly and maybe even a bit wistfully, part of him wished he was eighteen years old again.

My father was very fond of Izzy, who he said was still remarkably hardy; despite his age the old man walked the forty blocks to his office and back every day, enjoyed fine wines and an after-dinner cigar. Much of my father's early success was thanks to Izzy's encouragement.

The evening of the party was perfect; the humidity was low and there was a cooling breeze coming off the bay. Guests were invited for five in the afternoon. There was a band dressed in white dinner jackets, mountains of oysters and shrimp, cases of champagne. Later the Gruccis would put on a fireworks display over the water. My father wore a new linen suit. A pale green tie. Sideburns in the fashion of the time. He looked surprisingly debonair.

He had insisted I wear a blazer and tie, to show respect to Izzy and his family. On the drive there, I was mute with anticipation. Even opening the car door was an effort. I was nervous but eager, like a skydiver on his first jump, one leg dangling in space, the other safe inside the fuselage. There was only one way down.

The driveway was lined with cars. Young valets with longish hair and red polyester vests took keys and handed out tickets. The party was on the wide green lawn overlooking the sound. Tables with white cloths and chairs had been set up. White balloons. Flowers. Hundreds of people were already there. Many of them quite elderly. As soon as we arrived, my father saw someone he knew and waved at them.

"I'll be right back," he said. My mother rolled her eyes. He was already gone.

"Honestly," she said. "Let's find the bar, shall we, darling?"

It was my job to order for my mother. She had an abhorrence of ordering her own drink. She would rather die of thirst than do so. I brought her vodka and water, and we inspected the crowd from one of the tables. I couldn't leave her now.

"Babes, darling!" We turned around to see Roger approaching, his smile wide in welcome. He was beautifully dressed, as always. A silk handkerchief jutting elegantly from the breast pocket of his blazer. White Gucci loafers. "How are you? Is Mitch here?" he asked, referring to my father.

"Roger," she said, accepting his quick kisses on each cheek, a maneuver she found affected. "Mitch deserted us as soon as we arrived."

"Lucky me, then." Roger winked. "I get you all to myself." Then, as if noticing me for the first time, he said, "Wylie. Good to see you. What a beautiful boy."

He had a way of shaking men's hands with his right and feeling their biceps with his left. He couldn't keep his hands off people. It was part of his charm. He always acted as though he hadn't seen you for a while, even if you had only seen him the day before. It was not unlike a Labrador retriever I owned later in life: I would only step out of the room for a little while, but when I came back he was, tail wagging furiously, beside himself with joy. The only exception was that Roger behaved that way with everyone. "Oh, you're getting strong, young man."

"Thank you, Uncle Rog."

"Wylie's been rowing crew," my mother said.

"Rowing crew? Have you now? Excellent."

I nodded.

Roger kept his gaze on me and said, "You know, there are a bunch of other young people here. Kitty's kids and some of their friends. By the pool. You don't want to hang around with the old farts. Why don't you wander over?"

"That's a fine idea, Roger," my mother said. "Wylie, darling, I'm sure you can make some friends. I'll come find you before we leave."

"Great." Roger grinned, patting me on the cheek. "They'll love you."

I walked in the general direction Roger had indicated. Despite my height, I am a naturally shy person. Large crowds, strangers intimidate me. But if Cesca was anywhere she would most likely be here. There were a dozen or so young people around the pool, all wearing bathing suits. Some were in the water, others lounging nearby on the grass or on chaises. There was lots of laughter, and rock music coming from within the house. This was clearly a party within the party. In the way young people can, I immediately sensed that most of them were older than me.

I walked past one of the chaises, on which reclined a handsome youth, naked to the waist, long brown hair to his shoulders, lithely muscled. His tan legs were sprawled out in front of him and he was drinking a beer. Leaning against him was a girl in a blue-and-white checked bikini. Her wet, blond hair spilling down her back. They ignored me.

Standing out uncomfortably in my blazer and tie, I looked for a recognizable face. A deeply tan girl with long dark hair moved away from a group and came up to me, smiling. It was obvious she was a child of the family. But she was not Cesca. I assumed it was Carmen. "Hi," she said. "Can I help you?" She would be just as friendly to a deliveryman who had lost his way.

"I'm Wylie Rose," I said. "I was told to come over here."

Her looks were striking, and it was easy to imagine men falling in love with her. We were the same age but she seemed older.

As though she had already done and seen things that I could only imagine.

She laughed. "You're Mitch's son, right?"

I nodded. I couldn't help being struck that someone my age would refer to my father like that.

She looked around. Having placed me now, she was losing interest. "Aurelio," she called. Then something in what I took to be Spanish, although later I learned was Catalan. In either case, I wouldn't have understood. The only foreign language I had studied by that point was French.

A tall boy turned around. He was taller than me, with glossy black hair and an aquiline nose. I remembered him from years before. He was now almost a man. He had been kind to me then, friendly. Around his slender hips he was wearing only a pair of cutoffs that were smeared with dried paint. He walked over. "Hello," he said. His teeth white. There was a melancholy about his eyes despite his friendly smile.

"Lio, this is Mitchell Rose's son."

"Wylie," I reminded her.

"Wylie. Hello. How are you?" he said. Then, "Have we met before?"

I hesitated. "Yes, a long time ago. When I was a kid." I paused again. "I fell out of your tree and broke my arm."

He laughed. "That was you! Now I remember. I always wondered what had happened to you. I was afraid we had scared you off."

I grinned, trying to conceal my shame. "No."

"That must have hurt."

"A little."

His eyes revealed genuine concern. He was not making fun of me, as I had feared. "You're welcome to join us," he said.

"Thank you."

"Aren't you hot in that jacket and tie?"

"Yes."

"Well then, take them off. Make yourself comfortable. Come on, let me introduce you to some people. That was my sister Carmen," he said. As I removed my jacket and loosened my tie, he escorted me to a picnic table at which sat another young man, not as tall as Aurelio but equally handsome. The face more powerful, the shoulders bulkier. Around his neck a string of coral shells. There was a guitar in his lap; several girls surrounded him.

"Cosmo," said Aurelio. "This is Wylie. He's Mitchell Rose's son."

Cosmo did not get up but only lifted his chin in greeting, impossibly cool. "You're the one who fell out of the tree, right?" To the girls he said, "This guy is the son of one of my uncle's best friends. You see that tree, there?" He pointed. The rope was still in place. The tree didn't look as tall as I had remembered. If I stretched out my arms above my head, I could probably touch the branch. "A long time ago we dared him to climb up the rope and jump onto the roof. It was a game we played all the time. I must have probably done it fifty times. He was the only one to ever break his arm." He laughed, and the girls did as well. "It's good to see you again, man."

I said nothing. As I had feared, I was quickly becoming the "guy who fell out of the tree."

"Let's go inside," suggested Aurelio. "I think Cesca's there." At the mention of her name, I had to suppress a surge of panic and doubt. This was what I feared and wanted most.

"Bring me back a beer," said Cosmo, strumming his guitar.

"Get your own beer," laughed Aurelio.

Anxiously, I followed him up a short flight of stairs to a deck and then through an open sliding glass door into a living room. "Cesca?" called Aurelio. *"Ets aquí?"* The living room was empty, the toys and Spanish cartoons long gone. Instead, now there were empty beer bottles on the table and rolling papers. On the walls concert posters. Pink Floyd. Bowie. Two girls in sundresses were standing in the kitchen, their hair damp from swimming. The fragrant smell of marijuana.

"Have you seen Cesca?"

"I think she's upstairs," one of the girls said with a giggle. "Want a hit?"

"No thanks," said Aurelio. "What about you, Wylie?" I shook my head. I hadn't smoked pot yet. I had friends who did. One of them was kicked out of Andover because of it.

"Um, no thanks. I'm cool."

Carrying my blazer and with my loosened necktie, I was plainly uncool, and this made the girls giggle again.

Aurelio walked to the foot of the stairs and called, "Cesca?" Then something else in Catalan.

A voice answered from upstairs, also in Catalan. The two siblings bantered back and forth. I caught my name mentioned once. "She'll be right down," said Aurelio, without explaining the rest of their conversation.

I stood there, expectant as a disciple. Upstairs I could hear feet pounding on the floor, doors slamming. Aurelio asked me where I was at school, but I was barely listening. He was going to be a senior this year, he told me. There had been a number of schools. He had struggled. Had difficulty reading. College was not for him, he said with a smile. What he really wanted to do was paint. This did interest me, however, and I was about to ask him more when a figure appeared at the top of the stairs.

Turning my head, I looked up and saw her. She was in a short, tight pink dress carrying a pair of sandals and walking down toward us barefoot. Even the photographs I'd seen did not do her justice. Cesca at eighteen. All my old fantasies burned up in the heat of reality. There would be no rescues, no fairy tales. I couldn't help but stare, my jaw slack.

She walked right by me. "Lio, don't tell me you aren't going to change?" she asked sharply in English.

She was shorter than I was but had the kind of presence that made her appear taller. Her hair was combed but still wet. No makeup. Brilliant brown eyes, dewy lips. A faint aroma of jasmine and roses. The resemblance between the siblings, the same dark beauty, the same physical intensity, was striking.

"Change? For what?"

She rolled her eyes. It was as though I was not there. "For Gog's party. Mare wants us all to be there. She wants a picture."

"I don't have anything to change into," he said with a helpless laugh.

"Oh, you're impossible."

He shrugged, still smiling. I could tell these were roles they played. She the elder sister, he the hapless kid brother.

I saw my moment and took it. "We're about the same size," I said.

For the first time, Cesca turned and looked at me, her brow furrowing. She was already accustomed to ignoring men, taking their attention for granted. A rich man does not stoop to pick up a penny from the sidewalk.

"Who are you?" she asked.

"This is Wylie . . ."

"Wylie Rose," I said, not wanting to be referred to as "Mitch's son" or, worse, "the guy who fell out of the tree."

"What I meant is that Aurelio could wear my blazer and tie," I continued.

Cesca stared at me for a minute, then smiled and said, "That's brilliant. Take off your shirt and give it to him."

Aurelio began to protest, but she cut him off. "Do it. I'll get Cosmo and Carmen in here as well. Mare wants us ready for seven." She turned to me, put her hand on my forearm, and squeezed it gently. Even if I had never met her before, just that faintest of pressure would have made me hers. "Thank you," she said and gave me a little wink before walking out.

I stared after her, watching her cross the lawn to where Cosmo was sitting.

"Lucky for me you came," laughed Aurelio.

I unbuttoned my shirt and handed it to him. It was a standard Brooks Brothers white button-down. My father had been taking me there every year since I was a child. The wooden, club-like walls, the stacks of shirts. It was always quick when we went there. In my father's eyes shopping was effeminate. You went to the store with a purpose and then you left. Across the broad floor men inspected the ties. *Would Mr. Rose care to see anything else? No thanks, we're just here for the boy.* Nick was his special salesman who always helped us. He was an old man with bad feet. Years before, my father would have smiled, happy to be recognized. Back when he had only three suits in his closet. Now he had dozens.

Aurelio slipped on the shirt. Despite his being a bit taller than me, the shirt fit him surprisingly well. I have long arms, and my neck had filled out because of rowing. "Perfect," he said. I then handed him the tie and the blazer.

"Can I keep my pants?"

"Don't worry about pants. I'll stand in the back row," he said with a wink.

We left the house and went out back to where the photographs were to be taken. Along with several dozen other guests, I watched as the family posed, Izzy and his wife, Ruth, seated in the middle surrounded by their children and grandchildren. Aurelio was grinning hugely in the back with his hair in a ponytail, my tie snug against his throat. From the waist up, he looked like a Spanish princeling. They were all there: Cesca, Aurelio, Cosmo, Carmen, Izzy, Ruth, Kitty, Dorothy, Roger and his

wife, Yvette, although it would be only a matter of time before there was another Mrs. Roger Baum.

The only one absent was Ugo, but he had been split from Kitty for years now, even though his presence was clear in the face of each of his children. There was also Randall, Kitty's new beau and future second husband. A political science professor at NYU. I have seen the photograph many times since then, taking special pride in my own small role in it.

Later that night, I was standing around a bonfire wearing a black Rolling Stones T-shirt, I am not sure whose. The iconic lips and tongue. Aurelio had thrust it at me, saying, "Here. Wear this." He was still wearing my clothes, enjoying the new persona. The light had faded. After the photographs and the speeches, the party within a party at the Playhouse continued as the adults sat down to dinner. I had already had several beers and was feeling pleasantly tipsy. Although I kept looking for Cesca—who was apparently mingling with the adults—Aurelio wouldn't let me leave his side.

He was a great talker, appreciative of new audiences. And I was a great listener. He explained to me his theories of art. He spoke with the enthusiasm of youth, sure in the uniqueness of his discoveries, like someone thinking that no one else before them had ever fallen in love or theorized about the stars. The eternal and ageless mysteries. I didn't mind. I was flattered by the attention. When he started talking about Japanese composition, ukiyo-e and Utamaro, I hung on every word. It was all new—and fascinating—to me.

I confessed to him that I was also interested in art. Since childhood I had loved to draw knights, Civil War soldiers, and, for the entertainment of my friends, fantastically naked women with improbably long legs and pneumatic bosoms. I knew I had a little talent, but it had never occurred to me that I could do

anything with it. Until that moment, I just thought of it as a trick, like being able to wiggle your ears. Certainly my family knew no one who was in the arts.

It had always been assumed that, like all my classmates, we would follow our fathers to Harvard—or possibly Yale or Princeton, depending on affiliation—and then to Wall Street or the law. In extreme cases, Washington, although public service was something one did after one's fortune had already been made. There was no reason to think I would ever deviate from this path. After all, it promised security, respectability, and the comforts of wealth. In due time I would have children of my own and offer them the same advantages. There was no room for creative expression. It was about responsibility to family and society. To take a different route would have been heretical— somehow unmanly. Wanting to be an artist would be even worse. But what Aurelio was saying made perfect sense, and I had to know more.

Excitedly he led me to an old shed. "Are you sure?" he asked. "You'll be honest, right?"

He switched on the light. It was a simple room, the walls un- painted, the joists exposed. There was an easel that held an un- finished canvas, and more canvases were lining the walls. A large table made from a door was covered with painter's tools, includ- ing old coffee cans smeared with paint. The place reeked of tur- pentine. A tall roll of unprimed canvas was leaning in the corner. A stool stood in front of a wall draped with green material.

The canvases were bold, beautiful. That last word is one I might overuse, but nothing else substitutes. The browns, golds, and blues. Deep blacks. As rich as Rembrandt, but with a modern artist's vibrancy and movement. Who am I thinking of? Picasso in one of his early periods. A wisp of Modigliani, the palette if not the execution. My painterly vocabulary was at that point virtually nonexistent.

Today I would suggest Corot, Velázquez, maybe even a little Goya, with a bit of Pontormo thrown in for good measure. I was struck by the confidence, the maturity of the works. They were almost all portraits. I recognized his family. Izzy, looking both tired and noble, like a Jewish Lear. His wife, Ruth. Roger. Kitty. A brooding Cosmo. Carmen, sultry and aloof. He'd done many self-portraits. Not surprisingly, I was immediately drawn to one of Cesca. It was only of her head and shoulders, but Aurelio had captured a quality to her smile and her eyes that was at once both familiar and unknown. I stared at it as I dared not stare at her.

"These are amazing," I said, wanting to adequately convey my delight and admiration.

"You're very kind. They are merely studies. I have a long way to go."

That was my introduction to his famous modesty. He was like the perfect host, who wants to share everything with you but refuses to accept compliments on the quality of his linen or the excellence of his wine. It is an almost Oriental attitude, one brought by the Moors to Spain and then down through the generations. The king who welcomes a guest to his palace with the words "Please do me the honor of entering my humble abode."

But Aurelio said it without irony. At the age of seventeen he knew that he had still a long way to go. To me, however, he seemed so far down the road as to be almost invisible, a mere wisp of smoke on the horizon indicating the degree of his progress from my own.

"No, I mean it," I insisted. Maybe I wouldn't have been so forward if not for the beer, but also there was a quality about him that seemed to require extra care, a natural reticence that needed, like an exotic plant, more water than others to truly thrive.

"Maybe," he replied enigmatically.

"Where did you learn to paint?"

"My father taught me. He is a painter, you know."

I remembered my father talking about him. The tone wasn't very flattering. My father held artists in low esteem, especially those who abandoned their families.

"But you didn't go to art school?"

"No. They don't teach you how to paint in art school. At least not in New York. The art of painting is dying there. Today it's all about minimalism and video and radical lesbianism. That's why I am going to study in Barcelona. At the same school where my father studied."

I was suddenly tremendously envious of him—of his talent and his opportunity. I wished I could have said those words, had people gape when they saw a painting of mine. I felt the flower of ambition opening within me. "When do you leave?" I asked.

"At the end of the summer. I'm dropping out of school."

"Would you show me?" I asked. "How to paint, I mean." Looking back, I am embarrassed by my presumption, but at the time I felt like a beggar asking a millionaire for a handout; he had so much and I had so little. He looked at me and pulled a face, sucking in his cheeks. "You don't want me. I don't know enough."

"You know more than I do. I can draw, but I've never used oil paints before. I have no idea how to mix them. Or anything."

Aurelio nodded his head and said, "Okay, why not? Why don't you come back tomorrow, and I can at least show you how to build and prime a canvas. That's how my father started with me."

I happily agreed. It was like hearing a piece of music for the first time and feeling as though you already know it, that it resonates within a part of your soul that you didn't know existed. I was excited, like a convert brimming with newfound faith. But this was not the only way in which my life was destined to change that night.

5

AFTER DINNER, THERE WERE THE FIREWORKS. I HAD LOST sight of Aurelio. Maybe having extracted a commitment from him, an obligation, I had scared him off. But for the moment it didn't matter. Someone had passed me a joint. I can't remember who. It was an evening of new beginnings. I took my first hit, trying to imitate the others, and, to their amusement, began coughing. When it was my next turn I tried again, this time successfully. I remember laughing and feeling a pleasant, unfamiliar lightness. We were all standing around in a circle. There was even an adult with us, wearing his jacket and tie. He inhaled greedily. "Good shit," he said, holding his breath.

One of the girls giggled, and I followed helplessly while the starbursts and Roman candles whistled and exploded overhead. The crowd applauded. I saw my parents in the distance and avoided them. They would want to know where my shirt and jacket were. Smell the beer and dope reek on my breath.

Then I stopped caring.

"Hi," a voice said. "There you are."

It was strangely rough and cracked, but had an underlying femininity, like someone who laughs and shouts more than most people. I recognized it immediately, even though I had only heard it for the first time that night. It was Cesca. She was still wearing her dress, but her feet were once again bare. She held a glass of red wine in her hands. "I've been wanting to thank you all night."

"For what?"

"For giving Aurelio your clothes." She smiled, her head nodding in encouragement. It was an amazing smile. Welcoming and suggestive. It is easy for me now to see that nothing about her was simple, but then I was too callow to know better. As I came to learn, it was impossible for her not to flirt, to seduce. It didn't matter who it was. A waiter, her dentist, the man who sold newspapers in the kiosk on the corner. They just had to be male. To her flirting was as natural as breathing. But this being my first time experiencing it, I couldn't help but think she was turning it on just for me.

"You were brilliant. And he looked so handsome in them too. My grandfather was very happy."

I told her I was glad I could help, uncertain of what else to say.

"Wylie, right?"

"Right."

"You want to get high?"

"For sure." The words sounded unnatural coming out of my mouth. That was how I had heard the stoners at my school talk. Boys with long hair who played Frisbee and strolled through the woods when they thought no else was paying attention. Rash with impunity, even though they were all destined for expulsion. Still, I thought it made me sound cooler, more experienced. What did I know?

"Great," she said. "Come with me."

We walked away from the party, toward the dunes overlooking Gardiners Bay. The fireworks were done now, but the whiff of cordite hung in the air. The band had started playing again, and people were dancing on a wooden dance floor that had been installed on the lawn.

I took off my shoes and followed Cesca through the beach grass. A nearly full moon cast a silvery glow over the beach. When we sat down she was so close to me that I could feel the skin of her arm on mine.

Scarcely believing where I was and with whom, I was reluctant to speak, to say anything that would break the magic of the moment. For years I had imagined what I would do when I saw her. How I would tell her I loved her and take her in my arms. It would be easy. But such confidence is an illusion. It takes little to shatter it.

She sat there barely visible, producing a joint and a pack of matches. As she lit a match, for an instant her face was illuminated, her eyes shining at me conspiratorially, like those of a child with a secret. She took a deep drag and handed the joint to me. I remembered to inhale and hold it, trying not to cough. Desperate to impress her. Again.

"Where are you going to school?" she asked, leaning into me. I told her.

She nodded. "I thought you were older. You look older."

"What about you?"

"I'm going to Barnard in the fall." She told me that she wanted to major in theater, specifically set design. Her mother often took her to shows on Broadway, the *Nutcracker* at Lincoln Center during the holidays. More than the actors or the dancers it was the sets that appealed to her. "I love the idea of creating my own little world," she said. "It's art you can walk through, you know?"

I said nothing. Aurelio was a painter. His father also. Cesca wanted to design sets. A family of artists. The freedom, the creativity, the beauty. I envied her the life I imagined she lived.

"I'd like to be a painter," I declared impulsively, putting into words for the first time an ambition that had only that night occurred to me, thinking this would somehow impress her, make her look favorably on me.

"You?" She seemed to find this hysterical, and we both started laughing. "What do you know about painting?"

"Nothing," I confessed. "But I've always liked to draw."

"Are you any good?"

"I don't know. I guess so. People have always said I was."

"You'll have to show me some of your work then. Do you have a studio?"

"No."

"Where do you work?"

I shrugged. "Wherever I can."

"It's a hard life, being an artist," she said, suddenly serious. "It's not for everybody."

I nodded my head. I knew nothing. "I'd like to try. When I saw Aurelio's paintings tonight it made me think that maybe I could do it too. But I don't know if I could ever be as good as him. He's incredible."

For a moment she was silent. I stared at her profile and listened to the rhythmic breaking of the waves below. Then she said, "You know what's really incredible?"

"What?"

She snickered and leaned into me, her face inches from mine, and whispered in a low voice, "This pot is incredible. Shhh. Don't tell anybody." Then more laughter. "God, I am so stoned," she said.

I laughed too. Everything was tremendously funny and terribly important at the same time. Emotions, sensations, barely imagined thoughts, one quickly replacing the other, crackled through me like electricity. And there was Cesca, her knees touching mine, laughing with me. The moment was perfect.

I had to say something, had to express a little of what I was feeling. If I didn't, I would implode. "You're the most beautiful girl I've ever seen in my life," I blurted out.

"You're sweet." I knew instantly it was a compliment she had heard many times before, and it had lost its novelty.

But I was young, made brave by the combination of the pot and her proximity. "No, I mean it. You are. I thought you were the day we first met. Do you remember?"

She shook her head. "No."

"I was a kid. I came over to your house. I fell out of the tree and broke my arm."

"That was you?" She laughed. "Sorry. I don't mean to laugh. I remember that. You were such a sweet boy. We had no right to make you do that. I felt terribly about what happened. Hearing you cry. It made me sad."

"I was trying to impress you."

"Me?"

"Yes."

"Why?"

"Because I fell in love with you."

She said nothing.

Feeling foolish, I said, "Look, forget it. I'm sorry. I didn't . . ."

"Shhh," she said. "Don't be." Then she got to her feet and took my hand in hers. Astonished, I said nothing.

"Do you want to go for a swim?"

"Sure. What—"

"Good," she said, interrupting me. "Come on."

Still holding my hand, she led me down to the shoreline. The water of the bay is always calm. It is popular with parents and children too young or scared of the ocean waves. At night it is even more placid. "Can you help me with my zipper?" she asked, turning around.

Wordlessly, I reached out. I had never unzipped a woman's dress before. Not even my mother's. I fumbled unfamiliarly and found the zipper, lowering it carefully. She stepped away from me and shrugged out of her dress. I watched as she placed a hand on my shoulder for balance and removed her underwear. She stood before me, naked, but I could barely see a thing. Two vague dark points on her breasts and another darker patch between her legs. She laughed and wiggled her hips. "Come on, slowpoke. It's your turn."

Quickly I removed my clothes and dumped them in a pile on the beach, but she was already in the water. The last thing I removed was my eyeglasses. For a moment I debated leaving them on but feared losing them in the water. Without them her body would be a blur.

I entered the water, the tiny waves cold and gently lapping at my feet, feeling the hard edges of shells. "Where are you?" I called.

"Over here."

I swam toward the sound of her voice, her head just visible. The water was shallow. When I stood it was barely to my waist. The air cool on my skin.

"Don't you just love swimming at night?" she asked. "Isn't it heaven?"

She was floating on her back, her body laid out like a table. I had never been this close to a naked woman before. I approached like an initiate. My ignorance shaming me.

She waded over to me. "Hey you," she said, and to my surprise she reached her hand below the surface. Instantly I became excited. She giggled, holding me with her hand. Without letting go, she reached up and kissed me, slipping her tongue into my mouth. "Do you like that?" she asked. "Do you want to touch me?"

"Yes," I croaked.

She took my hand and placed it on her breast. The softness indescribable. She kissed me again. This time I pulled her toward me, confident in my physical strength, in the belief that she wanted me, that there could be only one outcome. But she ducked away with a splash.

"You're going to have to catch me."

She dove under the water and I couldn't see her. "Over here," she called, nearer the beach.

"Where are you?" I called.

"Here," she said, now right behind me. She embraced me and again we started to kiss. Her tongue darting in and out, sinuous, alive. I was erect now. She let out a low moan, and I reached between her legs.

"Come with me," she whispered. She took my hand and led me back to the beach. On the sand, she stopped and kissed me. I reached for her. "Not here," she said.

We gathered our clothes and walked naked across the sand. Even though I could still hear the music and noise from the party, I felt entirely alone with her, as though we had slipped through a crack in the wall. "This way. Come on."

We ran up the beach to a low structure that was apparently changing rooms. There was a short flight of stairs and then a deck that felt rough underfoot. She giggled, saying, "Here we are." She pushed open a door and I followed her inside.

Moonlight illuminated the room through a skylight in the ceiling. I saw a massage table. A basket of towels. She lay down, her legs apart. My moment of truth. My watershed, the dividing line of my life. Everything that came before and everything that would come after.

"Now," she whispered, pulling me toward her, encircling me. The pressure of her thighs. The tautness of her belly. Her body still cool from the water. She grabbed my shoulders. Her hips rocked back and forth and I along with her. "Yes, yes, yes," she said, in a voice halfway between a command and a mantra. I was trying to not lose my balance. Trying to not disappoint her. Trying, unsuccessfully, to not finish too soon.

"That's all right," she said. "We can go again."

And we did. This time I was better. Less nervous, more at ease. She demanding, knowing what she wanted. By the time we were done I could feel beads of perspiration from my exertions running down the small of my back.

We sat there side by side on the bench. "Your first time?" she asked.

I nodded. "Yes. That obvious?"

"No. I think it's sweet," she said, leaning over and kissing me on the cheek. Her breast rubbed against my chest, arousing me again. We made love a third time. Slowly. Pleasurably. When it was over we were speechless, our chests heaving, unable for several minutes to even move.

We dressed and walked slowly back to the party, her arm around my waist, my arm about her shoulder.

The party was coming to an end. I had to find my parents. "Can I see you again?" I asked.

She kissed me. "Of course. Come for a swim tomorrow."

6

I RETURNED THE NEXT DAY AFTER WORK. AND EVERY DAY after. We swam in the pool, played tennis, went to the beach. Cesca entering the ocean like a naiad. Hair up, neck bare. Diving cleanly into the waves, laughing in the spray. Wherever she went, men's eyes followed her. At night we made love but never in her bed. We returned often to the changing room. There was also an old stable with a loft. Once in her car. She kept me apart from her family. Only Aurelio knew. Or at least I thought he did. "Pretend you are coming to see him," she told me. When no one was looking she would kiss me.

And I did see Aurelio. We talked about painting. He showed me how to stretch and prime a canvas. Some of the basics. Composition. How to mix colors. He had books with color plates that he would bring out to the studio. "Look at that," he'd say. "See how the line follows?"

If Cesca was busy, he and I would sit outside and take turns sketching each other. As we sat we talked. He was curious about everything. Had I ever been to North Africa? What was boarding school like? Did I know anything about butterflies?

He had a way of questioning that was both childish and pro-found. Because of his dyslexia he got most of his information from people instead of books. Over the years I would be on the receiving end many times, when he would just look at me and ask, "Why?" And he meant it. He wanted to understand the deeper rhythms of life, the subtle undercurrents that pulled us all along. Why people did things, what our motivations were, our desires.

Wherever he went he would engage complete strangers in conversation, learning about their lives. His face open and handsome, his manner pleasant and trusting. It was almost im-possible to say no to him. Drunks, passengers on trains, dinner partners, the homeless, girls on the beach. Whoever life placed in his path. Often he would even ask them to pose for him. Taking out his sketch pad and drawing them while they talked. Many times I would just leave him, knowing he could be there all night. And they couldn't help talking to him. He just had this way about him. He could get them to tell him things they wouldn't reveal to anyone else.

For several weeks I saw Cesca every day. The summer days and nights crackled with promise. Warm, silken evenings. Every-thing was new, splendid. Wrapped in the glow of youthful inti-macy, we lay on our backs and shared our dreams and fears. She told me about her family, her childhood. How when she was a little girl she had a puppy, an Alsatian, she named Nadó, which means "baby" in Catalan, but it was hit by a car. She had cried for days, she told me. A tear appeared in her eye as she spoke. "I really loved that dog, you know?" Her favorite poet was Neruda, but she also loved Auden. She wished she could sing but said she had a terrible voice. I didn't believe her and she said, "Oh yeah? I'll prove it," and began to sing "Me and Bobby McGee." She hadn't been wrong. I started laughing and had to agree with her. "Cosmo has an amazing voice," she said. "I'm so jealous."

I listened eagerly, intently, to everything she said, still unable to believe that it was she who was in my arms, gazing at the curve of her cheek, the luster of her skin. Occasionally she brought me a present. Once, a book of Picasso drawings. Another time a set of graphite pencils. I have the book still. It is inscribed, *"Amor, amor, hasta la noche abrupta,"* It is by Neruda, although I didn't know it at the time. Translated it roughly means "Love, love, until the night collapses."

One evening after dinner we walked the beach all the way to Louse Point. "I love this old beach," she said. "My parents used to always bring me here when we were children. Sometimes I wish I never had to be anywhere else. I wish I didn't have to go to college."

"Don't you want to go?"

For a moment she didn't say anything. Then, "I don't know. Not really, no. I don't really see the point of it."

"Why?"

"Because it kind of terrifies me. The thought of devoting myself to one thing, even to something I love, seems so final. I mean, what if it's not what I end up doing? Why waste all that time? It's so forced, so artificial. Making people decide about the direction of their lives so early. It doesn't make any sense."

I nodded. I was still two years away from having to face such a decision. But the thought of not going to college, of not going to Harvard, had never occurred to me. It would have been un- natural, like snow in summer.

"Don't you worry about such things?" she asked. "What you want to do with your life and being wrong?"

"Aurelio seems to know what he wants."

"Yes. He's lucky in that way. It's always been easy for him. The truth is that he'd be crap at anything else." She laughed.

"And you?"

"That's the thing. I don't know if I wouldn't just be crap at everything."

Several nights later she couldn't see me. There were other friends. She had been neglecting them, she told me. She'd call me tomorrow night, for sure. But then tomorrow came and again she was busy.

The next day I went to the compound after work. There was no point in calling. "We never answer the phone here. We just expect people to show up if they want to see us," she had told me. It was true. There was a constant stream of people moving in and out of the various houses throughout the summer. German boys in small bathing suits helping themselves in the kitchen. Pretty girls sunning themselves by the pool. Musician friends of Cosmo's. Old friends of Roger's, sleek-looking men with side-burns and second wives. Mercedes convertibles parked on the grass. Delivery vans dropping food, wine, and flowers. Kitty presiding over lunch for a dozen. A Babel of languages. Usually when I arrived Cesca would hurry to meet me, saying, "Thank God you're here. All these people are driving me crazy."

Today, though, there was no sign of Cesca or her car. People I didn't recognize were playing doubles on the tennis court. I skirted the Playhouse and found Aurelio in his studio painting a still life. I watched him work for a little.

"Have you seen Cesca?" I asked after a while.

"Not since she left."

"Left?"

"Left. This morning."

"What?"

"She left this morning," he repeated.

"To go where? For how long?"

"She didn't tell you?"

"No."

"Last night at dinner she said she was leaving today for France for a few weeks. Some friends of hers have a château somewhere. They invited her and she went. She's always doing things like that. Here one moment"—he dabbed his brush in the paint on his palette and then applied it to the canvas—"and gone the next. Poof. Still, I would have thought she'd have told you, seeing as how you've been spending so much time together lately."

I stared at him, incredulous.

"Wait. I almost forgot. She did leave something for you though," he continued. "She dropped it off before leaving but I wasn't really paying attention." He put the brush and palette down, and wiped his hands with a turpentine-soaked rag. "Here it is." He handed me a purple envelope, leaving behind a smudged thumbprint. "Sorry." He grinned.

I took it, still confused. Mumbling my excuses, I stepped out of the studio and walked toward the beach, where I sat on the sand and tore open the envelope.

Dear Wylie, it began.

> *Sorry to do it like this. I'm terrible at this sort of thing. Fear of commitment, I suppose. Of giving too much of myself. Sex is one thing but feelings are something else. Whenever I feel someone getting too close it's time for me to move on. For what it's worth, I really do like you, Wylie. Maybe a little too much. And then what happens when I break your heart? Because I would. Or make you feel weak or inadequate? I can't help myself. It's how I'm made. I'm not a bitch all the time I swear but I can be when it suits me. What you need is a nice, normal girl who will be sweet to you. Buy her crappy presents, take her to the movies. Break up with her. Do it a few more times with a few different girls. Learn how to love someone who wants to be loved. By that time you'll have forgotten all about me.*
>
> *Con amor,*
C.
>
> *P.S.—Why do you have to be so handsome?*

I stupidly read the letter several times, searching in vain for clues or answers that weren't there. But it was all there. It took me years to really understand what she was saying. Like many people I preferred my own interpretation, choosing to decode her words in a way that caused me the least pain.

For several days I sulked, brooding over her betrayal, the abruptness of her departure. At first I hated her, called her names. If I was older I would probably have gotten drunk, but I didn't drink much in those days. Instead I went for long runs, pushing myself, replacing psychic pain with physical pain. Playing over my revenge in my head. What I would do or say when I saw her next. With each footfall repeating the word *bitch bitch bitch*.

But my anger wasn't real and it didn't last. The fact of the matter was that I couldn't just cease loving her. My love wasn't like a stove that could be turned on and off. It was a seed that had been planted years before, a living thing that had taken root. At night as I lay in bed I relived every moment of our weeks together in my head. Sometimes I cried, other times I asked the darkness why, but mostly, on the verge of sleep, I thought about what it would be like to be with her again and gradually became determined that I would win her back. That all that was required was to prove to her that she was mistaken. That she could love me as I loved her. After all, hadn't I seen it in her eyes as we made love, heard her whispered words of endearment, felt the caress of her fingers, the radiance in her smile? I was sure I had, and I knew I would see her again.

It was a week or so after she left that I returned to the compound. If I couldn't see her, being in her home, surrounded by her family, was a poor but necessary substitute. There, at least, I could console myself with the memory of her, easing the sting of her absence even if it kept the wound fresh.

And Aurelio was glad to see me. Soon, I was going every

day. His companionship was palliative. We went on field trips. We painted the sea, the sky. Ripe fields. His canvases were effortless, mine clumsy.

Sometimes I stayed for dinner. Kitty welcomed me as the son of an old family friend. Carmen and Cosmo both largely ignored me. He had a band. He spent hours in his own studio. Every week there seemed to be a new girlfriend, each more gorgeous than the last. When he came to the table he made everyone laugh. He was the family clown, could tell jokes, mimic voices. If he hadn't been a musician he would have been a terrific comedian.

Carmen sunned herself by the pool, attended by a constant stream of young men and equally pretty girls. Then they would all drive off somewhere. Parties that I was never invited to in houses where parents were away.

After Labor Day I returned to school. Even though I had promised myself that I wouldn't, in a moment of weakness I wrote a letter to Cesca at her address in the city. In it I wrote that I would be back in New York over Christmas and maybe I could see her then if she was around.

I knew enough to realize there was no point in remonstrating with her, asking why she had done what she did or the way she did it. People are the way they are. You have to take them or leave them, and I wasn't ready to leave her yet. Like a traveler to Shangri-la, I had discovered a new world, and, having lost it, all I could think of was how to return. I wished her good luck at Barnard and signed it "with love."

Of course, I never heard back.

7

THERE IS AN OIL PAINTING ON MY WALL NOW OF SAMPANS on a pearlescent river. They could be Chinese but just as easily Thai. There are nine sampans in all, very small. I don't know who painted it, but I have spent many hours staring at it, wondering about the lives of the people on the boats, where they are going, where they've been. Do they know each other? Are they in competition?

Two seem to be chatting in a friendly manner. Maybe they're related. I have made up a story that a man in one of the boats is in love with a woman in another. She is young, bareheaded, alone, possibly a widow. Her face would be weathered but there would be traces of an early loveliness. She is also obviously quite tough or else she couldn't operate that sampan by herself and survive. It is easy to see why someone would fall in love with her. But she is torn between having her independence and subjugating herself to a man. If she were to marry again, he would have to be strong but also understanding. Someone who loved her for herself, not for her strong back or child-birthing potential. She has noticed the man in the other sampan stare at her. He seems like a decent man, but she cannot tell. A hard worker like her, but what would he really be like? Her first husband had been a brute, and she was not sorry when he drowned. Maybe she is better off on her own, the master of her own fate even if it means a life of loneliness. It is impossible to know. Theirs is a story without consummation. Fixed in time like Keats's Grecian lovers.

We can never really know another person. A couple can be married for decades and still keep their secrets. The long years before they met. Childhood. Other lovers. Then there are the small things, things not quite remembered, the banal. Rainy days. A childhood room. Fourth of July celebrations. Trips to the dentist. The death of a dog. All the myriad events and en-counters that shape our lives, like water flowing over stone.

These are what make us. I have tried to capture Cesca as I knew her. What I experienced firsthand and what I learned, either from her or from those who knew her. Others may not approve of her, may find her too selfish or irresponsible. I have a friend who married a girl that I never liked. She was dull and plump but he adored her. They were very happy together. It doesn't matter what I thought of her, after all. It is impossible to tell the heart what it should want.

CESCA NEARLY GOT MARRIED HER FIRST YEAR AT Barnard. There had been a boy, a few years older than she, soon to graduate from business school. He had given her an enormous yellow diamond that had belonged to his grandmother, who was an Astor. Cesca had accepted, amused by the novelty. She liked the idea of being engaged. It was a portal to adulthood. She was always in a hurry. To be first. To define oneself by sweeping gestures and contradictions. She was still young enough then to believe that life was only a series of grand chords.

Kitty told her she was too young for marriage but knew there was nothing she could say to dissuade her daughter. But Izzy also disapproved and promised to intervene. You're too young, he argued. They were having lunch at his regular table at La Côte Basque. He had invited her to discuss the matter. The waiter discreetly serving the *délices de sole Véronique*. Pouring the Montrachet. Izzy loved his eldest granddaughter but knew she lacked discipline. There was a wild streak in her. It was what made her noble, he thought, but also reckless. This fatal flaw had ruined all his children, although he had enough discipline for them all even if did them no good.

Cesca resisted. She told him that her fiancé had been offered a job at Morgan bank. Marriage was an attractive notion. Like many children of divorced parents, she was torn between her desire for a secure home life and the disbelief that such security was ever possible. She might have moved on from wanting to be the wife of a Catalan pharmacist, but she hadn't lost the craving for consistency, for a settled life where circumstances could impose a kind of order on her. It was the dream of a child, like wishing for snow at Christmas or a happy ending.

Izzy urged her to wait until after she'd graduated from Barnard. "Then if you want to get married, you'll have my blessing," he said. "But maybe by then you'll change your mind. Think about it. You are destined for bigger things, my dear. Marriage is not yet part of the equation. One day but not yet."

He pointed out that she still had much to accomplish before she should consider such things. Husbands, after all, were demanding. Children even more so. Would she be able to pursue her dreams? Did she still want to study theater design? He knew the Nederlanders, the theater owners. He could make introductions. If necessary, he would even invest in a show. She would be a triumph. Broadway would beat a path to her door. But only if she remained single.

Izzy's nature was to expect the exceptional from his offspring, but that also meant he was destined to be disappointed. Like many self-made men, he believed that anything was achievable through the power of hard work and determination. But when his children inevitably failed to fulfill his ambitions for them, he kept urging them on.

Roger had been the first. From a young age, Izzy had set him such a high bar that it would have been nearly impossible to succeed. Not for any son of Izzy Baum was it good enough to simply do well or lead a productive life. No, from Izzy there was always the constant pressure to be great. "You can be great!" he would tell Roger, and later his grandchildren, even my father. "You can be great!" And he meant it too. With his scrapper's will, he truly believed that greatness was attainable with enough effort and encouragement.

In his own way, he had become great, but he never thought so. He knew he had become a success, had money and houses and the trappings of wealth, but those were not great things to him. They were simply the benefits of a lifetime of toil, combined with a certain pecuniary cunning. By the time his children had come along, he no longer aspired to greatness for himself, but he believed he could give Roger the tools to become great. More than power and influence, that would be Izzy's ultimate reward. To be pointed at and hear said, "You see that man, Izzy Baum? He's the father of Roger Baum." Nothing would have been sweeter to him. This had been his dearest wish since the moment he had first held his son, amazed by the pink-skinned perfection of the boy.

So he gave Roger all the advantages he had never had. Private schools. Lessons in French, riding, and sailing. Extra tutoring in geometry. He would invite different men—corporation presidents, politicians, college professors, architects, artists, doctors—for dinner at the palatial house on East Sixty-Eighth Street and have his son sit with them to absorb their knowledge. And at the end of every evening, Izzy would stop by Roger's room and, as the boy was drifting off to sleep, would ask, "Did you learn anything tonight?"

"Yes, Papa," was the answer.

"You will be great!" repeated his father, stroking the boy's hair. "I know it."

And as the boy grew, Izzy kept an eye on him, wondering what shape the spark of genius would take. Would he become a scientist, a doctor, a poet, a political leader? The first Jewish president even? Anything was possible. Unlike his own father, Izzy was irreligious. He had no ambitions for his son to grow up to become a rabbi or Talmudic scholar. His years in the business world had taught him that the only thing to believe in was one-self. But he wouldn't have minded if Roger became a university professor or even a critic. It did not matter if his profession of choice was lucrative or merely consequential. After all, he did not have to worry about sullying his hands with labor. Money would never be an issue for Roger. Izzy had already drawn up with his lawyers extremely generous trusts for each of his children, but his real hope was with Roger.

And for years that hope appeared to be well founded. During Roger's prep school years, he was a star, winning prizes in a wide range of academic and athletic pursuits. He was captain of his football team and president of his student body. Boys liked him, and girls found him exciting. Even his teachers, normally so jaded by the constant change of faces every year, envisioned great things for him. When Roger graduated from private school in New York, Izzy threw a huge party at the Stork Club to celebrate. Eddie Fisher sang, and among the luminaries in attendance were the mayor of New York, Ernest Hemingway, Bishop Fulton J. Sheen, Rocky Marciano, and Jackie Gleason. It was covered in the *Times*. Roger's graduation present from Izzy was a Jaguar roadster.

Izzy would continually send letters to Roger, citing recent remarkable actions he considered of the same caliber as the ones that would one day redound to him. Of particular interest at one point was Dr. Salk, and during this time Izzy actively encouraged Roger to identify other diseases that might be cured as well. *Just think of it,* he would write, *one day to be mentioned in the same breath as Jonas Salk. You can do it! With your brains and my money, there's no reason you can't find a cure to any of the terrible diseases currently afflicting the globe. Have you thought about changing your studies to science or even medicine? If so, I will have a word with the president immediately. Should you decide to pursue this course of action, I might even see my way clear to donating a new laboratory.*

If Izzy had actually left Roger alone, it is entirely possible that his own intelligence and inborn abilities would have assured him of a good, if not a great life. But Izzy couldn't help meddling. It was in his nature to control.

It was different with Kitty. Izzy had tried to control her too, but, unlike Roger, she rejected him. Even as a child, she fought him. When he said he admired her blue dress, she'd wear the green one. She would come home from school and, instead of doing her homework, would read Nancy Drew stories or listen to programs like *The Romance of Helen Trent.* As she grew older her rebellion manifested itself in her choice of men. She went to Vassar and was nearly kicked out after her freshman year for having a man in her room. By the end of her junior year, she quit school entirely and moved to Paris, where she rented an apartment overlooking the Tuileries and studied painting. She went to nightclubs on the Left Bank and became the mistress of a married politician.

Her father was furious, but he never stopped sending her money every week to the American Express office on Rue

Scribe. In spite of it all, he still doted on his eldest, and nothing could put him in a better mood than a word or a smile from his daughter.

She and my father had even been lovers for a period, although I did not find that out for many years. My father was Roger's bosom friend, his regular crony. In college they would travel down to New York from Cambridge on Fridays and go to "21" with girls Roger knew, and Roger picked up the tab every time. For many summers, while my father worked first as an intern and then as a young attorney at various Manhattan law firms, he would come out most weekends to stay with the Baums, his first introduction to the East End of Long Island. He thought it was paradise. Izzy liked to live well and enjoyed sharing his pleasures with the people he loved.

Some nights, if she was alone, Kitty would knock on my father's door. The first time it had happened my father was startled. She was his friend's sister, and Izzy's daughter. "Don't be silly," she said, unhooking her bra. "Look, do you want to or not?" Afterward, she said, "I'm not interested in dating you, Mitch. You're cute, but you're not really my type. If there was another man here, it just might as well have been him." Over the course of that summer, whenever they both happened to be in the house, she would knock again if she felt like it, and she usually did. Occasionally, at dinner, when no one was watching, she'd slip her hand onto his thigh. For my father, it was like living in a French novel.

If Roger had too much of his father's attention and Kitty scorned it, the youngest, Dorothy, was virtually ignored. Prettier than her sister and more delicate, Dot was treated like a doll by her father. He never made demands of her, never expected much of anything from her. She, in turn, tried everything she could to please him, to not have him treat her like a baby. In the end the only thing she could do was shock him. She took lovers. Drugs. Dabbled in left-wing politics. Became a hippie. Lived on an ashram. Protested the war. She wasn't married. Didn't have children. Apparently my father also slept with her.

Like an old jockey training for a last race, Izzy was not yet ready to give up. He was determined that one of his descendants would be great. Nothing was more important to him. He would spend whatever it took. It was a pact he had made with a god he didn't believe in. You make me rich, Lord, and I'll make someone great, someone who can give back, who can make the world a better place. Who can be a better person than I. Even if his own children would never be great, there were still Kitty's children. If he couldn't succeed with his own, he would make one of them great. But now he was an old man. He might not live long enough to know what his grandchildren could, or could not, achieve.

Sitting at lunch, Cesca knew her grandfather would give her the old speech about how she could be great. She had heard it all before. But unlike some, she actually believed she could be great. She already knew that Aurelio would become a great painter. That Cosmo would become a great musician. Carmen was brilliant as well as beautiful. She could be anything.

Cesca just didn't know what direction her own life would take. There was so much that impassioned her but not any one thing more than another. From a young age she had learned how to draw, but she never felt the same love for it that Aurelio did.

Yes, she could do theater design, as Izzy suggested, but there were other things that interested her too. Fashion, for example. She had always been told what a good eye she had. And what if there was something out there that she hadn't come across that was to be her destiny? To commit to one thing now would be a mistake. She couldn't afford not to be ready when it announced itself. If only she could be sure. What she needed was a sign. In the meantime, why not marry? If she was destined to be great, what did it matter whether she was married or single?

After lunch, she started walking down Fifth Avenue, weighing her grandfather's words, determined to prove him wrong. She loved him, but she thought he was a bully, wielding his money like a weapon. It had been easier when she was a little girl. She could always get what she wanted then, but her desires were basic, childish. A cookie, maybe. A new party dress. This was a different matter. It was a big decision—but it was her life. She knew he had never listened to anyone and had always followed his own course. Why couldn't she do the same? It made her angry.

She wished Aurelio was in the city. He was the only one of her siblings who would understand. He would listen, would help her weigh the pros and the cons. Despite his cavalier attitude toward his own life, he possessed an instinctively philosophical nature. Ethics were important to him. What is right and what is wrong? "What is the real reason you want to get married? Your motive for moving away?" Many times they had stayed up late plotting an adventure or agonizing about the future. In most cases he would decide that the best course was direct action. Fear was never a factor. Something always had to be dared, to be risked, for it to have any meaning. That was the crucial consideration. The gesture had to have import, if not it should be abandoned.

Cosmo and Carmen could never offer such counsel. Cosmo was still too brash, too unformed, too selfish. He would not care where she went but would only miss her after she was gone. And Carmen? All her life she had brought her problems to Cesca, seeking an older sister's advice. Cesca had never brought her problems to Carmen. It was important to be strong, to show no indecision. That was the basis of their relationship. No, only

Aurelio could help, but he was in Barcelona. She hoped he was taking care of himself and remembering to eat.

She found herself in the Twenties and decided to walk the rest of the way home. Crossing Fourteenth Street, she became aware of a man following her. Young, brown, Puerto Rican or possibly Italian. Hollowed cheeks.

New York was more dangerous then. Muggings a frequent occurrence. It was important to not let down your guard. She walked faster and thought about turning in to a store when the man crossed to the other side of the street. She was only a few blocks from home now. She turned a corner and he was there, a knife in his hand. A single thin blade. "Gimme all your money, bitch," he said.

Even during her freshman year, Cesca had chosen to stay with her mother and siblings in the house in the Village. Crime, she knew, was everywhere, but this was her neighborhood. The familiar brownstones and stoops. The people who worked in the shops, the pizzeria, the hair salon around the corner all knew her. The old lady who spent her days leaning out of the window watching for trouble. They waved at each other. She felt safe here. Suddenly the street was empty.

He thrust his hand at her, and she reached into her purse to remove her wallet. Here, she said, almost in slow motion. She was not afraid. Not exactly, though she was unable to bring herself to look directly at the man.

"Now the ring."

She looked at her hand, at the engagement ring that had belonged to an Astor. Money was one thing. There could always be more. But not this. It was unique. It was hers. It was out of the question.

"No."

"What do you mean no? I'll cut you."

It was as though someone had woken her up. Suddenly alert

to what was happening, she looked at the man. His eyes shifting side to side, desperate to get away. Standing there foolishly, impotently, brandishing a small knife. She sensed his weakness, his cowardice, and despised him for it. An impulsive fury rose within her. "I said no," she repeated and began screaming at him in Catalan. The vilest things she could say. *"Bastardo! Ves a la merda! Poca polla!"* Swinging her purse at him. Surprising him, hitting him in the face.

There were other people on the street now. *"Fill de puta!"* she screamed and swung again. Her house keys spilling on the street. Her makeup. She didn't care. The purse came down on him again and again, as he shielded his face, dropping his knife.

"Concha!" he shouted and ran.

"Cabro!" she screamed after him.

By now there were other people around her. "Are you all right, lady?" asked one of the men.

Shaking with fear and anger, out of breath, she started picking up her things from the street. A handle on her bag had snapped. The man's knife lay there, but she avoided it. Even the money was still there. One of her shoes had come off. She picked it up and wedged it back on.

"I'm fine," she said in English, but she knew she wasn't.

She just wanted to get out of there. To leave this place, the halfhearted solicitude of strangers, now that the danger had passed. Hot tears burned her cheeks as she ran off in the other direction. Someone shouted she should wait for the cops, but there was no point in that, even if they ever came.

She told no one about what had happened. Her mother would overreact and tell her she needed to be more careful. That she shouldn't walk and should only take cabs. Her fiancé would be equally alarmed. There was nothing any of them could do, though. No one can really protect you from danger if the danger is meant to find you. You are the only person who can do that.

She was proud of herself for having stood up to the mugger. She knew she was brave. No one else she knew would have done it. Aurelio would have given him everything. Offered it. Here, take my coat too. That was the way he was. And it would have been different too if she was a man. A man who fought back might have been stabbed. But she had caught the mugger unprepared. He had thought she was a helpless woman, but she'd turned into a fury. She almost wished he hadn't run away. She was the descendant of Catalan women who had castrated French troops and nailed them to trees in reprisal. Vengeance and cruelty were in her blood.

The next day she began taking karate classes. The sensei was a large black man with an Afro. She was a willing pupil, learning how to disable an attacker and where on the body were the best places to strike. She went every day, proud of her ability to deliver a roundhouse kick high on the body bag.

It was not enough to defend herself though. She began to seek out danger. It was easy to find then. Park Avenue was as unsafe as Harlem. I remember my father telling me about one of the older members being attacked right outside of the Harvard Club in broad daylight. He was a veteran of the First World War. He was knocked down and his wallet and watch were taken. He had a gash on his forehead.

Cesca refused to be intimidated. At night she would stride down the middle of the street, waiting for someone to attack her. Silently willing it, her hands flexing, a can of Mace in her pocket. *Let them try it,* she thought. *I am ready. You can't scare me.* Fortunately, no one ever did. Possibly any assailants sensed the fight in the beautiful young woman and passed her over for an easier target.

There was more. Someone told her it was possible to climb to the top of the Brooklyn Bridge, walking up the sloping cable using the auxiliary cables as handrails. It was a simple matter of scaling a gate intended to keep out potential suicides. She would go up often, either alone or with friends, late at night. Her fiancé tried to go once but suffered from acrophobia and had to turn back. To the horror of those of her friends who were able to make it to the top, Cesca would sit on the edge, her feet dangling in space, staring out over the twinkling city, flicking her cigarette ash into the night sky while the East River rushed blackly by far below.

She also took up skydiving and heli-skiing, anything that could provide an adrenaline rush. And she conquered them all. Proving to herself that she could overcome fear. Her fiancé tried to put his foot down. They would have arguments. He yelled at her to stop taking such crazy chances. He told her she was going to hurt herself seriously one day. She called him a coward. *Covard. Marieta.* Unforgivable words. Doors slammed. His calls went unanswered.

The wedding was to have taken place in June. There would be a marquee at the Baums' compound just like at Izzy's birthday. Bigger. In the end it never happened. Cesca called it off. She returned the Astor ring that had started everything. Izzy took her to lunch again and told her how proud he was of her. She smiled at him and told him she was taking karate; there were scabs on her knuckles. She had never felt better.

Independent again, she became more social than ever. There were late nights at Max's Kansas City, where she became a regular. The celebrities who frequented the place quickly accepted the beautiful girl, her shirt unbuttoned to her waist. She possessed the same qualities they did. She played by her own rules, made people laugh, didn't ask for anything and didn't take.

One night she would sit at Warhol's table, another night at Larry Rivers's. She saw the New York Dolls perform and then partied with the band after. Also Iggy Pop, the Talking Heads, the Ramones, Tom Verlaine. One night Mick Jagger came in, and she sat on his lap. Much more. Cocaine. Casual sex. She almost went home with Lou Reed. She never went to bed with anyone she didn't want to—except for a few times. In the mornings, she slept late, past noon. She was taking a leave of absence from Barnard.

8

IT WAS THE FOLLOWING AUGUST WHEN I NEXT SAW CESCA. I was seventeen now, she nineteen. Once again I was working as a carpenter.

Over the course of the year Aurelio had sent me several letters and postcards from Spain, the spelling appalling but the handwriting exquisite. In each one he asked how I was, told me his latest news, filled the margins with charming drawings and doodles. The last one said he would be back in Amagansett for several weeks at the end of the summer, giving me the dates and telling me that it was important I come as soon as he returned. "I have a surprise for you," he wrote. I marked the day in my calendar and when it arrived drove over after work to the compound in an old Ford pickup I had bought for $500 at the beginning of the summer.

I did not know if Cesca would also be there. Since Memorial Day I had wondered if I would run into her, but we did not move in the same circles. Hoping to see her, I visited places where we had been together. A bar in Amagansett where they played live music and where she knew the owner. The beach at Louse Point. But not once did I attempt to contact her directly. She had made it plain that our brief romance was just that, as relevant as the pages of last year's calendar.

I had tried to forget her. Taking her advice, I'd dated several other girls over the year, but none of them was as exciting as Cesca. They were all attractive, privileged. There was a field hockey player from Grosse Pointe. Another girl whose father was a senator. Others whose details now escape me. But they all bored me, and I broke up with them. Cesca had spoiled me. I was like the heir whose first taste of wine was Margaux: Every other vineyard would only suffer in comparison.

And now, in the days leading up to Aurelio's return, she was more in my mind than ever.

I parked the truck and walked across the wide lawn toward the studio. It was a beautiful summer day. Hot. The sky solid blue. Butterflies flitted in the meadow. "Hello," I called, knocking on the studio door. Inside, it was darker, cooler, smelling of linseed oil and turpentine. There were two figures in the room. Standing next to her brother, laughing, wearing an orange bikini, was Cesca.

I had fantasized about this moment for almost a year. Rehearsed it over and over again. I had prepared what I would say, how I would stand. I remembered none of it at that moment, of course. The reality of her obliterated everything else.

What I did remember was her beauty. She was another year older and, if anything, even more beautiful. Her long, brown, sun-streaked hair. Her tanned, taut skin. The strength in her legs. The golden hairs at the declivity of her spine. The small mole just above her navel. Her hands on me. Moments of intimacy, the secret jokes of lovers.

They both stopped talking when I entered and turned to look at me.

Cesca spoke first. "Wylie," she said with her bewitching smile, as though nothing could have made her happier than to see me.

I was unable to speak. All I wanted to say was unsayable.

"Welcome, amigo," said Aurelio, stepping forward and embracing me. He had grown a beard. If anything he was leaner than before, the smile more beatific. He looked like one of Zurbarán's monks. "I am so glad you could come. I have much to show you."

"How are you, Wylie?" asked Cesca.

"Good. You?"

"Great," she answered, coming toward me and presenting each cheek to be kissed in turn. "You look so handsome. Doesn't he, Lio?"

"Down, girl," laughed her brother. His teeth were white. "He came here to see me to talk about art, didn't you, Wylie?"

Turning to me, she said, "Have you been painting, Wylie? I remember you had talked about it. Did you do it?"

I had been painting. In the art studio at school. The teacher, bored and probably a drunk, preferred painting scenes of duck hunting. I knew I could learn nothing from him except what not to do. So instead I worked alone on weekends or after study hall, whenever I could. I had brought some of my canvases. They were in the truck.

I nodded. "Yes," I said. I knew they were terrible. But I had brought them to show to Aurelio the way you consult a doctor. It hurts here. Can the limb be saved? What course of treatment do you recommend?

"Good for you," she said. "Would you let me see them?"

I hesitated. My mouth opened but no words came out.

"Really, Cesca," said Aurelio.

She laughed. "Don't worry. I can wait. Anyway, I have errands to run." As she walked by me, she passed her hand under my chin, casually, knowing that I could be had at a touch, a glance. "I'll leave you two boys alone. Bye, Wylie. Nice to see you again. You'll come back, no?"

I watched her leave, longing but unable to follow. Nothing went as I had hoped. Already I was trying to think of a way to see her again. I don't know what I expected. Apologies? Unlikely. Tears? Kisses? It would be like asking a clock to run backward. A few moments later I could hear the sound of gravel scattering as she drove away.

"Ignore her," said Aurelio, shaking his head, as though reading my thoughts. "Come over here and let me show you some things. And, remember, you must be honest with me."

I SPENT THE REST OF THE AFTERNOON LOOKING AT AURElio's canvases. He had brought back many but left even more in Barcelona. "I am very happy there," he confided. "Everywhere you look, there is beauty."

The paintings were wonderful. I told him so, but he demurred, saying, "No, no. I am not there yet. But I am getting better." His smile of modesty. He meant what he said. Always.

At his request I showed him my work. Compared to his paintings, mine were crude, obvious. Flat. Derivative, inspired by plates in books, not real life.

Aurelio studied my three or four canvases seriously. If I recall they were vaguely modeled after Picasso's sad harlequins and acrobats. There was also one self-portrait. Moody and adolescent. In some way, they were all about Cesca. "Here's what I think," he said after a while. "You have talent, but you have no idea how to paint. It is like you were raised by wolves. I am taking you to see a painter," he said. "A real one."

A day or so later Aurelio called to say he had arranged it. We were going a few miles inland to Springs, to the studio of a great painter. I knew the name, had seen examples of his work in books and museums. "Paolo and his wife, Esther, are old family friends," said Aurelio. They had met at art school and fallen in love. Esther was a Jew. In 1939 they were forced to flee from the fascists, first from Milan, then Paris. Finally they had come to America shortly before the Fall of France. Destitute, living in a cold-water tenement on Eighth Street, Paolo at first was only able to support his family by selling hand-painted postcards on the street, while Esther looked after their infant son, Gianni. Through the community of other exiled artists they met gallery owners and patrons. The end of the war coincided with a flowering of the New York art world. Paolo's work was soon in demand. There were one-man shows, articles in magazines and newspapers. He enjoyed success, if not stardom. "It was a great time to be an artist," sighed Aurelio.

I was to come by the house on Saturday morning and pick him up. Aurelio was a poor driver and did not possess a license. He had failed each time he took the test. For a while there was an old bicycle he rode, but he gave it away or lost it. For longer trips he was dependent on his family and friends. Over the course of our friendship, I would drive him many times, often quite out of my own way, but I never regretted a single trip. He was always such good company that I actually looked forward to his phone calls, saying, "I need to go to New York" or "Can you take me to Montauk?" If no one was around, he was just as happy hitchhiking. Sometimes, he told me, he even preferred it because it allowed him to meet so many new people.

We drove down Springs-Fireplace Road, Aurelio chattering away happily, until we turned up a short driveway. I parked in front of a weather-beaten barn standing beside a small arbor decorated with abstract statuary. To the right across a lawn stood an old farmhouse, the shingles brown with age, the trim white. On the grass, there were two enormous cement apples, hip high, rounded like breasts. We walked across the lawn. Outside the door was a small ship's bell. Aurelio rang it twice and called out. A voice answered from inside. "I'll be right there!"

A few minutes later, the door was opened by a tiny old woman, her long gray hair swept up in a bun. A light shawl around her shoulders even though it was quite warm. A cameo brooch was at her throat. Reading glasses dangled from a thin gold chain around her neck. She looked like an old photograph of an immigrant who had just come through customs at Ellis Island.

"Ciao, Aurelio," she said, as he bent to kiss her on each cheek. We towered over her. "I am so happy to see you." Her voice was heavily accented, European, her smile broad. Her merry eyes sparkled with intelligence.

"Ciao, Esther," Aurelio replied. "This is my friend, Wylie. The one I told you about."

"Ciao, Wylie," she said, grabbing both of my hands with hers. "Welcome. Come in, come in."

We entered the kitchen. The house was bright and welcoming. They had been here since 1948. The land, thickly covered with scrub and pine, extended back many acres. It had been a poor neighborhood. The modest houses were built by the local baymen called Bonackers. When they bought it, the old farmhouse, which dated back to the eighteenth century, was derelict. Paolo had restored it room by room with his own hands. He had trained as a mason in his native Sardinia. Knocking down walls, patching the roof, rebuilding the chimney.

There was a long, yellow-painted kitchen floor that ran the entire width of the house. To the left, a simple wooden table surrounded by chairs, its surface smooth with the memory of many meals. On it rested an open book, the words in French, the title unfamiliar. Teilhard de Chardin's *Le Phénomène Humain*. There were handwritten notes in the margins. "Sit, sit," said Esther. "Would you like some tea?"

Aurelio laughed. "Even if I wouldn't, I know you'd bring me some anyway," he said, squeezing her hand affectionately. To me he said, "It is impossible to leave here without Esther trying to feed you. If you're lucky, she may have even just baked some cookies or a loaf of bread. And you can't say no. She won't allow it."

Esther grinned and said, "You are too skinny. You need to eat more. I'll be right back." There was a large black stove in the middle of the room. Next to it a red rocking chair. The rear wall was painted white, and on it hung several round baskets the color of wheat. Old sash windows looked out over the sides and back of the house. A steep flight of stairs, also yellow, led up to the second floor. The ceiling was so low Aurelio and I almost had to stoop. Esther bustled around the kitchen, reaching into various cabinets, asking Aurelio about his mother and father, his sisters, his brother. Aurelio had been coming here since he was a boy.

"Is it all right if we go see Paolo?" asked Aurelio.

Esther looked at the clock on the wall. "Wait a little. He is still working, but he will be coming in for lunch soon."

She placed a trivet and a teapot on the table, followed shortly by two mismatched teacups. The tea smelled sweet. "You still take it with lemon and honey?"

Aurelio nodded.

Esther then turned her attention to me. "So, tell me about you, Wylie. Aurelio says you are a painter."

I hesitated. "Not really. I mean, I like to paint but . . ."

Aurelio, sensing my embarrassment, came to my rescue. "Wylie is very talented, but he needs some guidance."

"I see."

"I wanted him to meet Paolo. I thought it would be helpful."

"Good. Paolo is always interested in meeting young people."

We continued chatting for half an hour, drinking tea. It was now past noon. "Why don't you show Wylie around?" suggested Esther. "I have to finish getting lunch ready."

Aurelio led me out behind the house. "Paolo made all this," Aurelio said. It was a garden of wonders. Cypress trees. Sculpted fountains. Abundant shade. I had never seen anything like it before, like a dream come to life, but a happy dream, the product of a beautiful imagination. The outdoor space divided like a series of rooms. Here is the bedroom, here the kitchen. All open to the stars. Later in life I would visit similar gardens in Tuscany, Èze, but this was all new to me. This Mediterranean sensibility. The love of being outside, the harmony with nature. A long, freestanding wall covered in an abstract mural, another with a single window through which poked out the branch of an apple tree. The lattice of an arbor, strewn with knurled grapevines. A whitewashed brick oven, its aperture black with use. A solarium, painted in the colors of the sea, where Aurelio told me Paolo liked to sunbathe nude in winter. Wisteria. Wire chairs placed strategically where visitors could take their ease. Willows, pine groves. In the distance more statues, peeking from behind the trees like nymphs in a myth. The grass was sweet with the smell of fallen apples.

"Pollock lived right down the road. He used to come here. They all did," said Aurelio. "Esther was a sort of den mother for the Abstract Expressionists. They always knew they could get something to eat here. They would have parties that began at lunch and lasted all weekend. Guests slept on the ground. Can't you just see it? Back in those days Paolo used to make his own wine. I understand it was pretty filthy."

I imagined the ghosts of the era. Who would have been there? Pollock certainly. His wife, who was also a painter. Maybe Rothko. Motherwell. The women in sandals and capri pants. Cat's-eye glasses. Their arms bare in the style of the day. The men, earnest, smoking, drinking, arguing about art, the contemptibility of critics, the latest show. Money was never a topic. Instead they reveled in their freedom, their talent. Some of them would go on to become household names, others footnotes, and some disappeared entirely. It was a different Hamptons. There were no millionaires. At least not many.

"Who are these two young handsome men in my garden? *Cos'è questa cosa?* Why aren't they with pretty girls instead of an old man?" boomed out a voice, the accent thick yet amused.

I turned and saw a short man with the face of a matinee idol walking up to us. He had rich black hair white at the temples and twinkling black eyes. He embraced Aurelio, who stood a foot taller than him. "I was *desolato* with you for not coming sooner," he said. "But now you are here. You must tell me everything about Barcelona, eh? Did you bring anything to show me?"

We had several canvases in the truck, wrapped in a tarp. Most were Aurelio's, but he had insisted I include at least one of my own, which I did, as well as a few drawings.

"*E chi è questo?* And who is this?"

"This is Wylie Rose. He is the son of Mitchell Rose, my uncle Roger's old friend. I think you've met him."

"Oh yes, the great businessman," he replied, making a face and then laughing. He pronounced it "busy-ness man." "Your mother is *molta bella*, very beautiful, no?" His voice lilting, like music.

"Yes," I answered.

"I once spent a charming evening sitting beside her at a dinner party. Alas, she wouldn't go to bed with me, no matter how much I pleaded. *Che tragedia.*"

I didn't know what to say to that.

"No matter," he said, laughing again. "Sometimes it is much better to dream of love than to have it. That way you can never be disappointed. Come. Let us go and see what delicious thing Esther has made for us for lunch. *Sono affamato.*"

We followed Paolo inside. The table was set for four. A loaf of homemade bread rested on a cutting board. Cheese. At each place a bowl of steaming soup. Red wine in thick tumblers.

"Ah," cried Paolo on entering and rubbing his hands together. "A feast! I knew it. We are only artists, but we dine like kings!" We sat, and Paolo turned to me and asked, "Wylie? Like the coyote? I love him. Always trying but never succeeding. He is very human. *Très sympathique, non?*"

"I never thought about it like that." Of course, I had been teased about the name my whole life. Children running up behind me and yelling "beep beep!" I was grateful to him for seeing it differently.

"You should! It is a very philosophical cartoon, no?"

Over lunch he drew me out. I tried not to talk too much, but I couldn't help it. I was drinking wine, which loosened my tongue. I told them about myself, about wanting to be an artist. School. What I wanted to do. What my father wanted me to do. Paolo told me that being an artist was about more than talent. It was about dedication.

Esther spoke up. "You should read Rilke," she said.

I hadn't heard of him and said so. "No?" was her reply, her eyes expressive with concern. As I was to learn, she had a poor opinion of the American educational system. "You Americans. You are all orphans," she would say. "Wait here," she said, rising from the table, and despite her age she nimbly climbed the stairs. A few minutes later, after the conversation at the table had resumed, she returned, carrying a small dog-eared paperback. "Here," she said. "You can borrow this if you promise to bring it back."

I looked at the book. It was entitled *Letters to a Young Poet* by Rainer Maria Rilke. I thanked her.

"Esther loaned me the book a few years ago," said Aurelio.

"What's it about?" I asked Esther.

"Rilke was a famous German poet in the early part of the century," she replied. "A young military student contacted him seeking his advice. The student was torn between being an officer and being a poet. He sent his poems to Rilke, who wrote back to him. Eventually there were ten letters. Rilke said that it is never a question of whether one should become an artist or not. You either are or you aren't. If you cannot live without creating, that is all you can be. If you can live without, then you aren't. But it also takes work. Much work. Many years. You have to *'gehen Sie in sich,'* as Rilke said. You have to go inside yourself."

I nodded my head, unsure of my commitment. These people were artists, even Aurelio. It cloaked them like religion, like a mother's love. It fed them, gave them purpose, joy. But I was in embryo. My path unknown, my devotion untested. I was like a traveler from another country. The customs were attractive yet unfamiliar. I was afraid of doing the wrong thing, of giving offense.

"Take the book. Read it," said Esther, her smile kindly yet meaningful. She was paring a peach with an old knife. "You are very young. Remember, being an artist is very hard. If you aren't careful, it can destroy you."

"*Bene.* Enough with the serious talk," announced Paolo, putting down his wineglass. Our bowls were empty, the last drops of soup mopped up with the bread. "You have some beautiful paintings to show me. Aurelio, why don't you bring them out to the studio?"

I followed Aurelio back across the lawn to the truck and retrieved the canvases. We then walked around the old barn to a modern, rectangular studio, its walls nearly all glass. Paolo was already there and had unlocked the door for us. He sat in a chair in front of a small desk by an unlit potbellied stove.

There were several easels scattered around the room with canvases in various stages of development. Some of his finished work was on the walls, more in racks. His paintings were beautiful, original. Rich with the colors of the Old World. The Mediterranean blue of the sky. The sunbaked brown of the earth. The black of widow's scarves. The older paintings were more figurative. Families on the beach, young children. Nudes. I wondered if they were of Esther and their children, now grown. The more recent works were more abstract but with the same marvelous colors, the same sense of life. They made me feel as though I was standing at an open window, seeing things I had never seen before but intuitively recognizing them. Bulls. Widows. Lovers. I could almost feel the heat, the smell of the sea. In the back, there were racks of more paintings. The studio had no electricity. When it got too dark, it was time to stop for the day. Aurelio had told me that in the winter, when the days were shorter, Paolo and Esther often traveled so he could teach in Rotterdam, Milan, Berkeley, Cambridge. He had paintings in collections all over the world.

"Show me," Paolo commanded. Aurelio had brought a dozen or so paintings. "Ahh," said Paolo, as he took each one in turn. He leaned back in his chair, his forefinger to his lips. *"Buono."*

When the canvases had been shown, Paolo said, "Bravo, Aurelio. You are learning well. But don't be too eager yet. You are like a horse that wants to run too fast. Learn to pace yourself. Otherwise, you may tire and stumble."

Aurelio stiffened but nodded his head, saying nothing.

"It is a question of finding your style. It is like Esther said: In order to find your own artistic voice you must go inside yourself. That is the difference between an artist and someone who moves paint around. You must learn to trust yourself, *si?*"

Aurelio nodded again. I was also speechless. To me, Aurelio's paintings were perfect, but after hearing what Paolo said I understood why he criticized them. Despite their beauty and the skill with which Aurelio had painted them, they were void of anything personal. I hesitated to show Paolo my own much less ambitious work, but he said, "Come, Wylie Coyote. Show me your paintings!"

Silently, I stood and displayed what I had brought. Again, Paolo leaned back in his chair, saying, *"Si, si."*

"I also have drawings," I offered.

"Bene. Let me see them, *per piacere,"* he said, reaching out his hand. Like the rest of him, it was small and finely formed yet strong.

He studied them. They were mainly pencil and charcoal drawings. A portrait of my mother drawn over spring vacation, friends from school.

"Prego. I have bad news and good news for you, Wylie Coyote," said Paolo with a smile. "The bad news is that you have no idea what you are doing. You are like a baby that has been taught how to walk all wrong. It is important for you to relearn how to walk and only later can you run, *si?"* He laughed. It was impossible to disagree. "But the good news is that you have talent. The question is whether you can do what is required, *si?"*

I nodded my head. "What should I do?"

"You need a teacher. A good one."

"Will you teach me?"

He bobbled his head noncommittally, making a steeple of his fingers. "We'll see. It is possible, but first you need to do certain things."

"What?"

"You must read the Rilke. Esther is right. If the book sounds true to you then you may have what is needed. There are other books. Arnheim, for example. John Berger. But start with Rilke. Also, you must draw all the time. Carry a sketchbook and pencil with you everywhere you go. Draw everything."

"Is that all?"

He laughed. "No. Also, you must spend a lot of time looking at paintings. Really looking at paintings. Go to museums. Visit ateliers. Educate yourself. When I was a student that's what we would do. We would look at everything. We wanted to know how it was made, what made it good, *si?* We were like wild animals, hungry all the time." He made a snarling face and then laughed. "If it is really good, you will know because those are the paintings you wish you had done yourself, and you will lust after them like a disappointed lover because you never did. You will feel an ache here." He held his hands to his heart. "And here," he added with a laugh, pointing to his crotch. "Now, come," he said, ushering us out. "I am an old man, and I need to rest."

"May I come back?" I asked as we strolled back to the house.

"Naturalmente," said Paolo. "You may come back tomorrow, if you wish. I could use a strong back. There is much work to do that I am either too old or too lazy to do myself. That is the best way to apprentice, no?" he added with a laugh. I said goodbye to Esther. She handed me the Rilke, which I had left on the kitchen table. "Good luck, young man," she said.

For the rest of the summer, I returned to their house in Springs every day after work. I read the Rilke. Swept the studio. Cleaned the brushes. Stretched canvas. Helped patch a leak in the roof. Weeded the garden. Ran errands. Afterward, Paolo and I would have a glass of wine under the willow tree that grew near the front door, Esther joining us. They would critique my drawings. Sometimes there would be other friends. A famous artist lived across the street, a Romanian whose clever drawings frequently appeared on the cover of *The New Yorker.* There were also former students. A gallery owner from the city. Admirers from Europe who spoke only Italian; they would sit there in the garden wearing their jackets over their shoulders like capes, smoking cigarettes while Esther waited on them.

Most of their friends came to them, but once I was asked

to drive Paolo to the house of another painter, a short distance away. It was de Kooning, white-haired and disheveled. "Bill," said Paolo as the old men embraced. I sat in the background while the two artists talked, each in his own accented English. Their friendship spanned decades.

Many of their friends were dead, though. Pollock, whose name they pronounced "Po-lack," Rothko, Gorky. Pollock had given Paolo and Esther one of his early paintings as a sign of friendship when his career was just beginning to take off. The famous *Life* article had already appeared. They hung the painting in various rooms in the house, but after a few months they returned it, saying it didn't work anywhere. Pollock was not offended. He understood. Esther laughed when she told the story. The loss of a painting that would one day be worth in the millions was of no importance to her.

There were other works of art in the house by friends. A Rothko sketch. A small Kandinsky, from when they met in Paris before the war. A Calder mobile. In the corner was a tall Giacometti. Most staggering of all, an entire wall covered in a mural painted by a man who was more famous as an architect but which was still stunning. Otherwise the house was very simple, almost empty. Everything was precise, nothing extraneous, like a Zen garden. There was only one bathroom, with an enormous iron tub that had ball-and-claw feet. This was harder on the women than the men, of course, who were happy to do their business in the bushes. Over the many years I visited, the house never changed. The only additions were new books, new friends, and new grandchildren.

I saw less of Aurelio than I would have liked. He now possessed a reserve that hadn't been there before. He may have been hurt that I was spending so much time with Paolo. Or he may have been embarrassed that I was present when Paolo critiqued his work. That is the problem with modesty. Too often it masks deep ambition. It would have been one thing if Paolo had complimented his work. Then Aurelio could have been self-effacing. But to hope for one reaction and receive a lesser response not only is truly humbling but can also be truly disappointing.

When we drove home that afternoon, we just barely talked about what Paolo had said to him. "He's right, of course," said Aurelio glumly. "My work is too imitative. I need to find my own way." I did stop by on several occasions, hoping to find him in. He was always friendly but more introspective, less confident.

On those occasions, I would catch glimpses of Cesca, but always from a distance. Walking into the house followed by a tall man with long blond hair. Talking in the garden with her grandmother. Carrying groceries. There was never a convenient opportunity to speak to her. Once, I stopped to watch her play doubles with her mother, Roger, and another guest. She was wearing a short white tennis dress, with her hair tied back. Long legs. Pink pom-poms on her socks. She bounced the ball twice with her hand on the clay before delivering a rifle shot of a serve down the line, past her uncle, who couldn't lay his racquet on it. Pleased, she turned and winked at me, then shifted to the other side of the baseline and served again with equal power.

Roger yelled out some comment, half in jest, half in frustration. I lingered a few more moments for the sheer pleasure of watching her move.

As Paolo suggested, I had bought a sketchbook, and soon I was filling its pages. At lunch, I would draw the men I worked with. They were locals. Initially they were annoyed about being asked to sit still, but they usually liked what I showed them. Most of them asked to keep their portraits. I also drew groups of girls on the beach, seagulls, children playing in the waves, old couples strolling together. Some were quick studies, others more finished. Like Paolo I was drawn to the beach for its good light, variety of subject matter, and natural compositional qualities.

The days melted into one another as I began to have an understanding of myself, no longer as son or student or team-mate, but as someone apart. This, I said silently, this is what I want. To watch as something beautiful emerges on a blank page, to get something right, to make a mistake and go back and try again. It was like the thrilling early days of love, when everything is possible.

9

As the end of summer neared, I was invited to a farewell dinner for Aurelio. He was returning to Barcelona in a few days. Cosmo was the cook. He was one of those people who seemed to be good at everything. Good student, star athlete. Once I had been leaving Aurelio's studio, and I heard piano music. I followed it to the main house. There, through an open window, I could see and hear Cosmo playing, his head bowed in concentration, the fingers flying over the keyboard, the notes lingering in the air. For several moments, I stood there mesmerized. Finally, I had to remove myself, concerned he might suddenly stop and see me.

At the dinner were Izzy and Ruth Baum, looking older and frailer, Paolo and Esther, Roger, Dot, Kitty, and Randall. All the Bonet children, of course, and a few of their friends. I felt flattered to be asked.

Cesca was dating a tall, handsome Greek named Pavlos, who lived in Southampton. He wore a gold chain around his neck and a heavy mustache and drove a vintage Maserati. I had never been so close to a car like that before. I couldn't help admiring its sleek design, the polished wooden steering wheel and leather seats. "How are you, Wylie?" asked Cesca, her hand on my forearm. Her voice familiarly raspy. I had barely seen her. She appeared always to be in motion, elusive as music from another room.

She was wearing a white peasant-style blouse with embroidery in the front, showing off her deep tan. It hung off her shoulders, revealing her clavicle. "I like your hair longer," she said. I had been letting it grow. She reached out and touched the back of my head. "So handsome." She talked to me now the way an adult does to a child or a horse. I resented her trying to keep putting distance between us. Did she regret our time together so much? "Aurelio says you've been seeing a lot of Paolo. He's a friend of Pare's, you know."

I nodded my head. We were standing out on the porch. She was smoking and held a wineglass in her other hand. I had drunk nothing so far. The police had started cracking down on drinking and driving.

"They all knew each other in Paris," she continued. "Have you ever been to Paris, Wylie?"

I shook my head. "No."

"You should. I'd be happy to give you names of people there."

"Thank you. I'd like to go." What I really wanted to say was: I'd like to go with you. She would wear a kerchief around her head, shop in the little stores along cobblestoned side streets, in the evening we'd have aperitifs at a sidewalk café. I would paint. Every night we'd make love in our small bed. We'd be together again. Like before.

"Let me see your sketchbook," she said, removing it from my back pocket. I didn't try to stop her even if I could have. She put her glass down on the railing and flipped through the pages. "Not bad."

"Thank you."

"You should draw me sometime." It was part invitation, part challenge.

"When?"

"Why not now? I'm an artist's daughter. I know how to pose." Taking me by the hand, she led me to a small white metal table with several chairs scattered around. "You sit there, and I'll sit here." She leaned back in her chair, took a final drag of her cigarette, stabbed it out in the ashtray, and, finishing her wine, winked at me. "Okay. Ready when you are."

Portraits are very difficult. Paolo had told me: "To do a good portrait of someone, you must either draw them hundreds of times or know them for hundreds of years." There is a difference between capturing a likeness on paper and capturing a person. The former requires skill, which is hard enough in itself, but the other requires knowledge, which is even harder. More challenging still is to draw someone you are in love with.

"Mind if I scratch my nose?" Cesca asked after ten minutes. I nodded my head and reviewed what I had so far. It was not terrible. "Don't worry," she said. "I won't ask to see it until you're done."

I continued to draw her. It is an extraordinary freedom to be able to sit and stare without fear of being caught at someone who you love but who may not love you back. The eye can linger over every facet of their face, the planes of their shoulders, a nostril's delicateness, the curve of an ear, traveling wherever it wants. To a bare knee, a slender calf, the rise of a breast. To hands joined together on a lap. Occasionally your eyes will travel to theirs and meet, and, for a few seconds, there is an exquisite, unspoken intimacy.

"You know, Wylie . . ." she began to say.

"There you are," cried a voice behind us, shattering the moment. Cesca smiled as Pavlos walked up. "I've been looking for you." He had no accent. His father was Greek, his mother American, I learned later. He was raised in New York but worked for the family business. They owned an island in the Aegean.

"Wylie's almost finished," said Cesca.

Pavlos looked over my shoulder. "Hmm. Yeah. Not bad."

He took the book from my hand without asking and showed it to Cesca. "See? It almost looks like you."

The drawing was incomplete, I wanted to say. I needed more time. I was furious with Pavlos but said nothing.

"I love it," said Cesca. She stood up and bent over to give me a kiss on the cheek. "May I keep it?"

"But it's not finished."

"I'm getting stiff from sitting. Can we finish another time?"

"Only if you let me come back and do it again. I can do a better job."

Before she could answer, Pavlos came up and said, "Come on, babe. It's dinnertime." As he led her inside, she turned back to look at me, mouthing a silent "Thank you."

The rest of the evening passed in a haze. Like an opium eater, I knew it was important not to overdose. I kept clear of Cesca, exchanging only occasional glances with her. Just being in the same room was exhilarating. But it was also painful watching her sit close to Pavlos, his hands on her. I tried to ignore it, to rise above it, and to show her that I was the better man. So I performed for her, chatting with everyone, making them laugh. Izzy and Ruth, whom I respectfully referred to as Mr. Baum and Mrs. Baum, even though the family referred to them as Gog and Bushka. Paolo and Esther.

At dinner I sat next to Carmen, who normally was so reserved, but I managed to entertain her with a few jokes. She was going to be a senior in high school next year and was trying to decide whether she should go to Harvard or Oxford. She already knew she wanted to be a doctor. On my other side was Dot, who drank too much, and at one point put her hand on my thigh under the table.

After the dishes were cleared, Aurelio rose to make a toast. He thanked everyone. His mother first. Then his grandparents. To my surprise, he also thanked me. We all said "Salut" and took a sip of wine.

Roger found me. He was as jovial as always. Yvette and he had split up. His hair was turning gray. He asked after me. About school. As always, he expressed himself with his hands as much as his voice. He could not help touching the people he talked with. It was a trait the whole family shared. Constantly roaming over people's shoulders, patting a knee. He was a little drunk, and his eyes were glassy. "Good, good," he said in response to my answers to his questions. He also asked after my father. They were no longer as close as they had been.

"Tell Mitch I said hello. It's been too long since I saw him. Tell him I miss him." He had a pained look in his eye that focused in for a moment and then disappeared. "What about girls?" he asked, changing the subject. "Bet a handsome young man like you must have plenty of girls. You should have seen your old man. He was a real pussy hound."

Aurelio came up. "Take a walk?" he asked.

I said good night to Roger and promised I'd tell my father to give him a call. I looked around for Cesca, but I didn't see her. She must have left while I was talking with Roger. Disappointed, I followed Aurelio outside. He had a bottle of wine and offered it to me.

"Thank you for coming tonight," he said, as we walked under the stars. "I will miss you."

"I will miss you too."

"You know, you are one of my only friends."

This surprised me. He had the gift of friendship. People were drawn to him. Men, women, old, young. I had seen it. His charm and his soulful eyes. It was easy to like him.

"Why do you say that?"

"I know many people, but that doesn't mean they are my friends. Or that I respect them. I respect very few people. Almost none my own age—except for my family, of course. That is why I suppose I prefer older people like Paolo and Esther. You are one of the only young people I have met whom I respect."

I said nothing. "That's just it," he continued. "You know when to be quiet. When to say nothing. You are content to just accept things as they come and learn from them. That is very difficult. It takes people lifetimes to do that, but to you it comes naturally."

I had never looked at it that way. To me, it was simply shyness or good manners. My mother always told me that people don't like someone who talks too much. I was, however, pleased that Aurelio thought so highly of me. He was certainly the only person around my age whom I respected greatly. I had other friends—classmates and former classmates. Fellow oarsmen. I was even moderately popular. At least no one seemed to actively object to my presence. But none of them knew of my interest in art or understood it so perfectly. Even the girls I had dated knew nothing of my ambitions, thinking instead that I was destined for a nice, safe, normal career like the rest of my peers.

I thanked Aurelio and took another drink of the wine. We were sitting now on the same stretch of beach where I had gone swimming with Cesca the year before. The moon shone above the water.

The memory was bittersweet, and I probably drank more of the wine than I should have. We talked about Barcelona, art school, the insidious effect that money had on the art world—one of his recurrent themes—the importance of creating something beautiful not for fame or reward but for the thing itself. Aurelio did most of the talking. I mainly sat there thinking about Cesca and getting drunk. I desperately wanted to talk about Cesca, in the annoying way that young men feel compelled to share their romantic aspirations, but every time the subject was on my lips I said nothing. He was her brother after all. His first loyalties lay there.

At one point I lay down on the sand, listening to the waves gently lap the shore, staring up at the stars, feeling at peace. It was good to have a friend like this, I reflected. I was so grateful to him, for his companionship, his encouragement. And for introducing me to Paolo and Esther. The future seemed a little clearer. Maybe Cesca would also be there in some way. I couldn't see it yet, but it was a nice thought. Aurelio talked on.

"I love you," he said, disturbing my reverie.

These were not words I was accustomed to hearing, especially from a man. My mother had said them to me when I was a child, tucking me into bed with a kiss on the forehead. Or as a form of apology or to soften the blow of a punishment. "You know I love you, but . . ." That was how my father spoke to me, throwing the phrase out in passing, as though it would be embarrassing not to adumbrate it with a qualification, avoiding any whiff of sentimentality. I took it for granted that my parents loved me, as I loved them, but we were not a family given to regularly professing our affection for one another.

Certainly I had never heard these words uttered to me by a girl of my own age, even if I did yearn to use them myself and hear them reciprocated. Most of all from Cesca. When we were together I had told her that I loved her and had felt in her touch what I believed to be love, but the words never came. Sometimes she would pretend not to hear me, other times she would stroke my head and say, "Thank you, Wylie."

I was unsure how to respond to Aurelio. Maybe in Europe

it was more conventional, like topless sunbathing. Didn't French men kiss each other on the cheek? I didn't want to insult him.

"I—I love you too," I said, meaning that I felt deep affection for him, which was the truth.

He put his hand on mine. It was dark, and I could barely see him, but I heard him shift closer to me. Felt his breath on my face.

I stood up, and he pulled away.

"I have to go," I said, stumbling back over the dunes, wanting to get as far away as possible.

"Wylie, come back," he called.

I didn't listen. I had heard about guys like that. We made fun of them. They compromised us. But I was young then and didn't know that love could take more than one form.

10

I AVOIDED THE BONETS AFTER WHAT HAPPENED THAT night with Aurelio. That meant I never finished my drawing of Cesca, though it remained in my sketchbook. That whole year I would go back and stare at the unfinished drawing of Cesca I had made that night. While I had soon filled up my first sketchbook and had worked my way through several more, like a postulant with a favorite psalm I would return almost nightly to the portrait of Cesca. I had sketched the broad outline of her face and hair but only finished one of the eyes. It stared at me, beautiful and restless. The rest of her features were ghostly, lightly penciled in, the mischievous smile just barely perceptible, the dark hair only a vague mass. It was far from a perfect likeness but it was all I had.

There were other concerns that year. After I had returned to boarding school in the fall for my senior year, my mother went to my father and told him she wanted a divorce. The news had come as a surprise to both him and me. I had never thought of my parents as particularly unhappy. But I had never really thought of them as particularly happy either. In the selfish way of children, I had just assumed that nothing would come along to disturb my world. Other children's parents might get divorced but not mine.

But my mother was unhappy. Unlike my father, who was naturally gregarious, she didn't have many friends, and during the summers her days, especially the ones when my father was working in the city, were lonely ones. She was southern and missed her home, her friends and family, and did not like many of my father's associates. She found them ill-mannered and their humor crude. Their women were loud and overdressed. She was like a cat living in a nation of dogs.

When I was a child she was my best friend. We would raid vegetable stands together, hunt for frogs in the mud, dig holes in the backyard, attack the local beach on our bikes. She, not my father, was the one who taught me how to bait a hook and catch crabs with a chicken leg. How to bodysurf. During summer weeks she would sit out on the back porch with her vodka and cigarettes, my absent father's chair unoccupied until the weekend, while I played on the floor with my impressive collection of toy tanks. She would tell me stories about her family, about her own childhood. Memories of faded plantations and foxhunting, large Christmas parties and sledding in Richmond during rare but ecstatic snows. About her father, who was a hero in the war and had been killed at Saint-Lô. On her desk was a black-and-white photograph of him, handsome in his captain's uniform. She kept the Silver Star that had been posthumously awarded him in its box in the top drawer of her little writing desk.

My father was crushed by her demand. He had felt that the marriage was a success. That they were as happy as ever. "That's the point, Mitch," she had sighed. She was not vindictive, though, letting him hold on to the East Hampton house while she kept the New York apartment. This she would soon sell in order to return to Virginia. My father, meanwhile, was living in a small rental apartment near Beekman, but I never saw it. The rest of the details, the process of cutting away the dead tissue from the live, were spared me.

I did have a single visit from my father late that fall. He appeared unannounced at my school on a Saturday and took me out to lunch at the local inn, where instead of eating he just alternated between saying how much he still loved my mother and telling me how she was a bitch who had ruined his life. Naturally, I couldn't agree with him but sat there nodding, letting his anger wash over me, sensing the pain of his wounded pride, the wreckage of his life. It was only years later that I learned of his affairs.

I was spending my first Christmas break after the divorce at our soon-to-be-sold apartment with my mother when I ran into Cesca at a New Year's Eve party. She was on her way out with a group of people as I was coming in. "Wylie," she exclaimed. "How wonderful to see you. We're late for another party. Give me a call. Happy New Year!"

I took her at her word and called the number late in the afternoon on the first. The phone rang four or five times before an unfamiliar voice answered "Bonet residence."

"Good afternoon. Is Cesca there?"

"Miss Cesca no here."

"Do you know when she'll be back?"

"She be back later."

I debated leaving a message but decided against it.

"Thank you. I'll call back later."

When I did call back, the same voice answered. It was around seven o'clock. The time after naps and before dinner, at least in Manhattan.

The voice on the other end said, "You wait. I see if she here."

"Please tell her it's Wylie."

I waited several minutes before Cesca came on the line. "Hello? Wylie?"

"Hi. Yes, it's me. Sorry to bother you. You did say that I should give you a call."

"Look, I have to run out."

"I was hoping I could see you."

"I don't know. I'm very busy."

"Please? I have to go back to school soon."

She sighed. "Okay. Tell you what, can you come downtown tomorrow around four? I know a little café."

"Great. Where?" She gave me an address on Waverly Place.

I arrived early. The café was dark and smoky inside. The walls held faded photographs of long-dead opera singers. I sat at a small empty table in a corner. A waiter approached. I didn't know what a cappuccino or latté was, so I just ordered a cup of coffee. "American or French?" the waiter asked. "American," I answered, unsure of the difference.

Ten minutes passed. Twenty. There was no sign of Cesca. I wondered if I should call her from the pay phone on the wall. Even if I could remember her number, I debated whether it would do any good. If she were coming, she would have already left. The thought that she might not come depressed me. I felt foolish and then slightly angry, at myself for thinking she would be interested in seeing me and at her for letting me think it.

I had finished my second cup of coffee and was about to leave when Cesca walked in. "Sorry I'm late," she said, giving me a quick kiss before sitting down.

She was wearing a long oatmeal-colored sheepskin coat, blue jeans, and Frye boots. Her head was covered by a light wool cap. Her cheeks were rosy from the cold.

"It's been a crazy day," she said, taking off her cap and shaking her hair out, an act that cut me like a knife. There was a simplicity and naturalness about her that made her even more beautiful. The waiter hurried over. She stood to give him a kiss. "Ciao, Danny," she said. She asked him to bring her a cappuccino and took a pack of Marlboros from her purse.

"So how are you?" she asked.

She was like that and knew it was easy to forgive her. Her presence exonerated her.

I told her about school, painting, applying to college, my parents' divorce. She was empathetic, recalling her own parents' divorce. "It was hard at first," she told me, then shrugged. "My father was never around much anyway, so it didn't really seem all that different at first. You'll learn."

I asked her about herself. She was taking time off from Barnard. Maybe she would not go back to college after all. She was thinking about transferring to an art school. Somewhere that offered a degree. Possibly Parsons or SVA. Maybe London. She had heard good things about Saint Martins. Or maybe the Beaux-Arts in Paris. It was a big decision.

I was envious of her opportunity, wishing I was in a position to alter my life the same way. I would be going to college in the fall. If I told my parents I wanted to go to art school, they would oppose it. My father because he would think it was a stupid, airy-fairy idea—and he'd be damned if he was going to pay for it. My mother because it wasn't what one did, dear.

I told Cesca this, and she laughed. "We don't have that problem in our family," she said. "My grandfather would love it if we became artists. Or actors. Or anything. Aurelio will become a great painter," she said. "Cosmo a great composer."

What about her? I asked.

"I'm not sure yet. Maybe a set designer. Maybe a painter. Whatever it is, I'll be great at it." She laughed and looked at her watch. "I have to go."

She put down her cup and opened her purse. "No, please," I said, fishing around in the pockets of my khakis for my money.

"Let me." We'd barely been talking for half an hour. I didn't want it to end. "Please don't go just yet," I pleaded.

She gave me a sympathetic but resigned smile. "I have to go, Wylie. Another time."

"Wait, one second. Can I ask you something? It's important. It's about Aurelio."

She resumed her seat. "What is it?"

"Um, I don't know quite how to say this."

"Say what?"

"Aurelio. Is he, I mean, does he like girls?"

She laughed. "Of course he likes girls. Why do you ask?"

I blushed. "I just wondered. He, um . . ." But I couldn't finish.

She looked at me evenly and leaned in, smiling. "He also likes boys," she whispered. "I think he'd do it with a turnip if he was attracted to it."

I sat back and took this in. It was not information I wanted to hear, but I supposed it was better, if only slightly, than the alternative.

"You look confused," she said.

I nodded my head. "I am confused."

"Why?"

I proceeded to tell her about what had happened on the beach. How surprised and angry I had been.

"I can understand that," she said. "I hope you forgave him."

"That's just it. I don't know if I can."

"Of course, you should. He's still Lio."

"Yeah, but he's a guy. He shouldn't be doing that kind of thing at all. I freaked out, you know? I haven't seen him since, and I don't know if I want to."

She looked at me, her dark eyes amused, bold. "So what if he made a little pass at you? You're lovely. I don't remember you complaining when I did it."

I looked away, embarrassed and annoyed. I didn't want to discuss what had happened between us quite so casually.

She laughed. "Don't be too hard on Lio. He's a sweetheart. He didn't mean anything by it. I know how fond he is of you." She stood up. "Look, I really have to go. How long are you in New York for?"

I told her. Only three more days and then back to school.

"I'm going skiing in Utah tomorrow so I probably won't see you before you leave. But you'll be back out next summer, right? And if Lio's around, I hope he won't freak you out too much."

She bent over and gave me a kiss, not on the cheek, but this time, to my surprise, on the lips, lingering just a second longer than necessary. The softness of her lips, their warmth; I remember them still. Standing up, she ran her fingers through my hair. "So handsome," she said. "I'll see you in the summer, okay? *Adéu.*"

BUT I DIDN'T SEE HER THAT SUMMER. I DID, HOWEVER, SEE Aurelio.

It was at Paolo and Esther's. I was living with my father, once again working as a carpenter and painting in the evenings, but I still went to see them every Saturday. Paolo would critique my work while Esther fed us. Most days I would help in the garden, planting or weeding. Sometimes Paolo and I would walk to the beach, where he would make fantastic sand sculptures and flirt with the pretty girls. Once, a beautiful blond woman in a bikini rode by on a horse. I had never seen him so excited. He walked up to her. *"Ciao, bella donna,"* he cooed in his heavy accent. "You are a goddess, no? Come and sit with us miserable mortals and tell us what it is like up in heaven."

To my astonishment, she dismounted and sat with us, and

for an hour she helped Paolo with one of his sculptures while the horse wandered about in the background, nibbling on beach grass. Paolo kept her laughing with a running string of stories and compliments. It was a delicious moment. He was at that age when a man can charm a woman without being a threat. Certainly if he had been younger, he would have charmed her right into bed. With his short legs and handsome face, he never failed to remind me of a satyr.

I always felt honored when Esther asked me to stay with them for dinner. There would often be other guests coming. Other artists, a magazine writer and his wife. A famous photographer. Novelists. Everyone gathered outside, where the slanting sunlight glinted against the leaves of the trees. People of all ages. White-haired lions of the Abstract Expressionist movement with scarves around their necks, pretty girls in strapless dresses. Paolo and Esther's son, Gianni, and daughter, Ginevra, were there with their families; a three-year-old grandchild running naked through the garden squealing with laughter. There is nothing like a party at the home of an artist. Esther was cooking a seafood stew in the outdoor oven in a large copper pot: squid, fluke, cod, striped bass, and monkfish. "Mon-key fish," as Paolo called it.

Tables had been laid under the arbor, and lanterns had been lit in the branches. We were all about to sit down when a lone figure appeared at my side. It was Aurelio. I had not seen him since that night.

"Hello, Wylie," he said.

"Hello."

"How are you?"

"Good. And you? When did you get back?"

"A week ago. It's good to see you."

I said nothing.

"Look, about what happened," he continued.

"Forget it."

"Are you sure?"

"Yes."

He broke into a huge smile. "I am glad. I've thought about you often. You must come over tomorrow. I have many things to show you."

It was impossible for me to remain angry with him. I remembered what Cesca had told me about him. He was still my friend. We talked about Barcelona. Art School. How beautiful it was. How fine the people were. I asked after his family. After Cesca.

"She hasn't been here this summer," he told me. "She's somewhere in Europe right now but she's threatening to go to art school in London. I hope she does. She's much more talented than she gives herself credit for."

"What do you mean?"

"She draws quite beautifully but she's very secretive about it. When she was a little girl she'd always be drawing in a corner and when Pare asked to see it she'd try to hide whatever it was she was working on. He could be critical, you see. He'd say things like 'That leg is too long,' and he'd be right, but she'd start crying anyway. She hates criticism. Always has."

I nodded, trying to picture such a scene. "How did she seem to you when you saw her?"

He laughed. "Pretty much as she always seems. Leaving a trail of disappointed men in her wake."

I changed the subject. "Is everyone else well? Are they all around?"

"Come by tomorrow. They'll all love to see you."

"I will."

"Come to my studio first. I want to show you my new work."

I went the next day. He was very excited. It was easy to see why. His paintings were better than ever—luminous, sensual, moving. Portraits of men and women, most of them nude. He told me that many of them were prostitutes. Some defiant, some vulnerable. One had a tattoo of a butterfly on her shoulder. A man, thin as a blade, had an enormous member. There were a few others. An old man, his hands bent with arthritis.

"What are you going to do with these?" I asked.

"I've got a meeting with a gallery owner in the city next week. I finally think I'm ready. If he likes my work, he may represent me."

I breathe out silently. "That's very exciting, Lio. When do you go in?"

"I will take the train in Tuesday. The gallery's in the East Village."

"Would you like a lift to the station?"

"I was hoping you'd ask," he replied with a smile. It was like old times.

A few days later at the station, I helped him onto the train, his canvases tied together. "Good luck," I said, shaking his hand. I meant it. I was happy for him. No one I knew worked harder than he did, or cared more deeply. The success of a friend runs two ways. It can cause jealousy or it can inspire. I saw Aurelio as a light on the path, leading me on. If he could do it, maybe I could too. When one is young, anything is conceivable, no matter how ambitious it seems. What is not yet understood is that most fail, even the talented ones.

As the summer wound down, I visited the Bonets often. Aurelio let me work in his studio with him. He would spend the whole day there, forgetting about eating, about everything else. Only Kitty could rouse him. "Come in for lunch," she would say. "Wylie, make sure he doesn't forget." When he finally ate, he would fall on his food like a starving man.

One night I was invited to dinner at the big house. Roger was there with his new wife, an Englishwoman named Diana. Dot was by herself. Kitty was with Randall. Cosmo, Carmen,

Aurelio, and me. The only one missing was Cesca. Izzy was faltering. He used a cane now, around his shoulders a shawl. His hair was thinner, the skin like paper. There were sores on his forehead and hands. His mind went in and out. I shook hands with him gently, introducing myself. It was like holding bone.

"Mitchell's son," explained Kitty in a loud voice.

The old man nodded his head and said, "I always liked your father. Give him my best, will you?"

Ruth sat there like an empty shell, recognizing no one. Dot led her in and out. At dinner she carved her food for her.

After dinner I found myself talking with Dot, her dyed blond hair outlined in the lamplight. She had many bangles on her wrists, which rattled when she moved. She also wore long earrings and a reddish halter dress tied at the neck revealing leathery shoulders. Her face was lined and tired, but there were still traces of her former prettiness. Everyone else had gone inside. The stars were out, and it was time for me to go. There was no sign of Aurelio. I kept craning my neck to look for him. He had probably slipped away to his studio. Dot was saying something.

"Excuse me?" I said.

"I said I used to fuck your father." She drew on a cigarette.

I had no idea how to respond.

"He was pretty good. What he lacked in technique he made up for in enthusiasm."

"Well . . ."

"What about you?" she continued.

"What about me what?"

"You want to fuck?"

"Um . . ."

"Still a virgin, right? I thought so. You can always tell. Come on. We'll fix that."

"I'm sorry. I don't . . ."

She put out her cigarette and stood up. "Suit yourself. You're missing out though."

"Thank you. But . . ."

"Are you queer?"

"No."

She leaned over and grabbed my crotch. "Well, if you change your mind, I'll leave my door unlocked. I'm in the little red house."

I watched her leave. When I told my father about it the next day, he laughed and told me it had been a long time ago, but it was true. "What a family," he said, shaking his head. "They're beautiful, talented, rich. It's all very seductive. But they're like spoiled children. They'll take everything and give nothing in return."

11

IN THE FALL I WENT TO COLLEGE AND CESCA DID MOVE TO London. Ostensibly she was there to study painting at the Chelsea School of Art, but it seems more likely now that she was lost and was simply trying to give her life some direction. Studying set design at Barnard and living in New York had not proved to be satisfactory. Aurelio was in Barcelona. She wanted to make her own way. London seemed as good a place as any. This was in the early eighties. The King's Road swarmed with punks in Mohawks and Doc Martens. Nightclubs and pubs pulsated with loud, angry music. Thatcher was in office, the economy was beginning its long climb out of recession, and the IRA had bombed Harrods. As for the reason for studying painting, Cesca told me once later: "You know I'm not a bad painter. The problem is that there were people in my family who were much better than me."

She moved with the aristocracy, as she would. Most of them were old friends of the family, new friends she met at parties. Her face was her passport. Every Monday she would come to class exhausted and hungover from the weekend. Most of her classmates were serious students who didn't know what to make of her. She rented a furnished apartment on Lower Sloane Street that belonged to a friend of her mother's. It was on the first floor and looked out over the Duke of York's Barracks. There was shopping at Vivienne Westwood and Harvey Nichols, late nights at Tramp and the Cod. Ronnie Scott's. Dancing at Annabel's. Once she flirted with Richard Harris, who took her to a pub he knew near Billingsgate that was open all night and where fishermen and dockworkers would come in for an early pint and say, "Awright then, Richard?" and he would tell a joke or sing a song.

She had one friend in particular, a heavy girl who had recently come down from Oxford. Emma was her name. She dyed her spiky hair purple and wore ripped stockings and heavy leather bands studded with spikes on her arms. Her father was a cabinet minister. They lived in a large house on Cheyne Walk. In the dining room was a Canaletto. "You have to meet Ems," one of her friends in New York, an English woman Cesca had met at Studio 54, told her. "She's simply outrageous."

A week after arriving in London, Cesca rang, introducing herself. "Do come round," said Emma. "We'll have a spot of lunch."

She took Cesca to an Italian restaurant near her house where they drank two bottles of Pinot Grigio. Emma loved New York, especially the club scene. She also knew Spain a little. Had been to the Marbella Club but in general the country was too full of Arabs for her tastes. Had she been to Venice? Cesca had not. "You must go," Emma declared. "I'll take you. We'll go together and stay at the Cip. That's where we always stay. They always make a big fuss about Daddy. And the boys are divine. Just watch them. Remember, they're all buggerers at heart." She giggled. "*Anale,* they call it. Haven't you ever done it?"

"Never."

Emma winked and smiled. "Filthy beasts. They do it all the time. The girls do it to preserve their virginity. I know a principessa who did it with her cousin up until the time she was married. Takes some getting used to, but you learn to enjoy it. The trick is to relax."

Emma introduced Cesca to many of her friends. Through the fall, she took her to weekend house parties in the country. Emma's family had a "pile," as she called it, in the Cotswolds, near Chipping Campden, but she preferred visiting other people. Most days it rained, the men shooting pheasant while the women walked along behind and watched. After her first weekend, Cesca bought a Barbour jacket and Hunters. At night the men wore black tie at dinner, and the women smoked Silk Cut and danced barefoot. The rooms were large and drafty, and the hot water ran out quickly.

Most of the men she met were Old Etonians working in the City or managing their own estates. They struck her as overgrown schoolboys who drank too much and had bad teeth. But not all of them were like that. Emma had a friend whose family owned a large Georgian villa in Buckinghamshire. He played guitar in a rock band that had yet to release an album. His name was Desmond. He was her third cousin. Emma shrieked: "We used to play doctor!"

Desmond occupied one wing of the house. The rest was shuttered and the furniture covered in dust sheets. The rooms unheated. There were dirty dishes in the sink and dirty sheets on the beds. They arrived while the band was rehearsing. Desmond was the lead singer. He had long blond hair and wore leather pants. Emma had told Cesca he was a viscount. His parents were divorced. The earl lived in Italy for tax purposes. The mother, a fading beauty, had remarried. The sister lived on an ashram in India.

Cesca thought Desmond very handsome. They all huddled

in a large, nearly empty room in front of an impressive mantel in which burned an inadequate fire. She was wearing a short skirt that showed off her legs. There were two other men and a young woman. The men had long hair. One was German, and he played bass. He had a high forehead and a long pinched nose. The last name well known to students of history. They sprawled on a few old chairs and sofas, drinking vodka. Desmond was looking at her and ashing his cigarette on the floor. "There's no food," he announced languidly. "It's boring, but we'll have to go to the pub before it closes if we want any supper."

Cesca rode in his car, an old, mud-spattered Land Rover. It had almost been a command. "You," he said, "you can ride with me."

She had looked at Desmond and then at Emma, with whom she had driven down. "You don't mind, do you?" she asked Emma as Desmond started the engine. Already she knew that she would sleep with him.

After dinner, back at the house, they were once again sitting around. There was wine. Someone had produced a hash pipe. The German was strumming a guitar. It was getting late. Cesca was tired and looked around for Desmond, but he had disappeared from the room. "Have you seen Desmond?" she asked. No one had. Emma was missing too.

She went upstairs. There was a long hallway decorated with dusty old prints with several doors leading off it. On the other side were sash windows. She called their names. The hallway was dimly lit. She knocked on each door and then opened it. The last one she opened revealed Desmond and Emma sitting on a bed together. Desmond's forearm was extended, pale and veiny. A rubber hose tied tightly around it. In his other hand he held a syringe that he was pressing into his arm. When she entered, they both looked up in surprise.

"Close the fucking door," said Desmond.

"What are you doing?" she asked.

"What does it bloody look like I'm doing?"

"Sorry," she said, quickly closing the door behind her and running downstairs. That night she slept with Clemens, the German, instead. In the morning, while it was still early, she had him drive her to the station. She never spoke to Emma again. Several years later Cesca read about her death in the newspaper. PEER'S DAUGHTER FOUND DEAD IN DRUG DEN, ran the headline. Desmond had been arrested and convicted for supplying the heroin. He spent six months in jail.

Shortly after Christmas, Cesca met Freddie Blackwood. Tall with rakish, dark hair and a long pointed nose, he was half-American and half-British. His mother was the daughter of a baronet, and his father was a film producer who had returned to the States after the divorce. Freddie had gone to Harrow and then Yale. Now he was at Cazenove, the Queen's brokers. That was his job, but his passion was speed, as he liked to say. At his mother's house in Surrey he kept a small collection of vintage sports cars. At a nearby airfield, an old Sopwith Camel. Cesca first saw him at a nightclub surrounded by girls, several empty champagne bottles on the table, his black tie slightly askew.

"What's your name?" he asked. His eyes shone with good humor and self-assurance.

He drove her home that night in his 1963 Alfa Romeo Giulia Sprint Speciale. She invited him up. "Never on a first date," he said and asked if she had any plans at the weekend.

She did.

"Cancel them. You're coming with me."

"Where are we going?"

"I'm not telling. But now I know where you live. I'll pick you up around nine on Saturday morning. And dress warmly."

He walked her to her door and kissed her lightly on the lips, smelling of musk and cigarettes and something else she couldn't quite define but which she liked very much.

He picked her up in the same car. "Ready for an adventure?" he asked. "I've brought all the necessary supplies. You look absolutely stunning, by the way. There's a rug behind you in case you get cold. I bought the car for her graceful lines and powerful engine, not for her heater."

They turned up the Brompton Road to the M3, heading south. The car sped along. The day was cold but fair.

"Where are we going?"

"It's a surprise. One of the most beautiful places in England, maybe even the world."

While they drove, he told her about his life. He was very funny and put her at her ease. He was only a few years older than she was. He thought it was amazing they had never met. He had lived in New York for a few years as a young child. His parents had owned a large farm in Connecticut before the divorce. He was an only child.

"Weren't you lonely?" she asked him.

"Alone but never lonely," he said and smiled.

She told him about her family, her brothers and sister. It was impossible to imagine her life without them. She tried to describe them. "They say being an only child makes you selfish: Is that true?"

"Absolutely. I must always have my way. Fortunately, what I want is usually good fun so no one complains."

Like many Englishmen of his class and background, he was uninterested in art. His taste in fiction ran to Dick Francis and Ian Fleming. In paintings, to portraits of horses and race cars. Music was to dance to. He did, however, have style. He dressed beautifully. His suits were from Huntsman, his shoes from Lobb. He knew how to entertain, even cook. There were one or two dishes he could whip up quickly. Balsamic chicken. Herb-crusted rack of lamb. And, of course, the right wines. He could ride, sail, shoot, and fox-trot. He was a decent fast bowler, and had played polo at Yale and now at Hurlingham. After college he had worked for a year on a vineyard in Bordeaux. He was never happier than when he was elbow deep in grease fixing an old car.

They drove to Salisbury, the great spire of the cathedral white against the sky. "Have you ever been inside?" he asked.

"Never."

"Let me show you."

He drove into the car park. "Come on."

They entered, necks craned up to the vaulted ceilings. "Not bad, eh?" he asked. For the first time, she took his hand and gave it a gentle squeeze.

There was a tour already under way. They followed close behind, giggling like naughty schoolchildren. "The spire is the tallest in England," the guide said. "It is 123 meters high. The cathedral was built in only thirty-eight years. The foundation stone was laid on the twenty-eighth of April 1220. The clock"— they all turned their heads—"is the oldest working medieval clock in the world. It is no longer possible to climb to the spire."

On the way out, they passed the little gift shop. He bought her a postcard of Constable's painting. "Here," he said, "to remember."

They parked in a field, the cathedral in the distance. He spread the rug on the grass. She sat, bundled in her coat, a thick scarf around her neck. "Look what I have," he said. He withdrew a hamper from the boot. Inside, a cold chicken. A loaf of bread. A tin of foie gras. A bottle of Saint-Émilion. Two glasses. "Here, try this," he said, smearing a wedge of foie gras on a hunk of bread. "Best in the world, eh?"

"Mmmm, delicious," she answered.

He opened the wine.

Later, they drove home in the rain. That night he did come upstairs with her. The next day was Sunday. They both slept in. When they awoke, they made love again. Later, he went to the store and brought back eggs, bread, and cheese, and they had a picnic in bed. Miles Davis and Roxy Music on the stereo. She didn't put her clothes back on until she left the next morning.

He took her places. They drove through Cornwall to Arthur's castle. The Brenner Pass. The Ardennes. The cold coastline of Normandy past the unending forest of white crosses. They stayed in a hotel in Caen, and Cesca could barely suppress a giggle as he registered them as Mr. and Mrs. Frederick Dickwood, her hands in her pockets. His French was better than hers. They could hardly wait to get upstairs.

Before dinner they wandered the streets, admired William the Conqueror's castle. In the restaurant they ordered *tripes à la mode* and goose *en daube*. In between courses, they drank calvados, which was, as he explained, the local custom. They finished the meal with Pont-L'Évêque and a ripe Camembert, washed down with even more calvados. He admired the way she could eat, heartily like a young girl or an athlete in training yet never gaining an ounce.

Some weekends they didn't drive at all. Instead one time they flew from Heathrow to Verbier, another to Lech. He was a good skier. But so was she, maybe even a little better. Other weekends they did nothing. Went to a movie, dined at London restaurants. She met his friends. Slept in on gray London mornings and while having tea in bed listened without guilt to the peal of church bells.

Some of the trips were less successful. In early spring on a drive through Holland, the Alfa broke down in Scheveningen, and they had to wait three days in a nearly empty, hideous modern hotel that was operating with a skeleton staff because it was off-season. The stretch of beach was deserted, the chairs stacked. Freddie was constantly on the phone with his mechanic back in London. They spent a lot of time drinking Bols in the bar and watching the roil of the North Sea through the windows. The manager, a plump blonde, kept apologizing and telling them to come during the summer. "You wouldn't recognize it," she said.

"Never trust a country that doesn't make its own wine," Freddie said on their second day. "England excepted, of course."

"It's not so bad."

"I wouldn't mind being stuck in France, but this is bloody awful."

Finally on Tuesday the spare part arrived. Freddie wouldn't let anyone else touch it. He disassembled the engine, lying its parts in an orderly fashion on a clean sheet in the hotel car park. "The Dutch also don't make cars," he said. "It's like that old line from the Orson Welles film about the Swiss and cuckoo clocks. What have the Dutch done? Edam and tulips. Dreadful country."

By Wednesday evening they were back in London. For the rest of the spring Freddie refused to drive anywhere near the Low Countries. "If we wanted wet weather and foul food, we could just stay in England," he said.

Spring melted into summer. Cesca had decided not to return to Amagansett. She would visit Aurelio in July, and then she and Freddie had a big trip planned in August. They were going to drive from Paris through Dijon, Mâcon, and Lyon to Geneva and across the alluvial plains of the Po Valley past Milan to Venice. He told her it would take several weeks. His annual holiday. There are many chefs along the way who would be gravely disappointed if we did not stop by, he said.

Kitty flew to visit her for two weeks before the Venice trip. She had been in Barcelona first, visiting Aurelio. Cesca insisted that she stay in her flat as she was spending most of her nights at Freddie's, on Lowndes Square.

"I like him very much," said Kitty. "Go easy on him."

She and her daughter were having lunch on Beauchamp Place. The previous evening she had met Freddie for the first time. He took them to a restaurant on the Royal Hospital Road, and insisted she order the pig's trotters with chicken mousseline, sweetbreads, and morels. It was fabulous. "English food is getting better every year," he said, "even if it isn't English food at all." At the end of the meal the proprietor, who was French, sat with them and had a brandy. He tore up the bill. Freddie had been one of his early investors.

Kitty had many friends in London. A Persian woman who was married to a Cambridge don and was the London editor for a well-known American literary journal. Several art dealers. The director of the Royal Ballet. The second wife of a duke. The head of a large advertising firm who had once been her lover. A Rothschild. Even a member of the Royal Family whom she had met in Mustique. She invited Cesca and Freddie to several events. A gallery opening at the Serpentine. A dinner party at Spencer House.

At the end of her visit, Kitty asked her daughter if she knew the old wives' tale about Venice. No, Cesca answered. Kitty laughed. "It's probably nothing. But they say if you go to Venice with someone you aren't married to you'll never marry them."

Then it was July. Cesca had never been happier. The trip to Barcelona was like a homecoming. Aurelio, although too thin to her eye, looked wonderful. He was still the handsomest man she'd ever seen. Handsomer than Freddie even. As usual, he was dressed in old clothes that hung off his tall frame. His pants were spattered with paint, and he wore a Basque sweater and a thin cotton scarf around his neck. Espadrilles. He had been waiting at the airport. He ran to her when he saw her and picked her up in his arms with a whoop. He had hired a gypsy band to serenade her as she entered the arrivals hall.

They chatted in Catalan all the way to his apartment. When the cab stopped, people on the street greeted Aurelio. He lived on the top two floors of a house along the narrow corridor of the Barrio Chino, the city's red-light district. Laundry hung drying between the buildings, blocking out the sun to the street below. There were several women standing around outside his building smoking. "This is where I live," he said, grabbing her suitcase. "Come on up."

"Are those?" she asked on the stairs.

"Yes, prostitutes. This street is for the regular ones. A few blocks down you find the transvestites. Sometimes they model for me."

It was a simple apartment, neat as a Carthusian's cell. The lower level consisted of a combination bedroom, kitchen, and living room. There was a bed in the corner, with a blue blanket stretched across it. An old sofa. A stove and a small refrigerator. There was no phone or television. In the center was a small square bathtub that doubled as a sink. The toilet was on the landing. By the bed were a few well-thumbed books in Catalan. Unamuno. Saint Augustine. Vasari's *Lives*. Several photographs. A notebook. She looked inside the cupboards. They were nearly empty. Boxes of pasta. Tins of sardines. Tea. Salt.

"No wonder you look so skinny," she said.

"You sound just like Mare." He laughed. "Don't worry about me. Come. Let me show you my work."

He led her up a circular metal stair to the top floor of the building. It was a wide-open room bathed in natural light. There were canvases stacked everywhere. It was obvious at once that he had made a breakthrough.

She was both proud and envious. Her own work would never come to this level, she knew, even if she had been working as hard on it as she should have. The final months at school had been a blur. She found herself going to class less and less. One or two of her teachers had tried to talk to her, encourage her to be more focused, but she wasn't interested in the limitations being forced on her. It became increasingly obvious to her that the whole notion of art school was artificial and absurd. How could one grade creativity? The only purpose was to provide young artists an environment to work for several years and a way for the instructors to earn a living. Art school was an oven, a proving ground. Nothing more. At the end you simply emerged. It distressed her. Aurelio was the one who knew how to do it.

He had many friends. They sat at a café on the Ramblas. Several people came up to them and stayed for a drink. "This is my beautiful sister," he would introduce her. *"Ella ha vingut aquí a trencar cors."* She has come over here to break hearts. Everyone laughed.

The first night she took him to dinner. "They serve the best paella in town," he said. All through dinner, he talked excitedly about his work while she sat and listened. He had always been like that. She marveled at how easily they slipped into their old roles. "I know many people here," he said, "but I only feel truly comfortable around my family. I am so happy you came."

Later, after they had consumed several bottles of wine, they returned to his flat. "I am very drunk," he said. They both laughed hysterically when he nearly tripped over the sofa.

"Sorry there's so little privacy," he said. "I'll go upstairs while you change."

"No, it's all right," she said. Normally she slept naked.

"Suit yourself."

She watched him as he removed his shirt and trousers. She could see his ribs, the boniness of his hips, the flatness of his belly, the long whiteness of his fingers with paint under the nails. He brushed his teeth in the sink.

"Mind if I take a bath?" she asked.

"Of course not. There are towels in the cupboard."

She ran the water. It came out hot and in bursts.

"The plumbing's not much here. Sorry."

"Stop apologizing." She slipped out of her clothes and walked past him.

"You sure you don't want me to go upstairs?"

"No," she said, settling into the tub. "Can you light me a cigarette? My hands are wet."

She sat there in the small square tub, her knees almost touching her breasts. There was no room to get her head wet. She would have to be a contortionist. "How do you wash your hair?" she asked.

"With this." He handed her a small bowl.

She put out her cigarette and dipped the bowl in the water, raising it and pouring the water over her head several times until it was wet. She then lathered her hair and rinsed it again with the soapy water.

"Not exactly the Ritz, is it?" he said.

"It's all right. Can you hand me a towel?"

She stood up, her body glistening, specks of soapsuds clinging to her stomach and thighs. She toweled off standing up. He looked away.

Stepping out of the tub, she left a trail of wet footprints on the wooden floor and wrapped herself in the towel. "Thanks," she said. "I really needed that."

"Of course."

He watched her as she brushed her hair, still wearing the towel.

"Good night," she said, walking over to kiss him on the top of his head. Before getting into bed, she removed the towel, letting it drop to the floor, and then slipped under the covers.

For a long time, she lay there listening to his breathing, staring into the darkness. Fifteen minutes. Twenty. Maybe more.

"Are you asleep?" she asked.

"No."

"Neither am I."

"Go to sleep."

"I can't."

"Try."

"It's not working."

"Try counting sheep."

"That never works."

"Go to sleep," he insisted.

He lay there for several minutes and heard her moving about. "What are you doing?"

"Getting dressed."

"Why?"

"I'm going out."

"Do you want me to come?"

"No," she said, standing in the doorway. "Don't wait up."

In the morning, he was up before her. He hadn't heard her come in when she returned shortly before dawn. When she came upstairs to his studio, he was working.

"Morning," she said. She was wearing one of his shirts.

"More like afternoon."

She shrugged.

"Have fun?" he asked.

"Yes," she said, lighting a cigarette. "I met some people. We went to a club."

"Ah."

"You disapprove?"

"Of course not."

"Good," she said. "Then let's go out and get some breakfast. I'm starving."

He took her to one of his favorite cafés, where they had *truites de patates* and sausage and large bowls of *cafe amb llet*. "What should we do today?" she asked.

It had been years since she had visited Barcelona. She remembered the palm trees. The elegance of the city. Its lights burning from the interiors of shops and restaurants. The colonnades. The mild weather. She was surprised by how many tourists there were. He took her all over on his motorcycle. "I feel very daring," she said. "Like Marlon Brando."

"I have a favor," he asked.

"What's that?"

"I want to paint you."

"Again? Aren't you tired of painting me? You've been doing it since we were kids."

"Not at all. You are one of my favorite subjects, but this time will be different."

"In what way?"

"This time I want to paint you nude. You gave me the idea last night."

She giggled. "How risqué."

"No, I think it would be a great painting."

They started the next day. Aurelio had already built the canvas and prepared the surface. It was to be a large painting. He had her reclining like Manet's Olympia, her left hand covering her pubis. "You are a nocturnal creature so I will paint it as though it is nighttime," he told her.

"How appropriate," she smiled.

A few nights later, they were at a party where Cesca met

Felip. He was a tennis player with muscles like rope, piercing blue eyes. From the moment he entered the room, she couldn't keep her eyes off him.

"Who's that?" she asked Aurelio.

He told her. Felip had just returned from Roland Garros, where he had lost in the semifinal round.

"Introduce me."

"I don't know him that well but all right."

The reaction was chemical, almost explosive. Everyone in the room could feel it. In a few moments, they left the party together. Cesca didn't return to Aurelio's apartment for three days.

"I was getting worried about you," he said when she walked through the door. "Where's Felip?"

"He had to train. He has another tournament coming up. His coach was furious. I just came back to get my things. You don't mind, do you?"

"Not at all. Will I see you again?"

She threw her head back and laughed her rich, hoarse laugh. "Silly. Of course you will. Felip has to train every day, so you'll see plenty of me. In fact, let's have lunch now. I'm famished."

"Then can we work on the portrait again? It's nearly finished. I was afraid you were never coming back and that it would stay that way forever."

That became their routine for the remainder of her stay in Barcelona. She would spend the night with Felip and the day with Aurelio in Barrio Chino. On the last night they all had dinner together. Uncharacteristically, Aurelio ordered champagne.

"I'm going to miss my two handsome boys," she said, her hands on both their shoulders.

"We will miss you too," said Aurelio.

"What about Felip? Will you miss me?"

Felip laughed. "I will miss you. My coach will be happy to

know you have left. He says I have been playing like an old man ever since I met you."

She went home with Felip that night, and then, in the morning, Aurelio took her to the airport in a taxi.

"Thank you for everything," she said, kissing him. "When will you be back in the States?"

"I am planning to come for Christmas. I promised Mare."

"Good. Then I will too. By the way, I love the painting you did of me. I hope you don't think this sounds incredibly vain, but I think it's the best thing you've ever done."

He smiled. "I think so too."

He watched as she walked through passport control, aware that his were not the only masculine eyes following her. Several other passengers, airline employees, porters, security personnel followed her movement. It was almost impossible not to. Every one of them imagining for a second what it would be like to possess her. She turned and waved at him, flashing a brilliant smile. He waved back, the smile identical.

"*Adéu,* Lio!" she cried.

"*Adéu,* Cesca!"

"See you at Christmas! I love you!"

"I love you too!"

He took a bus back to the city. On returning to his studio, he stared at the portrait of his sister. He had decided to title it: *Cesca en la llum de la lluna.* Cesca in the moonlight. She was right. It was the best thing he had ever done.

12

THE MOTORBOAT SCUDDED SOUTH ACROSS THE CLOUDED waters of the great lagoon past wooden pylons driven into the soft mud. In the distance rose the domes and towers of the glittering city. To the left, the island of Murano, famous for its glass. Most people arrive in Venice through the back door, like a secret lover. The glories of Santa Maria della Salute, San Giorgio, the Piazza San Marco lie unseen on the far side. Drawing closer, the boat slowed and entered a maze, down one narrow canal, then another, under arched footbridges, past ancient walls green with algae, crumbling brick walls, black shutters, obscure Palladian churches stained with soot, their Latin inscriptions now all but indecipherable. Glimpses into private enclosures of ancient epicurean luxury. Tall cypress trees. *Caffès* where white-jacketed waiters carried drinks on trays. Boutiques staffed by pretty girls.

Everywhere there were tourists, and the city's famous cats. Navigating in between water taxis, barges, the occasional gondola, until suddenly the shadows fell away, the canal opened up, and the boat picked up speed again out on the open water, looking back over the trailing wake at the famous basilica of Saint Mark's and the arches of the Doge's Palace. Then the engine cut and the launch glided to the private dock where the hotel's greeter stood waiting to help them ashore with their luggage.

They walked under a canvas loggia to the front desk. The receptionist, elegant in morning coat with a soft gray tie, swiftly acknowledged their reservation and politely requested their passports.

"Welcome back, Signor Blackwood," he said.

"*Grazie.*"

"*Grazie a lei. Prego,* the porter will show you to your room."

"Come along, darling," Freddie said. "What did I tell you? Beautiful, eh?"

"Beautiful."

The suite looked out over the lagoon. Cesca stepped onto the balcony. "God, what a view."

Freddie tipped the porter and followed her onto the balcony. "What do you feel like doing? Are you tired? Hungry?"

They had been driving for several days. Each night in a different hotel. Lyon. Monaco. Last night they had slept in Genoa. Every night they ate well, hungry after a long day of driving, stopping in churches. Every night they made love. In Lyon the manager had to call up and, in an embarrassed voice, ask them to make less noise. They would be in Venice for a week.

"Let's stay in and order room service," she said, turning and facing him, her arms around his neck. "Is that all right?"

At dusk they emerged from their room sated, showered. "We can have a drink on the terrace," Freddie said.

The terrace was crowded. They sat next to another couple, a handsome older man with a dark mustache and an attractive woman. Cesca recognized him but couldn't place him. She could tell he was used to being stared at. His hands were beautiful, almost feminine. He wore plenty of gold. Gold watch. Gold rings. Gold reading glasses. Even a gold bracelet. Despite this, he still seemed supremely, effortlessly masculine.

The tables were so close together it was impossible not to chat with each other. He did not offer his name, as though to do so would be superfluous. He explained that he was in town for a backgammon tournament. His accent was refined, foreign, but he was not Italian. He recommended a restaurant in the Cannaregio. He said it was where the real Venetians went. It was too far from the city center for tourists. They drove from Genoa? He had always wanted to go. One day. He loved Monte Carlo. He went every year. Backgammon was his game. He had many friends there.

Finally, he stood up to leave. "Come, my dear," he said. "Or we'll be late. Enjoy your stay. You are a lovely couple. *Ciao.* Good night."

"Good night," said Freddie, rising in his chair and shaking hands. "Thank you."

They watched them leave the terrace. Other guests watched them as well. For a moment the terrace was silent.

"Was that?" she asked.

"Yes." Freddie nodded. "I always loved his movies."

The days slipped by in a pink haze. In the mornings they sleep in, the sheets rumpled. They feast on each other's bodies. They could never tire of one another. Every moment was ripe with carnality. He slipped the pillow under her stomach. "There," he said. "Comfortable?"

He entered her with long strokes, sunlight seeping through the curtains, his strong arms planted on either side of her, pinioning her to the bed. She never wanted it to end. It was more than pleasure.

They played tennis at noon. It was too hot for most of the guests. They were both brown from the sun, their limbs strong. He was surprised by how competitive she was. Every set was a battle, with neither willing to let the other win easily. Sometimes other guests watched them and clapped when a particularly good point was scored. By the end they were breathing hard, sweat glistening on their foreheads and arms. At lunch, they drank Negronis. He had introduced her to them. They sat outside. The waiter brought octopus carpaccio. *Filetto di branzino.* A bottle of Gavi di Gavi chilling in an ice bucket. They ate like hunters, their insides hollow from the exertion of love and sport. Then they lay by the pool, occasionally diving in to cool off. They were the couple everyone watched. Their beauty invited speculation. People wondered who they were. Rumors abounded. He was an English lord. She was a famous model. They had run away together. They were married to other people. They could barely keep their hands off each other. They moved in a halo. The rest of the world seemed drab next to them, even in Venice. What was known about them was their youth, their faces, and their passion. It was impossible not to envy them.

They only left the island at night. They went to restaurants. Harry's Bar.

"What about the churches? The Titians? Don't you want to see them?" he asked.

"No. Too many people. I don't want to feel like a tourist. I want to feel like I live here."

"Wouldn't it be something to live in Venice?"

"Then every day you could walk out of your palazzo and go look at the Titians any time you wanted. In January or October or sometime when the streets aren't crawling with sunburnt Germans or fat Americans or little Japanese going click-click-click with their cameras. That's what a real Venetian could do."

"I wonder if you wouldn't go a little mad after a while though? All that water."

"Absolutely. I think that's the whole point. I think you need to be a little crazy to live here. Exposure to so much beauty can't be good for one's mental health."

"That's how I feel about you," he said. "Now I understand why people say they're crazy for someone."

"Stop," she said, pushing him gently. "Don't get all gushy on me. I thought you English were meant to have stiff upper lips."

"I'll show you what's stiff." He laughed and reached for her.

For them night couldn't come fast enough. The rest was diversion, distractions to keep them from devouring each other utterly. They waited all day. Until, after dinner, they were ready to begin again. The bed with its crisp, cool sheets beckoned. Every night they returned to it, like pagans at an altar.

"Have you ever tried it?" she had asked in the restaurant.

"No, we used to joke about it in school. You know. English schoolboys."

"I had a friend in London who said the Italians were crazy about it."

"Well, Italians."

"We should try it."

"Are you sure?"

"Yes."

"I should get something."

"Maybe the concierge."

"Wouldn't that be too obvious?"

"Does it matter?"

"No. Let's go. Pay the bill. Hurry."

They returned by the hotel's private launch. When they reached their room, he called down to explain what he needed. That he had a burn on his hand. *"Prego,"* the concierge replied. "Of course. I'll send it up right away, *signor.*" Would he like a doctor?

"No, that's all right."

They had a drink while they waited.

"I've never done it either," she said. "I want to do it with you."

He smiled and said nothing. He felt like a champion. It was a reward.

Fifteen minutes later, there was a knock at the door. He gave the porter a generous tip. *"Grazie,"* he said.

"Grazie a lei."

"Cheeky bastard," he said after closing the door. "It's like he knows what we are up to."

"So what? It's not like it hasn't happened before."

"I suppose not."

She finished her drink. "I'm going to go get ready," she said.

The room was dark when she came to bed, her strong body warm and pliant. "Are you ready?" he asked.

"Go slowly."

He began as usual, taking his time. There was no rush. They had all night. All morning. All the time in the world. She writhed on the bed. "Now," she begged. "Now."

Slowly he obeyed.

"Let me know if you want me to stop."

"Ah," she said. "That hurts."

"Do you want me to stop?"

"No. Stay there. Just go slowly. Ow. More slowly. Stop."

He waited, stroking her back, feeling himself in her. Restraining himself.

"Okay," she said.

He began again. Slowly, infinitely slowly.

"Better?"

"Yes." She nodded. "Keep going," she said.

He went deeper, then deeper still.

"Oh God," she shouted. There were tears in her eyes. She was on the edge of a cliff. Her heart was racing. The line between pleasure and pain had blurred. "Don't stop."

Afterward they lay spent in bed. "Are you all right?" he asked.

"A little sore but I loved it," she replied softly, gently stroking his chest. "It's like nothing else. I don't think I could do it all the time, though. It'd be too much."

He kissed her head as it rested on his shoulder. She was more precious to him than ever now. They had signed a secret pact. They were bound to each other forever.

Venice ended. Once again they were in the car with the top down. The return trip was faster. He needed to get back to the office. They had been away two weeks. It was almost September. They passed Brescia, Milan, Aosta; drove through the foothills of the Alps, Mont Blanc looming massively in the distance, overshadowing everything else. Then Chamonix and down into the rolling vineyards of Burgundy. The first night they spent in Dijon, staggering out of the car at their hotel. They had been driving for nearly nine hours. They had planned a gourmet meal. Booked a table months in advance.

"Do you mind if we just eat in our room?" he asked. "I'm fagged out."

The next night they reached Paris, where they stayed for one night at the Ritz. "I'm feeling better," he said. "Let's go dancing."

He took her to Castel, on the Left Bank. "My father used to come here," he said. "He was a good friend of Jean, the founder."

They met a Frenchman at the bar. He was with a beautiful blond woman. She had pixyish hair and a sleeveless, backless dress that revealed her lean, well-toned arms and shoulders.

"Where are you from?" Cesca asked in English.

"Norway," she answered. "Oslo. Have you been?"

Cesca shook her head.

The room was full, the music loud. It was after midnight. Freddie leaned over and asked if they could leave, but Cesca was having fun. She wanted to stay. She was charmed by the Frenchman. He was very elegant, older. He wore a thick gold watch on his wrist. His hands were perfectly manicured. They too had just returned to Paris. He had a château near Menton. "You should come," he said to her. "You would love it."

"Maybe I will."

He asked her to dance. She looked over at Freddie, who smiled and said, "Of course." They moved to the small dance floor. Freddie followed them with his eyes until the Norwegian girl said something, and he turned to look at her. When he looked back to the dance floor, he didn't see them.

"Is anything the matter?" the girl asked.

"No. Sorry."

A little while later Cesca and the Frenchman returned to the table. They had been in the bathroom together. She was wiping her nose and laughing.

"*Encore?* Another round?" asked the Frenchman, signaling to the waitress for a new bottle of champagne.

"That's awfully good of you but we really have to go," said Freddie, taking out his billfold from the breast pocket of his jacket. "Isn't that right, darling?"

"Nonsense," said the Frenchman. "Stay. It's my party."

"Please, Freddie," Cesca said. "It's our last night."

"Oh, all right." He smiled, trying to look like he didn't mind.

It was now two in the morning. They were on their fourth bottle of champagne. Cesca and the Frenchman, whose name was Arnaud, had disappeared again.

"How long have you known Arnaud?" Freddie asked the Norwegian girl. Her name was Beate.

"Not long."

"Where did you meet?"

"In Nice. On his yacht."

"Oh? Jolly good."

"He is a lot of fun."

"I can tell. Are you staying in Paris long?"

She shrugged her naked shoulders. "I don't know. It depends on Arnaud."

Cesca and Arnaud returned again and Freddie said, "Darling, I really think it's time to go. We have a long day tomorrow and an early start."

She was trying not to hear him. She wanted him to go away, didn't understand why he was behaving like this. It made her angry. "Don't be such a drag, Freddie," she said, finally.

"I would be happy to drop her at your hotel if Cesca wants to stay," Arnaud said.

Freddie ignored him. "Come on, Cesca. Time to go."

For a moment her eyes flashed, and he feared she would refuse. The thought of a public scene appalled him, especially in front of Arnaud.

She huffed and quickly stood up, making the point that she was being inconvenienced. "Fine," she said, her mouth tense. "Have it your way."

She turned away from Freddie and coquettishly presented her cheeks to be kissed by Arnaud. "It was lovely meeting you," she said. "I'm so sorry Freddie's so boring. Thank you for everything."

He waved his hand like a lord. *"Rien,"* he said. "It was my pleasure, *chérie.* Don't forget. You are always welcome in Menton."

In the taxi going back to the hotel, she was sullen, angry as a spoiled child denied a toy.

"Look," he said. "I'm sorry that I had to break up the party but it's ridiculously late."

"Oh, don't pretend like you were having such a bad time. I saw you flirting with Beate."

He rolled his eyes. "Don't be silly, darling."

"I am not being silly. I saw you. I didn't know you liked blondes so much."

He sighed and said nothing. "Please, darling. Let's not fight."

"Why not? Why can't we fight? What are you scared of?"

"I'm not scared of anything," he replied in a hushed tone. "I just don't think it's something we need to fight about."

"You're an uptight, pompous, British asshole."

They arrived at the hotel, and she strode out of the car, past the night doorman, and through the revolving door before Freddie could pay the driver. When he got to the room, the bathroom door was locked. He knocked gently. "Darling?" he asked. "Are you all right?"

"Leave me alone."

"Please? Let's not fight."

"Fuck you."

He sighed and sat on the bed. "How much longer will you be?"

"As long as I want."

"All right, I'm going to go back to the lobby to use the loo there. I'll be right back."

There was no answer. When he returned, the room was dark, and she was curled on the bed, her face to the wall.

"Darling?" he asked.

"I'm asleep."

Wearily he got into bed.

"Don't touch me."

"I won't. Good night, darling. Sleep well." He rolled over on his side and was asleep within minutes. It was the first night they had not made love.

The telephone rang at eight o'clock with their wake-up call. *"Bonjour, monsieur."*

"Bonjour, merci," he said groggily.

The room was still dark, the late August sunshine barely

able to penetrate the heavy curtains. "Darling?" he asked.

She grunted and pulled a pillow over her head.

"We have to catch the noon ferry," he said. "I'm going to call down for room service."

"Go 'way. Sleeping," she muttered.

He took a shower and quickly shaved. When breakfast arrived, he was waiting in a bathrobe. Still, she had not moved. He signed for the check and poured out a cup of coffee. "Darling," he said. "Black coffee for you?"

No response.

He placed the cup and saucer on the nightstand and sat down carefully next to her on the lip of the bed. "Darling, we have to begin to wake up. It's another big push today, I'm afraid. Nine hours."

She let out a low groan, then said, "I'm dying."

"No, you aren't. Just feeling a little under the weather. What you need is some food in your system. I've ordered up eggs, bacon, toast. The lot."

"I'm going to be sick."

"Really?"

"Yes, really."

He stood up quickly as she threw off the sheet and dashed for the toilet, closing the door behind. The heavy door was so well balanced it didn't slam.

He gave her a few minutes and then knocked. "Everything all right in there?"

"I'll be right out."

She emerged a few minutes later, wrapped in a towel, her hair tousled, the sides of her mouth turned down. Streaks of dried mascara ran down her face. He was sitting at the table, the breakfast laid out before him. She sat down and picked up the coffee he had moved there.

"I hope you don't mind if I started," he said. "It's jolly good."

She sat there and sipped the coffee in silence.

"Have a croissant."

He handed her the basket, and she took one, tore off a piece, and placed it gingerly in her mouth, little bits of pastry clinging to her lip. Slowly she chewed. Then another bite.

"Oh God," she said. "What happened?"

"We went to a nightclub."

"I remember."

"We met some people. You took rather a shine to the man. Apparently you have big plans to visit him at his château in Menton in the near future. His name was Arnaud."

"Oh Christ."

"You kept disappearing to the loo together. No doubt to do cocaine. I really don't understand what you see in that drug. It always just makes me jittery."

"What else?"

"Well, that's about it."

"Did we have a fight?"

"We did."

"What about?"

"I'm not really entirely sure. I think it had to do with me wanting to leave and you wanting to stay."

She cradled her head in her hands. "It's coming back to me. I think I owe you an apology."

"Don't be daft. You don't owe me anything."

"I think I was a bitch. I'm sorry if I was."

"Think nothing of it. Water under the bridge."

She finished the croissant and lit a cigarette. "I think we might need some more coffee," she said.

They missed their ferry. Traffic getting out of Paris was terrible, and then they were snarled by road works on the A1, taking them twice as long as Freddie had planned. By the time they got to Calais, it was too late. There was another ferry leaving two hours later, so they had lunch at a little café overlooking the harbor.

"France doesn't want us to leave, obviously," she said, smiling. "Maybe we should turn around and go back to Paris?"

"Or Venice?"

"Yes, please. Let's go back to Venice."

He smiled. "I wish."

They arrived in Lowndes Square after ten. A gentle rain was falling, and for the first time in days, he had to put up the car's cloth top. It was his third straight day of driving. They both collapsed on his bed. Freddie still in his clothes. She would return to her flat tomorrow to sort her laundry, check her mail. For the second night in a row, they didn't make love.

In the morning, she let him sleep and slipped out to buy milk, bread, and *The Sunday Telegraph*. When he awoke, she had tea and toast waiting for him. "Morning, sleepyhead," she said.

"Morning."

"Better?"

"Yes, much. Thanks. Lovely tea. Can't get a proper cup anywhere but England."

Like Br'er Rabbit in his briar patch, he was plainly happy to be back in London. The gray autumn skies, the rain, the food all appealed to him, reminding him of home. Life resumed. They went out most nights. Dinners, the theater. Weekends in the country at friends'. One of his best friends from Harrow was a duke. In the fall they went shooting, and she watched with the wives.

She had given up art school, and her future was now uncertain. She could go one way or another but didn't know what she wanted. Already she felt dissatisfied. Small things annoyed her. She was all but living in his flat. She hated the red lacquered Chinese cabinets that had belonged to his mother. The salmon-colored walls and golden curtains framed the view over the square, in her opinion one of the dreariest in London. She felt oppressed by the Dresden figurines over the mantel. The rows of engraved invitations. The vintage cartoons in the guest loo. There was no youth here.

She was getting bored, like a wild animal that has been domesticated but still sniffs the air, yearning for the ability to run free. She missed warmth, her family. When the phone rang often it was a woman asking, "Is Freddie there?" It was tempting to smash the receiver back on the hook. Her days drifted by in idleness. Waking late. Doing the shopping. Buying a frock on Bond Street or a book at Hatchards in Piccadilly. Going to matinees. Getting dressed for the evening. Occasionally she took the tube to the City and met him for lunch. But it was only at night that she felt alive, consumed by passion, and sometimes even that was not sufficient. She had few friends of her own. English women were very tribal, she felt. She was an outsider, with her American accent and exotic looks. Most of the women they knew were already mothers. Very few of them worked. They struck her as little more than brood mares whose lives were already half over. Leaving school at the age of sixteen and then working as an au pair or at one of the auction houses as an intern for a year or two while they trolled for a husband.

And then it happened. She was late. To be certain, she waited a few days to confirm, but by then, there was no mistaking it.

That night, when Freddie came home, he did just as he always did and threw off his jacket and gave her a light kiss, saying, "Hullo, darling." Then, sensing her mood, asked, "What's the matter? Why aren't you dressed?"

She was sitting on a chair in the bedroom, her feet tucked up under her. A cigarette burning. "I don't feel like it," she said. "You go without me."

"Are you sure? Don't you feel well?"

"Just a little off. Women troubles."

"Ah, right. You don't want me to stay?"

"No, you go on ahead."

For a week she carried around her secret. Staring into the water of the Thames. Sitting in Green Park. Feeling the rain on her face. She called him at work. "Can we cancel our plans tonight?" she said. "I want to have dinner. Just us."

He knew something was wrong. She had been distant for days. They sat at the table in their regular Italian, a glass of wine in front of each of them. He told little jokes, filling up the awkward pauses, waiting for her to start.

"I'm late," she said.

"You mean?"

"Yes."

"How did it happen? I thought you were . . ."

"I am. Sometimes it just happens."

He sat there for several seconds digesting the news, his face a blank. "But that's wonderful," he said eventually, breaking into a smile.

She looked at him. "I'm sorry," she said.

"Sorry? What for?"

"I don't want it."

His head jerked back slightly, his eyebrows lifted. Even more surprised now. "What?"

"I said I don't want it. I don't want to be a mother yet. I want to get rid of it."

"Are you absolutely sure?"

"Yes."

"My God."

"I want you to understand."

"I don't know if I can."

"I want you to find a place. Where I can get rid of it."

His face was pale. He couldn't look her in the eye.

"Will you help me or not?"

"I—I don't know. Do you have any idea what you're asking?"

"Yes."

"And it doesn't bother you—or how I might feel about it?"

She looked away. "Either way I'm going to do it. If you won't help me, I'll go to New York."

He slumped in his chair, staring at his now empty glass, his mouth compressed. "Don't I have a right? It's my child too, after all."

"Of course it is. But it's my life, and I am not ready yet. Please don't make this any more difficult than it already is."

"I'm sorry if I am making your life so damned difficult. This all comes as rather a blow."

"I know. Maybe I shouldn't have told you. Maybe I should have just taken care of it by myself."

"Maybe you should have."

"Look, will you help or not?"

"What if we got married? Would that change things?"

She shook her head. "No."

"No to what exactly? Getting married or changing things?"

"Both."

"I see." He sat, absorbing the shock. "I love you," he said finally.

She said nothing.

"Do you love me?" he asked.

She looked away, saying nothing. "Right," he said.

"I'm sorry."

"Not half as bloody sorry as I am."

She reached out her hand to take his, but he drew away. For several seconds, she left her hand in the middle of the table, but it remained there untouched.

"Okay," she said, picking up her purse. "I'll spend the night at my flat. Tomorrow I'll send round for my things. I'll leave your key."

She stood.

He looked up at her, resenting her.

"Good-bye, Freddie," she said and walked out of the restaurant.

All night and the next day, she sat in her now unfamiliar flat staring at the telephone, waiting for it to ring. That it would be Freddie, saying, "I'm sorry, darling. I understand. Of course you're not a monster. There's no point in rushing things. We have plenty of time. I've found a doctor. I'll pick you up, and we'll go there together."

But he never called. Within a week she was back in New York. Within two weeks she was in Amagansett, recovering from her operation, wrapped in a blanket, her toes in the sand, watching the night descend over Gardiners Bay.

She did not know it was possible to feel so empty. But not for a moment did she regret it, any of it. Her mother waited for her inside. So did her grandfather and grandmother and Carmen. She did know that she needed her family. There was really no one else. She finished her glass of wine, dropped her cigarette, and went back inside.

13

BY THE END OF MY FRESHMAN YEAR AT COLLEGE, CESCA had become a healed wound where only a scar remained. To touch it was to remember. It was best to forget.

To my family's and my disappointment, I had not been accepted by Harvard. Despite good grades and success rowing, there had been, as my genial college adviser put it, "too many qualified candidates."

Instead I had enrolled at my second choice, a very respectable, albeit small, liberal arts college in New England. One of the attributes that drew me to it was that it had boasted a reputable fine arts department. However, I had seriously discussed with Paolo and Esther if they thought it made sense for me to go to art school instead since at that time I envisioned my eventual career as one of a painter. We were sitting outside under the shade of their willow tree. In the background two of their grandsons were playing soccer.

"Wylie Coyote," said Paolo, after thinking carefully. "You should go to college." He pronounced it "co-lage."

"But you didn't. You went to art school," I retorted.

"Yes, but I was an ignorant peasant boy. All I knew was that I had to get out. I won a scholarship and I went. Pah! *Beato me!* Lucky me! I learned how to draw better maybe. I learned how to paint better. But it didn't make me smarter. There was no Plato, no Descartes, no Tolstoy! Reading makes you a better artist than taking a life drawing class, no?" He laughed, showing his radiant smile.

I listened to Paolo. I knew he was right. I could always go to art school later if I still wanted to. But secretly, mistrustingly, there was the doubt in my heart that maybe Paolo was letting me down gently. That he was saying in the most diplomatic way he knew that I lacked the talent to succeed as an artist and that college was my best option. I burned to ask him what he truly thought of my abilities but knew that he would only wave away so direct a question. He would have told me it was impossible to know. It was like predicting the weather years in advance or winning the lottery.

So in the end I went to college. I was reasonably happy there. Dated a girl from Scarsdale. Took Painting 101 from a Russian woman whose family had emigrated years before. Broke up with the girl from Scarsdale. Drove into New York many weekends. Hung out on the Lower East Side. Went to Save the Robots, the Holiday, the Pyramid. I made friends. In the spring, I rowed crew. To make Paolo happy I took philosophy.

In the summer after my freshman year I traveled to Europe for the first time with two friends from prep school, Nelson and Brady. We hit the usual spots: London for a few days, Paris, Florence, carrying backpacks, using Eurail passes, staying in cheap hotels and pensiones. We had introductions to family friends. We were even invited to a few parties. I went through several sketchbooks during the trip, spending hours in the Tate, the Louvre, the Uffizi, and the Scuola Grande di San Rocco.

My friends had only just so much interest in museums. Brady, who had a nervous laugh and a wicked sense of humor, had a cousin in London who took us to a nightclub in Soho where all the beautiful women onstage were men.

"I'm telling you," insisted the cousin. "That's not a girl. Bloody confusing, what?"

In Paris we visited the Ritz Bar, feeling like the spiritual heirs of Hemingway, shocked by the prices and ending up having only one drink apiece. In Venice we slept the first night in the central square outside the train station along with hundreds of other young people, clustered in small groups like remnants of an exhausted army. Also in Venice, I had my first Campari and surreptitiously drew a portrait of a lovely girl with dark hair sitting in a café on the Riva degli Schiavoni while she stared out over the Grand Canal. I never spoke to her, but whenever I look at the drawing, which is one of the few I still have, I wish I had. My friend Nelson, who was very handsome, the grandson of a bishop, ran into a girl he knew, a relative of the poet T. S. Eliot whose name was Eliot. We made plans to meet up with her and her friends in a bar later that night near Saint Mark's, but they never showed up.

From Venice we went to Barcelona, where we saved money by staying with Aurelio, who was delighted to welcome us. I loved the city from the first. Its palm trees, its architecture. The energy on the streets. It was my favorite of all the cities we had visited. More than Paris, more than Venice. Maybe it was because I knew it was where Lio lived, the city he loved best. He revealed it to me, like a secret. He knew where to find the best cheapest coffee, the cheapest bread. He walked down the Ramblas, greeting people by name, stopping and chatting. It was a procession of pretty girls, young men on motorcycles with dark glasses and long hair, cafés and bars, each one more interesting and welcoming than the last. In the evenings, magical sunsets with Montjuïc in the background silhouetted against the sky. Even the occasional wave of stench from the sewers merely added to the ambience. Everywhere people seemed happy, content in the knowledge that they lived in such a special place.

In a bar near his apartment, we talked about his family. Cosmo's triumphs. He was becoming a successful musician. There was talk of an album. Unlike me, Carmen had been accepted at Harvard. Her ultimate goal was medical school.

"And Cesca, how is she?" I asked cautiously.

He laughed. "Cesca is Cesca. *Plus ça change* . . ."

"What do you mean?"

"She is engaged again."

"To whom?"

"He's a cousin of some kind, apparently. Somehow related to Bushka's side of the family. He's a successful businessman, too."

"What's his name?"

"Gavin. Gavin Oppenheim."

"Have you met him?"

"Years ago. When I was a kid. He was already an adult."

"So he's older?"

"Yes, he's got to be at least forty now."

"How'd they meet?"

"I think it was when Cesca went skiing in Switzerland earlier this year. Gavin lives in Switzerland. She looked him up. One thing led to another and bang."

"Ah well, that's great. Really great."

In a way, I meant it. The thought of Cesca being married soothed me. It had been so long since I had seen her I had almost forgotten the hold she had over me. It was like avoiding a street that held certain memories. By not turning down it I was safe. But streets so often have more than one way to access them, and suddenly, without thinking, it is possible to enter from a different direction and find oneself once again among the familiar sights and shopfronts. That's when it all comes rushing back.

We lingered in Barcelona, not wanting to leave. It was a place where I would have gladly lived. Waking every morning to paint. Long talks into the night with Lio and his friends. On our last night there, we all got very drunk and got home late. After we had all gone to sleep, Aurelio woke me whispering, "Come upstairs. There is something I want to show you."

I was still drunk and only half-awake. For a moment, I hesitated, remembering the night on the beach.

He sensed what I was thinking and chuckled. "No, nothing like that. I want to show you something. I wasn't sure I was going to, but I want you to see it."

He led me up the spiral staircase. There was an easel turned to face away from me holding a large canvas. "Tell me what you think," he said, indicating that I was to walk around to see what was on the other side. "I hope it won't upset you."

It was Cesca's nude. The nude. Seeing it was exquisite torture. He had captured her perfectly. It was like showing a painting of a forgotten feast to a starving man. Each morsel deliciously rendered, tantalizing in its verisimilitude. I remembered that body. For a brief moment in time it had become as familiar to me as my own. Now it was just a memory—but a memory stirred to life by Aurelio's skill. I could not take my eyes away.

"What do you think?" he asked.

I told him I loved it. It was true. The painting was a masterpiece. He grinned with satisfaction. "I thought you'd like it," he said slyly. "My sister's a beautiful woman. Loving. Fierce. Honest. But also dangerous. I think I've captured that. This is no mere housecat. This is a lioness. She can strike at any minute. Do you see?"

I said I did.

"Of course," he said. "You know better than most what her claws can do."

"It's all in the past," I lied. Inwardly, I felt the old ache at her absence.

"Bo," he said. "Good. I am very happy with it. But it is also very private, very personal to me. I will never sell it. I think I am going to give it to Cesca, and if she wants people to see it, then she can show it. If not, she can keep it hidden somewhere and, when she is old, go back and remind herself of how beautiful she had been."

14

I RETURNED TO EAST HAMPTON A FEW DAYS BEFORE I WAS due back at college and drove over to the Bonets'. I was sure they would want to hear about the time I spent with Aurelio and that it would be pointless to telephone ahead and so just decided to show up. It was a perfect late August afternoon. The sky was endlessly blue.

I took the back roads, past the potato fields, to avoid summer traffic. I hadn't been for a year, but it was all instantly familiar to me. The long driveway, the large white neoclassical clapboard house where Izzy and Ruth lived, the various outbuildings, the tennis court, and the infamous tree. And beyond it all was the slender cobalt ribbon of Long Island Sound stretching endlessly eastward.

I knew Aurelio would not be there, so I bypassed his studio and went straight to the pool, where I found Kitty and Randall sunbathing.

They greeted me warmly. "Wylie dear, how nice to see you,"

replied Kitty, putting down her book. "What a lovely surprise. You look so grown up."

I walked over and gave her a kiss on the cheek and shook Randall's hand. "How's your father?" she asked.

"Very well."

"Good," she said. "We haven't seen him for so long. He used to practically live here."

"Yes, I know."

"And we haven't seen you for some time either. What brings you around?"

"I just returned from a trip to Europe. I visited Lio in Barcelona for several days. I thought you'd like to hear about him. He looked very well."

"Oh, that's adorable of you, Wylie. Yes, we'd love to hear all about him. You wait here. I know the rest of the family would like to hear too."

Holding up a small bag, I added, "He also gave me little presents to give to everybody."

"What fun. Just wait there. I'll get Cesca, Carmen, and Cosmo. Randall, can you see if Wylie would like something to drink?"

Putting a wrap over her bathing suit, she walked on her still-good legs to the Playhouse. A few moments later she returned, saying, "Cosmo isn't here, but Cesca and Carmen will be right out. They're very excited to see you."

A short time later both girls appeared. Cesca, wearing a black bikini, looking brown and lean, walked up and embraced me, a big smile on her face. "Wylie. Oh my God," she cried. "Look at you. Even handsomer than ever!" She smelled, as always, of jasmine and roses. If anything she was more beautiful, the memory of Aurelio's painting carried before me like a flag.

Carmen's welcome was less emphatic. She stood there, allowing me to kiss her. There were some who thought that she was the lovelier of the two daughters, but I would never agree.

"So you've seen Lio," said Cesca, sitting on one of the lounges. "Tell us all about him."

I proceeded to and began with how well he looked.

"Is he too thin?" asked Kitty. "I hope he's eating enough."

I told them about his work and his spirits. "I have something for you all from him," I said. I picked up the small bag. "There is one for each of you." I removed small paintings the size of postcards, each depicting a different site in Barcelona. For Kitty, Sagrada Familia. For Carmen, Tibidabo. For Cesca, a café. On the back of each card was the person's name and a message in either English or Catalan. They were charming.

"Where is that?" Kitty asked Cesca.

"It's a little place that Lio and I used to go to on the Ramblas. How sweet."

"What does your card say?"

"'Qui no s'arrisca no pisca.'"

"What does it mean?"

"It's Catalan. It basically means, 'If you don't take risks in life, you will never succeed.'"

Kitty laughed. "That's perfect for you."

They passed around the postcards for all of us to inspect, making comments, laughing at the comments he wrote. "I have a few more," I said. "They're for Mr. and Mrs. Baum, Cosmo, Roger, and Dot."

"Cesca, darling, can you take those from Wylie, please?" Kitty asked.

"Yes, Mare."

I gave Cesca the bag. "It's so good of you to bring these for us," she said, squeezing my hands. "And so good to see you again."

"It's good to see you too."

"There's something different about you. You aren't wearing glasses anymore."

"Yes, I switched to contacts."

"*Molt maco.* Very handsome."

I blushed and looked down at her hands, still clasping mine. There was a large diamond set in platinum on her left hand. "Congratulations," I said. "Lio told me the good news."

She removed her hand to look at her ring. "Yes." She smiled. "I'm engaged. Again," she added with a laugh.

"The wedding's going to be held here," said Kitty. "On the lawn. A big white tent."

"You'll have to come," said Cesca.

"Thank you. When is it?"

"Next June."

"I'll be there."

"As long as we're planning ahead, what are you doing to-night?" asked Cesca.

I had no plans.

"Mare, is it all right if Wylie stays for dinner?"

"Of course. I'll have Rosita set another place."

"Good. That's settled," said Cesca, excitedly patting my thigh.

The touch of her hand made me blush. "Should I go home and change?" I asked. I was wearing shorts and a tennis shirt.

"No need," answered Cesca. "We're very casual. Stay, have a swim. You can borrow one of the boys' trunks. Come with me."

She took me inside the house to the room that Lio and Cosmo shared. I had never been upstairs before. There was a hallway with several doors off it. The emptiness of bedrooms in the quiet of midafternoon. Shyly, I stepped into their private lives. The intimacy of seeing pillows where people laid their heads, the drawers where they kept their clothes silenced me, like a novitiate being shown the Holy of Holies. Out of the corner of my eye, I looked into what I took to be Cesca's room. It was messy, the bed unmade, clothes on the floor. Carmen's door was closed. I moved with respect, following Cesca, achingly aware of her nearness.

We were in a masculine room. There were two single beds, one Cosmo's, the other Lio's, untouched. Two chests of drawers. Two closets. On the walls, there were posters for a soccer club and a large Miró reproduction. She rummaged through one of the chests and produced a pair of swim trunks. "These should fit," she said, holding them up against my waist. I looked at her. She smiled at me. We were alone in the house. But the moment slipped by and she walked out the door, saying, "Come down when you're ready."

When I returned to the pool, Cesca was there. Carmen, Kitty, and Randall had gone, and in their place was another woman. She was puffy, with reddish hair and pale skin, the kind that burns easily. She wore a white sundress and a broad-brimmed straw hat. She was next to Cesca on the chaise where I had hoped to sit.

"Have you met Wylie?" Cesca asked her as I approached.

I introduced myself. Her name was Caro, and she was an old friend of Cesca's from New York. She was in her first year at Harvard Law School. She had just popped by. She would be staying for dinner too. Immediately I resented her. Not only because she would deny me the chance to be the sole focus of Cesca's attention, but also because her presence made mine appear foolish.

Unsure of where to sit or what to do, I dove into the pool. The water was salt, clean, cold. I swam several laps hard, showing off a little. When I emerged, I felt less angry and walked over and sat on the ground.

Cesca turned to me. "So tell us about what you've been up to, Wylie. How long has it been since I saw you last? Two years? Three?"

I knew how long it had been. That day in the café in Greenwich Village. But I said nothing. As if I would ever forget.

For her part, Caro also said nothing and just smiled.

So I told them about myself. About college, my trip to Europe. I tried to make it as entertaining as possible, encapsulating the past several years of my life into a series of anecdotes.

"Where did you stay in Paris?" Caro asked.

I told her we'd stayed at a little hotel near Saint-Germain-des-Prés that one of my friends knew. We'd shared a room. The toilet was down the hall. The Deux Magots around the corner.

She shrugged and looked away, unimpressed. "I don't know it." Either she had sensed my resentment of her or she was as unhappy at my presence as I was at hers.

"It sounds like a lovely trip, Wylie," commented Cesca.

"And you, Cesca?" I asked. "How are you? What are you up to these days?"

She shifted on the chaise and lit a Marlboro, deflecting my question easily. "I'm good. Really good." She never did like personal questions.

"Where are you living?"

"In New York and here, for now. Until my marriage."

The conversation lagged. I asked Caro about herself. Where was she from? How long had she known Cesca? They had met in school. Later I would find out that they had much in common. Each came from a family of mixed backgrounds. Her father was American. A banker. Her mother, a famous beauty, Georgian but raised in London. A princess of some kind, according to Cesca. At one point there had been vast estates, serfs. All Caro had inherited from her was disappointment. It must be hard to be a plain girl. It must be harder still to be plain and have a mother who was beautiful. It is the same for short men who have tall fathers. There is something cosmically unfair about it. It is difficult not to be bitter.

After dinner I was in the kitchen, helping to clean up, scraping uneaten food into the garbage, washing dishes, happy to have a distraction, to feel useful. It was late. The family lingered long after the meal ended, finishing the wine and talking. We were in Kitty's house. The rooms large and airy, filled with big stuffed sofas, paintings, African fetishes, Mexican mirrors. The dining room looked out over a potato field, which was now too dark to see. Everyone else had gathered around to hear Cosmo play.

Cesca entered the kitchen carrying empty wine bottles. She had changed before dinner and was now wearing a long, green, light cotton dress embroidered around the neck with a pattern of tiny red beads. It was the first time we had been alone since the Playhouse. "Hi," she said.

"Hi."

"You okay?"

I nodded. "Sure. Thanks again for inviting me for dinner."

"I'm sorry about Caro," she said. "I didn't know she was coming over."

"That's okay," I replied disingenuously, intent on the pot I was scrubbing. "No reason to apologize."

"You sure?"

"Yeah." I meant it.

"I know I promised we'd go for a walk."

"It's okay. Next time."

"God knows when that will be," she said with a laugh. "At the rate we're going it could be years."

I laughed too.

"Caro will be leaving soon," she said, touching my arm.

"Do you want me to stay?"

"Yes, that would be nice." She was about to leave but stopped and said, "Meet me outside in fifteen minutes. By the stairs to the beach. Caro should be gone by then."

As I waited in the darkness, I heard the sound of feet crunching on gravel and the cough of a car engine as it ignited. Several moments later, faintly illuminated by the lights from the house, I saw Cesca walking toward me.

"Hello you," she said, slipping her arm through mine, leaning slightly into me. It was as if she had been doing it every day for our entire lives.

We walked down to the beach. It had been years since I had first come here with her on the night of her grandfather's birthday party. As if reading my thoughts, she said, "You know, even back then there was something I couldn't resist about you. You were so handsome. But there was something more. I felt an instant connection with you."

I said nothing. Holding my breath. Waiting to see what she would say next.

"Were you very angry with me?"

"Yes."

"And now?"

"Now? Less angry. But still you might say confused."

"Is that a problem?"

"Yes."

"Wylie, what do you want me to say?"

"An apology would be nice. An explanation."

"Sorry, I don't do either. And if I did, you'd have to get in line behind all the other people." She let out a little laugh.

"So what do I get?"

"What do you want?"

"You."

"I'm not available."

"Because you're engaged?"

"Yes. That's part of it."

"What's the other part? What did I do wrong?"

"Poor Wylie. Don't you see? You did nothing wrong. Quite the opposite."

We walked on a few steps in silence. "I was in love with you, you know," I said.

"I know. And it was lovely. But we were both so young. What did we know about love? My God. I'm not sure I even know now."

"So why are you engaged?"

She laughed. "That's a good question."

"Do you love him? Gavin, I mean. That's his name, right?"

"Yes, that's his name. And yes, I suppose I love him in a way."

"Where does he live?"

"Geneva, but he has apartments in New York and Paris."

"Will you move to Geneva?"

"Probably."

"So what's the problem?"

"Oh, I don't know. Lots of things, I suppose."

"Such as?"

"Such as how do you know? How do you know you can love just one person for the rest of your life? And is it madness to even pretend to try?"

"Can you?"

"I don't know if I can. I mean, all I'm thinking about now is how much I want you to kiss me."

I stopped and looked at her, taking her hands in mine. "Do you want me to?"

She laughed. "Of course I do."

Stepping forward, she raised her lips to mine. Her breath was sweet, her tongue soft. It was all as I remembered. Better. Her hands went under my shirt. My hand reached for her breast. She was not wearing anything under her dress. Through the cotton I massaged her, feeling the hardness of her nipple.

"Cesca," I said. "I've missed you so much."

She stepped back. "Stop," she said.

"What's the matter?"

"I shouldn't . . ."

"Shouldn't?"

"You know."

"Why?"

"Too many reasons," she said, shaking her head but clutching my shirt, holding me away.

"Do you want to go back inside?"

She nodded her head. "Yes."

"You know, I still love you," I said. "I never stopped."

"Don't, Wylie. Please."

"No. You told me that I would forget you, but I haven't. I don't care if you're getting married. I will always love you."

She stepped forward and kissed me passionately, quickly.

"Good night, Wylie," she said. "Thank you."

I stood there watching her walk away. My disregarded words still hanging in the air, the taste of her still on my lips.

15

ON THE SCALE BETWEEN LOVE AND LUST, THERE ARE MANY stops. It is nearly impossible to define *love*, in English at least, because its definition, not to mention its place within our culture, is so broad. Unlike the Eskimo's famous fifty words for snow, in English the word *love* means everything from how a person may feel about chocolate cake to the devotion a couple may feel after many years of marriage.

Then there is maternal love, sexual love, patriotic love, aesthetic love, and much, much more besides. When John Lennon sang "All you need is love," he was playing it safe. *Love* can mean just about anything. It is a word of infinite nuance, but for that very reason also has a stunning inadequacy. The ancient Greeks had four words for love: *eros*, for physical love; *agape*, for spiritual love; *philia*, for social love, and *storge*, for familial love. Even that doesn't seem like enough though.

Lust, however, is love's younger sibling. It is uncomplicated, straightforward. It relies on only one thing: egotistical desire. Lusting after something means wanting to possess it whether or not it wants to be possessed. Certainly, it is possible to desire an inanimate object, such as a car or a painting, but mostly lust is physical. The hunger one human feels for another.

As with all desire, there are gradations of intensity. There are the thousand small lusts we feel every day. A man may spot a pretty girl sitting by herself at a bar, and, for a moment, he lusts after her, wonders what she would be like naked, what size her nipples are, what her smell would be like. And then he loses interest as the conversation turns to a different topic. These lusts are easily forgotten. There are also grander lusts. Lusts that upend civilizations, destroy marriages and lives. Zeus's lust for Europa, Paris's lust for Helen. Later, Lancelot and Guinevere. Tristan and Iseult. Abelard and Héloïse. Invariably lust that is fulfilled seems to end badly. After all, there is a reason it is considered a sin.

The feelings I had for Cesca lay between lust and love. There is no question I lusted after her. For days after I would see her I could think of nothing else. I would lay awake at night and masturbate with her image in my head, wishing she were with me. I did not do this with every pretty girl I knew. There were girls, and later women, who were extremely attractive, some even beautiful, but none of them affected me in quite the same way Cesca did.

Why the brain fixates on one person instead of another is a mystery. Our synapses fire, our hormones surge, our hearts beat faster. Granted, Cesca was exceptionally beautiful, but that wasn't it entirely. There was something else about her that drew me to her as much as her beauty did. From the very first minute I saw her before I fell out of the tree, something inside me knew that in some indiscernible way she would be inextricably tied to my life. It was like tasting a food for the first time and not only liking it but recognizing it, as though in a past life it had been your favorite dish. That was how I felt about Cesca: As though I had already known her and loved her for many years.

What I didn't know, of course, was whether she felt the same way about me. There were times when I thought it might be possible, that maybe she loved me too. Other times I felt that loving Cesca as I did indicated that there was something flawed about me. What was it that attracted me so deeply to her? Why was I so willing to love someone who caused me such pain? Someone who was willful, stubborn, selfish—but also capable of great warmth, loyalty, and vivacity. By fixating on her, did I render myself emotionally unavailable to other potential relationships? Or was I simply like the stubborn gambler who believes that by always betting on the same number, one day I will hit the jackpot?

It was in December during my sophomore year. Returning after dinner one evening, I found a piece of paper slipped under my door. We had a communal telephone on the floor and took messages for each other. "Call Cesca," the note read, followed by a Manhattan phone number.

"Carlyle Hotel," answered a voice on the other end. I knew the Carlyle. It was not far from our old apartment. It had a famous bar with paintings of animals on the wall. Bobby Short sang there at night. My parents had taken me once years ago.

Confused, I said, "I'd like to speak to Cesca Bonet, please."

"One moment, please." Silence. Then, "I'm sorry, sir. We have no guest here under that name. Might there be another name?"

I thought. What was the name? "How about Oppenheim? Gavin Oppenheim?"

"Thank you, sir. Connecting you now."

The phone rang. There was no answer. "I'm sorry, sir. There doesn't seem to be an answer," interrupted the clerk. "Would you like to leave a message?"

"No. Please let it ring some more."

Finally, Cesca answered.

"Hello, Cesca? It's Wylie."

"Wylie," she said. Her voice sounded panicked. "I've been waiting for you to call. I left you a message hours ago."

"I know. I just got it. I was out. Are you all right?"

"Yes. I don't know. I'm so confused. Can you come over? Where are you? I need to see you."

I hesitated. My college was two hours away.

"Please come. I'll wait." She gave me her room number.

It was nearly nine on a Tuesday night, and I had classes the next day and an early morning training run with the heavy-weight crew. "Of course. I'll come. I'll be there as soon as I can."

"Thank you."

I sped down the Merritt Parkway. I still had my old pickup. The roads were empty, and I made good time. Less than two hours after I had spoken with her, I was driving through the familiar streets of the East Seventies, and, not wanting to waste time hunting for a parking spot, I put my truck into the garage next to the hotel. I checked my wallet and hoped I had enough to cover it. I would also need to buy gas.

Just before eleven, I walked into the empty lobby. No one challenged me, so I went to the elevator and took it to her floor. At the door, I rang and then knocked. There was no answer. I rang again, leaning on the buzzer. Once. Twice. Finally Cesca came to the door. Her eyes were bleary.

"You came." Her voice thick.

"I said I would."

"Sorry. I fell asleep."

I followed her into the suite. There was a bedroom on the right. We went into a little sitting room. There were boxes and bags everywhere.

She sat on a sofa. A table in front of her had an empty vodka bottle and a full ashtray on it. She was wearing only a long dark T-shirt. Her legs and feet were brown and bare. Red toenails.

When she uncrossed her legs, I could see a glimpse of white lace.

"Do you want a drink?" she asked. "I have more vodka in the kitchen."

"Sure."

She stood and wove to the little kitchenette. I heard her grabbing ice from an ice maker. The sound of ice falling on the floor. Then, "Oh shit."

"Can I help?" I called.

"No. Everything's fine."

She returned carrying two glasses filled with vodka and sat next to me on the couch, where she lit a cigarette.

"Thank you for coming. I didn't realize how late it was."

"I was happy to come. I was worried about you. You sounded terrible on the phone. What's the matter?"

She leaned forward and buried her face in her hands. "Oh God. I'm such a mess."

I put my hand on her back. "What's the matter?" I asked again.

She began to sob.

"Cesca?"

"I don't want to get married."

"Why not?"

Another sob. "I don't love him."

"What do you mean?"

"Gavin. I like him. He's rich. Good-looking. He treats me well. We have great sex. But I'm not in love with him."

"Where is he now?"

"Who fucking knows? I can't remember. Europe. Australia? He travels all the fucking time. This is his apartment. I've been hiding out here for a week, not wanting to see anyone. He's never here."

"When did you talk to him last?"

"Yesterday. No, two days ago, I think. I can't remember."

"Did you ever love him?"

She leaned back and took a sip of her drink. "No," she answered, shaking her head. "No, I don't think so."

"So why did you agree to marry him?"

"Oh, I don't know," she groaned. "I suppose it seemed like a good idea at the time."

"But not anymore?"

"No."

"Does he love you?"

"I don't know. I guess so. At least, he tells me he does."

"But you don't feel like he does?"

"How do you know when someone loves you? I mean, really know. Does it mean they treat you differently? Are they kinder to you? More patient? More honest? I really don't know. You know what I think it means? I think it just means that you lie more to people. You pretend more to spare them pain until one day you can't lie and pretend anymore and your real feelings come out and then it's all over. My parents were in love and looked what happened. Your parents too. And don't even get me started on Uncle Roger. The only perfect relationship I've ever seen is my grandparents'. But I don't know that for a fact either. They come from a different generation. My grandfather never hid anything from my grandmother. She knew everything because he told her, and she accepted it because what choice did she have? Back then, people married for life. They were braver."

"And you don't think that Gavin and you can be that brave?"

"I know I can't. And I don't want to get married to someone who I have to lie to. When we're together, he's always so polite, so considerate, but I know he's not telling me everything either. Why get married just to be miserable?"

"Then don't."

"It's not as simple as that. I was nearly married once before, and I called the wedding off. That was awful. I promised myself I'd never do that again."

"So what are you going to do?"

"I don't know. It's so fucked up." She lit another cigarette.

I sat there silently for several moments.

"So why am I here?"

She looked at me. "You're here because I trust you. For some reason, you're the only person I've ever met who has never judged me. Even my family. My mother would be furious. Gavin's handsome, rich, charming. He's also family. My third cousin or something. I don't know." She waved her hand vaguely in the air and took another drink. "Whatever."

I reached out for her hand and gently massaged it, stunned by her words, grateful for them.

"So what do you think I should do, Wylie? Where did you get that name, anyway? Wylie, Wylie. It's a hell of a funny name. It's like being named Sly or Tricky, isn't it? Are you sly or tricky, Wily Wylie?"

"It's an old family name. From my mother's side."

"An old family name. Aren't you grand? We don't have any old family names in our family. We're a new family. I'm getting another drink. Excuse me."

When she returned, she sat on the couch next to me, her feet tucked up under her legs, and asked, "So what should I do, Tricky Wylie?"

"Well, would you consider marrying me?"

She laughed and put her hand on my cheek. "You're so sweet. But I'm trying to get out of a marriage, not into one."

"Okay, is there anyone else you'd rather marry?"

"No. I don't want to get married. The whole idea scares the crap out of me."

"So what brought all this on now? The wedding's months away, isn't it?"

"Yes, but all the planning. I received samples of stationery yesterday. Jesus. That's when it hit me. I thought, I can't go through with this."

"Well, it seems to me that you've only got two choices: marry Gavin or not. If you don't want to, then you should tell him as soon as possible so you don't drag things out."

"Fuck, I don't want to think about it," she groaned and lay sideways on the couch. Then, sitting up: "Am I a bitch? Am I a bitch for wanting to marry someone for love?"

"No, of course not."

"Wouldn't you want to marry someone for love?"

"My offer still stands."

She smiled. "Of course it does. Dear, sweet Wylie. Maybe I should take you up on your offer. Would you like that, Tricky Wylie?"

This time she leaned over and kissed me on the mouth. Her breath tasted like vodka and cigarettes. She was on top of me. We kissed on the couch for several minutes before she stood up and said, "Come with me," and led me by the hand into the bedroom. The room was dark, the only light from the living room. The bed was unmade. Clothes were scattered over the furniture. I nearly stumbled on a shoe.

"Sorry it's such a mess. I told the maid not to come today," she said. "I'll be right back."

She went into the bathroom and closed the door.

I stood there, staring dumbly after her. Thinking that if there was a god of second chances, I should be thanking him.

I was sitting on the bed when she emerged from the bathroom, naked. More glorious than ever. The light from the bathroom shining behind her.

"Come here," she said, biting her bottom lip and giggling. "I know this is what you want." She grabbed my belt buckle, pushing me onto the bed. As before, she engulfed me, devoured me. Hers was nothing like the limited, tentative lovemaking I had encountered with other girls. It was fierce, passionate, relentless. She left me drained, spent, unable to move. All the time I was thinking, This is Cesca's neck, Cesca's breast, Cesca's hand, this is her, this is her, this is her. I remembered it all.

In the morning I lay on the pillow staring at her while she slept, her head on my chest. I didn't ever want to move. I wanted to burn the perfection of the image into my brain. It was like finding out that God is real or how Columbus must have felt when he did not sail off the edge of the world and instead put his feet down on the dry sand of San Salvador. The overwhelming relief. The gratitude. The immeasurable, unalloyed joy. Later, when she stirred, we made love again, slowly this time, fearlessly, our bodies revealed by the sunlight coming through the window. She shuddered in ecstasy, demanding everything I could give her.

We slept more and then ordered room service. College was forgotten. Unimportant in comparison. Crew practice was long over, so were most of my classes. I would have to answer for my absence later, but at this moment I had the outlaw's scorn for the orthodox. "Stay," she said, over coffee. "Please. We'll make a day of it. I don't want you to leave just yet."

I needed little persuading. We spent what remained of the morning naked, and then, in the early afternoon, we went out. On Madison Avenue, I felt like a tourist even though I had been raised in this neighborhood. With Cesca by my side, everything became unreal, new, possessing depths of beauty and fascination I had never perceived before. The familiar buildings seemed different, the items in the shop windows particularly alluring. She was pulling me along, caught in her gravitational wake like an asteroid around a planet. The force of her will, the extraordinariness of her beauty, the way that strangers would stare at her in the street, all seemed somehow bigger, more significant; compared to her the rest of the world was dross.

New York in early winter. There was no snow on the ground yet. The trees were barren. Already women were wearing furs, marvelous scarves. It was cold. I had on only an old tweed jacket of my father's, turned up at the collar. Cesca offered to buy me a coat. I refused, but she insisted. We walked into a store where I tried on several Italian cashmere overcoats. Blue, tan, black. All of them rich and warm. They cost hundreds of dollars, a thousand or more. It was an absurd amount of money. We left the store laughing, coatless. "We should have stolen one," she said.

In the Frick. There were groups of schoolchildren. Senior citizens. We passed by Lippi's *Annunciation*, Gainsborough's pale beauties. "These are my favorites," she said in the Fragonard Room. "You see?" she said, standing in front of a large canvas depicting a young woman in a long silk dress leaning against a column in the middle of a lush pleasure garden. "That's me, dreaming of love."

We walked through Central Park and later had a drink in the Carlyle's bar. I had noticed with great pleasure that she had removed her engagement ring. We sat side by side at a banquette in the corner, our thighs touching, holding hands. "Do you like martinis?" she asked. The room was dark, and faintly magical in its late afternoon emptiness. We were the only ones there besides the bartender, who was busy polishing glasses, and our waiter. Tables stood waiting for evening. A grand piano sat unplayed. On the walls elephants skated and giraffes doffed their caps. The world outside had ceased to exist. It could have been four in the morning. Time no longer applied to us, we were superior to it.

I laughed with delight. Everything was new, sparkling. I would have done anything for her, tried anything. Upstairs was our bed. The rest was forgotten. "I don't know. I've never had one."

"Never? Well, then, it's time to introduce you."

"Two vodka martinis," she ordered. "Up. With three olives."

They made me quite drunk. I was still learning how to hold my liquor. Like most college students, I was more familiar with beer, my father's Jack Daniel's, and sweeter concoctions, such as rum and Coke. The martini's taste was aseptic, strong, yet there was something about the directness of it. After the second, my head started to swim. The room went in and out of focus. I started kissing Cesca, who kissed me back and then said, "Enough. Let's go upstairs."

I tried to pay, but she laughed and said, "Don't worry. It's all on Gavin."

Dinner was from room service that night. She ordered a magnum of champagne. Caviar. We made love many times. She was tireless. Crying out, not caring if anyone heard. We knocked over a table. Several lamps, the telephone. Later we lay in bed, casually naked, and talked—about Gavin, Aurelio, her parents. She unburdened herself, sometimes drifting into long moments of silence. I said nothing. Then she would stop, and we would make love again. This went on for hours until, exhausted and satiated, we finally slept.

In the morning I awoke late, realizing I had to get back to school. No one knew where I was. I had obligations, work to catch up on. Cesca tried to get me to stay. She had assumed I would. We hadn't talked about it. Looking back on it, I wish I had stayed. But I had to leave.

"Gavin doesn't come back until tomorrow," she said. "We can have one more day. Please stay. It'll be fun."

"I wish I could, but I can't."

"Fine," she replied, covering herself with the sheet and sitting up in bed to light a cigarette.

"I'm sorry. It's Thursday today. I can be back tomorrow night."

"That won't work."

"Why not?"

"I told you. Gavin is coming back. I have to see him."

"What are you going to tell him? That you can't marry him?"

She blew smoke out of her nose. "I haven't decided yet what I am going to tell him. But I think I am going to go ahead with it."

This surprised me. It shouldn't have, but it did. After what had just happened between us, I thought that the marriage would definitely be off. How could it not be? Didn't it mean as much to her as it did to me? "I just thought . . ."

"What did you think? That I'd break my engagement to Gavin because we slept together?"

That was exactly what I had thought. But I was clearly wrong. I didn't know what to say.

She laughed. "You just don't get it, do you?"

"I understand that I love you. What more do I need to understand?"

She shook her head. "Let's not go there, okay? I've got my own problems to sort out. Please don't make my life more complicated than it already is." She sighed. "Excuse me," she said, standing up and walking to the bathroom, letting the sheet slide to the floor. She closed the door behind her and locked it.

I sat there for a while, feeling foolish. My cheeks were burning. Slowly I pulled on my pants. I knocked on the bathroom door. "Do you want me to go?"

From inside: "No. Wait a minute. I'll be out soon." The sound of running water. Eventually she emerged, her head and body wrapped in towels. She went to the bureau and withdrew a black bra and panties. I couldn't help but watch her. The perfect line of her leg. The curve of her breast. Trying to memorize them, suddenly aware that they were about to be taken away from me again.

"Turn around," she giggled. "You're embarrassing me."

When I turned back, she was dressed in black jeans and a long black shirt. Her feet were bare, her hair still wet.

"Are you mad at me?" I asked.

"Don't be silly," she said, coming over and giving me a kiss on the cheek. "I shouldn't have snapped before."

"It's all right."

She put her hand soothingly along the side of my face. "Don't think that this didn't mean anything to me, Wylie. It always has. It's always very special being with you. If I do wind up marrying Gavin, I'll never forget."

"Cesca, I . . ."

She placed her index finger across my lips. "Shhh. I know. You should go now."

"May I call you?"

"We'll see."

Rising up on her toes, she kissed my cheek. "Thank you for everything. Good-bye, Tricky Wylie."

Somehow the door closed, and I was in the hallway, carrying my jacket. Then I was in the elevator and out on the street, with the doorman tipping his hat, offering to get me a taxi. It was all a dream. No, it wasn't. It had been real, but there was nothing to prove it had happened, no physical evidence. No souvenir, no keepsake. Not even a book of matches to remind me of it all. I went to the garage next door. Handing over my ticket, I braced to learn how much I owed, fearing the bills in my wallet would be hopelessly inadequate. My bank card only worked in Connecticut. I could have gone to my father's office and asked him for the money, but it would have been awkward. Why wasn't I at school?

"That's okay, mister," said the attendant. "It's been taken care of. Mrs. Oppenheim already called down. It's on Mr. Oppenheim's tab."

16

CESCA MARRIED GAVIN, AS I WAS AFRAID SHE WOULD. IN the end, I wasn't invited to the wedding. I wrote to her often. Long, passionate, youthful letters. Occasionally she wrote me back a short note. Once I got a postcard from Spain with a photograph of the sea on the other side. It began *Dear Tricky Wylie* . . . But eventually we lost touch.

I cherished her memory. I dated other women, but none of them touched me the way she had. I was just going through the motions. Fumbling in the dark, the creak of bedsprings, bad breath in the morning, forced gaiety to pretend that what I really wanted was for her to be gone. Cesca was the apogee. No one else came close.

After college I returned to New York, rented a small apartment downtown near Wall Street, where the streets in those days were empty of life at night, and tried to paint. I took classes several days a week at the Art Students League. My father gave me a year to succeed. After that, who knew? He mentioned law school, but I never gave him any reason to think I would really do that. To his credit, he was surprisingly supportive of my wanting to paint. He seemed proud of my talent, one he lacked. I think that, not unlike Izzy Baum, he would have been pleased to be the father of a famous painter. He even steered a few of his friends and colleagues to me, and they obliged him by paying me to paint portraits of them, or their wives or children. Once even a favorite Pekingese dog.

At the same time, he constantly reminded me of how difficult a painter's life would be. "There's no money in it," he would say over dinner. "How do you ever plan to support a family?" I had no proper response and always assumed there would be money from somewhere, whether I earned it myself or was given it. He had been raised without such assumptions, earning every penny. He warned me about the dangers of being a rich man's son. That was why he wouldn't give me more money. He pointed to Roger as an example of early privilege having ruined his life. I had no answer to that.

I worked as a bartender and a copy editor. I lived as cheaply as possible, eating primarily pasta and canned soup. I completed a cycle called "The Life of the Poet." It was a series of ambitious canvases depicting different aspects of a poet's life. The poet with his family. The poet at work. The poet in love. There were eight in all. Aurelio formed my mental image of the poet—tall, gaunt, handsome, slightly tortured, wholly dedicated to his art. The paintings were large. I labored over them with everything I had. I made slides and showed them to several galleries. The only one that evinced any interest was run by an old queen, who took me for dinner one night and, after several bottles of wine, he started to say how handsome I was and suggested that we go to bed. I left him at the table, calling after me to come back. That I'd be sorry. It was a time when galleries displayed works with broken china on them or cartoons of barking dogs. Those galleries meant nothing to me, and I meant nothing to them.

In the spring Aurelio called me. He was back in New York for several weeks, also talking to galleries. He was not having much more luck.

"The art world has gone insane," he said. "Beauty is dead. All they want is ugliness."

We went out to a little coffee shop near his mother's house. He looked well. Older, of course, but still the same gentle soul he had always been. He said that coming back to New York was depressing. It wasn't just the art world. It was the city, the crime, the drugs, the filth. He sat there drinking his coffee.

"If it wasn't for my family, I wouldn't come back at all," he said. "By the way, have you heard about Cesca?"

"No. Why?" I answered. I had been careful not to ask after her, waiting to bring her up at the end.

"She left Gavin. Ran off with some French actor."

"Where? When?"

"A few months ago. In Paris. Mare was furious, of course. Personally, I was amazed the marriage lasted as long as it did. Cesca's not the kind of person to be tied down by one man."

"How is she? Have you seen her?"

"She's well, I think. We spoke the other day. She's already left the actor."

"Is she still in Paris?"

"No, she's back here now. In Amagansett. I'll be seeing her this weekend."

I wasn't sure if this was good news or not. Instead of asking more, all I said was "Give her my best."

Two weeks later my intercom buzzed. It was late, and I had just gone to bed. "Who is it?" I said into the intercom. At first I only heard static. "Who?" I repeated.

"It's Cesca. Come down."

"What time is it?"

"Who cares? Come down. We're going out."

Quickly, I pulled on my jeans and a T-shirt, grabbed my wallet and keys, and locked the door behind me. She was in front of my building, sitting in her red BMW convertible, wearing a revealing black dress. She looked terrific.

"Hello, Tricky Wylie," she said. "Get in."

I slid into the passenger seat. "How are . . ." I began to say when she reached over and kissed me deeply.

"Oh, I've missed you so much," she said.

I didn't know what to say. Thoughts and emotions spilled through my brain. Had I missed Cesca? When had I not? Had I not thought of her every day? Had I not put her face in front of every girl I met and found them all wanting?

But I also remembered everything.

She had been married.

Her life had become unknown to me.

She had ruined me.

And now she was sitting here opposite me, smiling her brilliant smile, her short skirt revealing those miraculous knees.

"What are you doing here?" I managed to say.

Already she was pulling away from the curb, taking us into the night. She drove a stick, shifting fluidly.

"We're going dancing," she replied. "There's a great club in Tribeca."

There was a large crowd milling in front, some of the people wearing outlandish costumes, like contestants on a game show. We parked across the cobblestoned street. "Come on," she said. Pushing past the crowd, she walked up to one of the bouncers at the door and said, "Hello, Tommy."

He replied, "Hey, Cesca. How's it going?"

"Great. He's with me."

I followed her through a long hallway decorated with surrealistic images. An insistent bass beat pulsated through the room. The dance floor was packed. Beautiful women, effeminate men.

Celebrities. Movie stars. Investment bankers in pinstripe suits, club kids. Grace Jones strode past me, tall as an Amazon. "Let's get a drink," Cesca shouted into my ear. There was a bar in the back. People made way for her as she approached. She greeted the bartender with a kiss on both cheeks. "Hello, darling, two vodka martinis, up with three olives."

"You got it, Cesca." She slipped him a twenty-dollar tip.

"So how are you?" she asked me, lighting a cigarette. It was only slightly less loud here.

"Fine, fine. Really good," I shouted into her ear. I was still feeling disconcerted, as though I had woken up in the wrong bed and had no idea how I had gotten there. "Lio told me about you and Gavin."

"Yeah, well. *'Ai xí és la vida,'* as we say in Catalan. That's life." She shrugged her shoulders. "Do you know? I never even took his name. What do you think that says about me? What do you think that says about him? Maybe I should have taken you up on your offer after all." She smiled. "You know, sometimes I think you're the only person who really gets me. I think you'd put up with anything I did, wouldn't you?"

It was true. But I wasn't an idiot. I knew what damage she was capable of doing. It was like those stories of people who adopt lion cubs and raise them as pets. Then, one day the lion has grown and it mauls you. The lion's not to blame. Such behavior is in its nature. But inside us there is the belief that we are different, the exception. The ones who don't get into car accidents, or are never diagnosed with cancer or mauled by lions. Until we are, we think we are invulnerable.

I nodded, but she was no longer paying attention. She drank her martini in nearly one swallow and placed the glass back on the table. "Drink up, Wylie. Let's dance."

I was never much of a dancer, but it didn't matter with Cesca. She was a marvelous dancer. Sensual, spirited, moving perfectly to the music, knowing that everyone in the room was watching her, admiring her. It was impossible not to. She danced with the entire floor, moving from partner to partner. I was just a member of the audience. Occasionally, like a leading lady on the stage, she would catch my eye and wink at me before resuming her role. I kept dancing on the periphery, keeping time to the music, not comfortable enough to stop but not feeling comfortable where I was. I knew there was no point in saying anything. I was just supposed to be happy I was there. It was what she wanted.

At some point, Cesca grabbed my hand and said, "Come with me." Her hands were slick with sweat. She led me to a large ladies' room filled with people of both sexes, some smoking, others making out. Cesca found an unoccupied stall and pulled me in. Instantly, urgently, her arms were around me, her tongue down my throat, grinding her hips against me. Then she placed my hands on her breasts and began to fumble with my belt. "Fuck me, Tricky Wylie. Fuck me."

I did. Against a wall. But I didn't want to. I remember looking up at her face, her eyes closed. It was only later that I realized I could have been anyone. Then, all I wanted was to please her. I don't know which of us was sadder or the more confused. Her, for treating life so cheaply, or me, for being so easily in her thrall.

Later she drove me home through the early morning streets. "I'm so happy to see you again, Wylie," she said, running her fingers through my hair. *"Molt maco."*

"What are your plans?" I asked. "Will I see you again?"

"Oh, I don't know. I'm not sure where I'm going to be one week to the next. I've always wanted to go to Fiji. Maybe I'll go there."

"What would you do there?"

"I don't know. What I do now, I suppose. Maybe I'll learn to surf."

"Would that make you happy?"

She threw her head back and laughed. "Shit, I don't know."

"What if I came with you? To Fiji, I mean."

"That's incredibly sweet but a terrible idea. I'd drive you crazy in a week. If you spent too much time around me, you'd get sick of me. I wouldn't want that. I like the way you see me. It's the way I'd like to see myself, I think."

"How do you think I see you?"

"Beautiful. Interesting. Desirable. Did I leave anything out?"

"No."

"That's the problem, Wylie. I did. I'm also angry, frustrated, spoiled, stubborn, occasionally cruel and self-destructive. There are days when I hate myself so much I can barely get out of bed. And, when I do, all I want to do is try to obliterate everything in my path. That's why I don't want to see more of you. I don't want to obliterate you too."

"Shouldn't I be allowed to decide that for myself?"

"No. I wouldn't ask that."

"What if it was what I wanted?"

She shook her head. "No, you wouldn't. Believe me."

"Aren't you being too tough on yourself?"

She shrugged. "Am I? Who's to say?"

"Me. Let me in, Cesca. I love you. I'll love you no matter what."

She drove in silence for several minutes. "I don't know. Maybe. One day. Not now. Okay?"

"Okay." That was enough for me. For the first time I felt like we had an understanding, an acknowledgment that there might be a one day.

She stopped in front of my building. The street was deserted. Trash littered the sidewalk. The windows in all the buildings were dark. Few people lived there. It was not a residential block.

"By the way," I asked. "How did you find me?"

"Lio told me where you lived." I had given him my address so he could write to me.

"Lio did?"

"Yes."

"Did you say why?"

"I said I wanted to see you."

"What did he say?"

"He said, 'I think Wylie still has a crush on you.'"

"What did you say?"

"I said I still had a crush on you too." She reached out and took my hand. "See, it's not just you." Then she kissed me delicately on the cheeks, the eyelids, and the lips. "Good-bye, Tricky Wylie."

I stepped out of the car and leaned back in. "When will I see you again?"

"I don't know. Probably not for a while."

"Now that you've got my address, can you at least write to me and let me know how you are?"

"I'll try. In case you don't remember, I'm not very good at writing letters." She smiled one last time and then started the ignition. "Take care of yourself."

"You too."

I watched her drive away. In the east the sun was already rising.

17

Izzy died. No one told me. I read about it in the *Times*. isidore baum, philanthropist, is dead at 90. The obituary described his life, primarily his business career and good works. It mentioned his three children by name. Of his grandchildren the only one singled out was Cosmo. "One of his grandsons is the musician Cosmo Bonet." The funeral would be private. A memorial service would be held at a later date.

I sent a letter of condolence to Roger, but that was all I felt was appropriate. I assumed the whole family had returned for the funeral, but I could not bring myself to contact Cesca directly even if I knew how. Her life had once again closed to me. For all I knew she had ran off with someone else or even remarried. Even Aurelio had dropped away, making good on his promise to avoid America.

It was June. I was having my regular monthly dinner with my father in New York. He had recently remarried. His new wife, Patty, was younger than him and pretty. She was also a good cook and a passionate entertainer, two attributes my mother lacked. I had never known him in better spirits.

My year to become a painter had become two and I was no closer than before to selling my work. I dreaded our dinners, knowing he would inevitably bring up my lack of success and my dire financial situation. There was a steak house on Third Avenue he had been going to for years. It had beige-jacketed waiters who all knew him and greeted him by name. "Service. That's the most important thing in a restaurant," he would tell me. "These days you can get good food in lots of places, but if they don't know you they won't take care of you the same way." The maître d' was a short Italian guy in a sharp suit. His name was Joe, and he always led us in to my father's favorite table. I watched as my father thanked him with a neatly palmed twenty-dollar bill. My father no longer needed to look at a menu. They knew what he liked. Jack Daniel's. The chopped salad. New York strip, rare. House fries. I had the same.

After grilling me about my life and finding my answers unsatisfactory as usual, he decided to move to other topics. Not that I blamed him. The subject of my life was depressing even to me at this point. I was stagnant, broke, even if I wasn't willing to admit that to my father yet. I remembered listening to Esther and Paolo tell me about the camaraderie they had enjoyed with fellow artists in New York in the late forties and fifties. Many of these artists had, like them, escaped the threat of Nazism to find safety and a new place to work in New York. This motley group of Frenchmen, Germans, Italians, Romanians, Dutch, and even a few Americans had been at the forefront of an artistic revolution. Yet they were all friends. They all socialized with one another, critiqued each other's works, had affairs with each other's husbands and wives.

There was none of that around now. At least not that I saw.

Artists were more competitive, more secretive. As Esther said, "Artists these days don't care anymore about creating art. Art has become a commodity, like pig bellies or steel. Something to be bought and sold. They just want to make money," pronouncing the last word "mo-nee."

"By the way," my father said as the steaks arrived. "Izzy Baum died a few months ago."

"Yes, I know. I saw the obituary."

He looked philosophical for a moment. "He was quite a guy. I owe a lot to him."

"I'm sorry."

"No, it's okay," he said, waving his hand as though it were possible to brush mortality away like a gnat. "Izzy had a full life. It's just hard to believe how fast it all goes. It seems like only last week that I met him for the first time. And now he's dead. Makes you think."

I nodded my head. I was too young and self-absorbed to give much thought to death. In those days, life seemed to stretch out forever, and I was just beginning my journey.

"Anyway, the reason I brought up Izzy is that his memorial's this weekend," he said. "In Amagansett."

"Are you going?"

"Of course."

"When was the last time you saw him?"

"A few years ago. He was already looking old and feeble. He'd had a stroke. I went over to the house once, and he was in a wheelchair. The left side of his face was paralyzed, so it was a little hard to understand him, but he was mentally all there. He knew who I was. Asked about business. Told me he was proud of how I had turned out." He stopped chewing.

"What about Roger? When did you see him last?"

My father nodded his head and resumed eating. "About the same time. I haven't really had much to talk about with Roger lately, you know. He'll call me up every now and then and try to pitch me some crazy idea. He had one about making paper out of garbage. There were some people he had met. They had invented the process. All they needed was some start-up money. So I met them. They came to the house one day. They had brought along prototypes. Not only would it find a use for the billions of tons of garbage produced every year but also think of the trees that would be spared. A win-win for everyone. The only problem was that the prototypes smelled like shit. We can fix that, they said. That's what we need the money for." My father laughed and shook his head.

"So what happened?"

"I told them if they could find someone to invest in their shit paper, I wished them luck. Roger said I was being too harsh. I didn't get the big picture. Some crap like that. That was the last time I talked to him. I told him to quit wasting my time. Roger was always kind of a schmuck when it came to business. He was a real disappointment to Izzy."

I let his last comment hang in the air. It was obvious he felt the same way about me. There was nothing I could say.

"Anyway, do you want to come with Patty and me to Izzy's memorial? It's this Saturday. You knew the family, right? As I recall you and Kitty's oldest boy were friends. What was his name again?"

"Aurelio."

"Aurelio. Right. It will be at the compound. Why don't you come out on Friday, and we'll go over."

Several days later, at a quarter to two in the afternoon, I was driving behind my father onto the Baum compound. There were scores of other cars on the grass. It reminded me of Izzy's eightieth birthday. That had been ten years ago. I handed my keys to a valet, and followed my father and Patty to where another man, this one in a gray suit, was handing out programs and showing us where to go.

It was a lovely June day. There was a large open tent on the lawn shading rows of folding chairs facing the water, most of which were already occupied. At one end of the tent was a lectern surrounded by a semicircle of more chairs that was flanked by flowers. To one side, on an easel, was a large, framed, black-and-white photograph of Izzy. On the other side was a black grand piano. Several photographers milled around the crowd. There was no sign yet of the family.

We found three seats together near the back. The noise of dozens of people talking filled the tent. Most of them were quite old. My father knew several of the guests and stood to shake hands and speak with them. He introduced Patty and sometimes me. I looked through the program. On the cover was the same photograph of Izzy that now stood on an easel at the front of the tent. Underneath was his full name, the date of his birth, and the date of his death. Inside, the left side contained the words to the Twenty-Third Psalm. The right side listed the names of the people who would be speaking. I saw Roger's and Cosmo's names. The rest were unknown to me.

The tent fell silent as the family walked in. Roger came first, in a dark suit with a serious expression on his face. Diana on his arm. Kitty and Randall came next, followed by Dot. Then Cesca, Aurelio, Cosmo, and finally Carmen. They were all soberly dressed, which contrasted sharply with the lush green of the lawn, the sparkling azure of the water, and the light blue of the sky.

They kept their gazes forward without looking at the crowd. After they had all taken their seats in the first row, a rabbi in a black suit with a shawl around his shoulders stood and intoned a prayer in Hebrew. Many of the mourners murmured along with the words, my father included. Then Roger rose and addressed the crowd. Like many of the other men under the tent, he was wearing a yarmulke. He thanked everyone for coming and then explained that his mother was not able to attend. She was too weak, but she was grateful that so many people had loved Izzy. Roger then led the crowd in reciting the psalm.

When he finished, he removed several folded sheets of paper from the inside pocket of his jacket, put on his reading glasses, and proceeded to eulogize his father. He talked about how strong a man he was and how much he loved his family, and that they were everything to him. At several places Roger's voice broke. When he sat down another man stood up. He was elderly and stout with a heavy accent. He had been Izzy's business partner for many years and spoke of his acumen and told a few funny stories that lightened the mood of the crowd. The other speakers included men who remembered Izzy's philanthropic work, his support of education and his contributions to the arts.

The last to stand up was Cosmo. But instead of going to the lectern, he went to the piano. "This was a favorite of Gog's," he said and then started to play. It was beautiful. The mourners were rapt. He played like an angel. When he finished, he stood up and without bowing returned to his seat. Roger then returned to the lectern and thanked everyone else again for coming and invited anyone who wished to join them for some refreshments inside.

There were more than one hundred guests, many of them elderly, so it took them a long time to file into the house. I hung back, trying to look inconspicuous.

"I thought I saw you here."

I turned around. It was Lio.

We embraced. He looked very well. Clean-shaven. Dressed in a dark suit.

"I'm sorry about your grandfather."

"Thank you. I loved him very much."

"How is everyone else?"

"They're all right. We've all had time to let it sink in. He had been ill for a while. Some are more upset than others. Cesca's been taking it particularly badly."

"Why?"

"I'm not sure. She always felt very close to Gog. Might have something to do with being eldest grandchild."

We talked for a little about his work, and he asked about mine. He seemed excited about what he had been doing and promised to show it to me. I wished I could have been as enthusiastic. In recent weeks I had come to feel as though I lacked the talent or the vision or the drive or whatever it was that was required to be a successful artist. I would stare with grim dissatisfaction at my canvases. I had all but stopped working, walking guiltily past my easel on the way in or out of my small apartment, staring into space, drinking too much, and generally feeling depressed. When I did work, it was often only to scrape away and repaint something I had already done.

I wanted to share how I was feeling with Aurelio. He of all people would understand and could lend a sympathetic ear. Maybe even provide some useful advice. But I was hesitant to tell even him. To do so would have been an admission of my inadequacy. To doubt was to admit that I wasn't up to it, like a seminarian questioning transubstantiation.

"And you, Wylie? How is your work?"

"It's going well," I lied. "Will you be in New York at all? Maybe you could come by? It would mean a lot to me to have you critique them."

It had been months since I had shown my work to anyone. I was working alone, virtually living alone. Most of my friends had entry-level jobs at banks or were going to graduate school. We were on different schedules. The young bankers worked late hours, and when they went out, they usually opted for expensive nightclubs like the Palladium. I rarely joined them because I was always short of funds.

"I might be in next week if I have time before I return to Barcelona."

"When are you going back?"

"Wednesday." Today was Saturday. "I'll let you know. Come on in," he said. "If I don't start mingling with the guests, Mare will be furious."

He led me inside the house. I saw Cesca across the room. She was talking to some guests. She looked tired. Her hair was pulled back and she wasn't wearing any makeup. I wanted to say something to her but didn't want to intrude.

Instead I bumped into Cosmo.

"Sorry about your grandfather," I said.

"Thank you," he responded, not even taking the time to talk to me and pushing ahead through the crowd until someone he actually wanted to speak with detained him.

Standing there alone, I scanned the room. It was packed, the guests spilling out into other rooms. Some children were playing on the lawn. I spotted my father and Patty as they chatted with another couple in a corner. I also saw Roger and his new wife shaking hands solemnly. Kitty. Carmen.

"Hello, Wylie," said a voice behind me. I turned and recognized Gianni, Paolo and Esther's son. He was as handsome as his father but in a softer way, and taller, though not as tall as me. He was about twenty years my senior. It was said that when he was a student at Harvard he dated Edie Sedgwick. Now he was a professor at a small college in New England. I had recently heard that his marriage had broken up.

"Are your parents here?" I asked.

"No, my father wasn't feeling well so Oma stayed to take care of him," he answered, using the nickname the family called Esther.

"Nothing serious, I hope."

"His back has been bothering him lately."

I felt guilty about not having seen them for a while.

"Would it be all right if I visited them?"

"I'm sure they'd love to see you. Just call ahead of time. Oma will let you know if it's okay."

At this point Cesca walked up to us and slipped her arm around Gianni's waist.

"Hello, Wylie," she said.

It was done so naturally it took me a second to realize what had just happened, and then it became obvious. "Hello," I replied.

"I forgot you two knew each other," she said, giving Gianni a kiss on the cheek.

"I'm sorry about your grandfather."

"Thank you. It's been rough. Poor Bushka. She's taking it all very hard."

I nodded my head. There wasn't much I could add.

"And you, Wylie?" she asked. "How are you?"

"I'm fine."

"Excuse me, Wylie," said Gianni. "Sweetheart," he said, turning to Cesca, "would you like something to drink?"

"That would be lovely. White wine."

"Wylie?"

"No thanks."

Gianni disentangled himself and walked through the crowd to the bar.

"It's good to see you," said Cesca, placing her hand on my arm. "You look skinny, though." It was true. I hadn't been eating well.

"Well, you look beautiful."

"Thank you."

"How long have you been with Gianni?"

"A few months."

"How did you two meet?"

"Oh, we've known each other all our lives. I used to have a mad crush on him when I was a little girl. He was the most beautiful man I'd ever seen. Even more beautiful than you."

"Are you happy?"

"Yes."

"I wrote you a few times."

"I know. Your letters were sweet. I hope you weren't too disappointed when I didn't write back."

"No." I smiled. "I knew better. And I'm happy for you. Gianni's a terrific guy."

She smiled back. "You're a dear, Wylie. You always have been. Thank you for understanding."

Gianni returned with Cesca's white wine. I took this as my cue to leave. "My condolences again," I said as I leaned in to kiss Cesca's once-familiar cheek. Jasmine and roses.

I then shook Gianni's hand and said I hoped I'd see him soon and that I'd call Esther tomorrow to see about coming over. I had meant what I said about him to Cesca. I had always liked Gianni enormously. It was easy to see why any woman would fall for him. I was happy for them both. When you love someone and you can't have them, there is at least a kind of comfort in knowing that they are with a person you admire. I felt as though a chapter in my life had closed, that it was finally time to forget about Cesca.

Other things came to a close instead over the next few months. I decided to give up painting. It was something that had been coming for a long time, but I had been too stubborn to accept it. My plan now was to apply to architectural school. That way I could still make use of my artistic talents but in a context that would provide me with a more secure career. Harvard was my first choice, but I also was looking at Columbia,

Cornell, and the University of Virginia, although I would have considered myself lucky to get into any of them.

My parents were relieved. My father immediately reached out to friends of his. He knew several members of the faculty at the Graduate School of Design. He even invited me to move out of my apartment in New York and stay at the pool house in East Hampton rent-free, which I accepted gratefully. They would not be there long, however, as they now left after Thanksgiving to spend the winter in Palm Beach, where my father had recently bought a house off South Ocean. I soon got a job working with my old boss building houses. It was good money and practical experience for what I now thought of as my new career. In the evenings I studied, boning up on my calculus and physics. I took out several volumes on architectural history from the library. Wrote flash cards with words on them like *clerestory* and *gambrel*. I was feeling good at last, convinced that my life was on the right track.

I was also able to spend time with Paolo and Esther. Winters on the East End of Long Island are bitter, and their house was old. When the wind blew, you could hear it whistling through the cracks. They bundled themselves up in heavy sweaters and stoked their wood-burning stove. When it snowed, I drove over to shovel their driveway and the path from the house to the old shed where they kept their tiny car. Many days I brought them groceries when the roads were too icy for them to drive. Once a week I split wood for them.

In the past they had gone away during the winter to a more hospitable climate where Paolo could teach. But not this winter. Paolo was feeling too weak. He had a bad cough, the result of too many years breathing in cement dust and tobacco smoke. They were not disappointed in me for having turned away from painting. They had many friends who were architects. Sert, Corbusier, Bunshaft. Paolo had even collaborated with some of them. For Sert he did a huge mural. For Bunshaft another. Paolo told me proudly that those commissions had helped pay for Gianni and his sister to go to college.

"And how is Gianni?" I asked over tea in their kitchen.

"He has been involved with that Bonet girl," said Esther, who was knitting a sweater. Her voice reeking with disapproval.

"Is anything wrong?"

"She is magnificent," said Paolo. "Like a wild animal." He then started coughing.

"Yes, she is quite lovely, but I am not sure she is right for Gianni," sniffed Esther.

"Pah," said Paolo. "Have you ever known a mother who thought a girl was right for her son?"

"Victoria was right for him," she replied, mentioning the name of Gianni's first wife. A pretty heiress he had married when he was still in grad school. "She is also the mother of his sons. He should never have left her."

Paolo leaned over to me. "It was the Bonet girl who broke them up. She saw him at a party. Bang!" he said, smacking his palm on the table. "She is a siren. Like *Ulisse e sirena, no? Che cosi fai?* What do you do? He had no one to tie him to the mast, *si?* So he crashed upon the rocks. Pow!" He slapped his hands together. More coughing.

Esther shook her head and sighed. "It has been very difficult on the children."

"I'm sorry," I said. "I had no idea."

"He has asked her to marry him," she said. "Once the divorce comes through."

"What did she say?"

"She said maybe—not definitely no, not definitely yes," laughed Paolo. "But I told him to forget about her. A siren doesn't marry. She can't stop being a siren. It is what she does. It is her *natura, no?* You may as well stop asking a horse to be a horse or a fish to be a fish."

In early March, Paolo and Esther invited me for dinner. Gianni would be coming out, and he was bringing Cesca with him. When he was there, I was demoted. He was the true son, after all.

"Thank you for all the help you gave my parents this winter," said Gianni. "They said you were wonderful to them."

"They are wonderful to me. It is the least I could do."

I would steal quick glances over at Cesca. She looked subdued, distant. When she caught me looking at her, she would give me a brief smile and then look away. Gianni was very solicitous of her. Could he get her more wine? Was she warm enough? He could bring her a sweater. She barely responded to him.

"So what are you doing up here by yourself, Wylie?" she asked midway through dinner.

I told her. Applying to architectural school. Working construction. Rising at dawn, putting on my quilted canvas jumpsuit to keep out the cold, and driving to the work site while it was still dark. The ground was rock hard. It was worse when it snowed. My hands were red and chafed; dirt circled my broken fingernails no matter how hard I scrubbed.

"Sounds awful," she said.

"No, I like it. For the first time in my life, I feel I'm doing something really useful. I have a plan."

"What about at nights? Don't you get bored?"

"I study most nights. And I'm pretty tired, so I'm in bed early. This is the latest I've been up in weeks."

"What do you do for fun?"

"I don't know if you could call it fun, but it does get lonely some nights. There's a bar in town near the railroad tracks. Big Al's. Sometimes I go there after work. There're also a few places in Sag Harbor. The Sand Bar. Murf's."

"I've never heard of them."

"They're all local places. Nothing fancy."

The conversation turned to other things. The corrupting influence of television was one of Esther's favorite topics. Also politics. Esther was liberal, Gianni more conservative. To his mother's horror, he had voted for Reagan. Sometimes they would argue. This was one of those nights.

"I'm sorry," Cesca said at one point, addressing no one in particular. "I've got a headache. I think I'm just going to go to bed."

Gianni stayed up with us, finishing the wine. Later, after he and Paolo had gone upstairs as well, I helped Esther wash up. "Wylie," she began, "do you have any girls in your life?"

"Not exactly. There is one girl, but she doesn't feel the same way about me." I dried a dish and placed it in the rack.

"How do you know? It can be hard to tell sometimes what girls are thinking. Many times they say one thing and mean something else."

"Well, she's with someone else."

"Ah, are they married?"

"No."

"Engaged?"

"No."

"Then there is still hope."

I shrugged my shoulders. "Maybe."

"Does she know how you feel about her?"

"Yes."

She laughed lightly. "There is nothing that makes a woman happier than knowing a handsome young man is in love with her. But, remember, she doesn't have to do anything else but be beloved. It is up to the handsome young man if he decides he wants more."

A few nights later, I walked into Big Al's bar. As usual, I had been agitated by seeing Cesca and was in no mood for reading about barrel and groin vaults and their place in Romanesque architecture. I was craving companionship, even if I spoke to no one. The thought of spending another evening alone was unbearable. Seated at the bar were several regulars, most of them former baymen, who were silently nursing their beers or shot glasses. I nodded to them. Big Al, a stout octogenarian who was blind in one eye and spoke in a gruff squawk, greeted me with a "Hey kid," and opened a beer for me. It took me coming there for several months before he deigned to recognize me, to know what I liked to drink. He had never bothered to learn my name, but I was grateful simply to be treated as a regular. I sat there, watching a game show on the television above the bar, lost in my thoughts. I had another beer and was about to go when I felt a hand on my shoulder.

I turned around, and there was Cesca.

"I was hoping to find you here," she said.

Big Al immediately brightened, hustled over as quickly as his girth would let him, and said, "Hey, beautiful, what can I get you?" I had never seen him move so fast or be so animated.

She smiled at him and said, "Stoli rocks."

"Ain't got no Stoli. Sorry."

"Absolut?"

"Coming right up."

Then to me she said, "All right if I sit down?"

I was too astonished to see her to say anything more than "What are you doing here?" Then, realizing that might have sounded rude, I added, "I mean, hello. I'm surprised to see you."

She laughed. "I'm sure you are. I remember you said this was one of your hangouts."

"Here you go, beautiful," said Al. "On the house."

"Aren't you sweet?" she replied. "Thank you."

"You want something else, kid?"

"Another Bud." Al limped off to the cooler, lifted the lid,

fished around for a while, removed a bottle, opened it, and set it down in front of me.

"What's your name, sweetheart?" he asked. The rest of the bar had gone quiet. All the men were staring at Cesca.

"Cesca." She put out her right hand.

"I'm Al," he said, taking her hand in his.

"Pleased to meet you, Al."

"You a friend of his?"

"An old friend."

"Hope you don't feel you gotta come in only when he's here." He winked.

"Why, thank you, Al. I can't believe I've never been in here. I must have passed it hundreds of times."

"Well, nothing wrong in making up for lost time," he chortled.

"I'll do that. How long have you been here for exactly, Al?"

"Almost sixty years. I've seen a lot of pretty girls walk in through that door, but you got 'em all beat, you know that?"

"That's so sweet of you to say."

"Sweet, hell. You're just lucky I ain't twenty years younger."

"You married, Al?"

"Yeah, but what she don't know won't hurt her," he said with a wink to the rest of the bar, drawing an appreciative laugh from the other patrons.

"Well, we'll just keep this our little secret then, won't we?" she said and, leaning over the bar, kissed him on the forehead.

Big Al beamed and turned red. The others whistled and clapped. "Big Al's in love," shouted someone.

"Aw, get out of here," he responded, obviously pleased.

"Al, I hate to love you and leave you, but Wylie here and I have to get going. I'll see you next time."

"I'll be waiting, darlin'."

I held the door for Cesca and followed her outside. The night was cold and brisk. Through the bare branches of the trees on the sidewalk, stars twinkled against a deep blue sky.

"I can see why you like that place," she said. "You want to get something to eat? I'm famished."

"Cesca, why are you here?"

"Aren't you happy to see me?"

"Of course I am. I'm just surprised, that's all. I might not have been there."

"Guess I just got lucky."

"What if I wasn't there?"

"Well, I'd have tried those other places. What were they called? The Sand Bar and Murf's, right?"

"Right."

"And if you weren't there, I'd've just driven to your house. I've never been there before, but I figured I could find it okay. So, if you're done questioning, what do you say to dinner?"

We drove separately to a little Mexican place in town. Cesca spoke in Spanish to the busboys, who grinned and blushed.

"Where's Gianni?" I asked.

"He flew home. He has a seminar to prepare for."

"How's it going?"

"The seminar? I have no idea."

"Not that. You know what I mean. Between Gianni and you."

She shrugged. "It could be better. The sex is good but . . ."

"You can spare me the details."

"Embarrassed or jealous?" She grinned.

I leaned back in my chair and grinned. "Maybe a little of both."

"But let's just say I don't see myself spending the rest of my life being a faculty wife in some small New England town where they roll up the streets at ten o'clock."

"So why me?"

"Why you? I'd thought you'd be happy 'why you.' "

"I am. I'm very happy to see you. I hope you know that. It just gets a little confusing sometimes, you know?"

She reached out her hand and grasped mine, rubbing her thumb along my palm. "Ooh, calluses," she said, leering at me. "That's a real turn-on." Then, "Poor Tricky Wylie. I can be a real pain in the ass, can't I?"

I left my hand where it was. "Honestly?"

"Of course."

"Yes."

"Does it matter?"

"It should but it doesn't."

"So why do you put up with me?"

"You know why."

She played with my hand in silence for a few moments. "You are too sweet, Wylie. I'm very flattered."

"I'm not trying to flatter you," I said, taking my hand back. "I'm trying to prove to you that you don't have to keep playing these games with me. We aren't teenagers anymore. Damn it, I love you and I think you should start loving yourself too."

"I'd like that. Do you think it's possible?"

"Yes."

"Well, you always were the more optimistic one."

I signaled for the check and paid. Outside, Cesca didn't say a word but came right up and kissed me. "I've wanted to do that all night," she said. "Come on. I'll follow you in my car. Take me to your place."

I AWOKE IN THE COLD AND DARK AFTER ONLY A FEW HOURS' sleep. She stirred and asked groggily, "What are you doing?"

"I've got to go to work," I whispered. "You sleep some more. Sorry if I woke you. I was going to leave you a note."

I sat down on the edge of the bed, feeling the warmth of her skin. I stroked her hair and kissed her on the cheek softly. She purred and pulled the covers around her. "Will I see you later?" I asked.

"I don't know. Would you like to?"

"Of course."

"Then maybe—but would you forgive me if I didn't?"

I stood up and sighed. "Probably not, but it would be about what I'd expect."

I walked to the door and opened it.

"Wylie?"

"Yes?"

"I just want you to know one thing."

"What's that?"

"You're the longest relationship I've ever had in my life. I hope that counts for something."

I closed the door behind me.

When I returned to the pool house that afternoon in the fading light, I found the bed unmade, an empty coffee cup in the sink, and a few cigarette butts ground into a plate. But otherwise there was no sign of her. I tried calling her at the Playhouse and then at the main house. The only person who answered was the nurse who looked after old Mrs. Baum. When I asked for Cesca, she said, "I have no idea. Sorry."

I even got back into my pickup truck still wearing my work clothes and drove to the compound. Except for a light in the main house where the nurse was keeping her vigil over a television set, the rest of the houses were dark, idle as children's toys on a shelf. There was no sign of Cesca's car. Once again she had vanished from my life.

18

IN THE SPRING I WAS ACCEPTED TO THE HARVARD GRADU-
ate School of Design. My father and Patty took me out to dinner
to celebrate. The restaurant on East Fiftieth Street was French.
My father had told me to invite a date if I wanted, but I didn't
have anyone to ask.

That night I stayed in the unfamiliar guest room of my father's new apartment. Even though I'd had plenty to drink, I
wasn't tired. I stared at the phone. It was late. I picked it up and
dialed Cesca's number. It rang four times, five. I was about to
hang up when I heard a sleepy voice.

"Hello?"

"Cesca?"

"Who's this?"

"It's Wylie."

"Wylie? What are you doing? Do you know what time it is?"

"Sorry. I just wanted to tell you something."

"What?"

"I got into Harvard architectural school."

There was silence on the other end of the line. "That's great, Wylie." Then the sound of another voice.

"Are you alone?"

"No."

"No, of course not. Look, I'm sorry I bothered you. I just wanted you to know."

"Good night, Wylie. I'm very happy for you." Before I could ask her anything else, she had hung up.

I moved to Cambridge in May to take summer courses to prepare myself. My father was more than happy to pay my rent and give me a stipend on which to live. I found an apartment on the top floor of a house on Craigie Street owned by a retired music professor. In the afternoons, she would play Chopin.

For the next three years, Cambridge would be home, but I would come whenever Cesca beckoned. There was a pattern to our reunions. She would be incommunicado for several months, or more, and then I'd receive a phone call or letter telling me to join her wherever she was. Gianni was by now a memory, not even the latest in a long line of men who had tried, and failed, to win her for themselves. At least, I remained a constant, probably because I was always ready to drop whatever I was doing and hasten to her side. Mostly I was summoned to New York. A few times it was to Amagansett in the dead of winter, when we were the only ones there. The snow deep on the ground, the refrigerator empty. Logs blazing in the fire. Once I met her on Cape Cod in the off-season in a large, gray modern house overlooking Cotuit Bay. There were vintage cars parked in the garage, expensive paintings on the walls, personal photographs on the shelves. An extensive wine cellar to which we liberally helped ourselves. We were all alone.

"What are we doing here? Whose house is this?" I asked.

"Shhhhh," she said. "Come to bed."

Wherever we went, she was always mysterious about her

recent activity. While there were certain subjects that were off-limits, she was happy to bring me up to date on her family. She told me about Cosmo's continued success and Carmen's rapid progress through medical school. Lio's disillusionment with the art world. He had been in a group show in Barcelona and had sold a few of his paintings. That he had not sold them all came as a surprise and disappointment to him.

Sometimes when we lay in bed, I could get Cesca to tell me about herself, her life. She told me about Freddie, the boy in Cadaqués. Others whose names I have forgotten. Why do you want to know all this stuff? she would ask. I don't know. I just do, I would respond, believing, falsely, that such knowledge could be to my advantage. It was like Scheherazade in reverse. I figured that if I knew her better than anyone, she would prefer me over anyone. It was just a matter of patience. Eventually she would be ready.

But each time I was wrong. There were mornings when I would wake up and be surprised to find she was still there sleeping next to me. I would hope for this day at least that she wasn't leaving. A few mornings, I even awoke to an empty bed but then found her making coffee. She told me once with regal insouciance that it was the only thing she could make. Like her mother, she abhorred domestic chores. After a day or two, whichever room we were staying in would be covered in her clothes. Underwear draped over a chair. Stockings balled up in the corner. Once I asked if she wanted some help cleaning up, and she looked at me quizzically. "Why would you want to do that?" She seemed genuinely perplexed. Hers was a life where people picked up after her or not at all. Chaos was preferable to order. She was a dropper of rocks in still water, the reflections in the ripples more interesting than a placid surface.

And then, inevitably, without warning, just as I was beginning to get used to her, and was even thinking this time she would stay, like a cat rescued during a rainstorm she would be gone. We could have been having dinner one evening, talking about how much fun it might be to live in, say, Amsterdam or Rio, or at what moments we were happiest—and I would always tell her truthfully they were the times I was with her—and there would be no hint from her that her bags were already mentally packed and she would be leaving the next day. Maybe she didn't even know herself. Maybe she was adhering to her own internal timetable, the circadian rhythms that ordered her life. Her disappearances, however, became more bearable over time. I grew to accept them as part of a natural order, like a bird's migration or the peregrination of the stars. After she had left, my life resumed its normal course, like a town after a hurricane. Slowly, I would rehang the signs, repair the windows, pump out the basement.

If I was overcurious about Cesca's life, there was no corresponding interest from her about mine. Rarely did she ask me a personal question. She didn't want to know how I felt about my mother or why I had quit painting. When she first reappeared, she would inquire in a desultory way about how my studies were progressing, but she rarely listened long enough to hear what I said. Nor would she have been interested if I went into detail about the differences between Brutalism and Futurism, who my favorite professor was, or whether I felt that my thesis adviser should have more flexible office hours. I was not offended by her attitude because I knew how solipsistic she was. We learn to make allowances for those we love most. In Cesca's case, she asked nothing from me she did not ask from herself.

After three years I graduated and, through a connection of my father's, found work at the Paris office of a New York firm. When I told Cesca of my move, her response was "Paris! I love Paris."

"Will you visit?"

"Of course, darling. Just try to keep me away."

Through a friend of my mother's, I rented a small, furnished apartment on the top floor of a house on the Île Saint-Louis that was a short walk from my office. It was charming, if cramped, and I had a view of Notre Dame. I went to work, struggling to adapt to my new job and my new culture. I had studied French in school and had a passable accent, but I was not a natural linguist, and it took me several months to get used to the speed with which the average Parisian spoke.

One night I returned home to find a message on my answering machine. Cesca's voice saying: "Wylie, it's me. I'll be passing through Paris in a week or so. I'll let you know. Big kiss. *Adéu.*"

I tried to call her back, but, as usual, there was no answer.

For the next week, I worked distractedly, rushing home from the office, wondering if that night there would be another message from Cesca, telling me to meet her at such-and-such a hotel on the Rue Whatever. Or to say her flight was arriving in the morning and to meet her. Or to just stay where I was—she'd be right over. In preparation for any and all such exigencies, I laid in a store of champagne, pâté, good coffee, even a small, enormously expensive tin of Russian beluga, all of which put a sizable dent in my meager weekly take-home pay.

But then there was the night I returned home to find another message. "Hi, it's me. Look, I'm sorry. I don't think I'll be able to see you. I've got to go. They're calling my flight. Next time, okay? Big kiss."

So, I drank the champagne and ate the caviar by myself and tried not to be angry or disappointed. I consoled myself with the belief that there would be another call, another promise of a meeting, and that, at some point, I would see her.

Like so many before me, I soon found myself seduced by Paris's charms. I was willing to overlook the challenges the city presented—the washer and dryers that don't really work, the inadequacy of the toilet paper, the bureaucracy, the perennial strikes, the inefficiencies, the dog waste on the streets, and the expense. As I settled in I made friends with colleagues, expats, a few old college friends who, like me, were temporary émigrés. I was doing well at the office. My projects included a Spanish bank, a Swiss shopping mall, even a hotel in Tokyo, where I was sent to visit several times. While I wasn't lead architect on any, my work on them had gotten me noticed.

And then I met Selene. It was at a party one night at an apartment in the First Arrondissement. The ceilings were four-teen feet high. Gilded boiseries. Ancient herringbone floors pol-ished from years of use. The host was American, from Texas. Another classmate of my father's, which was why I was invited. He had married a Frenchwoman, now in her fifties. Her tanned arms were like sticks, and she wore a chain of expensive-looking emeralds around her neck.

"*Enchanté, Monsieur Rose,*" she said graciously. "*Bienvenue chez nous.* Please have a drink."

I knew no one there and instead wandered from room to room, admiring the décor until I heard someone speaking in English. It was a tall, ash blond girl with large green eyes and a lovely figure. She was talking to an older couple.

"Excuse me," I said. "I hope you don't think me very rude. But I don't know anyone here, and my French isn't good enough to just strike up a conversation. I heard you speaking English and hoped you would take pity on me and let me join you."

"But of course," said the ash blonde. For the first time I no-ticed she spoke with an accent. The older couple drifted away.

"Are you French?" I asked.

"Yes."

"You speak English very well."

"Thank you. I lived in New York for two years. That helped."

"I'm from New York."

"You are! I miss it."

"Where did you live?"

"On Central Park West. My aunt has an apartment there."

Some men might have found her nose a bit too large, but I found it rather attractive. She was studying acting at nights and to support herself worked for a public relations firm. We flirted happily, and one thing led to another. There were dates, quick lunches, sex in semipublic places. For the first time in my life when I looked at a woman, I didn't see Cesca instead.

After we had been seeing each other for several months, she invited me to stay with her family in the Vaucluse for Easter. We drove in her little car, and I was honestly surprised to see us turn down a long avenue lined with poplars and pull up in front of a good-size château. Two dogs, an old Alsatian and an equally ancient terrier, ran out to meet her, barking in mad delight. She knelt down to embrace them and let them lick her face. They then began barking at me, although their tails were wagging the whole time.

"*Tais-toi!* Stop that, you old idiots," she commanded fondly, and gave me a kiss on the cheek to show them everything was all right.

As I was beginning to unload our luggage, two young men came down the front steps as well. Selene embraced them no less eagerly than the dogs and then introduced me. "These are my brothers, Achille and Horace."

The former, who was very handsome with blond hair and electric blue eyes like those of Peter O'Toole in *Lawrence of Arabia*, gave me a firm handshake. As I was to find out later, he had just earned a commission in a French cavalry regiment after graduating from Saint-Cyr. The latter, the baby of the family, was still at university. He had his siblings' good looks but seemed to conceal them behind large glasses and a shock of unkempt brown hair.

We put our bags in our rooms—Selene's in her bedroom and mine in the guest room down the hall—and then she took me for a walking tour around the estate. It was a fine spring afternoon, just cool enough to require a jacket but not so cold one couldn't detect the ripening of the earth. In the little village, we had an aperitif. There were only a few other patrons in the café, but she seemed to know them all, and was treated with a mixture of fondness and deference.

"I didn't want to say anything to you before," she said. In her accented English "anything" became "anyzing," for example. "But my father ("fazzer") is a count."

"Does that make you a countess?"

She shrugged. "Yes, in a manner of speaking, but it doesn't mean much anymore. The titles these days are purely courtesy."

"Why didn't you tell me before?" I really couldn't understand. I secretly congratulated myself on having slept with a countess. Despite my democratic background, I was still young enough to be impressed by things like titles and châteaux.

"Because it can make things awkward. I had hoped you would like me for me and not because of my family."

"I do." I smiled. "It doesn't matter to me at all."

Afterward we strolled back to the château and, giggling like schoolchildren, snuck up the back stairs and made love on her childhood bed. It was an old room with old furniture. There was a cassette deck, a few porcelain horses on a shelf, a tattered Rolling Stones concert poster in French on the wall, a nearly empty closet, riding boots propped against a corner, and the small, creaky four-poster bed that barely fit us both.

I met her parents that night at cocktails. Still giddy from our lovemaking and the bath we'd shared, we walked into a long drawing room with eighteen-foot-high ceilings and tall windows that let out onto a view of a wide park. The furniture, carpets, and paintings, which had once been quite grand, were worn with age and use. The silk on some of the cushions was threadbare, and, in places, the wallpaper was peeling. There was a large water stain on one of the walls. Still, it was quite a room.

A dapper looking man of late middle age, balding yet still quite trim and handsome, stood by the bar. He was wearing a velvet jacket of a deep purple, crisp white shirt, dark blue necktie, and pearl gray trousers. His slippers, too, were velvet, and they had little coronets on the toes.

"Ah, you must be the American," he said good-naturedly in nearly perfect English. "I hope you'll join me in a martini. How do you take it?"

Before I could answer he smiled and continued, "I prefer it dry myself, or, as Noël Coward said, I just like to wave the finished concoction in the general direction of Italy."

Despite Cesca's attempt to inculcate me, I was not much of a martini man, but I felt it best to go along with my host.

"Daddy loves America. He spent four years there. He was at Harvard architectural school—like you." I was surprised to hear this. This seemed like something she would have already told me. But she had told me very little about her family. I had formed a completely different impression of them.

Selene had never attended university, which was not unusual for young ladies from privileged backgrounds then. I already knew that, after leaving convent school at sixteen, she had worked as an au pair for a family in Austria and later in Italy. The ostensible reason was to improve her languages, of which she spoke five, but the primary goal was to find a husband. There had been an engagement, but it had broken off, something she didn't like to talk about. She had been in her twenties when she discovered acting, while living in New York.

"That's right," put in her father, "I was Class of 'Sixty. Selene tells me you were there as well."

I told him that I had been and the name of the firm where I was working in Paris.

"I know it. Very good," he said with a smile, handing me my cocktail. "Bottoms up."

After drinking the cold, clean liquid, I asked, "Are you still an architect?"

"Being an architect is like being a drunkard. You are never not one—even if you don't practice. But to your question, it is no longer my occupation. Once I fancied myself a new Corbusier. But then my father died, and I had to come back to take care of this place, *hélas*. I still like to keep my hand in. This is an old estate with old buildings. It needs constant renovation so . . ." he said, trailing off with a shrug.

"Daddy's being modest," said Selene. "A few years ago he converted an old monastery outside of town into a hotel. It's beautiful."

Pleased by the compliment, the comte allowed himself a little smile but, with tact, changed the subject. "You must tell me about some of your work, Wylie. What is Tokyo like? *Le japonais*. Are the women all like dolls? Selene tells me you've been there. I have always wanted to go."

At that point Selene's mother appeared. I hadn't heard her approach but turned and saw at my side a tall, still very beautiful woman. Her hair was white blond, and she wasn't wearing any makeup. She must have been well into her fifties but easily looked two decades younger. Selene more closely resembled her father.

"You must be Wylie," she said, with a faintly amused expression, as though laughing at some private but good-natured joke. There was an ethereal quality to her. Her eyes were so blue they were almost translucent. "Don't let Jacques make you drink that drink if you don't like it," she said in an amused voice. "He is always looking for someone to share them with. He thinks all Americans love them because that's where he learned to drink them. Most Frenchmen think they're disgusting."

I blushed and stammered, "Really, it's quite all right. I do like martinis."

"Nonsense, darling," chimed in Selene's father with a smile. "Let me know when you want the other half, Wylie," he said, rattling the shaker.

The next several days were full of excellent meals, long walks, parties, Easter celebrations and masses, horseback riding and picnics. The weather was marvelous, and the family couldn't have been more welcoming to me. Even though I wasn't much of a horseman—and everyone in Selene's family could ride beautifully, except for Horace, who was studying for final exams at Sciences Po, and rarely seemed to venture out of his room and usually only then in a ratty old dressing gown and slippers— they were able to find a tame old mare for me.

Selene and her brother Achille both rode like jockeys, as did their father, who, maybe unsurprisingly, had also been a cavalry officer. The mother could also ride but seldom did. In fact, she appeared to spend most of her time napping, which could have explained why she looked so young. In spite of being so languid, there was still something beguiling about her, and I wasn't sur-prised to learn that she had graced the cover of French *Vogue* several times in her youth.

My initial fears that the family would resent—or be cool to—me proved utterly groundless. Never had I met people so charming or who lived in so charming a way. There was an easy elegance about them that I had never encountered before. There was no yelling, no slammed doors, no bitterness.

"I love your family," I said to Selene as we returned to Paris the following Monday. After that we spent many weekends driving the seven hours or so down and back to her château, and we spent almost the entire month of August there. We swam in the old swimming pool built by Selene's grandfather, ate lunch outside every afternoon, went on day trips to Avignon, and listened to Verdi or Puccini every night under the stars after dinner. Selene and I became brown as nuts. She sunbathing topless. Every Saturday we went to watch Selene's father and Achille play polo in a local league and spent the matches on the sideline cheering on his team, stamping in the divots, and drinking champagne with her friends, many of whom were now becoming mine. On Sunday mornings I joined them for mass at the local Catholic church and then for a traditional French lunch at a restaurant in the village. For the first time in my life, I had created a happiness that did not involve Cesca.

19

WHEN SEPTEMBER CAME, I WENT BACK TO WORK, ALONG
with the rest of France. One day at the office, Aurelio called.
"Hola!" he said. "I am in Paris. Can you meet me for dinner?"

"Of course," I said. Selene had an acting class that night,
and I had no plans. On those nights, we slept apart because her
class ended so late.

Aurelio and I agreed to meet at a little auberge near my apartment on the Quai de la Tournelle. I dined there several nights a
week. It was cheap, reliable without being excessive, and the staff
had come to treat me like a regular. It was still warm enough to sit
outside, and I was waiting at a table reviewing some papers when
he walked up. The streetlights were just coming on, but I could
see that he looked thin, even more gaunt than usual. We greeted
each other warmly; under his coat he felt like bones. There was
a bottle of house red on the table. Lio poured himself a glass and
swallowed the wine in several enthusiastic gulps.

"You look well," he said, wiping his mouth with the back of
his hand. "Being an architect suits you."

"I wasn't much of a painter."

"It isn't much of a time to be a painter."

"And you? How are you?"

"I've been better. I think I'm fighting something. A flu, probably."

"What about your work?"

"It is coming. I have a gallery in New York interested in my work at last. A good one too."

"Will there be a show?"

He nodded. "There is talk of a group show next spring."

I ordered dinner for us both. Even though I am sure he was probably far richer than I, I insisted on paying for it. I would have been amazed if he even possessed a credit card. I had seen him in cafés, emptying his pockets like a beggar, a jester, searching for crumpled notes and loose change. We both had the escargots and the *pavé de boeuf.*

I ordered us each a cognac after dinner, and we each smoked a Gauloise bleu. I was not a regular smoker, but in those days everyone in Paris smoked.

I was on the verge of telling him about Selene when he said, "I have a surprise for you."

"Oh really? What's that?"

"Cesca is joining us tonight. She is working for a fashion house in New York these days, and they are sending her over to spend a few months in Paris in order to work at headquarters."

I wasn't sure what my face looked like, but for the first time in my life I was actually unhappy to hear of Cesca's presence. The timing could not have been worse. "When will she get here?"

"Any minute. She had some work function she had to attend; otherwise she would have come with me. She told me to make it a surprise."

"How long has she been here?"

"I'm not sure. A week or so. She said she didn't have your phone number or else she would have called."

I nodded at the obvious lie, letting it slip past like flotsam in the current. My mind was still trying to comprehend what it all meant.

A quarter of an hour later a large black Mercedes pulled up in front of the restaurant. The driver held the door open, and Cesca emerged, her lithe brown legs first, wearing a short, elaborate dress in a kind of dove gray. She lingered for a moment, chatting with the person in the backseat, and then swept over to where we sat.

"Look at these two handsome men!" she exclaimed, reaching out both arms wide to embrace us. "I am the luckiest girl in Paris!"

The waiter appeared instantly, and Cesca ordered vodka on the rocks. "How are you, Wylie?" she asked, her hand on mine, as though we were old friends who'd simply happened to run into each other.

"Lio told me about your new job," I said. "It sounds very exciting. How long will you be in Paris?"

"I don't know. A few months for sure," she answered, "and I'm counting on you to be my escort."

With Cesca's arrival, the evening was reenergized. She insisted we go somewhere. Did I know anywhere fun? I knew some places. In Pigalle, in Montmartre. We took a taxi to the first place, where we drank some more. There was music. Cesca danced with every man in the bar, while the other women, wives or girlfriends, looked on angrily. We went to other places and drank more. It became a blur.

Some people we met took us to yet another bar. They were Eastern European, possibly Arab. It was impossible to tell because their accents were so thick, the music so loud, and we had all had too much to drink. They wore their shirts tight and unbuttoned to the solar plexus. Gold chains. They had mustaches and flashed a lot of cash. At one point, we lost Aurelio. It was just Cesca, me, and the Eastern Europeans. Cesca and I were dancing slowly, her arms around my neck.

"Don't leave me, Wylie," she giggled. "I think they want to sell me."

"That's not all they want to do to you," I joked back.

"What would you like to do to me? I think I'd like that much more," she said, reaching up and kissing me deeply. "Oh, Wylie, I've missed you so much."

I'd like to say I thought of Selene at that moment, but I didn't. As usual, I was helpless, utterly in Cesca's power, pulled in like a dinghy in a maelstrom. I don't remember much more. The protestations of the Eastern Europeans. A cab ride home kissing. Laughing up the stairs to my apartment. Pulling off our clothes. Falling into bed together. I cannot be certain of the number of times we had made love over the years, but I had learned her body well enough, knew what she liked. I was familiar with her smell, and the heat of her flesh, the supple strength of her limbs. And she also knew what I liked.

In the morning, my alarm went off after less than three hours' sleep. She groaned and pulled a pillow over her head. I showered and dressed as quietly as I could, my head throbbing. I was even tempted to call in sick but instead took several aspirin. As ever, on those days when I woke to find Cesca next to me, I couldn't help feeling a kind of pride, like a freshman who had slept with the homecoming queen. She was precious to me. Her elegant dress of last night lay tossed in a corner. I leaned down to kiss her lightly on the temple, which made her grunt and roll over. I closed the door behind me.

Only when I began to sober up did I realize what I had actually done. I had forgotten all about Selene. She and I had plans to see each other that night. As usual she would come to my apartment rather than going back to hers, which she shared with two roommates. She even left a few items of clothing there. A pair of shoes. Makeup. A toothbrush. And I had left Cesca there!

All morning at the office, my mind raced with fury at myself for betraying Selene, aghast at the thought of her finding out about Cesca. I wondered if Cesca was still in my apartment. And if she had left, would she come back? And she was going to be here for several months now. Was she going to reenter my life at the worst possible moment? And what did I want? Who did I want to be with? Until the day before, until Cesca reappeared, I thought I knew. But now I was no longer sure.

I rang my apartment several times, but there was no answer. Was she still asleep? Had she left? Was she being discreet? Or was she simply displaying her usual disregard for the telephone? I dared not leave a voice message in case Selene might chance to hear it. At one point my office phone rang. It was Selene. My innards contracted when I heard her voice, terrified she might have somehow found out, and she was calling to tell me we were through. But I was letting my imagination get the better of me.

"*Bonjour, chéri,*" she trilled. "How are you today? I missed you last night. I almost came over."

A bolt of dread passed through me. "Uh, I'm glad you didn't. An old friend was in town from Barcelona, and we went out. You remember, I told you about him, Aurelio? I didn't get home until late."

"Naughty boy. I turn my back for one minute and off you go."

"Well, I'm paying for it now. My head feels like it's in a vise."

"Do you want me to come over tonight?"

"Can I let you know? I may just need to go to bed early. I'll call you later, okay?"

At lunch I dashed home to see if Cesca was still there and was relieved there was no sign of her. The sheets were rumpled, and they smelled of her. Hurriedly, I stripped them and thrust them into the wretched washing machine. I remade the bed with my only other set of sheets, and folded it back into a sofa. I then checked around for any signs of Cesca. An earring. A stray hair. An unfamiliar cigarette butt. Possibly, although it would be unlike her, a note, something scrawled in lipstick on the bathroom mirror. Luckily she had remained true to form. I checked the messages, and examined the medicine cabinet and the wardrobe to see if any of Selene's things had been touched, but they appeared fine. I closed the door behind me and hurried back to the office, my apartment expunged of all traces of my betrayal.

Now I could only wait. What if Cesca were to return? For the first time in my life I hoped she wouldn't come. I had no idea where to reach her. I didn't even know the name of the fashion house she was working for. Or that of her hotel. Once again, she had managed to preserve her secrets from me with laughter and a touch. That was all it ever took.

I returned home again after work, nervous and exhausted and penitent, hoping for a quiet night. Earlier I had called Selene back and told her truthfully that I was too tired to do anything and just needed to sleep. I said we would definitely see each other the next night. She offered to come over and nurse me, but I told her that wouldn't be necessary.

"Okay," she said, a little disappointed. "Feel better, *chéri. Bonne nuit.*"

"Good night."

"*Je t'aime.*"

"*Moi aussi.*"

I hung up, feeling guilty. The truth was I didn't exactly know how I felt. After all, what was not to love about Selene? She was beautiful, clever, caring, and had a family I adored. But then there was Cesca. I had never told anyone exactly how I felt about Cesca, as if to talk about it was to cheapen it. She was the partner of my secret self. Like a magical world accessible only through a door in an attic, I wanted to keep her all to myself. Not even in college, when it is common for men to brag about their conquests, did I say a word. The only person who knew of the depths of my feelings was Cesca herself, and I wasn't sure she quite understood. I certainly hadn't ever said anything about her to Selene. What I wanted was to keep my lives separate, to have both women. But I knew that was impossible. At least for Selene. It would crush her. She would despise me. Scream at me. I would lose her completely. I had no idea how Cesca would react, but I suspected it would make little difference to her as long as I came when called.

When I got to my apartment, I began staring at the phone, willing it not to ring. Knowing that, whoever was on the other end of the line, it would not bode well. Finally, as if challenging me, it erupted with that insistent chirrup that all French phones make. I looked at my watch. It was almost nine.

It was Cesca's voice.

"Hey, Tricky Wylie. Want to grab a late bite?"

"Cesca. Hi. Look. I'm sorry. I've already eaten, and frankly I'm too tired to go out." It was only half a lie.

"Then I'll just come over there."

"Cesca . . ."

"See you soon." She had hung up.

An hour later my intercom buzzed, and I let her up. I stood at the top of the stairs, listening to her walking up the five flights.

"Sorry I'm late," she said. "I stopped off to pick up some goodies." She walked in, looking beautiful. In her hand was a shopping bag. "Here," she said, giving it to me, like a rich aunt at

Christmas. "I noticed you didn't have any so I took the liberty." Inside the bag were a cold bottle of champagne and a small box containing two flutes. Duck liver pâté. Two cold lobsters.

"Be a love and open the champagne, will you?" she said, sitting on the sofa and kicking off her heels, but leaving on her trench coat. I uncorked the bottle with a soft pop and poured out two glasses, careful not to spill any. "Delicious," she said, taking a sip. "No one knows how to live like the French. So how was your day?"

"I was feeling pretty rocky this morning. How about you?"

"God, the same. I didn't crawl into work until around noon."

"I wasn't sure if you'd still be here when I came home."

She laughed. "Don't think I didn't think about it. You were wonderful last night, by the way. And what about those awful people who picked us up? What were they? Armenian? They were too funny. But it would have been heaven to lie here all day, thinking about you, waiting for you to come home. In fact, it's exactly what I did think about all day." She reached over a foot and tickled my lap with her toes, arousing me. "What have you been thinking about all day?"

"I was thinking about trying not to throw up at the office." I laughed, and she joined me.

"I thought that might be the case. So that's why I came over. In case you needed a little moral support. And I thought this would help," she said, slowly getting to her feet and removing her trench coat so it fell to the floor, revealing her nearly naked body, covered only by diaphanous black lingerie. Bending over, she kissed me and slowly lowered her head, undoing my shirt one button at a time and kissing my chest, my nipples, until she came to my lap and, with a smile, opened my fly.

Later, around midnight, we lay in bed, feasting on the lobster and the rest of the champagne, Cesca wearing one of my shirts. "You need better shirts, Tricky Wylie," she said.

"It's the best I can afford. Junior architects don't make a lot of money, you know."

"Nonsense. Tomorrow I'm taking you to Charvet. I'll have a dozen made for you. Now that's a shirt."

"I can't ask you to do that."

"You aren't asking. It would give me pleasure. That way every time I saw you wearing one, I'd know you were thinking of me."

"Cesca," I said. "There's something I need to tell you."

"What is it?" she said, wiping her chin.

"I've been seeing someone. A French girl."

"Is it serious?"

"Yes. I think so."

"Is she good to you?"

"Yes."

"Do you love her?"

I hesitated. It should have been so easy to say yes. Any man would have considered himself fortunate to have Selene, to share her bed, to hear her little jokes. The adorable way she snorted when she laughed. And yet I said nothing. When I compared how I felt about Cesca to how I felt about Selene, it was like holding a bright flame next to a shimmering one. It wasn't that I didn't feel elements of love for Selene. I just didn't love her as much. To claim otherwise would have been a lie.

"I'm not sure" was my gutless response. Such an admission was, in my mind at least, a bigger betrayal than sleeping with Cesca.

Cesca smiled. "Well, then . . ."

"What?"

"Does that mean you still love me?"

"Yes."

"Good," she said and reached over to kiss me. She was all I had ever really wanted, even though she gave me nothing. Yet she gave me everything.

The next day I broke it off with Selene. I called her at work, saying it was important we have lunch. She asked if it could wait until that night. She was very busy, but I was insistent.

We met at a little café near her office where we had occasionally lunched. She was waiting when I got there.

"What is it? You're scaring me," she said, sitting down.

"I'm sorry, Selene . . ." I began, but she could tell immediately what I was going to say and buried her face in her hands.

"Why? *Pourquoi?*"

"I just don't think it's going to work out. It's better to end it now."

"But that's not a reason. I thought you loved me. You know I love you. I don't understand. It just makes no sense. *C'est pas possible.*"

"I'm sorry," I repeated. It was all I could think to say.

"*Non, non, non, non, non,*" she said, shaking her head, tears running down her face. "It's another woman, isn't it?"

I looked away. I was not going to tell her about Cesca. What would I say? Yes, I've been in love with another woman my entire life. I never know where she is or when I will see her. I don't even know how she feels about me, but I can't help myself.

"It is. *Bâtard!*"

"Selene . . ."

"Don't talk to me. Don't look at me. *Menteur!*" she screamed at me. People were staring at us. "*Je vous déteste! Con!*" She stood up. "Oh my God."

I stood up too. "Please. Sit."

"*Va te faire foutre!* Fuck you! I don't ever want to see you again."

Wiping tears away, she ran off down the block, leaving me there alone getting dirty looks from the other customers. As I watched her recede into the crowd, I wondered if I hadn't made the biggest mistake of my life.

All afternoon I wrestled with the idea of calling Selene, telling her that I had made a terrible mistake, throwing myself at her mercy. It was still not too late, I reasoned. I had a narrowing window. But each time I reached for the phone I also thought of Cesca. I had made my choice. I had to live with it.

That night Cesca and I were in bed. "I broke it off with that girl," I told her.

She was lying flat on her front, her head resting on her hands. "I'm sorry," she said. "I'm sure she was a very nice girl. I hope she didn't take it too badly."

"I felt terribly. She was very upset. I really hurt her."

"Do you wish you hadn't?"

"No," I said, kissing her silken back.

The next three months passed in a haze. Every night we were together. And not just at my apartment but at hers as well. She was renting a high-ceilinged flat on the Boulevard Malesherbes, which was around the corner from her offices. There were dishes in the sink. Cigarette burns in the cushions. A maid came in once a week. It was the only time the bed was made.

Some nights I would meet Cesca after work, and we would go out to parties, sometimes several in the same evening. Other nights she would attend functions and meet me after. But every morning, we woke up next to each other. I no longer had to worry whether I would be seeing her that night. It was understood. I felt she was slowly letting me in. When I left for the office, she now said, "See you tonight." On the weekends, we had no other plans. She had somehow obtained a membership at the Tennis Club de Paris in the Sixteenth Arrondissement, where we would play, and invariably she would beat me.

We explored the city, the long boulevards, the parks, Richelieu's tomb, Roman ruins, the Musée Delacroix, discovering little restaurants and markets, bringing back cheese and vegetables. Cases of wine. Art Deco chairs. Antique hats. Dog-eared first editions. Money meant nothing to her. It flowed through her fingers. In her apartment were unopened boxes from Chanel, Hermès. She signed bills without looking at them. We did eventually go to Charvet, where, to my embarrassment, she insisted on buying me a dozen shirts of every hue. Blues, lavenders, magenta, yellows. Stripes, checks. I was taken to the fitting room on the second floor, an Aladdin's cave of fabric, shown a chart with different collar patterns. Monsieur is tall, said the tailor. May I suggest this one? What thickness of wristwatch did I prefer? It was important that the cuff hung just so.

I did not think about Selene. I know I should have felt a pang of remorse, guilt that I had irrevocably hurt a girl who had given me so much of herself. A girl who I could have spent my life with under different circumstances. Like an aborted fetus, our future life together had already begun to take shape, here a nose, there a heart, until it was cruelly terminated. If I had for a moment reflected, I might have realized how shabbily I had treated her, could only imagine the angry reaction of her father, the disappointment of her mother. They had all been so good to me, and I just took and shattered it as though it were nothing more than a clay pot. But I did not think about anything else except Cesca. Like a junkie, I thought only of my next fix and the euphoria that came with it.

There is a monstrous selfishness about love, especially in its primal stages, when nothing else matters, when lovers create an artificial world which only they inhabit. The language, the customs, the currency, are known to them alone, and no one else is permitted inside. It is a form of bliss but also a kind of corruption. Everything else is forgotten. Food, friends, work, responsibilities, all become subsumed by obsession.

When I look back over my life to decide when I was happiest, I would unhesitatingly pick those months in Paris with Cesca. I was a prospector who had finally struck gold. The seam was rich beyond imagining. Not only was Cesca beautiful, and more beautiful to me every day, but she was also wonderfully intelligent and funny. Aspects of her personality that I had never had the chance to experience before were now revealed to me; it was like learning that someone you already like is rich or can play the piano. It is more than a pleasant surprise. It makes them more interesting, more nuanced. If you love them already, it makes you love them more.

She could grasp the essence of an idea immediately, describe it perfectly, put people at their ease, make them laugh, make them think. We would go to dinners in restaurants with people in the fashion industry, sitting at long tables in golden light, and, always side by side, our hips or feet always touching, I would listen to her tell stories, imitate people. Like Cosmo, she was a natural mimic, a talent I had never seen in her before. The others at the table would be bent double with laughter. When she left, it was as though someone had dimmed the lights.

At the end of those evenings I had the pride of taking her home, of escorting her out the door, my hand on the small of her back, helping her into a waiting taxi, of receiving her kisses, while every man in the room envied me, and imagined what it would be like if they were me.

But of course everyone has their demons. It is impossible to be intimate with someone for any extended period of time without coming across them. It is like the first time you intrude on them when they are on the toilet: There is the initial embarrassment, a mumbled apology, but then a gradual acceptance of something perfectly natural, if not necessarily pleasant.

It was the end of December, and Cesca's time in Paris was nearly up. In January she would have to return to New York. "Let's stay in France for Christmas," she had said. Instantly, I had agreed. Not only would it save me the cost of a round-trip plane ticket to the States but also it would allow me to spend a few more precious days with her.

American friends of hers had invited us to spend Christmas in the Dordogne. We borrowed a car and drove down to a lovely medieval town called Sarlat. There was a light snow, and the air was clear and crisp. The French, like many Europeans, make a particular celebration of Christmas Eve. It is more than just a time to hang the stockings and sing a few carols. There was to be a midnight mass followed by *le réveillon,* a traditional feast of oysters and brandied roast goose, back at the château. We were told that those of us who wanted to attend the mass should be in the main hall by eleven, and then we'd all go together.

"Shall we go?" I asked Cesca, when we were up in our room. She laughed. "Why?"

"Why? I thought it might be interesting. I've never been to a Catholic Christmas mass before."

"Nor have I."

This surprised me. Religion was something we had never discussed. My own religious upbringing had been slight. There had been mandatory chapel at school, and my family went to church on Christmas, Easter, and for the occasional wedding, but, at that time, I had little interest in or practical use for faith.

"But I thought you were raised Catholic?"

"Well, that's just it. I wasn't."

"You weren't?"

"No, Mare's Jewish. In Judaism it's the mother's religion that dictates the children's. Except that Mare doesn't have a religious bone in her body. We never did any of the things that Jewish kids do. I've never even been inside a synagogue. None of us had a bar mitzvah or celebrated Hanukkah. For some reason we did have a Christmas tree, though. Probably Mare thought they were pretty." She laughed.

"What about your father?"

"My father had been schooled by priests in Catalonia, and so naturally he became a rabid atheist. To him all religions are lies designed to keep superstitious peasants docile." She shook her head and laughed again. "In our family, the only religion was art. That's what we worshipped. Who knows?" she said with a shrug. "Maybe one day I'll feel differently."

In the end I went, and she stayed. "While you're off sitting in some uncomfortable pew, I'll be here drinking champagne. Tell me, which of those two sounds more fun?"

The next day we exchanged presents. Cesca gave me a handsome set of onyx cuff links. It had been difficult for me to shop for Cesca. Like so many people who are rich, she already had everything she needed and most things she wanted. And such people tend to have expensive tastes. Using all my savings, I had bought her an antique Cartier wristwatch in rose gold at the marché aux puces in Clignancourt. As she slipped it over her hand, she said, "Ooh, Wylie. I love it," and leaned over and gave me a kiss.

I had never been happier to spend my money on anything. It gave her joy, which is all anybody wants. And she had accepted something of mine. It would now be part of her life, a physical presence in her life that would always connect us.

We returned to Paris, the days slipping away too fast. What had been months turned into weeks, then days, then hours. I was trying to slow time, to memorize every moment. This was the place where she took my hand and showed me Victor Hugo's house on the Place des Vosges, the expensive Bordeaux we drank one night in our favorite bistro, the way she touched her toes twenty times every morning. She was leaving, but I had to stay. I had my job, my career. It would have been impossible for me to leave with her, but that didn't stop me from seriously considering it. In my head, it was like the end of a movie when the hero runs after the heroine just as her train is about to depart, pushing past the guards, sacrificing everything for love.

Our last night. It was late. A sumptuous meal had been consumed. Then bed, where we made love with a shared urgency bordering on desperation. We were like warriors on the eve of battle; everything tasted better, life was sweeter in the knowledge that it might not last. Leave nothing back.

It was the moment. The next step was oblivion. "Cesca," I said, as she lay there panting, staring at the ceiling.

It took her several seconds to respond, as though she were returning from far away. "Yes."

"I think we should get married."

There was no immediate answer. "Do you mean that?"

"Yes."

She thought about that. "I've been married before, you know."

"I know."

"I'm not very good at it."

"You remember, I asked you years ago? Before you married Gavin."

"I've never forgotten."

"And I'm not Gavin."

"No."

"So what do you say?"

She continued to stare at the ceiling, and then turned her face toward me. For several minutes, we both looked into each other's eyes, questioning, wondering, before she smiled and said, "All right, Tricky Wylie. I'll marry you."

The next day I went with her to the airport. She was traveling first class on Air France. She looked lovely as always. Chic. A woman of means traveling by herself. Even though I was stricken by her leaving, the blow was softened by the knowledge that we would one day be husband and wife. I felt an enormous pride as well. This woman whose existence had so profoundly shaped mine for so many years had finally accepted me.

I looked at her face as we strode through Charles de Gaulle.

She was thirty now and I was not far behind. There were moments when I would catch her staring at her face in the mirror, stretching the skin back, or holding her breasts up to judge if they had incrementally drooped. True, there were faint lines on her face, but, in my opinion, they only enhanced her beauty.

Her mood had been somber all morning, which I took as sadness that we were going to be separated. It was not the time to talk of wedding planning. Lonely weeks stretched out before us. It had been months since either of us had slept apart. In the taxi I had begun a sentence "When we're married . . ." But she'd interrupted me by kissing me.

"Shhh, don't talk," she'd said. We were silent for the rest of the ride, her head resting on my shoulder.

I said good-bye to her at passport control. Her luggage had already been checked in. Most of the other first-class passengers were businessmen in dark suits. We kissed one last time, and she presented her passport to the official behind the desk, who inspected her with Gallic admiration before duly stamping the passport and returning it to her. Before the doors closed behind her, she turned and waved to me. I waved back, and then she was gone.

Once again she had disappeared from my life, sunk like a stone beneath the waters.

20

THAT WAS THE LAST I SAW OF CESCA FOR TWO YEARS.

In the days after she returned to New York my calls went un-answered. Sometimes it seemed as though the phone had even been taken off the hook. Initially, I was concerned that some-thing had happened to her, but soon I realized the truth. That she had no intention of marrying me. That once again she had played me for a fool. I was furious, hurt, resentful. I drank too much. I wrote bitter letters that I never mailed. For the first time I began to hate her.

Eventually, I regained my equilibrium, and threw myself into my work. When my office asked if I would consider a trans-fer to the Tokyo office, I leapt at the chance to dissociate myself from Paris and its memories. In that new city's enormous, alien sprawl, isolated by language and culture, I was able to put Cesca behind me.

I had a few affairs in Tokyo. Fellow expats. An Australian girl who worked as a bartender in Roppongi. A South African girl at my firm. Nothing meaningful. Just companionship and sex in a distant country, where most Westerners lived in hotels in the city center.

I returned to New York eighteen months later, feeling like a repatriated war prisoner. The city looked the same yet different. I too had changed and had grown older. When I dialed numbers, I found my address book was out of date. Friends had moved. Favorite stores and restaurants had shut down. The shop on Madison where as a child I used to buy model soldiers had become a gallery. My barber had gone.

Sean, the doorman in our old building, had retired or died. A long-familiar presence on the block, he was no longer there to say good morning to, even though he'd continued on long after my parents had moved out. When I stopped in to inquire after him, the new doorman eyed me warily and said he had never heard of Sean. And I had no home here anymore.

For the first few days, I stayed with my father, who had moved again, to an even larger apartment, this time on Fifth. It was as impersonal as a hotel suite. There were photographs of couples I had never met on a grand piano no one knew how to play. All vestiges of his former life had vanished. Chairs, paintings, even books had all been expunged and replaced by Patty's interior decorator. There was also now live-in staff, a Vietnamese couple, who slept in the back room off the kitchen. The husband was the chauffeur, and the wife handled the cooking and housekeeping duties.

On my first night back my father welcomed me home with a big dinner at the same restaurant where we had celebrated my acceptance into architectural school years before. He had aged. Grown heavy. His hair was making the inexorable transition from gray to white, but he was still possessed of the same enthusiasm, the same determination to wring as much out of life as he could. He was full of questions, bursting with paternal pride. I basked in it, grateful that I had become someone worthy in his eyes.

I knew none of the other people in the private room my father had booked. As cocktails were being served, my father led me around, introducing me. There were several real estate developers, who had been invited expressly for my benefit, with their wives. A famous architect who was now a neighbor of my father's in East Hampton. A few friends of Patty's.

Just before we sat down, Roger and his wife, Diana, walked in. "Wylie, my dear boy," he said, coming up to me, clasping my hand warmly, and rubbing my arm in the way he always did. "You look fantastic. Just fantastic."

My father came up. "I thought I'd keep this a surprise," he said. "You haven't seen your godfather since, when, Izzy's memorial, right?"

I nodded. It was good to see him. I could never tell who was in or who was out in my father's world. People would be dismissed for imagined slights or restored on a whim. Yet his friends adored him, aware of the value of his acceptance and the enmity of his contempt. Apparently, Roger was once again welcome, whether because of something Roger had done that had earned my father's esteem or simply because my father was mellowing, I never found out.

I had made it a point to try to forget about the Bonets. I had purposely lost touch with Aurelio. I was angry at Cesca but taking it out on the whole family. Roger, however, was his usual garrulous self. He informed me that his mother had finally died. That Kitty and Randall were well. They were living in the big house now. Dot was in India. Cosmo was terrific, wonderfully successful. Carmen was interning at St. Vincent's. What about Aurelio? I asked.

Roger's face looked uncharacteristically grim. "Not good," he said. "Poor chap's been sick. He came home a few months ago, and Kitty's gotten him the best doctors."

"What's wrong with him?"

"That's just it. No one really understands it."

"But he'll be okay?"

"That's what we hope. It's rotten luck."

I let myself absorb this news for a minute. Thought of Aurelio. How he never took care of himself, treating his body as though he were embarrassed by its perfection, as though he had no right to look the way he did. To him his own physical beauty was a distraction from his art. I am sure he would have much rather been ugly, like Lautrec. I felt guilty for not having seen him, for not having known that he was ill.

"Is he well enough for visitors?"

"Oh yes. Don't worry about that. I'm sure he'd love to see you. He's back at Kitty's. Along with his girl."

"His girl?"

"Yes. Some blonde he picked up in Barcelona. She won't leave his side. She's like a dog."

Finally I asked: "And Cesca?"

"Quite the career girl. She started her own perfume company. She has a store in Soho."

"Married? Kids?"

"Not that I know of. But it's a mystery to me why. Beautiful girl. What's the matter with men these days? Are they blind? When I was your age, a girl like Cesca would have been snapped up in a moment. Don't you think she's beautiful? Maybe you should date her, eh?" he added with a wink and a little jab in my side.

I laughed uncomfortably. To my relief, my father returned and said it was time to take our seats.

Like a recovering alcoholic, I told myself I would not contact Cesca. No good could come of it. I had the scars to prove it, the wasted years. That couldn't stop me from thinking about her, of still hungering for her. But I knew myself better now. Knew how destructive it could be. How there could be no such thing as just once. However, I did call Lio the next morning. A woman's voice answered, the accent European. "May I speak to Aurelio, please?"

"Who is this?"

"Please tell him it's Wylie."

"One moment, please."

A few minutes later, Aurelio came on the phone.

"Wylie, my old friend! I'm so happy to hear from you. I've been thinking about you." Beneath his cheery tone he sounded tired, as though I had just woken him.

"I've been thinking about you too. I'd love to see you."

There was a brief cough. His voice sounded tired. "Yes, I'd like that too. Maybe a coffee? I'm not really up for much more, I'm afraid. I've been ill, I don't know if you heard."

"Yes. I heard. I saw Roger last night. He told me. I'm sorry."

"Nothing to be sorry about. It's not your fault." He laughed but then started to cough, this time in earnest.

"When?" I waited for him to finish. He had coughed for nearly a minute.

"How about Friday morning?" It was now Tuesday.

"Perfect. Eleven o'clock?"

I had been working at my firm's midtown offices for several weeks now, and I was a senior associate. I had a bigger office, a larger salary, more authority, more people reporting to me. Feeling guilty about leaving in the middle of the day for a personal reason, I told my secretary I had a dentist's appointment.

When I walked into the café, Aurelio was already there. It was the same café where we had met years before. Now he was sitting with a small blond woman. I barely recognized him at first. Always thin, he was now skeletal. Despite the pleasant autumn, he was dressed as if it were winter outside. Over his head he wore a knit cap, and there was a thick scarf around his

neck. His cheeks were sunken, the skin like wax. Although I had no firsthand experience of it yet, I could sense death around him.

"My old friend," he said, slowly getting to his feet. It was as though he had aged half a lifetime in two years. We embraced. He was so light I felt I might crack his bones or lift him over my shoulder like a child. "This is Lulu," he said, introducing the blond woman. "She is my guardian angel."

I shook hands with Lulu and sat down. Lulu was elfin, with tattoos on both arms, a gold stud in her nose. There were also dark rings under her eyes. She looked exhausted. A waiter came over, and I ordered a cappuccino. They were drinking herbal tea. His lips were badly chapped.

"What's going on?" I asked bluntly, my concern outweighing good manners.

"That bad?" he said, grinning. "Yes, I know. I look like hell."

"I'm sorry I just . . ."

"Please don't worry about it. It's quite all right. It seems I am being very fashionable for the first time in my life. I have that terrible disease that is killing all the best people."

"How did you get it?"

"How? I don't know. Well, as they say, you're either gay or Haitian. And the last time I checked I wasn't Haitian." He managed a smile.

It was something we had never talked about. Not since that night years ago. I had never thought of him that way. That he was more omnivorous than that. "But I read it could be contracted lots of ways," I said. "Through intravenous drug use. Or if you had an infected blood transfusion."

He shrugged. "Yes, it's possible. I have never done hard drugs. I had anemia a few years ago. Spanish hospitals, maybe they aren't as good as the ones here. My mother had insisted that I come to New York for treatment, but I told her she was

overreacting. I suppose it could have happened then, but there's no way to check now."

Lulu spoke up. She had a slight accent. "There are new medicines being developed all the time. He is seeing the best doctors." She held his left hand with both of hers.

"It is an advantage of having a generous family." He chuckled. "Apparently there are a number of reputable hospitals that we have given a lot of money to over the years, and they don't want us to stop. So they are doing everything they can. My mother has become a she-wolf protecting her cub. I pity the doctors who aren't able to help me fast enough."

"He's on a new medicine now that could help him," said Lulu. "Isn't that right?"

Aurelio nodded. "Yes, it's true. Some days I feel almost normal. If you don't mind the side effects. Frankly, sometimes I can't tell what is worse, the disease or the treatment."

There was other, better news. He was finally being given a one-man show, his first. The gallery, in Soho, was one of the most respected in New York. It was what he had always wanted. The unsaid was that it may have happened too late. "There is so much work to do," he sighed. "It takes all my strength."

I offered to help in any way I could. "No, that's all right," he said. "I have plenty of help. Lulu, of course. My mother. Even Cesca. We'll be sure to send you an invitation."

He leaned back in his chair and sighed. Lulu sprang to her feet. "I think I should be going," he said. "I tire so easily these days."

"Of course."

"And I haven't even asked about how you are."

"I'm fine. Never better."

"Good."

He embraced me again, and, without thinking, I stiffened. "Don't worry," he said. "I'm not contagious."

"No, of course not. Sorry. Feel better, okay?"

"I'll see you at the show, right? Make sure we get your new address. And be sure to bring your rich friends," he added with a smile. "It'll be a good investment. They say an artist's work can triple in value after his death."

I did have a new address. I was now living in the West Village, in a small apartment in an old building on a tree-lined block near the river. The landlord was a fat, gregarious man named Tony who came by every month in his Cadillac to collect the rent. He lived in New Jersey and favored velour pullovers. He had bought the building in the 1960s, when the neighborhood was reeling from the loss of work on the piers. He had been raised on the block when it was still working class. The building had been a sailors' flophouse. Over the years, as the real estate market changed and prices soared, the value of his property rose into the many millions. "I won the frickin' lottery," he would laugh.

THE MOST SIGNIFICANT EVENT IN MY LIFE THAT FALL WAS that I met Kate. Tall, athletic, blond, she was from Philadelphia's Main Line. I had seen her at a party one night. There was a crowd of men in the corner, and, when one of them moved, I saw this beautiful woman standing in the middle. She was wearing a tight green dress and had a gorgeous figure. Long legs. I had come with someone else, a woman from my office who was always flirting with me, but I kept watching the other girl all night. She was never alone.

"Who is she?" I asked one of my friends, who was dating the hostess. "Do you know her?"

"Yes," he said. "Her name is Kate. Do you want to meet her?"

"No," I said. The girl was too popular. She was like someone standing in front of a pet store: All the puppies were pressing up against the glass, their tails wagging. And it was obvious she was enjoying the attention, was even used to it. One man got her a drink. Another lit her cigarette. But I remembered her. When I woke up the next morning, she was the first thing I thought of.

Over the next several weeks, I began seeing her around. Once, when I was sitting in a bar on University Place with some friends. "Oh, Kate's here," said one of the girls. I looked out the window and saw an old white Volkswagen Bug on the street. In the driver's seat sat Kate, her long blond hair visible from twenty feet away. "Get her to come in," said my friend. But she wouldn't. She had other plans.

There were other nights, other parties. At a black-tie event at the Public Library, I almost bumped into her by accident and said, "Excuse me," and she smiled at me before moving on. Each time I was tempted to talk to her, to introduce myself, but invariably she was with someone else or just leaving.

One Saturday in early October, I met some old school friends in Central Park to play football. After the game, I was invited to go with them for dinner. A Thai place downtown. Some other people would be joining us. In we walked, and there at a large, empty table in the center of the room sat Kate. For the first time, we were formally introduced.

"I'm Wylie," I said.

"I know. I've seen you around. I'm Kate."

I sat next to her. We spent the whole night talking to each other exclusively. Our interests and experiences overlapped to the point that we found ourselves laughing at the coincidences. She had lived in Paris during her junior year. At Princeton she had rowed crew. She had even gone to the same girls' boarding school as my mother.

We continued the conversation long after dinner ended, back in her loft. Rummaging under her sink for whisky, looking at blurry Kodaks in old photo albums, she told me about her father and her brothers. About her mother, who had died when Kate was a child. "That's me with the pigtails," she said, indicating a skinny towhead on the beach with a pail and shovel. Pictures of her father, rakishly handsome, in a convertible wearing a tweed jacket and dark glasses. Her oldest brother in a football uniform. A black-and-white of her grandparents sitting on the lawn in front of a large Georgian Revival house. Kate playing field hockey. Rowing on Lake Carnegie. Another of her whole family taken at Christmas.

This became a pattern. Over the next few weeks, we met every night after work and stayed up late talking. The loft she was renting in Tribeca was decorated with furniture inherited from her grandmother. There was a large Japanese screen from the Edo period. When I had lived in Tokyo, I had spent many hours at the Imperial Museum in Chiyoda-ku admiring the collection. Hers was a fine example. It took up half a wall. She said it depicted a scene from *The Tale of Genji*. The young man kneeling on the lower right has come to ask a lord for the hand of his daughter in marriage. Is he worthy? Does the daughter love him? We'll never know.

The loft had no real bedroom. Her bed was in the corner. The first night I stayed over I slept on the sofa. We did not even kiss for several weeks. I wanted her to know I was interested in more.

She invited me to a Halloween party in Haverford, near where she grew up. Friends of hers gave it every year. They covered the pool and put up a tent. There was a band. People from all over the Main Line came and parked on the grass. It would be a chance for me to meet her oldest friends. Her family no longer had a house down there. The last one had been sold years before. Cousins had moved away. Pinehurst. Palm Beach. Montecito. Manhattan. At one time the family had owned hundreds of acres of land in the area. Also, banks, railroads, utilities.

The house where her father had been raised was now a golf club. Her great-grandparents' home, a convent. She no longer had a place of her own, so we would be staying at the house where the party was being held. She had gone down on Friday to help set up and in her costume picked me up the next evening at the local train station. I had never been to the Main Line before. We drove past grand estates, country lanes. She pointed out landmarks. "That's Ardrossan," she said as we passed a large wrought-iron gate flanked by two brick pillars.

There was glitter in her hair and on her cheeks. Under her coat she was dressed as a sea nymph. As were two of her friends, also beauties. King Neptune was the host. They were part of his court. He turned out to be a cheerful old gentleman with a large stomach and a little white mustache. My costume was a set of Japanese robes I had bought in Tokyo.

We arrived at a party already in full roar. The house was immense, an exact copy of a palazzo overlooking Lake Garda and built at the turn of the century by a railroad baron. Kate took me upstairs to change. "This is our room," she told me. "Is that all right?" It was a small room with a single bed. Apparently it belonged to one of the boys in the family, a few years older than Kate, who would be bunking in with his brothers. There were four brothers and four sisters. Kate was practically family.

The guests were of all ages. Everyone greeted Kate with affection. It was obvious she was a favorite. The most beautiful girl in town had lived up to the promise of her youth and become the most beautiful woman. She introduced me to her friends, who welcomed me. The older men were dignified, despite being in costume. The women well preserved. Some of the younger men were more guarded, maybe even envious. They had grown up with her. As comfortable as cousins. One of them came up to me at one point, a little drunk, and asked, "How did you do it? I've been trying to get into her pants for years." I nearly hit him but instead walked away. "'S matter?" he called after me.

We made love that night for the first time. The party had ended, and the last guest had gone home. After saying good night to our hosts, she had led me upstairs laughing, kissing me on the landing. The door closed behind me. "Keep the lights off," she said. The silver moonglow through the open window illuminated the room. I reclined on the bed, speechless, watching her remove her clothes, her back to me, before turning and revealing herself. I held my breath as she approached. "I choose you," she whispered in my ear, her arms around me as I took her in my arms. It was an anointment.

Like all new lovers, we escaped from the world, floating above, lost in ourselves. Gradually, we returned, reaching out to friends and family, eager to share our happiness. I got to know her friends, of which there were many. Lovely women from her childhood, from school, from her year in Paris, who all considered her their best friend. They would call her with their problems, valuing her advice, protective of her, eyeing me suspiciously. *You better be good to her,* they all seemed to imply as they smiled at me with their teeth bared.

I met her family. Her father now lived in a small apartment in New York overlooking Central Park and spent most of his time playing backgammon at his club. A genial old rogue with gin blossoms on his nose and a wandering eye, he had been married four times. "Each one worse and more expensive than the last," he liked to joke. Kate treated him like a child, always asking if he was eating enough, did he remember to wear his scarf? After her mother's death, that role fell to her. She quickly adapted. Learning how to cook, do the laundry for her father and brothers.

Although her father had nominally been a stockbroker, his primary income was derived from two other sources: a trust fund established by his grandfather and his gambling winnings.

The former was regular if, for his needs at least, inadequate. The latter fluctuated wildly, depending on how his luck was running. But he could not draw more than what the trust paid him on a quarterly basis, which while generous was not nearly as generous as he was to himself and others. By the end of most quarters his bank account would be empty, his credit limits reached. Nor could he touch the principal, an ironclad term laid down by his grandfather. As a result, some years they were flush, other years lean, depending on his success at the backgammon table or racetrack.

They changed houses constantly, sometimes a grand estate, sometimes a little cottage, reflecting her father's liquidity. He would acquire paintings, give his wives jewelry, take the family on holidays to Saint-Tropez. The next year the telephone might be turned off for nonpayment. Staff came and went. More than a few times there were concerns that he might not be able to cover school fees. His wives would get fed up with his profligacy with both money and other women, and eventually leave him.

Like all gamblers, Kate's father possessed a sort of reckless style. He played in backgammon tournaments around the world. Nassau. Cairo. Hong Kong. But also chess, poker, even baccarat. Once at Belmont his horse had paid 20 to 1, and he had won so much money he could barely fit all the bills in the pockets of his suit. On his way out he spotted a black Rolls-Royce, the kind with a long, elegant bonnet, and immediately walked up to the owner and asked, "How much?" This was in the sixties and the man suggested what was then an astronomic price.

"Done!" said Kate's father, handing him stacks of bills while still having plenty of his winnings left.

He laughed heartily telling that story. For several years, he even had a liveried chauffeur named Morris, who would drive Kate and her brothers to school every morning in the car.

"Do you still have the Rolls?" I asked.

"Alas, no," he replied. "I had to sell it years ago to cover a debt. It was a beautiful car but an absolute fortune to maintain."

Luckily for Kate, she had money of her own, a small trust established by her grandmother, who saw that her son's dissoluteness would leave his children without any inheritance. It came to Kate when she turned twenty-one, and she kept a careful eye on it, speaking regularly with her financial advisers and even, from time to time, giving her father money to cover his bills. He insisted on calling them "loans" and made a big to-do about paying her back, but Kate showed me a file of bounced checks from his account. "I just gave up a few years ago," she said with a smile. "He's my father. What else am I going to do?"

Kate's two older brothers were equally receptive to me, taking the line that if their sister liked me that was good enough for them. All three had the same mother, their father's first wife. They had forged a close bond, enduring his wives and unpredictable whims, realizing that their best chance for survival lay in presenting a unified front. In adulthood they had all gone their separate ways. Chauncey, the eldest, worked as a screenwriter in Los Angeles and had no intention of marrying. The younger brother, who was a year older than Kate, was Jack. He was a straight arrow, everything his father was not. A steady family man and lawyer who lived on the Main Line, he was a member of Merion, where he played golf on Saturdays, and on Sundays he went to St. George's Church. His son attended Haverford School, his daughter, Agnes Irwin. They both played lacrosse. Kate adored her brothers and they adored her. They comforted each other like veterans who had made it through the worst.

There was much I admired about Kate. Her decency, her kindness, her loyalty. Her strength of character. Her beautiful blue eyes. Her elegant hands. For the first time in my life, when I reached out in the night, it was not Cesca I was thinking of.

At the end of each day, we raced out to meet each other, either for a drink or for dinner near one of our offices or to her loft. Kate was a terrific cook, and she loved to throw dinner parties. To her the shopping was as much fun as the eating. We bought cheese from small shops in Little Italy where the mozzarella was made by hand in the basement. Every afternoon it would be brought up still warm in large trays, smoke emanating from the kitchen like the daily election of a new pope. There was a special bakery too. Another place that sold fresh pasta. Extra-virgin olive oil. Things I had never known about. She taught me how to chop vegetables, showed me how to tell that meat is properly cooked when it feels the same as pressing a finger against the ball of the thumb. Among her favorite dishes: whole orato roasted with fresh rosemary. Osso buco. Roast chicken with garlic shoved under the skin.

The guests would sit at her grandmother's old table, the dishes presented like a reward. If there were too many people, we ate off our knees. This was more than food. During those months, I always went to bed happy. I loved Kate. She loved me. My friends loved her too. Paolo in particular was smitten.

I had taken her over to their farmhouse for dinner one weekend in winter. Night comes on early that time of year, and we drove to Springs in darkness. It was bitterly cold but clear, the heater in Kate's old Bug barely working. A dusting of snow on the fields. "Take a left at the end of that fence," I said. She turned in to the now-familiar driveway. It had been years since Aurelio had first brought me there, but I had never lost the sense of wonder that Paolo and Esther's home instilled in me.

"I wish you could see it better," I said to her. "We'll have to come back when it's light. This place is magical."

They were waiting inside, the long kitchen bright and cheery despite the temperature outside. Both were now in their eighties. Esther's hair was snow white except for a streak of black down the middle. They had always been short, but now they seemed even smaller. Paolo looked frail, but he perked up when he saw Kate. "Wylie Coyote, you have brought me a beautiful woman!" he exclaimed, his charm as vibrant as ever, even if the voice was weaker. Embracing her, he said, "Come and sit by me and let me admire you!"

It was a lovely evening. Paolo twinkled with life and good humor. We drank red wine and nibbled olives. Over roast chicken, he recited poetry in Italian. Kate happily flirted back. He pronounced her name "cat." "What makes you purr, cat?" he asked. "Are you a catcher of mice or men's hearts? You have already caught mine, no?" Esther smiled patiently, loving her husband even more, happy to see that he still possessed the youthful fire that had attracted her so many years ago. It would be a bad sign when he became too old to admire a pretty girl.

"You must come tomorrow to see my studio, cat," said Paolo as we were leaving. "Come in the late afternoon, after my nap. I will leave a saucer of milk out for you." We did go back, staying for hours in his studio, listening to him talk until the light began to fade.

Before we left, he gave her a small canvas of a man and a woman, lovers, on a beach. "Please take it," he said. "Paintings are like little seeds. You plant as many as you can so that they live on long after you are gone. All I expect is a little kiss in return. A fair trade, no?" Kate was overwhelmed by the generosity of the act.

She had the painting framed and hung it in a special place in her loft. For she who had inherited so much, it was original, a gift meant only for her. "That's us," she would say, looking at the painting. "I want us always to be together like that."

21

THE NEXT MONTH I RECEIVED AN INVITATION IN THE MAIL. My name handwritten on the heavy envelope in calligraphy. It was to Aurelio's show. On the front of the card was a reproduction of one of his paintings, one I had never seen before. It was beautiful—the colors rich, the technique masterful—but menacing, almost brutal. It depicted a man obviously in great pain but suffering like a saint. On the reverse ran the words "Aurelio Bonet. *El retrats dels morts*. Portraits of the Dead."

Underneath in pen was a note: *Hope you can make it, Tricky Wylie. X C.*

There was no question that I would go, and that Kate would come as well. I wanted her to meet Aurelio. I wanted her to meet the whole family—and I wanted them to meet Kate.

I had purposely avoided speaking about them. And especially about Cesca. That was a part of my life Kate knew nothing about. I had purposely kept it hidden. When I told Kate about the show, I gave her a loose idea of who they were and why it was important we go. They were old friends. An astonish-

ing family. Gifted, beautiful, blessed. I had known them practically my whole life; they had in many ways helped shape the
man I had become.

I said little about Cesca, merely that she was the eldest of four.
But she would be there. Part of me was worried about seeing her,
another part was eager to meet the challenge head-on. After
all, look where I was now. I was an architect, a graduate of a
distinguished school, doing well, earning the appreciation of my
seniors and the respect of my peers. I had a beautiful girlfriend.
A decent salary. In my closet, good clothes. Money in the bank.
My life had never been better. I wanted to show Cesca what she
had missed. But also that I had moved on.

Kate was happy to go. She had heard of Cosmo and had
even bought one of his CDs, of which there were now several.
"I didn't know you knew him," she said. "Do you think he'll be
there?"

The night before the show, I woke up in a sweat. I had an old
dream. I was following Cesca through a house in the country, a
house I didn't recognize. She was ahead laughing. There were
other people there, strangers, but I felt as though I knew them. I
wandered from room to room trying to find her. Someone said
it was lunchtime. I saw my father at the other end of the table. I
was surprised to see him. There was something important I had
to tell him but couldn't remember what it was. Then I woke up.

"What were you dreaming about?" asked Kate drowsily.

"Shhh. Nothing. Go back to sleep." She rolled over. I lay
there for the rest of the night staring at the ceiling.

We walked to the gallery. The evening had a spring chill.
Outside there was a small crowd on the sidewalk, chattering and
greeting each other as though it were a cocktail party. There
was a guest list. The gallery was on the second floor, and you
had to take an old-fashioned elevator. Only a few people could
go up at the same time. Town cars and limousines dropped off

patrons and guests; some idled by the curb. It was a dramatic-looking congregation, deliberately bohemian. Women in black with pale faces. An elderly Englishman in a wide hat with a cigarette holder. Men with heavy, rounded eyeglasses. Fruity voices. Scarves. It was like the opening of an underground play. The work secondary to the satisfaction of being considered important enough to be invited.

Upstairs the gallery was already crowded. I looked around for familiar faces. In one corner I saw Roger, but he was too engaged in conversation to notice me. I purposely kept my head down, hoping to delay seeing Cesca for as long as I could.

"Let's look at the paintings," I said, guiding Kate by the arm.

They were horrifying, gorgeous. Larger than life-size. Faces painted with a feverish intensity, the colors lush, staring at you like those about to feel the noose slip around their necks or the pistol against the backs of their skulls. The torment of savoring a last moment of life and the determination to die with dignity. They were men and women, most of them young, black and white, at one time attractive but now wasted, hollow shells of their former selves. Lips were cracked. Skin ashen. Some wore clothes but most were naked, revealing stark rib cages, sores, mottled skin, slack breasts. One man held an IV stand. In the upper left-hand corner of each portrait was a first name, followed by, presumably, a birth date and a death date. Only a few looked older than forty.

I was stunned, and so were a number of the others in the room. It was like entering a charnel house. To my relief, Kate obviously had the same reaction. One never knows how others will respond in such situations. There is always the temptation to look away in discomfort, to do or say something inappropriate. But she said and did nothing as we walked slowly around the gallery. I was amazed at how loud the room was. On the wall next to each painting was a little piece of paper with information about the painting: its title, dimensions, when it was painted. All were done within the past few years. Many of them had little round red stickers affixed to them indicating that they had already been sold. The prices were available on request.

I spotted Aurelio sitting in the corner. He was in a wheelchair, dressed like an old man in a heavy coat that was now too large for him. On his head the knit cap. But still the same aquiline beauty. A dying prince. Kitty and Lulu stood by him like sentinels, shielding him from all but the most welcome of well-wishers.

"Hello, Lio," I said, after waiting my turn, kneeling beside his chair. "Your big night at last. It's a triumph. Congratulations."

"Wylie," he said, managing a smile. "I'm so happy to see you."

"Hello, Kitty. Hello, Lulu," I said. "Lio, I'd like you to meet someone. This is Kate. Kate, this is Lio. This is his mother, Kitty. And Lulu."

Kate smiled at each of them. I was learning that she always had the right reaction to everything. "Lio, Wylie's told me so much about you. It's an honor to be here. Your paintings are incredibly powerful. Thank you for sharing them."

Lio smiled weakly. "Thank you. Wylie, where did you find her? Not only is she beautiful, but she has wonderful taste in art."

There were more people waiting behind us. He was like a groom at a wedding. There was no time to talk at length. We moved on.

"You would barely recognize Aurelio if you'd seen him a few years ago," I said. "He was the best-looking guy I ever met. Tall, strong, passionate. Confident yet at the same time sweet."

"I'm sorry."

"We're all sorry. It doesn't seem fair, somehow. Look at the incredible paintings around us. He's a great painter. If he dies, what a loss."

It was at that moment I noticed Cesca. She was watching me, with a faint smile on her lips, waiting for me to notice her.

For a few moments she held my gaze and then returned her attention to whomever she was speaking with.

Even though I thought I would be, I was unprepared to see her again. Like the memory of a cathedral, it is possible to remember a woman but it is easy to forget how overwhelming the reality can be. It is only in the face of that reality that one can be fully conscious of the sheer physical presence, the exquisite beauty, the inexplicable awe, the irretrievable secrets. As the eyes take in what the mind recalls, memory is obliterated. All that remains is the beating of one's heart growing louder with every passing second.

I stopped momentarily, unsure of how to proceed. Cesca had no such uncertainty. She came right up to us. "Tricky Wylie," she said, leaning in her cheek for a kiss, first on the right, then the left. The warmth of her skin, the familiarity of her scent. Jasmine and roses. It was intoxicating. She had cut her hair. It was now shoulder length, which in the dress she was wearing emphasized her magnificent shoulders and clavicle. She looked tan and rested, like a movie star between films. "I was hoping you'd be here. It's been far too long."

"Hello, Cesca." I was almost reluctant to speak, fearful my words or my voice would somehow betray me, making it obvious to Kate who Cesca was and what she meant to me.

It was as though Cesca understood what I was feeling and was slightly amused by it. "And who's this?" she asked, with her brightest smile.

I cleared my throat. "Kate, this is Cesca. She's Lio's older sister."

"How do you do?" said Kate.

"Wylie, she's beautiful. Kate, it's very nice to meet you. I've known Wylie here since he was a little boy. When you fell out of the tree, remember?" She laughed, and I joined her. I was slightly annoyed that she would bring this up. "Has he ever told you about that?"

"No," answered Kate. "Should he have?"

"You should get him to. Even then he was ambitious," Cesca continued. "Always reaching a little higher. Are you still like that, Tricky Wylie?"

I blushed. "Well, yes, I suppose I am. What about you?"

"I never reach for anything," she said with a laugh. "You should know that."

"I heard you have a shop in Soho now," I said, changing the subject.

"Yes, you can design your own perfume. It was an idea I came across in Istanbul. I was in the bazaar, and there was this little shop where there were all these little bottles, all of them containing wonderful things with wonderful names like vetiver, ylang-ylang, burnished attar rose, and emerald jasmine. It was magical. We have nothing like it here, so I decided to do it."

"It sounds very exciting," said Kate.

"It is. You should come by. It's an incredible experience to have a perfume that was created only for you."

"How is Lio doing?" I asked.

Her expression tightened. "Not well. Mare and Lulu spend all their time taking care of him, but he just keeps getting sicker and sicker."

"I'm sorry."

"It's been hell, quite honestly. I thought that having this show would actually kill him it was so much work and worry."

"It's an incredible show," said Kate.

Cesca nodded. "Yes, it is. Look, there's a party after back at the house. Why don't you both come?"

Kate and I left soon after and had dinner nearby. "Are you all right?" she asked.

I told her that I had been upset by seeing Lio and his paintings, which was partially true. What I did not mention was my reaction to seeing Cesca again. But Kate wasn't entirely fooled.

"She's one of the most beautiful women I've ever seen," she said.

"Who is?"

"Cesca."

"Yes. Yes, she is."

"Is there anything I should know?"

I stared at her. "No. Why do you ask?"

"The way you acted around her. I've never seen you so nervous."

I laughed. "Well, I suppose I had a bit of a crush on her when I was younger. You never really get over that sort of thing. I see her, and I feel like I'm a kid again."

She then proceeded to tell me about a crush of hers, a boy from tennis camp. She was nine, he was eleven. He was golden, had a killer backhand. All summer long, she trailed after him like a puppy. She'd run into him last year. He was fat and already losing his hair. "So much for childhood crushes."

But Kate didn't mind going to the Bonets' for the after-party. She had a beautiful woman's confidence in herself; it was unthinkable that anyone else could be more alluring. When our taxi pulled up at their town house, every light was ablaze. The same limousines and town cars that had been in front of the gallery appeared to be there. The front door was open, and guests streamed in and out. Music blared. The high-ceilinged living room was filled with couples dancing. People were drinking on the stairwell. I saw Carmen and waved. To my surprise, Cosmo approached me, holding out his hand and smiling. He had put on weight since I had seen him last but was still darkly handsome.

"Wylie," he said. "Good to see you. Who is this beautiful woman? You must introduce us."

"Kate," I said. "This is Cosmo Bonet. Cosmo, this is Kate Henry."

"A pleasure, Miss Henry."

"Wylie said you might be here," she said. "I'm a big fan."

"Are you now? I'm flattered. It is one of my greatest joys to meet someone who likes my music—especially when they are as lovely as you. Tell me, which album do you like the most?"

She blushed. "*Land of the Castles* is my favorite."

"Is it? You know that's what many people think the word *Catalonia* originally meant."

"Cosmo's father is Catalan," I pointed out helpfully, but Cosmo ignored me. I listened to them chat for several moments. Or rather, to Cosmo talk about himself. Kate didn't seem to mind though. I excused myself to get a drink.

I found Lio in a small study surrounded by admirers. Lulu, as always, hovering in the background. On his right, a handsome older man who looked very familiar, but I couldn't quite place him. Lio was smiling, laughing, buoyed up by the success of the evening.

"I sold out, Wylie!" he exclaimed. "Every painting! Can you believe it?"

"Congratulations!" I said, leaning over and hugging him gently.

"Wylie, this is my father, Ugo," he said, indicating the older man. To his father, he spoke in rapid Catalan, pointing at me.

"I remember your father," said Ugo Bonet, offering a large hand, his accent strong. "You look more like your mother. She was a beautiful woman. I hope she is well?"

"Yes, thank you."

"I am glad to hear it. Please remember me to her."

"I will."

"There you are!" said a voice behind me. It was Cesca. She

came in, walking past me and kissing both her father and her brother. "Lio, it's a party in your honor. Everyone wants to see you, but you're hiding away in here."

Lio smiled. "When I was healthy, I hated parties. Now at least I have an excuse."

"All right, darling. I understand. I just wanted you to know how many people here love you. We are all so proud of you."

"I know. Thank you. I think I am just going to go to bed. I'm exhausted." He held out his hand. Lulu stepped forward and helped him to his feet. I also stepped forward, reaching out my hands. "It's all right, Wylie," he said. "I'm not completely feeble yet."

His father also rose to his feet, saying something to his son in Catalan, his hand on Lio's back.

"Good night, my friend," Lio said to me. "Thank you for coming." He weakly opened his arms, and we embraced.

Cesca and I watched him shuffle off, supported by Lulu and his father. She was silent. Thoughtful. "I don't know who I feel more sorry for," she said finally. "Pare or Lio."

"Why do you say that?" I asked.

"What's worse? To die or to watch a child die? I know which I'd think was worse. I don't know how my mother does it. If it was my son, I'd be a wreck."

"Lio's still alive. There's still a chance. They say there are new advancements all the time."

"I don't believe the doctors anymore. They've lied to us too much." She sighed. There was a little balcony off the study that looked out over the backyard. "Let's get some fresh air," she said, turning the brass handle on the glass door that led to the balcony. She lit a cigarette and exhaled. "Brrrr. It's chilly," she said. Taking the hint, I removed my jacket and offered it to her. "Always a gentleman," she said with a smile. She held up her arm. Around her wrist was the Cartier watch I had given her. "See, I still have it."

"How are you?" I asked.

"I'm all right. The shop has been good for me. Keeps me in one spot. How are you?"

"Good."

"Your girlfriend is very pretty. How long have you been with her?"

"A few months."

"Serious?"

"I think so."

"Do you love her?"

Memories of Paris. Of Selene. What I had thrown away. I had heard from a mutual friend that she had married. "Why do you care?"

"I didn't say I did. I was just curious. But I'd be happy for you if you did love her."

"Why? Would it make you feel better about what you did?"

She shrugged her shoulders. "I don't feel badly about what I did. You shouldn't have asked me to marry you. Who knows? Maybe if you hadn't, we'd be together still."

"That doesn't make any sense."

"Doesn't it? Then I guess you don't know me as well as you thought you did, Tricky Wylie."

I said nothing.

She was close to me now. Her cigarette extinguished. I felt helpless. As always, I wanted her. There had never been a time when I didn't want her. She knew that. Reaching up, she kissed me lightly on the lips, her eyes fixed on mine, lingering there for several seconds. An eternity.

"But I know you," she said. "You will come back to me if I want." She stepped back. "Here's your jacket. I'm going inside."

Then she turned and left the balcony, leaving me alone in the dark, the sounds of the party echoing through the big house. For several minutes, I stood there, feeling the cold, replaying the scene in my head, hearing her words, scared of the truth.

Finally I went back inside and rejoined the party. There were fewer people now. I had forgotten about Kate. Would she have missed me? Did she suspect anything?

I spotted her walking up the stairs. "Finally," she said. "I didn't know where you had gotten to."

"I was speaking with Lio. He's gone to bed."

"His brother is charming. You shouldn't have left me alone with him. He even asked me out. Would have served you right too for abandoning me if I had said yes."

"But you didn't."

"Of course not. I told him I was with you."

"And that worked?"

She laughed. "Well, it did take some convincing. He's not the kind of person to accept no for an answer. But I didn't trust him. I've known a lot of men like him. They always disappoint you."

"And I wouldn't disappoint you?"

"I wouldn't let you." She smiled.

That night, after we made love, I couldn't sleep. I lay there in the dark listening to Kate breathe, watching her breasts rising and falling. For the first time since we met I felt I could betray her. That I could take her love and trample it underfoot. And I hated myself for that realization. She was so trusting, so loving. I knew how lucky I was but also knew how weak I was too.

Was Cesca right? Would I go back to her? I always had in the past. She just had to snap her fingers, and I came. But I was determined to be better than that. To not let Cesca poison this relationship too. I loved Kate. Maybe not in the way I had loved Cesca, but that love had always left me heartsick and alone, staring at an empty pillow. With Kate I could have something healthier. Be settled. Maybe one day start a family. Was it really that hard to decide? It wasn't.

22

AURELIO DIED OF AIDS IN JULY. IT WAS CARMEN WHO TOLD me. I was in the office when the phone buzzed. "A Dr. Bonet for you," said my secretary. "Will you take it?"

Cesca had asked her to call me. They had been with him at the end. Cesca was too upset to talk to anyone, Carmen said. She was a doctor now and had learned how to distance herself. Her voice sounded modulated, professional. The funeral would be the day after tomorrow. In Amagansett. Only family and a few friends. Lio had specifically asked that I be there. Would I come?

"Of course," I replied, my heart heavy, sadness seeping through my bones like water in a sinking ship. I then added, "I'm sorry."

"I know. Thank you. If it's any comfort, there was plenty of morphine. He died peacefully."

I hung up and stared out the window at the bright blue summer sky forty stories above the sidewalk. I had been expecting this news, but that made it no less tragic. My eyes welled with tears, and for a moment I wept for my friend.

I called Kate to tell her the news. "Oh God, that's awful. I'm so sorry," she said.

"The funeral's on Thursday."

"Do you want me to come?"

"It's going to be small. I think I'm one of the only nonfamily members invited."

"So maybe I shouldn't come. It would be an imposition?"

"Maybe. Do you mind?"

"Of course not. I understand."

Early Thursday morning, I drove Kate's Bug out to Amagansett. It was a fine summer day, hot but not humid. Traffic moved relatively easily, and I made good time. I got there early so I just drove around. My father would be at the house, but I didn't go to see him. I didn't know if he would be at the funeral or not. I would have been surprised to see him. Funerals had always depressed him.

At eleven I drove up to the big house. Some cars were already there. I recognized Cesca's red BMW. Some others. A blue Mercedes coupe that for some reason I thought might be Roger's. There was no sign of my father's car. Around the back, I saw a white van with the name of a local catering company painted on the side. A man and a woman in white shirts and black pants were carrying trays into the kitchen.

I couldn't help thinking of Izzy's memorial. That had been the celebration of a long life. There was nothing to celebrate about a short life. Death had come too soon for Lio. There were too many people left who would miss him.

I knocked on the door and entered without waiting for anyone to answer. It had been years since I had last been here. Kitty had redecorated since moving in after the deaths of her parents. The interior had been modernized, lightened. The living room ceiling had been extended through the bedrooms above to form a large atrium. Now, with curtains drawn, it was sunless and quiet as a church. Lining the walls were Aurelio's paintings, both old and new, some hung on the walls, others on stands, still more simply tilted up. The first person I saw was Roger sitting in a chair. He looked pale and agitated.

"Uncle Roger," I said, feeling like an intruder. "It's Wylie. I'm so sorry."

"Wylie," he said, looking up, his normal ebullience dimmed. "Come in, come in. Terrible. Just terrible. What a waste. What a loss. Unbelievable. That beautiful boy." He shook his head.

"Carmen called and told me that Lio wanted me here today. I hope that it's still all right that I'm here."

"Of course. Of course. Everyone will be along soon. Just taking a bit longer than usual. It's been a terrible couple of days." He stopped speaking and looked out the window. Then he seemed to remember I was in the room. "Can I get you anything? A drink maybe?"

"No thank you. Please don't trouble yourself. I'll wait outside."

I stepped through the sliding doors onto the deck. There was no one else out there, and I breathed more easily. The sun sparkled on the sound, and I was warm in my jacket and tie. I was standing there staring out at the water, my hands in my pockets, when I heard the door slide open behind me. I turned and saw Cesca. Without saying anything, she walked up and embraced me. I had held her so many times, but never like this. She stood there and sobbed for several minutes, her arms around my neck while I stroked her hair.

"Thank you for coming," she said at last.

"Of course I'd come. I loved him too."

"I know you did."

She stepped back and looked at me. Her eyes were red. I noticed a single gray hair. Barely perceptible lines on her face. I handed her my handkerchief, with which she dried her eyes.

"Thank you," she said. "Always a gentleman. I must look awful."

"No," I answered. "Not at all. You look beautiful." I meant it.

She smiled and moved a hair from across her face. "Oh, Wylie. I am so glad you're here. It's been hell. I'm sorry I didn't call you myself. I was out of my mind. Carmen even had to give me a sedative to calm me down and help me sleep."

"How's your mother?"

"She's been amazing. There's so much to do when someone dies. I had no idea. The forms. The funeral home. We had him cremated, you know."

"I didn't know."

She nodded her head. "It's what he wanted," she continued. "Today we're going to scatter half his ashes over the water, and next week we're flying to Barcelona and scatter the other half there."

The rest of the guests began arriving. Esther came alone, a cane in her right hand. Paolo was not feeling well. A few other people I didn't know, friends of Kitty's. Aurelio's dealer. Carmen's boyfriend, who was Asian and also a doctor. He introduced himself as Jonathan and said he was a neurologist. They had met at medical school. We stood around in the living room chatting idly, but we were mostly lost in our thoughts while the bartender set up the bar, adjusting the folding table, laying out the heavy white tablecloth, pouring ice, unpacking the glasses. Carmen came out and joined us, standing next to Jonathan, who put his arm around her. Then Cosmo, who looked puffy and distraught. Roger and his wife, Diana. Finally, Kitty entered, head high, chin firm, like a queen in mourning. She had her arm around Lulu. Dot came next, followed by Randall and a haggard Ugo Bonet. On his arm was a handsome blond woman who held a little girl, also blond, by the hand. Last came Cesca, holding an urn.

Kitty stopped and addressed the small crowd. "My friends, thank you all for coming to show your love and support for Lio on this sad occasion. We will now go to the beach."

At the sand everyone kicked off their shoes, and some of the men rolled up their trouser legs. Cosmo carried a guitar. I gave Esther my arm and helped her over the sand. No one sat in the white chairs that had been set out.

When she reached the water's edge, Kitty stopped and said, "This is one of the places Lio loved most. When he was a child, he would spend hours in this very spot swimming or making elaborate designs or sand castles. Over the past few months, he kept saying he wanted to come back, but by then he was too sick. Now that he is gone, he can finally return here." She paused and then, speaking with effort, continued: "What we'd like you all to do today is step forward and take a handful of his ashes, and as you scatter them say a little prayer. It can be silent or aloud. It doesn't matter. Lio will hear you anyway."

Cesca stepped forward with the urn. Cosmo began to play, a mournful ballad that I assumed was Catalan. One by one we took our turns. Carmen went first, wading into the gentle surf, lifting her dress with her left hand, holding her brother's ashes in her right. She spoke in a soft voice, and I couldn't hear what she was saying. Then she flung the ashes over the water. One by one, the rest of us took our turns. When I stepped up to take my handful, Cesca gave me a quick, private smile and a wink. I walked into the water up to my knees. The ashes in my hand felt so light and inconsequential. "Good-bye, Lio," I said to the wind. "I will miss you. The world is a poorer place without you." Then I scattered the ashes, watching them quickly disappear.

I watched Cesca wade into the water, could see her body contract as she cried, taking deep breaths, and when she was finished, she threw the ashes with a defiant shout as far as she could.

Kitty went last. It was heartbreaking to watch. Most of us were already in tears, overcome by the emotion of the moment. Cosmo had stopped playing. Kitty stood there, almost up to her hips, the bottom of her dress floating on the surface of the water, and began to sob. Large, uncontrollable outbursts, almost screams, naked in their maternal agony. Finally, Cesca waded back out and put her arm around her mother, comforting her. Kitty grew quiet and then with an effort released her son's ashes.

Silently, we followed her back to the house, as Cesca supported her, stopping to retrieve our shoes but not bothering to wipe the sand from our feet. I had offered my arm to Esther. Cesca took Kitty inside, but the rest of us remained outside, subdued, staring back at the beach, alone in our thoughts.

"There is nothing worse than the death of a child," said Esther after a while, grimly shaking her head. "Poor Kitty. Their lives will never be the same again."

In the house, Roger came up, followed by a waiter, urging people to have a drink, something to eat. "We have lots of food and drink," he said. "Please. Help yourself. Just give the waiter your order, and he'll be happy to bring it."

Gradually, the pall lifted, and we began to talk again. I chatted with Esther, a little with Carmen's boyfriend. Helped myself to a ham sandwich. I had planned to return to the city but wanted to see Cesca before I left. Eventually she reappeared.

"Please don't leave yet," she said.

"I need to get back. I have work tomorrow."

"Just a little longer. I need to talk to the guests."

"All right."

She reached up and gave me a quick kiss on the cheek. "Thank you. I knew I could count on you."

Inside Cosmo was at the piano. Playing something sad yet beautiful, elegiac. Brahms maybe, possibly Chopin. The notes perfectly capturing the mood. While the others chatted in the dining room, where the food was, I sat to listen. Cosmo acknowledged me with a smile. There was nothing to be said. I stared at the objects around me. The sorts of beautiful knickknacks that the rich effortlessly acquire. Silver cigarette boxes. Beaten brass. Bronze Florentine sculptures of centaurs. A Murano glass ashtray. I picked up a small ivory netsuke and inspected it. It was of a boy, his hands bound, being fed by mice. I wondered what the story was behind it. How did he become a prisoner? What had he done to earn the mice's friendship? My mind ranged idly about the room, allowing me momentarily to forget why I was here. It was comforting not to have to talk, to be allowed to look at Aurelio's paintings and think about him, what he had been and what he might have still become.

Then Cosmo stopped and asked me: "Where's your pretty girlfriend?"

"She's not here."

"Ah. Too bad," he said and resumed playing.

Esther came over to tell me good-bye. Other guests were leaving too, hugging Kitty, carefully closing the door behind them so it wouldn't slam. They waved wordlessly to Cosmo, who kept playing. The bartender stood idly behind the bar, her hands behind her back. Nearly a whole ham, baskets of bread, untouched food sat on the dining room table. The waiter moved around the room, collecting glasses and emptying ashtrays.

"I told Mare she was ordering too much, but she wouldn't listen," said Cesca, slipping into the chair next to mine and lighting a cigarette. She leaned her head back and rubbed her eyes. "God, I need a drink."

"Can I get you one?"

"Would you?"

"What do you want?"

"White wine. No, make it a vodka on the rocks. A big one. It's that kind of day."

I returned with the drink. "Thank you so much." She took a sip. "God, I needed that." Another sip.

"How are you holding up?" I asked.

She laughed. "You don't want to know."

"Your mother was incredible today. So were you. And Cosmo. And Carmen. Lio would have been proud."

"He'd have told us to stop being so melodramatic because we were bumming him out." She smiled. "Mare asked me to see if you could stay for dinner."

"She did?"

"Yes. It would mean a lot to her—and to me as well. She knew how fond Lio was of you. I don't think we've quite gotten used to him not being here, you know. The empty seat at the table. If you could fill it tonight it would be a great help."

"Of course. I'd be glad to stay."

"Good. Thank you. I'll tell Mare. She'll be so happy. Wait here. I'll be right back."

I calculated the time. It was still possible that if I stayed for dinner I could drive back late. I would have to call Kate and let her know.

When Cesca returned, I asked if I could use the phone. "Use the one in the kitchen," she said. "Come find me when you're done."

I called Kate at work. When she picked up, I said, "Sweetheart, it's me."

"Hi, baby. How are you? I've been thinking about you all day."

"I've been better. It's been very sad."

"I'm sorry."

"Look, the reason I'm calling is that they invited me to stay for dinner. I hope that's okay. I know we had no real plans, but I just didn't want you to go to any trouble."

"No, that's okay. I was going to make you something nice for dinner because I figured you'd have had a rough day, but I can do it tomorrow. What time will you be back?"

"I don't know. I'm not sure. Late. Midnight maybe. At least traffic will be light that time of night. Do you want me to come over, or should I stay at my place?"

"Call me when you're leaving. If it's not too late, come over. If it is, then maybe you should just go home."

"Okay. I'll talk to you later."

"Bye."

"Love you."

"Love you too."

I hung up and went looking for Cesca. There was no one around except for the waiter and bartender, who were cleaning up. "Are you Wylie?" the bartender asked. "Miss Bonet asked me to tell you to meet her in the Playhouse."

I thanked her and walked over to the Playhouse. I knocked and called out, "Hello? Cesca?"

"I'll be right down," she answered from upstairs.

A few minutes later, she appeared. She had changed out of her black dress and was now wearing a beach cover-up and carrying a towel. "Here," she said. "Here's an old swimsuit of Cosmo's. It might just fit you. After you change, let's go for a swim. I need to get out of the house. I'll meet you on the beach."

When I joined her, she had spread out two towels and was lying on her back on one. I sat down on the other. The folding chairs that had been set out for the ceremony had been removed. The beach was no longer a grave site. The water rolled gently up and back, eternal and impervious. The only indications of what had just happened here were faint footprints in the sand.

"Let's get a little sun first and then go in," she said. It was hot, and already her skin was glistening. She was wearing a bikini, her body toned and brown. It was impossible not to stare at her. She was presenting herself, like a feast, a gift. I would have had to be a rock to not be aroused. My eyes traveled over her breasts, where little beads of perspiration had formed in her cleavage, down to the navel I had kissed so many times and to the swell of her mons. She knew I was watching and took pleasure in it, a coy smile curving on her lips.

"Thank you for staying," she said, lighting a cigarette. "I think I'd go crazy if I was alone right now. Mare has Randall, Carmen has Jonathan, and Cosmo never needs anyone. Normally, it would be Lio and me. He was always the one I turned to first. But now . . ." She sighed and sat up. "Fuck."

There was nothing for me to say. She already knew. I just reached out my hand to her, and she took it. "Wylie, you're always there for me when I need you. Why are you so good to me?"

"You know why."

She let go of my hand and nodded. "Let's go for a swim," she said, grinding her cigarette out in the sand and standing up. "Race you!" She started sprinting down the short strip of sand to the water. I jumped up and ran after her, but she had too much of a head start. We both splashed through the shallows and dove in, the water cool and marvelous.

"Here we are again," she said, coming up from the water, clearing her wet hair from her face. "That first night? The night of Gog's party? Remember?"

"I could never forget," I answered.

"That's good. Would you believe me if I told you I never forgot either?"

I shrugged. "I don't know. I never really seem to know what you think about anything."

"We were both so young. You were so sweet back then. Cute too. What a lovely body. We had fun, didn't we?"

"Until you left."

She shook her head. "Yes, I suppose I had that coming." Then, "That was stupid of me. I was wrong."

"And Paris? And all the other times? Were you wrong then too?"

"Shit, Wylie. Don't you understand what I'm trying to say?"

"I don't know. What?" She was close now, impossible to ignore. I was no more invulnerable to her than when I was a boy. Like Ulysses, I wished I could have had wax in my ears too, been tied to the mast.

"Well, when you figure it out, you let me know, okay?" she said and then dove into the water, swimming with fine strokes out to the old floating raft. I followed. She was already up on the raft when I reached it, her legs dangling in the water.

"So how's your friend? The pretty blonde."

"Kate? She's good."

"Kate. That's right. I couldn't remember her name. She made a big impression on Cosmo."

"She's a fan of his music."

"Are you going to marry her?"

"I don't know."

"Why wouldn't you? She's lovely."

I resented Cesca talking about Kate like that. I also felt guilty, and she knew it, daring me to say something, bring it out in the open. If anyone else in the world had asked me that question, I would have told them yes. But Cesca wasn't anyone else in the world. As always, she brought my deepest desires to the surface, kicking over my carefully constructed fictions and half beliefs as if they were so many sand castles.

"Well, if you don't know . . ." she continued.

"I don't know. You're talking about marriage. That's a big step."

"I know it is. I made the step, remember? And, boy, did I step in it." She laughed.

"Why did you marry Gavin?"

"Why? I don't know. I suppose I thought it seemed like the

right thing to do at the time. So much of life is like that, isn't it? Doing something and then regretting it later. I liked the idea of getting married. And he was successful, mature, handsome. On paper it looked perfect. In reality it was something else."

"What happened?"

"Well, I just couldn't make it work. In a way he was too perfect. I always felt as though I wasn't good enough. Not smart enough. Not successful. He put me on the mantel like a little statue and just expected me to look decorative. That's what he wanted from me. I had other ideas."

"I'm sorry."

"God, don't be. I'm not. I felt trapped. Useless. Couldn't really do what I wanted to do. It was always his friends or his plans. I couldn't even decorate my house because it was already decorated, and he didn't see the point in doing it over again. One day I just woke up and realized that if I stayed married to him for one minute longer, I'd go completely insane."

"How did he take it?"

"Surprisingly well. He wasn't what you'd call a passionate man. Everything was weighed. Analyzed like a business deal. Risk versus reward. When he realized it made more sense to cut his losses, he did."

"Do you think you'll ever get married again?"

"Why? Are you proposing again?" She smiled, daring me.

"No, what I meant was . . ."

"Oh, don't get your panties in a knot, Wylie. I know what you meant. Just having a little fun with you, that's all. Anyway, we should be getting back. Mare's expecting us for drinks at seven."

She stood up and dove into the water, clean as a knife. Once again, I followed her. On the beach, she picked up her towel and started drying her hair, before wrapping the towel around her torso. I remember watching her. Even when she was performing the most simple acts, it was impossible not to be struck by her beauty. The angle of a knee, the muscles in her arm, the shape of her toes. Like that of a great athlete, her grace was inborn. We walked back to the Playhouse, passing Aurelio's studio.

"Do you mind if we look inside?" I asked. "It would mean a lot to me."

"Sure. I've been in a few times."

"Was it strange?"

"No. It felt quite natural. It looks just the same. I still feel Aurelio there. His presence is so strong even though he hasn't been there in months. Poor Lio. Oh shit." She stopped talking and started to cry. I wrapped my arms around her, comforting her. Feeling her skin cool from the water, her wet hair, her closeness. I felt myself becoming aroused and shifted my hips so they weren't touching her. When she had calmed down and her breathing returned to normal, I let go.

"Oh God. Sorry," she said, wiping tears from her face. "It just hit me again that he's gone."

"We don't have to go to the studio, if you don't want."

"No, no. It's fine. I'd like to go."

The studio was dark, and, despite the still strong smell of turpentine and oil paint, it felt musty, like the room of a child away at college. Everything was left just so, waiting for the return. The brushes had been cleaned. The palettes scraped. I looked around at the sketches and photographs pinned to the walls, recognizing some from years ago, taking in more recent ones. The splotches of dried paint on the cement floor. The racks of canvases, some still primed and waiting for paint that would now never come. I searched through the older paintings. I found the one he did of me from years before.

"God, I look so young."

"Mmm, you were. Almost too pretty for a boy."

"What about now?"

"You've lost your prettiness. Now you look just the way you should look."

"I'll take that as a compliment."

"You should."

I then found the early portrait of Cesca that had so trans-fixed me the first time I had been here. It was perfect. The slightly crooked smile. The intelligence and fire in her eyes. It was all there. "You look just the same."

"Liar."

"I used to stare at this whenever Lio wasn't looking."

"You should see the nude he painted of me in Barcelona."

"I did."

"Oh, you did, did you? And? What did you think?"

I remembered when he had shown it to me. The pride in his work. For my part, admiration infused with acute embarrass-ment and lust. "It was miraculous."

"It was quite a painting, wasn't it? Did you get all horny when you saw it? I bet you did."

"I'm not going to give you the satisfaction of an answer." I smiled. "Whatever happened to it?"

"He gave it to me."

"He did? Where is it?"

"It's a secret. A girl has to be careful about who sees a paint-ing like that," she said with a smile.

I nodded and looked around the room. "So, what are you going to do with all of his other paintings?"

"That's something we've been talking about for months. Mare and I want to have a show, but Lulu's not sure what she wants to do."

"Lulu? Why does Lulu get a vote?"

"Oh, you probably didn't know. Lio married Lulu. He left her everything. Paintings, money, the apartment in Barcelona."

"Wow. Well, good. I suppose."

"Yes, she was incredible to him. I've never seen such devotion."

"When did they get married?"

"Two weeks ago. There was a little ceremony in his bedroom. He could barely talk. But he had asked her. He wanted to do something for her. To repay her for her love. He was like that."

"Were you there?"

"Yes," she laughed. "We all were. He was such a dear man. He was so weak, but he wanted to look special for his wedding day. There was an old top hat that had belonged to Gog and a white silk scarf, and he insisted on wearing those things in bed. Lulu wore a little white dress. We filled the room with flowers. Cosmo played the wedding march. A friend of Mare's who is a judge officiated."

"Where did Lio meet her?" I asked.

"In Barcelona. She's Danish. He saw her panhandling on the street. She had been backpacking around Europe for several months and had run out of money. There had been a guy, but they'd split up at some point. Lio was afraid she might soon start selling herself, so he invited her for lunch. The next thing he knew she had moved in."

"Was he already sick by that time?"

"Yes, I think so, but he didn't know it. You can only imagine how Lio felt about going to the doctor." She smiled. "He thought everything could be cured with tea and sleep."

"Could they have saved him?"

She sighed. "Oh, I don't know. Maybe. In a few years, they might find a cure. If he had lived that long. I've read a lot of articles about AIDS, talked to Carmen. She knows a lot about it. She's specializing in internal medicine at St. Vincent's now. There's so much about the disease they don't know and so many more people who don't want to know."

"So what is Lulu going to do with Lio's paintings?"

"I don't know that either. We brought it up with her after he died. Cosmo said we ought to organize a global tour. Hang them in hospitals in major world capitals. He'd go and play. He could get his manager to arrange the whole thing, but Lulu said no."

"Why?"

"She said she didn't want to lose any more of him. Each one of the paintings was precious to her, and she couldn't bear to part with them."

"That sounds a little nuts to me."

"Maybe. I don't know. I think she's grieving right now. Let's see how she feels about it in a couple of months. Come on, let's go back to the Playhouse, or we'll be late."

There was an outdoor shower, where she stopped and turned on the water. She undid the back of her bikini top to remove the salt and stood with her back to me. I couldn't help but stare at the sides of her uncovered breasts, which were as brown as the rest of her. Then she washed the sand from her feet. "Your turn," she said, taking the towel and wrapping it around her head, leaving her naked from the waist up. The casualness of it all annihilated me. I had never wanted her more.

She walked by me saying, "After you've finished, wait for me downstairs, and we'll walk over together, okay?"

There was no one else in the big house when we walked in half an hour later. Cesca walked up to the bar, put ice into two glasses, and filled each with vodka. "Here you go," she said.

"I have to drive."

"One won't hurt you."

Slowly, the rest of the family wandered in. Roger and Diana first. Carmen and Jonathan. Even Ugo and his new wife. Roger's mood had improved, and he began telling funny stories. He told one about my father and him when they were in college. "One night we were in a bar in the South End, and there was this fabulous girl. Redhead. Great tits. Both of us wanted her, and neither of us was going to give the other guy a crack at her. There was dancing. So each of us danced with her. While we were dancing, she whispered in my ear that she liked me better than your father. Naturally, I wasn't surprised to hear that. Later I drove her home in my car. I was at the wheel. She was in the middle. Mitch on the other side. The interiors of cars back then weren't as brightly lit as they are today. At one point I felt her hand snake over to my crotch, unzip my zipper, and begin giving me a hand job! Of course, I wasn't going to say anything. I didn't want to make your father feel bad. She finished before we got to her place, somewhere out in Watertown, and I was feeling pretty good about myself, as you can imagine. She gave us each a good night kiss, and as we were driving off your father turned to me and said, 'See, Roger? I knew she liked me better. She just gave me a hand job.'" Everyone roared.

Dinner was surprisingly lively. It was a simple meal, leftovers from earlier that day. A dozen wine bottles. A green salad. Served buffet style on the sideboard. Candles were lit on the long dining table. Kitty welcomed me warmly. It was the first time I had spoken to her all day. "I am so glad you could come," she told me. Roger and Cosmo took turns entertaining the crowd, telling uproarious stories, each more outrageous than the last. The wine flowed. Cesca and Carmen joined in. Many of the stories had to do with Aurelio. About the time he accidentally lit himself on fire, or when he had dared Cesca and Carmen to spend a night alone in a graveyard, and how he had pretended to be a ghost but had tripped and fallen accidentally into a hornet's nest. Even Lulu was weeping with laughter.

I sat next to Cesca, who kept refilling my wineglass. A part of me wanted her to stop, another part of me did not. I knew what she was doing. And she knew I knew, and that only emboldened her. *I am getting you drunk,* her eyes told me. *Too drunk to drive*. At one point she even slipped her hand under the table and held mine, leaving it there for several minutes, intimate and innocent at the same time, our fingers interlaced, as though we had been doing it all our lives.

At this point, I had only betrayed Kate in my mind. When I had sat down to dinner, I had every expectation of shortly getting in her car and driving home tonight. But with each hour, I pushed the time of my departure back even further. The conversation was too entertaining. The company too pleasant. Cesca's presence too intoxicating. Like everyone else at the table, I needed to lift the great sadness that had climbed on top of me since Lio's death. We all needed to laugh, to remind ourselves of the joys of life. To forget the pain and remember what it was about Aurelio that made us all love him so much.

Initially, I had intended to leave by eight. I would have a quick bite, say my good-byes, and virtuously be back in the city by ten if I didn't hit traffic, maybe even early enough to see Kate. Then, when it became obvious that eight was too early, I told myself nine. I'd be fine to drive. I'd only had a few drinks. But then nine came and went, and I was astonished to see that it was nearly half past when I next looked at my watch. If I left by ten, I could still make it back by midnight or so, as long as I drove steadily and didn't get stopped by the police.

The easiest excuse for a moral lapse is to claim inattention. To deceive ourselves. We want to feel that our sins are not our fault. That we were pushed, or stumbled, not that we made a conscious choice to hurt other people. At trial, few suspects plead guilty. There is always a mitigating factor. Someone else made me do it. I didn't do it. That wasn't me. It is simpler to live with ourselves if we can convince ourselves of our innocence. Of course, such justification is simply another word for cowardice.

If I had thought for a moment of Kate, things would have been different. But I didn't. All that I could think of was how privileged I felt to be there, sharing this moment with them. To be accepted by this extraordinary family that I had admired so greatly and for so long. Grateful that their love for each other also, in a small way, included me. Even Cosmo made me feel welcome. That in some way I had a right to be there. That there was nowhere else in the world I would rather be. No other people I would rather be with. Such a feeling was as intoxicating as the wine. The distinctions between truth and want become blurred, until we forget the one and focus only on the other.

It was easy, too easy. Like felling a tree that is already rotten; a simple push and it crashes down. That's all it takes.

"You can stay here tonight if you want," whispered Cesca, leaning over to me. The rest went unspoken. Nothing else needed to be said. The time for resistance was long past.

I nodded, I was complicit. Like a child trying to brazen out the broken vase on the living room floor, I said, "I have to make a phone call."

I went to the kitchen and found the phone. There were dishes in the sink. Normally, I would have helped clean but not now. I had a purpose. It was an old-fashioned phone, fixed to the wall. The dial pad on the receiver. "Kate," I said when I heard her voice. "Baby, hi. Sorry for calling so late. I think I'll be staying here tonight. I've had too much to drink. I'll just have to wake up early tomorrow and drive right to work."

"Okay. Are you all right? I've been worried about you."

"I'm okay. A little drunk. It's been an emotional day."

"I understand. Call me when you get to work."

"Good night."

"Good night."

I hung up, guilty but also unencompassed, fooling myself into thinking that I was free, that my actions were without consequence, that it was impossible to hurt someone who didn't know she was being hurt.

If my older self had been able to sit down with my younger self at that moment, what would I have said? Look at the decision before you. What do you really want? What is best for you? For the people you care for? Who is it that you really love?

On the one hand there was Kate. Beautiful, kind, affectionate, and good. There was nothing wrong with her and much to love. I enjoyed her company, and I think she enjoyed mine. I could imagine our lives together spooling out ahead of us. Children, holidays, dogs, a place in the country at some point. There would be money. Enough to live reasonably well, do as we pleased. Maybe I would start my own firm. Become an adjunct professor, lecturing to eager young design students on crisp fall afternoons in Cambridge while the orange and red leaves in the yard rustled in the wind. We would grow old together, our hair turning gray and then white. Grandchildren. At some later date, hazy in the future, there would be death, but only after a happy, well-spent life.

And then there was Cesca. I had no idea what a life with her would be like, if there would be one at all. It would be an invitation to chaos, to agony. What I did know was that since I had met her so many years ago, not a day had gone by without my somehow finding a way to think of her. She touched everything I did, believed in, or felt. In her presence, the world was richer, more exciting. Colors more vivid, senses sharpened. There was no one closer to me, who understood me so instinctually. Removing her would be like removing a vital organ.

And yet, like a cancer, a parasite, she had infiltrated me, siphoning off the nutrients that kept me alive. Time and again she had dashed my expectations, broken her promises. But I couldn't help myself from going back again and again like a bloodied boxer, hoping that this was the round when I could turn defeat into victory.

Why did I feel the way I did about her? There was no question that I loved her. But that then begs a definition of what love is and, more to the point, how I perceived it. Had I missed the lesson that taught us what love is? Or maybe something about me was broken. How could I love someone who caused me so much pain? Read the poets, however, and you find time after time examples of the pain of love. Like Prometheus, I had my innards regularly torn out, but unlike him I longed for the rock.

It would be too simple to say I loved Cesca because she was beautiful, that she was brave. True, I admired the way she confronted the world, challenging it on her own terms, refusing to compromise or doubt herself. If I had been a psychiatrist, it is possible I might have ascribed other factors to my fascination with her. Maybe I lacked the confidence she possessed in abundance and so hoped she could help make me stronger. Or maybe it was just as simple as wanting to make her love me so I could then reject her. But it was more than all of that. In my deepest heart I believed we were meant to be together, that fate or destiny had conspired to throw us together and we were meant to be, even if I was to be made miserable time and again because of her. Otherwise why would I have put myself through the emotional torture that over the years she had forced me to endure, seeking me out and abandoning me again, if not because I knew one day it would all be made right?

I could not believe that she was willful or capricious, although she could be both those things. That she was incapable of love. What I did believe, or what I wanted to believe, was that she was capable of love. It was just that she needed the right person to show her how, to reassure her, to rid her of her restlessness and let her be at peace. I believed I was that person.

Yet I also knew I was a fool, quick to forgive and even quicker to forget. What I didn't know was what she thought of me. Was

I simply a plaything, a diversion, or did she regard me in a different way? And how would I know, when she lied as easily as breathing? I had learned years ago that she told people what they wanted to hear, but was no more bound to her words than a musical note is to a violin.

All this rushed through my head as I stood in the kitchen, staring at the phone, hearing the voices in the dining room. It was not too late. I could still leave now. There was a gas station on the highway where I could get coffee, sober up. If I was careful, I would be all right. That way I could wake up in my own bed, clean of conscience. All I had to do was walk back into the dining room and tell everyone in a loud voice good night and thank you, exchange affectionate kisses and handshakes, and that would be the end of it.

I hesitated, my hand on the door, poised to push but unable to move. Would I choose Kate or Cesca? One promised stability, normalcy, a chance at a happy life. The other, passion and uncertainty. I knew I could live without Kate, that I would get over her just as she would get over me. There would be tears, recriminations. But Cesca was my passion, my craving, my magnetic north. Without her I would be lost. And she was waiting on the other side, ready to take me to her room and her bed, desperate to find release from the pain of her brother's, my friend's, death. She was looking for me now, needing me to help her to cope with her loss. If she sought my love and comfort now, after so long, would it be monstrous of me to spurn her and deny us both what would almost surely be an unknown period, days, weeks, maybe even months of cherished intimacy? And was I such a fool to keep putting my hand into the fire?

After a lifetime, I made up my mind and pushed the door open.

23

THE PAIN WE CAUSE OTHERS IS ALWAYS MORE DEVASTATING than the pain we cause ourselves. If we break our leg in a skiing accident, it's our fault. It hurts, but there is no one else to blame, which is a comfort of sorts. But if we were to break someone else's leg, we would be tormented by remorse and guilt. Of course, there are exceptions. Sadists, soldiers in wartime, the morally corrupt, the truly evil. But for the most part, we are predisposed to avoid causing pain of any kind. Where it gets complicated is when we must choose between inflicting pain on another and inflicting it on ourselves. The cowardly decision is to avoid the pain. Spare me, Lord, but take them, is a not infrequent supplication. It is the brave who take the pain on themselves.

I am not brave. Or at least, no more brave than the next man. I avoid unpleasantness. I don't want to hurt anyone or be hurt. Like so many people, I am content to be left alone with my life, to find pleasures where they come. I am not a political person or a man of strong opinions. Issues of huge import don't move me with any particular urgency. When students at my college rallied to compel the administration to divest from companies that were in South Africa, I walked past, agreeing on the one hand with the justice of their aims but also appreciating that the school needed to maintain a strong investment portfolio. It is also possible that if I'd lived in Berlin or Nuremberg in the early 1930s, I might not have been willing to speak out against Hitler, even as the warning signs grew unmistakable, hoping it would all just go away in the end and leave me in peace.

I know I am not alone. The great majority of humankind probably fits in my category. We don't want to cause pain but don't want to receive it either. For the most part, we would rather not think about it all. Unfortunately, there are times when we have to choose, to act. It would be so easy just to settle, to allow the waves to wash over us and take us. To postpone immediate discomfort or awkwardness for something equally bad, or possibly even worse, down the road. Like making a large purchase on a credit card that we might not be able to pay for when the bill comes due. We gasp and struggle for a few more moments to avoid the inevitable, clinging to hope and a childlike desire to wish unpleasant things gone, vainly trying to delay the reckoning as long as possible.

Courage is essential to action, but so also is conviction. If we don't know what we want, then we hesitate. Do I go left or right? In or out? It can be impossible to know until we have no other alternative. It is at these crucial junctures in our lives that everything comes down to a single split-second decision, when uncertainty is obviated and wisdom is supplanted by instinct. A Rubicon crossed, destinies altered. In the time it takes to draw a breath, for a heart to cease beating, for a leaf to flutter to the ground, everything can change. The only thing we know with certainty is that nothing will ever be the same again.

None of this flashed through my mind as I reentered the living room to rejoin Cesca. I pushed open the door, and she looked up from the table, expectant, smiling, happy to see me. There had been a time when that would have been all.

"Is everything all right?" she asked me as I slipped in next to her at the table, her hand enfolding mine.

"Yes," I said.

"You're staying?"

"Can we talk in the other room?" I whispered in her ear.

Her head drew back slightly, suddenly suspicious, uncertain of my intentions, but she said nothing. Instead, she shrugged, got to her feet, and walked ahead of me to the library.

"What is it?" she asked, her face stone.

"Look," I said. The words came out of my mouth, surprising even me. I had made my decision. It was almost as though someone else was speaking. "I'm sorry. But I really do need to drive back to the city tonight."

She pursed her lips and turned away from me. "That's too bad."

"I've got to be at work in the morning . . ." Even then I was being a coward for not saying that Kate was my reason. As though I was hedging, knowing that mentioning Kate's name would be unforgivable.

She cut me off, knowing I was not being entirely truthful and hating me for it. "I don't need your excuses, Wylie. If you want to go, go."

"I hope you aren't upset."

"Really?" she said angrily. "Is that what you hope? Well, let me tell you something: If a woman asks a man to spend the night, a woman, don't forget, who has just lost her beloved brother and is in need of comfort, and the man says no, what do you think the woman's response should be? And this from a man who has always told the woman that he loves her and now, when she really needs him, when he has the chance to prove himself to her once and for all, he refuses. Do you think she will be happy?

That she will say, 'Oh yes, *hombre*, go. Your job designing ugly buildings for large multinational corporations is so important, I understand.' That she will look at him the same way ever again? Tell me, Wylie. What do you think? I'd be fascinated to know."

I had seen many sides of Cesca. I had seen her happy, sad, excited, bored. I had seen her asleep and in the throes of passion. But I had never seen her angry. There was a glint of fire in her eye. A fire that could consume all the oxygen in the room in seconds, race up the walls and devastate everything in its path.

"I'm sorry. I . . ." What was I going to say? Was I going to change my mind? Even now I can't be sure. But there was no going back. Only the weak change their minds. A door had been closed. Nothing I said could matter now.

"Fuck you, Wylie. Get out."

Her disdain was withering. But I understood it. What else should I have expected?

I looked at her. We were beyond words. "Please give my best to your mother and Uncle Roger," I said feebly as I headed for the door.

"Get out," she repeated.

I walked through the front hall, skirting the living room, hearing the voices, the tinkling of Cosmo's piano, and let myself out. In an instant I had gone from being welcome in the bosom of this family to a pariah. I looked back to see if Cesca was watching, but she was nowhere to be seen.

The air outside was cool, the night clear. Overhead there were thousands of stars, but I ignored them, their beauty wasted on me. I was in shock. My brain still trying to comprehend what had just happened. For a while I just sat there in the front seat of Kate's Bug, staring dumbly through the windshield. Had I really just done what I had done? I felt sick to my stomach. The thought that I might never see Cesca again, hear her laughter, be swept up in her headlong rush through life, was impossible to imagine. Worse, I knew I had let her down. I had been tested and failed.

Eventually I started the car and backed it out, careful not to hit any of the other cars. A great tiredness came over me, and I remembered that I had actually had quite a lot to drink. I looked at my watch. It was only ten-thirty. I had called Kate just after ten. In the space of a half hour, less, my entire life had changed. I knew I should have been happy; after all, I had virtuously chosen Kate. But I wasn't. Not yet. Like a traitor, I still loved my betrayal. It would take time.

The car stood idling at the head of the driveway. I looked over at the Playhouse. There were no lights on. It was becoming increasingly apparent that there was no way I would be able to drive back to the city tonight. I had thought I could but now I realized it was impossible. I was too distracted, not sober enough. There was only one thing to do. I drove to my father's house.

It was too late to call. I knew my father and Patty were there but didn't want to disturb them. In the darkness I walked to the pool house and tried the door handle, but it was locked. The pool house, which had originally been a barn, had been recently converted by Patty. She had removed the old, heavy sliding door and replaced it with French doors. The kerosene stove that had provided heat had been ripped out. Changing rooms had been built. New furniture covered in expensive fabrics. My old bedroom in the former hayloft had also been upgraded. But now I couldn't get in. Even if I could, I knew my father had installed burglar alarms and hadn't shared the code with me. Retrieving an old blanket Kate kept in her car, I opted instead to sleep out on one of the chaises that lined the pool.

For a long time I sat there, playing back the last several hours in my head, worrying about whether I had just made the smartest decision or the worst mistake of my life. Eventually, under the stars, I fell asleep.

"WHAT ARE YOU DOING HERE?"

I opened my eyes. It was light. My father stood over me wearing a gray sweatshirt and holding a mug of coffee. He was always an early riser. Had his little rituals. Now that he was more or less retired, they gave structure to his life. Every morning he would get up, make himself coffee, and then with his Bernese mountain dog, Caesar, walk down the drive to retrieve the daily copies of *The Wall Street Journal* and *New York Times* that had only recently been delivered and lay there wrapped in blue plastic.

Evidently he had spotted my car and then me. The newspapers had not yet been collected.

I sat up and stretched. My neck was sore. The air was cool with the dampness of dawn. I figured it was around five-thirty. "Yesterday was Aurelio Bonet's funeral," I explained. "I wound up drinking more than I should have and decided to come here rather than drive back to the city. I didn't want to wake you so I just slept here."

My father grunted and nodded his head. "That was probably wise. Go on in the house and wash up," he said. "There's coffee in the pot. I'll be right back after I get the papers." He whistled for the large dog, and it followed him.

When he returned, I was in the kitchen, drinking the strong coffee he always made. He put the papers on the table. Then he scooped some dry dog food out for Caesar, who waited expectantly at his feet until the metal bowl was placed on the floor. Sitting down at the table, he opened the *Times*. He would have already scanned the front page of the *Journal* on the walk back up the drive. For a moment, we sat there in silence. "How's Kitty doing?" he finally asked, reluctantly snapping the *Times* shut.

"Not too well," I replied.

He nodded.

"I wasn't sure if you were going to be there," I said. "I thought you might be."

"I didn't really know the boy," he said. "And I haven't really been in touch with the family for a while now."

"But you see Roger."

"From time to time. We've gone in different directions. That's how it is."

I nodded. Then after a moment we both sipped our coffees. "I've made a decision about something."

"What's that?"

"I'm going to ask Kate to marry me."

He sipped his coffee again. "Huh. You sure?"

"Yes, I'm sure."

"Your call."

"That's it?"

He shrugged his shoulders. "You're a grown man now. You can do what you like. It's a big step. Try not to screw it up."

I looked at the clock above the stove. It was just six. "Okay," I said. "Thanks for the advice—and the coffee. I should get going if I'm going to make it to work."

"Okay. Drive safe."

"Thanks. Give my best to Patty."

"Will do."

I stood up and walked my now empty coffee mug to the sink. "Good seeing you," I said.

"Think you'll come out one weekend?"

"I'll try."

"Good luck with Kate. When are you going to ask her?"

"Tonight."

"Have you told your mother yet?"

"No. You're the first. I only made up my mind last night."

We shook hands, and I walked out of the kitchen to the front hall, opening and closing the door behind me. It was shaping up to be a beautiful day. If I drove fast and got ahead of the traffic, I could make it to work by nine. I might even have time to get home and shower quickly.

Once I was out on Route 27 heading west, the traffic moved briskly, and I passed the steady stream of pickups heading in the opposite direction to service the homes of the rich.

I had also surprised myself by telling my father about my intentions. To think about something is one thing, to announce it, especially to one's father, is another entirely. I had been thinking about Kate, my future with her, if there would be one, and if so what kind, for a while. But now it was obvious. There was no other course of action. I had been thinking about it last night while trying to get to sleep, alternately jumping from my shock at refusing Cesca to my conviction about Kate. I knew I would never conceive the same kind of passion for Kate that I felt for Cesca, and that was a good thing. After all, where had that passion gotten me? It had only produced brief moments of ecstasy followed by long periods of yearning and doubt. The more I thought about it, the more convinced I was that I had done the right thing. There could be no certainty with Cesca, no guarantee that in a week or maybe two she would not disappear on me again.

That night I took Kate out to dinner at a little bistro near her apartment. I had made no plans. There would be no gypsy violinists summoned at a strategic moment. No skywriter to form a proposal in the air. I didn't even have a ring. It was in many ways a perfectly ordinary evening. But I knew I had to do it. I told her about Lio's memorial, about Esther, about sleeping on my father's pool furniture. She laughed at that. After dinner we went back to her loft and made love. Later, when we were lying there together in the darkness, I asked her.

"Do you want to get married?"

"Are you proposing to me?"

"Yes."

She smiled and thought for a moment.

"All right," she said, rolling onto her front, so that her face was only inches from mine. "I'll marry you."

It is a wonderful feeling being engaged, especially during the first few weeks, when you both enjoy a kind of celebrity. Everyone is happy for you. Those already married congratulate you, and those who have yet to take the plunge regard you with a mixture of perplexity and awe. You are toasted at every dinner party—and some of the parties are even thrown expressly for your benefit. The other women coo over the ring, and the men smile knowingly and make lame jokes.

My mother, predictably, was thrilled. "Oh, darling, I'm so happy for you both," she trilled over the phone when I called her with the news. She was living in Richmond now, remarried to her second husband, a lean, handsome widower named Bill, who had retired as an Air Force general. "He was the one I should have married in the first place, darling," she had said. I had brought Kate down to meet her, and the two women had hit it off at once.

Those months were happy ones. Kate and I grew closer. I gave up the lease on my apartment and moved in with her. Work was going well. I still had to travel often, but we knew that merely indicated that I was moving ahead in the firm. Occasionally, Kate would join me. There were trips to London, one to Tokyo, where she met some old friends of mine. Everywhere we went, people were charmed by her. I knew how lucky I was to be marrying such a beautiful, warmhearted girl.

It was at a party in New York where I saw someone who looked familiar. We were in an apartment on Park Avenue with parquet floors and Chinese wallpaper. It was the birthday of a friend of Kate's whose husband worked at a large investment bank. It took me a few moments to place the face. The red hair. The pale skin. I remembered a summer day years before. Mutual dislike. Caro.

"I know that woman," I whispered to Kate.

By then Caro had caught my eye. Through the crowd, she came up to me. "Wylie, right?" she said. She was dressed in the theatrical way affected by many overweight women, the attempt to simultaneously deflect and conceal.

"Right," I replied, giving her a kiss on either cheek. "Gosh, Caro. Great to see you again." I introduced her to Kate and told her we were engaged.

"Congratulations," she said.

"Thank you."

"I haven't seen you in years," she said. "Isn't it awful about Cesca?"

"What do you mean?"

"You haven't heard?" Then slyly, "I always thought you two were so chummy."

"I, um, we haven't been in touch lately. What happened? Is she all right?"

"Hardly. I mean, I think she's all right now. But she tried to kill herself."

24

CARO CLAIMED NOT TO KNOW ALL THE DETAILS. WHAT SHE did know was that Cesca appeared to be especially upset by her brother's death. She drank more than ever. Where she had once been careless, she now became reckless, bordering on self-destructive. She ignored her family's pleas to stop. Then one night a suicide attempt. Fortunately the police had been called in time. It might have been pills. Possibly a razor blade. Caro wasn't sure. She had heard everything thirdhand. It had occurred several weeks before. Now Cesca was recuperating at a special hospital upstate. Caro didn't know where.

I had tried to conceal my shock from Kate, but she could tell I had been affected by Caro's news. "What a sad story about your friend," said Kate, as we were in a taxi heading home. "Are you all right? You've barely said a word since you heard about her."

"Sorry. Yes, I'm fine."

"You don't seem fine."

And of course I wasn't. I pretended that my reactions were

simply the natural ones you experience when you hear something sad about a mutual friend. Pity. Concern for them and their families. To a certain extent, curiosity and, most important, relief that the outcome was not worse.

But deep down I was also feeling guilt. I couldn't help but think I might have contributed to Cesca's behavior, and the idea pained me. That maybe if I had stayed that night, none of this would have happened. Part of me chided myself for being conceited enough to think that Cesca could be hurt enough by me to slip into a spiral of self-destruction. The other part assigned myself a lesser role: that I was merely a single straw out of the many straws that had broken her back. Regardless of the degree of my culpability, there was no denying that she had reached out to me, and I wasn't there for her.

Of course, I didn't know all the facts. I didn't know what other troubles might have been plaguing her. In hindsight it was possible to see that her wild behavior had always been erratic, manic, heedless, and a symptom of mental unrest. Yet it was these very qualities that seemed most to define her. Her boldness, her passions, her self-sufficiency, her unwillingness to be tied down to any one man or thing. In what had been a life spent desperately pursuing pleasure and avoiding pain, it was obvious that at some point something inside her would break. It was an impossible way to live. Such expectations are unrealistic, and eventually they reveal themselves to be false. The truth can be shattering. It would have only been a matter of time. Even if I had chosen her over Kate, even if she had by some miracle stayed with me, like that of an object thrown into the air, her fall was inevitable.

"Is there something you want to talk about?" asked Kate when we were getting ready for bed.

I had still never told Kate, or anyone else for that matter, the truth about my relationship with Cesca. At first, I had refrained from doing so because I was unsure of my commitment to Kate and wanted to keep Cesca a secret, aware of the power she held over me and not yet ready to forsake it. Then, after our engagement, feeling secure in our bond, I didn't feel the need to bring it up. It seemed extraneous, pointless, like paying in Confederate money. At times Cesca's image would come into my head, particularly when I passed by a place I had been with her. But these images rarely lingered. Not for a moment did I regret the choice I had made.

I sighed as I hung up my trousers. "I was disturbed by what that woman Caro told me about Cesca Bonet. How she had tried to kill herself."

"Yes, it's awful. The poor thing."

"Her uncle is my godfather, Roger. Remember? You met him at Aurelio's opening."

"Yes. He was charming. Very grabby."

I smiled. "That's him. I'm going to give him a call and see if I can find out what happened. It's just so hard to believe."

"Why?"

"Why? Well, you met her just that one time, at Lio's opening as well."

Kate nodded. "She was very beautiful. You told me you had a crush on her when you were younger."

"That's right. I did." It would have been madness for me to confess everything. I had never cheated on Kate. That was the point. No woman wants to know she has a rival. Nor did I think she needed to know I had faced an agonized decision in the kitchen that night in Amagansett. How close it could have gone either way. "The family has always been so good to me. First Lio and now this. They must be going through hell. I feel terribly that I didn't know."

"So give Roger a call in the morning," she said. "But I'm really not sure what you can do. I mean, wouldn't it just be nicer to write a letter? Sometimes people don't want to be bothered—although it can be nice to know that other people care. I mean, unless it was a very close friend, that's what I'd do."

I leaned over and kissed her on the forehead. "You're a genius," I said. I was continually impressed by her clear-eyed approach to life. Few problems were so big they couldn't be dealt with. Quite often the solutions were surprisingly easy. Like a sailor, she had developed her emotional sea legs early living with such a turbulent father. This bill has to be paid now, that one can wait. Don't answer the phone. Call the doctor. Make sure there's food in the fridge. Keep hidden when he's lost too much at the track.

"I think I'm going to stay up for a bit," I said. "You go on to sleep."

Kate lay there, her cheek on the pillow, her blue eyes watching me. Was she suspicious of something? Did she know somehow that I was leaving out the most important part of the story? "All right," she said, turning onto her other side. "Good night. Try to be quiet when you come to bed."

I poured myself a whisky and sat for a long time staring out of the window. Trying to imagine what had driven Cesca to such a desperate act. Wondering what, if anything, I should do—or could have done.

My first instinct was to see her. To reassure myself that she was all right and, most important, that she did not hold me to blame. I was aware of the vanity of this presumption, though, and suspected that she might not want to see me. That having let her down once, there would be no second chances. This was all assuming that I would even be allowed to see her. I had no idea where she was or what condition she was in or what constraints had been placed upon her. I wasn't family. I wasn't a husband. I had no legal connection to her. And what would I say to her? What would she want to hear? But selfishly, I knew I needed absolution. I couldn't imagine what she would want. But I knew I had to try to find out.

The next morning, after a fitful night, I called Roger from my office.

"Wylie?" he said, answering. "How are you, young man? To what do I owe the pleasure of your call?" He sounded as chipper and full of bonhomie as ever, even if the voice was a bit reedier than it had once been.

"Good morning, Uncle Roger. I'm sorry to bother you, but I was at a cocktail party last night, and I saw someone who told me that Cesca had tried to kill herself. Is that true?"

"Ah, yes. Terrible, terrible. She's all right now, thank God."

"Have you seen her?"

"I? No, no. But her mother tells me she is being well looked after."

"Do you happen to know where Cesca is? I wanted to write her a letter."

"That would be very kind. I am sure she'd appreciate hearing from you." He then gave me the name of a private institution upstate. "It's a lovely place, apparently. Caters to a select clientele. Rock stars, actors. That sort of thing. I don't have the address, but I am sure you can look it up."

I thanked Roger, asked him to give my regards to Diana, and hung up the phone. I then removed a box of personal stationery from my desk and wrote a short, cautious note to Cesca:

> *Dear Cesca,*
>
> *I saw your friend Caro last night at a party and she told me what had happened. I hope you are feeling better now and getting some rest. Today I spoke to your uncle Roger and he told me where to write to you. I hope that's all right. I feel terribly that the last time we saw each other you were angry at me. I know I let you down and I wish I hadn't. It is the last thing I*

would ever want to do. I don't know if you still are angry, but if
you aren't please let me know if there's anything I can do for you.
For that matter, let me know if there's anything I can do even if
you still are angry with me.

Wylie

The next week, I received a letter in reply, written in Cesca's
schoolgirlish hand. I had put my office as my return address.

Dear Tricky Wylie,

Thank you for your letter. It really cheered me up. Yes, it's
been a rough couple of months since Lio died. I'm in here because
they say I tried to kill myself, but it's really not true. I did think
about it, though, but that was only as far as I got. I mean,
doesn't everyone think about it at one point or another? But it's
something else entirely to act on it. Anyway, I'll tell you the
whole story sometime. The point is that everyone seems to think
I was and, to be honest, I had been behaving pretty badly so I
suppose, deep down, they were right in a way. That I was trying
to kill the pain by being self-destructive. And that if I had kept
up the way I was living I could have very easily killed myself
one way or another. My doctor says it was a cry for help. Isn't
that what they always say? How corny. My God, you'd think I
could show a little more originality than that. Anyway, I was
being incredibly stupid. I have no intention of doing that sort of
thing again. In fact, I haven't had a drink in three weeks and
obviously no drugs either. They let us smoke cigarettes here and
I still haven't been able to kick them yet but then again I am not
really sure I want to. How are you, Wylie? Are you still with
that pretty girl? If not, you should tell Cosmo because I could tell
he really fancied her.

You know what I'd like more than anything? For you to
come up for a visit. Except for Mare, and Carmen and Cosmo

when they can make it because they're both frightfully busy, I've had no visitors. I've alienated so many people in my life that there really aren't all that many I'd actually want to see—or who would want to see me. Ironic, isn't it? I'd like to think that even after everything maybe you'd be one of those people who would want to see me. I know I'd like to see you.

They'd prefer it if I didn't leave the grounds yet but maybe we could have a picnic or something if the weather isn't too foul. As you can imagine, the food here is pretty ghastly. Nothing like Paris, that's for sure. You remember Paris, Tricky Wylie? We had fun there, didn't we? I'd love a fresh baguette and maybe some lovely cheeses and a cold chicken. Yum. No wine though, alas.

Come whenever you can. I'm not going anywhere. Ha ha.

T'estimo. Adéu.

C

P.S.

Saturdays are best.

P.P.S.

Bring cigarettes. They cost a fortune here.

P.P.P.S.

Marlboro reds. X

I reread the letter several times. Cesca's personality crackled off the page. It was more than I had hoped for. Much more, too much. I had sought absolution and reassurance, but what I got was open, friendly, exculpating. But she was also vulnerable, a side of Cesca I had rarely seen.

There was no question that I would go and see her. I felt I owed her that much. But I told Kate, although I did not show her the letter.

"I'm not sure why you need to go up and see her," she said.

She was in the kitchen, chopping onions and garlic. On the stove was a large copper pot. "How close were you?"

Avoiding the question, I poured us each a glass of white wine and placed one next to her on the counter. "From what I understand, she hasn't had many visitors. She's probably lonely. It must be depressing being in one of those places. I can only imagine how important it would be to see a familiar face, to be reminded of the world outside."

"Yes, very sad. But why you?"

"It's a favor to the family. I've known them . . ."

"Yes, I know. You've known them your whole life. They're lovely people, et cetera, et cetera."

"There's no need to talk like that."

"Isn't there? I don't know. It just strikes me as strange that you'd be doing this."

"But you won't stop me?"

"Stop you?" she said, putting down her knife. "Of course I won't stop you. You'll do what you think best."

"Thank you," I said, walking over to her and kissing her. "I love you, you know that? No one else. If you had an old friend who was shut up in a loony bin and you wanted to go see him, I wouldn't mind one bit."

"Not even if he was really sexy?" She smiled.

"Not even if he was really sexy."

That Saturday I was driving up the Taconic in a light drizzle. Shortly after noon, I exited near Claverack and headed east down a succession of country roads. Eventually I spotted a small, discreet sign with the name of the clinic on it. I turned up the driveway and after several moments driving through dense woodland saw ahead of me a large, pleasant-looking, white, Federal-style clapboard house with a gambreled roof surrounded by deciduous and evergreen trees and a smooth expanse of lawn. Another sign read, VISITOR PARKING, and I pulled into the lot.

Most of the cars were late-model imports, primarily BMWs and Mercedes with New York and Connecticut plates. From the passenger seat, I removed a canvas bag that contained the lunch Kate had helped me make that morning and followed the path to the main building. Still more signs pointed the way to the theater, ceramics studio, community center, gym, and something called Potter Hall. I passed several people, who all greeted me and smiled. By now, the rain had stopped, and the earth had the rich, fecund smell of early spring.

I walked up the front steps, crossed a long porch with white rocking chairs scattered on it, and entered an airy lobby. To my surprise, it seemed more like a country inn than a psychiatric clinic. There were Oriental rugs on the floors, plants, chintz-covered window seats, and a fire in the hearth. On the walls were landscapes and portraits, I presumed, of the clinic's founders and former administrators; men with mustaches, earnest-looking women with strands of pearls. I hadn't been sure what to expect. There were no security doors, no large men in white uniforms. The air smelled vaguely of potpourri and wood-smoke. In the corner a couple sat on a love seat drinking coffee. A man in his forties or so—I couldn't tell if he was a patient or a visitor—was reading the *New York Times*. Behind the reception counter stood a short, round, middle-aged woman wearing a blue cardigan. Reading glasses hung from a thin chain over her ample bosom. She smiled and said, "Good morning. How may I help you?"

"Good morning," I replied. "I'm here to see Francesca Bonet."

"Ah, yes." She lifted her glasses to her eyes and consulted her ledger. "Mr. Rose, is it?"

"Yes."

"Wonderful. She's expecting you. She asked you to meet her in the Garden Room. It's just through there," she said, nodding her head toward the back of the house.

I thanked the woman and walked in the direction indicated. There were several other groups in the room. Saturday was visiting day obviously, and there was a low hum of conversation. The far wall was a row of French doors that overlooked a wide terrace and, below, a formal garden. As in the lobby, there were carpets on the floor, oil paintings on the walls, and the room was painted in a reassuring neutral color with white trim on the millwork. Directly in front of me was a trestletable supporting several electric urns labeled COFFEE, DECAFFEINATED, and HOT WATER, as well as rows of white mugs and little baskets containing tea bags, sugar and sweeteners, stirrers, and napkins.

I found Cesca in the corner on a large striped sofa. She was reading a book, but when she looked up and saw me, she leapt to her feet and smiling widely shouted, "Wylie!" Everyone else in the room stopped talking as she threw her arms around me and hugged me tightly.

25

SHE HAD BEEN IN BAD SHAPE. THERE HAD BEEN DRUGS. A lot of drugs. And men. A lot of men. She had sold her store and traveled. She had returned to Barcelona. To reconnect with Lio and walk in his footsteps. But the city had seemed devastatingly empty without him.

After a week she fled. Morocco was first, but she then returned to the States and went to Los Angeles. She spent the first few weeks at the Beverly Wilshire and later rented an apartment in Santa Monica. Her accountant called to tell her she was spending too much money, but she didn't care. She remembered wild nights in Palm Springs, driving down in an open car, high on peyote, the warm night air washing over her as she sang into the darkness. There were parties that lasted for days at a producer's house in Malibu. There were famous movie stars. B-listers. Prostitutes. Drug dealers driving up in Bentleys. Swimming naked, having sex in hot tubs with multiple partners. She would wake up with strange men in strange cities. Once in Las Vegas, another time San Francisco. Her clothes torn. One morning she saw she had a black eye. Other times men would steal her money. She didn't care. Clothes could be replaced. Bruises healed. Money replenished. And then she'd go back out and do it all over again. All the nightclubs knew her. She spent thousands of dollars. She crashed her car and bought a new one. At some point, nothing seemed to matter much anymore. This is what she told me.

"There was one night. I was back in New York. I was staying at the Plaza. I had been out with an old friend, but now she had gone, and there were a bunch of people up in my room doing blow. It was late, and I remember looking around and realizing I didn't know any of them. What's more I didn't want to. The whole thing suddenly seemed so vile, so pointless. Suddenly I felt that *I* had become vile and pointless. I just wanted to sleep, and I asked them to leave. At first they wouldn't. They just laughed and ignored me and kept on partying. So I started screaming for all of them to get the fuck out. I took off one of my shoes and smashed the mirror that the coke was on. Coke and glass went everywhere. After they left, I found myself staring out the window at the park. I was on the fifteenth floor."

She paused.

"It seemed so obvious. Just lean out a little. You know? It would be so easy. I would be dead, and everything would stop. So I climbed out onto the ledge. The park looked so pretty. I wasn't scared at all, I remember. But then a woman who had been in my room returned. She had left her purse behind. She saw me on the ledge and started screaming. "Oh my God! Oh my God! Help! Help!" You should have heard her. At first I shouted at her to shut up, but by then it was too late. By then I had come back in. The mood had passed. The thought of falling silently to my death had a kind of elegiac simplicity to it. Other guests came. Hotel security. Finally, of course, the police. But once she started screaming, it became a spectacle, something public and tawdry, which was just exactly what I didn't want. They took me to Bellevue that night for observation anyway. It didn't help that the police found traces of coke on the floor. Fortunately, Mare has a good lawyer. A couple of days later, here I was."

We were outside at a little table. The weather was cool, and we sat with our hands in our coat pockets. Cesca had gone back inside to get paper towels from one of the bathrooms to wipe off the little puddles of rain that still remained on the chairs.

She was smoking a cigarette from the carton I had brought. The food sat mostly uneaten in its containers. She nibbled at a piece of the bread and toyed with a drumstick. I asked her if she was hungry and she said she wasn't, at least not yet. She didn't have much of an appetite these days. Maybe later. But you go ahead. I told her I'd wait too. There was a slight tremor in her hand. Lines under her eyes. Her cheeks looked thinner. Her lips chapped. Still, she radiated beauty, like a flame burning out through a shadow lantern. Seeing her brought back a flood of memory. Unexpected, unrequested, but unavoidable. The kicked pebble that precipitates an avalanche. Within seconds whole towns can be wiped out, lives changed forever.

"How are you feeling now?" I asked.

She looked at me, sighed, and flicked her cigarette into the bushes. "Honestly? Very tired. But I don't feel like killing myself anymore—if I ever really did."

"That's good."

"Though there are times when I wouldn't mind killing a few other people." She smiled and I laughed. "Some of the people here are full-blown loonies. And that includes the staff. One of my doctors is desperate to sleep with me. But it's nothing I can't handle." She lit another cigarette. "Maybe I'll let him." She shrugged. Then, "I haven't had sex in weeks. I don't always mind not having the drugs and the booze, but I would like a good screw."

I looked away.

"Oh, Wylie, don't be bashful. We can go behind the bushes."

"I . . ."

"I'm just kidding. Actually I have almost no libido either. It's all because of the damn meds," she said. "They're supposed to make me feel mellow."

"Do they?"

She shrugged again. "I don't know. Sometimes I think they just make me boring, but, given the circumstances, maybe that's not such a bad thing."

"You could never be boring."

She smiled. "Thank you, Wylie. You always were sweet."

"How much longer will you be here?"

"I can leave anytime I want. It's an open hospital. No locked doors. I could get in your car with you and go, if I wanted."

"Do you want to?"

"Oh sure. In a lot of ways. But I've always had a thing about commitment, haven't I? I mean, I've never been very good at it. So I'm trying. My doctor and I have been talking about that. I think I'm going to at least stick things out here. Maybe if I can do that, well, who knows? Maybe when I get out, I'll get a cat or hamster or something. Start small." She smiled.

"That's good. So when do you think you will leave?"

"A few more weeks at least. Frankly, I'm in no hurry to leave. It's nice here. Quiet. You don't have to think. I spend my days in therapy: talking to my shrink, in groups, weaving, doing tai chi. I've made a few friends. If they had wine here, it would be perfect."

"Do you still want to drink?"

"You sound like my doctor," she laughed. "Of course I still want to drink. You never lose the craving, apparently. But you do learn to manage it. Some times are harder than others, like around dinnertime. I mean, could you imagine going to Paris and not drinking wine or champagne? I mean, what the hell?"

"What will you do? Will you go back to New York?"

"Well, that's kind of just it, Wylie. You've hit the nail on the head. I don't really know what to do next. So I'm just hiding out here, really. Afraid to do anything."

"But you could just go home, couldn't you? Out to Amagansett?"

She nodded her head. "I suppose. It just seems so pointless. What am I going to do there? Write bad poetry? Take a cooking class? I can only walk on the beach so many hours a day. Oh, I'm thinking about something else maybe."

"Like what?"

"I'm not really sure yet, but I have some ideas. I don't want to tell you in case I don't end up doing it, and you'll think I'm even more of a fraud than I already am."

"I don't know what you're going to do—and maybe you don't either. But that's not the point. The point is that the world is better with Cesca Bonet in it than not, I hope you realize that at least."

She nodded her head back and forth, and sighed. "Is it, Wylie? Is it really? Tell me. What have I got that's so great, huh? I mean, what have I done? Cosmo's a successful musician. Carmen's a doctor. Lio was a painter. They all did things. They all contributed. Made the world a better place. A more beautiful place. Me? I just flit about. Never serious about anything or anyone."

"You're being unfair to yourself."

She squinted at me for a moment, then looked away. With her left hand, she removed a thin lock of her hair that been caught in her mouth. "Am I? I don't think so."

"Look, just because you can't point to a canvas on the wall and say, 'There. That's mine,' doesn't mean you haven't done anything. Some people have different gifts, different talents."

"What have I got?"

"You have a gift that is more unique than being a painter, a musician, or even a doctor."

She looked at me. "What is that?"

"Think of the thousands of people who go to med school every year or paint. Most of them will just be mediocre. And that's okay because, as you say, they're making the world a better place, even if it's in a small way. But they don't have the gift you do, which is to inspire."

"Inspire?" She snorted derisively. "Sure. I inspire people to get fucked up."

"No. That's not what I meant. You enter a room and people notice you immediately. You have an energy, a beauty, that I've never seen in anyone else. You have inspired me. You always have, ever since we were kids. Whatever I have done, I have done for you. There was never a time when I didn't want your approval, your attention. Your love. Your image was always in front of me. Nothing meant more to me. And I'm sure I'm not the only one. You may not be a painter, but you can inspire painters. You may not be a poet, but you can inspire poets. It's because you contain the life they want to capture. They can only reflect what you are."

She kept looking at me, a serious expression on her face. Then she picked up my hand and squeezed it. "Thank you," she whispered.

We sat there for several minutes holding hands, saying nothing. Eventually she said: "You know, they force you to strip away your life, places like this. To tear down the artifice and see yourself for who you are, and only then can you begin to rebuild yourself. What I've realized is that my whole life has been empty. I've been able to stick at nothing. Commit to nothing. Apparently I couldn't even commit suicide properly," she added with a wry smile. "Now I have decided that I have to commit to something. I can't be a fuckup my whole life."

"What have you decided to commit to?"

She laughed. "That's just it. I'm not sure yet." She paused

and then looked at me. "Is it too late for us? Maybe that's it. What do you say, Wylie?"

I didn't say anything but instead just stared at my feet.

She laughed again. "I thought so."

It began to rain once more. Soft droplets. "Come on. Let's go for a walk," said Cesca, standing up.

The clinic was situated on about one hundred acres of land. Like many such institutions, it had once been a private estate. The old barns and stables had all been converted. Cesca pointed out the greenhouses and organic garden, where patients grew the vegetables that were used in the kitchen. We came to a large pond that was fenced off with wire. Signs warned against swimming. A family of ducks swam placidly on the surface. "They had to do that to prevent people from drowning themselves," said Cesca. "But I don't think that would stop anyone who was really serious about killing themselves, you know? It's one of the things about this place that makes me laugh. They pretend they're doing so much to help but really all they're doing is putting up a little bit of wire."

She laughed and shook her head.

"You don't still think about killing yourself, do you?"

"God no. It was a spur-of-the-moment thing. It appealed to my romantic nature."

She put her arm through mine. It felt so natural. That was the way things had always been with us. I had never been so comfortable with anyone in my life. We just slipped into a groove as though we had never been apart. "So how are you, Tricky Wylie? What's new with you?"

"I'm fine. Work's good."

"And love? Are you still with that pretty blonde Cosmo was so mad about?"

"Yes. Kate. Um, as a matter of fact, we're engaged."

"You are? Congratulations." She stopped and faced me,

smiling, and grabbed both of my hands. "That's wonderful news."

"Thank you." I was blushing with relief.

"When's the big day?"

"June. In New York."

"Good for you. Poor Cosmo," she said, shaking her head and smiling. "He'll be so disappointed."

We walked on a little farther. "That's why you left that night, isn't it?" she asked after several moments of silence.

"Yes," I conceded.

"I thought it might be something like that."

"I'm sorry. I . . ."

"Don't. Don't say that if you don't mean it."

"I do mean it. I am sorry I couldn't be there for you. But I had to make a choice."

She nodded. "So I guess we know whom you chose."

"It's not like that."

"Well, you're the one who's engaged to someone else."

I stopped and turned to her. "Damn it. That's not fair. I asked you to marry me. A number of times. And each time you shot me down. Remember Paris? That really sucked. I honestly thought you were going to marry me, and then you just disappeared. Do you know what that felt like? So don't go around acting as though I never asked. Because I did."

"I was wrong."

"What were you wrong about?"

She laughed lightly. "Oh, I've been wrong about a lot of things. But what was I wrong about exactly with you? I should have treated you better. And I should have said yes—and meant it."

"It's too late now. I'm already engaged. The wedding's in a few months."

"I understand. It's my fault."

This was not what I wanted to hear. Not now. For years it

was all I had wanted. Nothing more. I gazed about the woods, the silvery gray of the still-barren tree trunks. The milky white complexion of the sky. The compact dirt of the path at my feet. The dead, wet leaves lining the forest floor. Anything to avoid looking at Cesca.

"Don't do this. Please."

"Don't do what? We're encouraged here to apologize for our mistakes. It's part of the treatment. I know I've hurt you, and I want to apologize."

I looked at her.

"So, yes, I apologize for the way I treated you, Wylie. I know I played with your heart and took your love for granted. I guess I knew I could because there was so much love from you it would always last. For what it's worth, it made me feel wonderful. That no matter what I did, someone out there would always love me. Who forgave me. It was an incredible comfort. A luxury you can't imagine. It was like a wonderful jewel you keep in a special box and only wear on special occasions. But that doesn't mean I didn't love you too. I want you to know that. I did love you. Very much. I still do. At least in my own way."

I took a deep breath and exhaled. Our eyes met, searching. "I don't know what to say."

"You don't have to say anything."

"I've already hurt one girl because of you."

"And I apologize for that too."

"I'm not going to do it again. I can't."

"I understand."

"I let myself believe you in the past. Trusted you, and each time you just pissed on it. On me."

"Is that how you feel?"

"How the hell else am I supposed to feel?"

"How about thinking about things from my point of view, Wylie? It's always you, you, you. That's the one thing about you that always bothered me. You were always so passive, playing the victim and blaming other people when things didn't work out for you. You never thought about me as a real person, a person with flesh and blood and insecurities and a fucked-up childhood. I was always beautiful Cesca up on a pedestal to you. Don't deny it. If I ran away from you, maybe there was a reason. If I ran away from you, maybe you should have tried a little harder to run after me. Haven't you ever thought that it was always me coming to you? When did you ever come to me?"

She was angry now. Her chin thrust forward, her dark eyes flashing, defiant. I stared at her, stung by her accusation, pierced by my own vanity and ignorance.

"Oh God," I said. "I'm such a fool."

"Yes, you are, Wylie," said Cesca, her voice gentler. "You are a fool. But you're not alone. I'm a fool too. I just didn't want you to think that I was just a bitch."

"So what does this mean?"

"What do you want it to mean?"

"I don't know. I'm too confused. What do you want from me? What can I do?"

"I don't want you to do anything. You're engaged. You should marry her. That's what I want you to do. Have a family. Be happy." She gave me her little half smile.

"But I still have feelings for you."

"Good. I'm happy to hear that. If you loved me as you say you did, then you'd be a rotten sort of a person if you didn't. You can love two people at the same time, but you can't be in love with two people at the same time. It doesn't work like that. You've made your choice. It's a good one. You've got to grow up, Wylie. With me you'll always be a boy. That beautiful boy I knew so long ago. But now it's time for you to be a man."

I nodded my head. Knowing that what she said was right. "Thank you," I said.

"Come on," she said. "I'll walk you back to your car. I have to help prepare dinner tonight. It's part of our therapy. We all take turns in the kitchen. Can you imagine? Me? I've threatened to make paella. Pare sent me a recipe, but I can only imagine what a disaster it will be. At least, it'll be one of the few nights here when the food isn't some wretched vegetarian meal. That's the one thing about depressives and addicts. They really suck at cooking."

We both laughed, and once again she slipped her arm through mine. "Thank you so much for coming," she said. "I can't tell you what it means. Sometimes you just feel completely cut off and forgotten up here. As though life outside has continued on without you, and you've just stopped."

We retrieved the now-soaking bag with the mostly uneaten food in it. "Sorry you went to all that trouble," she said, laughing. "What I had was delicious."

I laughed too, holding up the soggy loaf. "Maybe you could use this to feed some of the ducks on the pond?"

"All right. We really aren't supposed to, but everyone does."

At the car, she said, "You know, there are a lot of good things I've learned up here. It's been very helpful. Taking responsibility for my actions, learning to confront my fears. For a long time, I didn't think anyone should love me. Or that I should love anyone. But I realize now you made me think otherwise. I can never thank you enough for that. What we had, no matter how fucked up it was in so many ways, was actually pretty special. I'll never forget that."

"Cesca . . ."

"Shhh," she said, leaning forward and kissing me lightly on the lips. Not a passionate kiss. A loving one. An intimate one. A parting one. "Don't say anything. Now just get out of here."

I looked at her. The familiar face, the lovely brown eyes. I had always seen beauty, passion. Something more. Something intangible, unattainable. Now I saw something wiser, kinder. She smiled faintly and nodded her head in farewell. "When will I see you again?" I asked. "Will you let me know when you're back in the city?"

"We'll see," she said. "You know I was never very good at planning that far ahead. Good-bye, Tricky Wylie. Take care of yourself and have a happy life. Thanks again for coming. You have no idea how much it meant to me."

She turned and walked away, back up the path to the main building. I watched her until she entered the house. At the door she stopped and gave a small wave. Then she was gone.

26

Shortly after Kate and I returned from our honeymoon, I received a letter from Cesca. It was postmarked from Barcelona:

> *Dear Tricky Wylie,*
>
> *Just a short note to congratulate you on your wedding and let you know I am fine. I am back in Barcelona but behaving myself (if you can believe it!!!). There is a hospice here for people dying of AIDS and I have started working there. It's pretty gruesome in many ways—as you can imagine—but also surprisingly wonderful. I feel like everyone here I am helping is Lio. I miss him every day but now I can still feel connected to him. I miss you too. Don't worry about me. I have never been happier.*
>
> *Molt amor,*
>
> *C*

And I was happy for her, of course, and relieved, but also a little skeptical. The notion of Cesca washing out bedpans or bathing the dying was as out of character as if she had written to say she was taking holy orders. I imagined that before too long she would grow bored with this new project, and the next thing I would hear from her was that she had taken up with a South American playboy and moved to Marbella.

But I underestimated her. Or, more accurately, maybe I was only now seeing an aspect of her I never knew existed—an aspect even she had not known about. She was like an athlete who had spent years building up certain muscles, while ignoring others. Now she was developing those muscles as well. And she was doing so with the zeal of a convert. It seemed to consume her, as though she was trying to atone for her wild years with an excess of selflessness, desperate to correct her deficits and bring her account back to zero.

To my relief, she was not overly pious about it. She wasn't like one of those reformed drinkers or meat eaters who become rabid teetotalers or vegans. She knew that not everyone would be able to, or even want to, do what she did. And, I think, that made her secretly proud, even if she never said as much. To take the hard road, to deny oneself ease or comfort or pleasure, was her penance.

Yet at the same time maybe I shouldn't have been so surprised. Cesca had always thrown herself into whatever she was doing, as determined as a dog with a bone. It was in her nature to be immoderate. It was a variation of Izzy's theme. If she was going to do it, whether that meant making love, breaking hearts, living the high life, or helping the dying, she was going to be great at it. Like a fearless gambler, she went all in.

Where once I had sent her letters as though into the void, posting them like prayers I never expected would be answered, she now became a lively, frequent, and often unprompted correspondent. Once a month or so for several years, a letter or card would arrive, their contents without presumption or agenda.

Some of her notes were quite short, a line on the back of a post-card. Others could be quite chatty and amusing, often with little drawings in the margins, and they formed a sort of long-running serial about her life. I have kept them all, but here's just one example:

Dear Tricky Wylie,

I hope this finds you and Kate well. It has been a good month here. I had a lovely visit from Carmen last week, who has grown into such a strong and wonderful woman. She was over here for a conference on AIDS—you know she has become quite an authority on the subject now, and I was very proud and impressed when I went to see her deliver a paper to the assembly. I kept thinking, That's my sister! That's my sister! *I remember when she was young and was terrified of spiders, even the most harmless daddy longlegs, and how I would have to hold her hand tightly and lead her trembling past a cobweb or scoop the spider up in my hands and take it out of the room before she could enter. I would never kill them because Pare had once told me that it was bad luck to kill a spider and besides they were the artists of the insect world, each web a miracle of creation. But now she is all grown up. She got married last year—did I tell you? I can't remember. It was a small affair. She emailed me afterwards apologizing for not inviting me. That it had been a spur-of-the-moment thing. One day she and her husband— David is his name. I haven't met him yet but he sounds lovely. He's also a doctor—they just went to the city clerk's office on their lunch break and got married. I probably wouldn't have gone anyway, you know? Not that I wouldn't have enjoyed it but my work here keeps me so busy and so many people need me that I don't see how I could have taken the time. Anyway, she has the best news of all: She is pregnant! When she told me we just laughed and cried at the same time, jumping up and down like a couple of lunatics. The baby is due in five months. How exciting! (When are you and Kate going to have a baby??? Quit wasting time!!!)*

I do have some sad news though. You remember my telling you about one of my patients, Alfonso? He died yesterday. It was a blessing really because he was in such discomfort. You could tell that once he would have been the most beautiful man—like Aurelio but blond—but now wasted and covered in lesions. He was good-humored about it until the end. I would joke with him that if he preferred I could get him a handsome male nurse to wash him but he would laugh and say, "No, I'm glad it's you. I wouldn't want the sight of my enormous cock to distract him from his duties." We would laugh about that and he'd make bitchy comments about some of the staff, even some of the patients. He had been an actor (remember?) and had friends coming by all the time. At the end he declined fast. So many of them do. When some first arrive they seem as though they could be here for months, but inevitably the end comes quickly. At night I just sit up and pray and cry for them. I feel so helpless sometimes. It's like trying to soak up the ocean with a sponge. When I wake up on those mornings it can be quite hard, but I go back and there's always someone there who needs me urgently. Death is both inexhaustible and impatient.

Everyone else is well. Mare is getting older, of course, but she is still as mad and charming as ever. She keeps promising to come. I see Pare all the time. He lives just outside of the city with his new family. My half sister Eulália is a perfect little angel. I am very fond of his new wife, Anna, too. He is mellowing now and hangs around his house like an old tomcat whose prowling days are over, happy with his memories of all the mice he has consumed over the years. In his old age he is even enjoying a modest kind of celebrity. There was an article about him in El Punt *and a local gallery has been selling his work, which makes him very pleased, as you can imagine. Cosmo just keeps doing better and better. Since he bought his house here up the coast I see a lot of him too. When he isn't on tour we have dinner regularly. I wish he had a girl. Too bad he didn't meet Kate first. No telling how things might have turned out, eh? Ha! Roger is just the same as always. He's not much of a letter writer but that's what Mare tells me.*

Well, that's my news. Write to me and tell me about yourself. There are times I miss Amagansett so much.

Més petons i abraçades,

C

I did write to her, but my own life was, while without drama, unfolding as lives often do, taking natural courses much as water from the spring runoff will flow down a dry streambed. We had our modest bourgeois adventures: Caribbean vacations, dinners with friends, small victories at work. The quotidian yet meaningful bricks that build up most lives. Kate did become pregnant. We moved out of her loft, which was fine for a couple but impractical for a family, and, returning to my roots, even if I had never truly strayed, bought a modest apartment on the Upper East Side.

While we gave up unfettered space and the daily glamour of living in Soho, our new apartment, in a fine old prewar building just east of Lexington, brought us a fireplace, a doorman, proximity to Central Park and good schools, and solid doors that we could close. I was now entering into the adult life, complete with its joys and sacrifices, my youth left behind me like a beacon for those coming after. Time, which I once seemed to have an abundance of, contracted, wearing down imperceptibly, like bone on bone.

I saw Cesca again. It was in Barcelona, several years after my marriage. I had been invited to speak at an architectural conference there. Kate stayed in New York with our son, Mitchell. I had told her I would be seeing Cesca, and she'd voiced no objection. But I still hadn't told her the whole truth about our relationship. Kate had her baby, after all. That is the purest bond. Everything else is secondary. My father, too, was smitten with his namesake. He and Patty invited themselves over frequently to our apartment, and if we were not regular weekend visitors to East Hampton, my father would call and ask, "When are you bringing my grandson out again?"

When I arrived in Barcelona, I was a more benign, staunch, and devoted man than I had been in my youth. I was moderately contented with my life, my growing family, my career. I was in my mid-thirties, going soft in the middle. I was beginning to notice resemblances to my father from when I was a child. He was about my age when I was born. My legs were his. Sometimes when I passed a shop window, it seemed as though I was seeing him in the glass.

The questions that had once dogged me had grown trivial as more serious matters took their place. When I thought of my youthful ambitions to be a painter, I shook my head in disbelief, barely able to recognize that person in the one I had become.

My hotel in Barcelona was old, elegant, the furniture in need of re-covering. It was the first time I had been back to the city since that August years before when I had slept on Aurelio's floor. Then it had been summer, now it was winter, the streets outside my room overlooking the Gran Via de las Corts Catalanes were wet with rain, the trees on the wide boulevard barren of leaves. The chairs outside the cafés empty. On the pavement Barcelonans hurried by, wrapped in scarves and heavy coats against what would be back in New York mild weather. I pressed my forehead against the glass, feeling its coolness.

It was my second day after arriving. Until then my time had been taken up with conference matters: meetings, panel discussions, breakfasts, lunches, breakout sessions, an official dinner. I had come with the founder of my firm, an elegant, white-haired man in his late seventies. He was staying in a palatial suite several floors above me. His shirts were handmade in Milan, his shoes in London. Each spring he taught a course at MIT. He served on important committees and boards. The firm was his whole life. It had cost him two marriages. His children barely knew him. Despite his age, he still traveled constantly. Seoul, Tokyo, Berlin, San Francisco. He was one of those men to whom work was a tonic. It kept him young. If he stopped, he would die. I knew I would never be him, even though part of me wished I could.

There was a client dinner that night, and I was expected to attend but had carved out a hole in my schedule in the late afternoon. I had called Cesca shortly after I landed. A woman answered in Spanish, and I asked to speak to Cesca Bonet. "Ah, okay, *sí, un momento.*" I heard the receiver being placed on its side and the faint tapping of heels on a floor. A few minutes later, I heard a voice say, *"Sí? Això és Cesca."* Yes? This is Cesca.

The sound of her slightly raspy, amused voice on the phone after so long came as a shock. Real time had passed, but suddenly everything seemed familiar again, as though it had only been a day or so since we had spoken. "Cesca, it's Wylie."

"Wylie! *Hombre!* You're here! I'm so glad. When did you get in?"

"This morning. Look, I'm sorry, but I don't have as much time as I had hoped. I'm with my boss, and he has me pretty solidly booked. I do have a window on Thursday in the late afternoon, around five, but I need to be at a dinner at seven. Does that work?" Most Barcelonans didn't eat until much later, but the hotel was used to accommodating foreign visitors.

"That'd be fine. Five, then. Shall I come to you?"

"Do you know where my hotel is?"

"Of course."

I was waiting in the lobby bar. Until this moment, I hadn't been nervous, but now I could feel my heart racing. With my foot tapping, I sipped my scotch and eagerly watched the door. I had been careful in choosing what I wore, my most elegant suit, a new silk tie. In my cuffs, the onyx links she had given me for Christmas years before.

In the past, Cesca would have swept in with a flourish, late, impossible to resist, and somehow managed to upend my world. This time I was prepared for her. My armor was thick. My resolve unbroken. This time the wax was in my ears.

So why see Cesca at all? Why not simply sail around the rocks and stay on the open ocean? I could have easily come to Barcelona without seeing her. In a city of this size, it is entirely possible that I could have spent my three days here without running into her. But it wasn't a sense of good manners or obligation that induced me to tell her I was coming, the way you might with an elderly female relative. No, when I wrote to Cesca, I convinced myself that my reason for suggesting we meet was entirely innocent. What, after all, could be the harm?

If pressed, I would probably say my reason for seeing her was to declare my manumission from her. To see in her face the realization of what she had lost in me and what I had become. To say: I have become a man, a husband, a father. This is what you could have had. To pay her back in a small way for all the agony she had caused me over the years.

But getting beyond my arrogance and petty pride, there was a deeper reason still. It was the most simple of all: I wanted to see her. With my own eyes. To again put a face I had once so cherished to her letters. To hear the sound of her voice again, the throaty laughter. In truth, I missed her. The way an exile misses his homeland or an old man misses his youth.

The deepest reason of all, as old as the race itself, was desire.

Though I did not admit it to myself, there was the secret hope that we were only a short elevator ride to my room, the quick shedding of clothes, the exquisite plunge into what was both known and forbidden, the urgent slap of flesh on flesh. It was a distinct possibility, a rekindling of long-lowered flames. It was the outcome I yearned for, and dreaded, most.

I had been there only a few minutes when, at the stroke of five, a woman appeared in the revolving door that led into the grand lobby. She had a scarf tied around her head and wore a long beige raincoat. At first I didn't recognize her. But when she removed the scarf, I knew it was Cesca. I came walking toward her, and, when she saw me, her face lit up with a wide smile. Raising both arms, she cried, "Wylie, *amor!*" I embraced her, inhaling the faint though familiar scent of jasmine and roses.

I led her to my table. "It's wonderful to see you," I said. A waiter had appeared, and I asked Cesca what she would like to drink.

"I'll just have some green tea," she said and, speaking to the waiter, ordered in Catalan.

There's something different about seeing someone after a while once we get past the age of thirty. Bodies change, skin begins to sag. For some it happens more quickly than for others. I met an old prep school friend of mine for a drink one evening after work. We hadn't seen each other since graduation. At school he had been lean, handsome, a gymnast. His hair long in the style that was current then. The man who came up to me saying "Wylie!" could not have been more different. Before me stood a fat, bald man, bearded and wearing glasses. It turned out he worked at our old school's development office. His purpose was not so much to renew an old acquaintance as it was to hit me up for a donation.

The Cesca who sat across from me now was not the same woman I had once known. The beauty was still there, but it was subdued, like an oil painting in need of restoring, the colors muted, the canvas slightly cracked. She was not yet forty but looked older. Her daily proximity to the dead and dying had leeched some of her natural vitality. There was a grayness to her now, as though she had spent too much time underground, deprived of light and air. She was thin, her jeans hung loosely about her legs. The lines in her face were more pronounced. Her hair was cropped short, and her clothes, I noticed, were worn, practical. On her feet an old pair of sneakers. The only ornamentation she wore was a small gold crucifix around her neck. She could have been a maid on her way home from work.

But time and usage had not damaged the crooked smile, the bewitching eyes. "Let me look at you," she said, smiling. She shook her head. "I can't believe it. After all this time. Here you are. You don't know how much I've been looking forward to it."

She asked to see photographs of my son, and I spent several minutes chattering about the mundane, unexpected joys of fatherhood, as well as the inevitable complaints of late nights, car sickness, the anxiety of getting into the right preschool. Already Kate wanted to have another.

"Is that what you want?" she asked.

"Yes, I suppose so. I never really wanted a child in the first place, but now that I have Mitch I can't imagine life without him."

"You're very lucky. I don't think I'll ever have children." She had told me about what had happened years ago with Blackwood.

"You still could."

She shook her head and smiled. "No. That's not God's plan for me, I think. A child requires a mother's full attention and love. I have too many other people that need me here. It wouldn't be right."

I didn't know what to say and filled the silence by ordering another scotch. "Would you like something to eat?" I offered. "They have some wonderful tapas here."

"No thank you. I'm not hungry. This tea is perfect."

There would be no elevator trip, I knew. The air of license that had once enveloped her like perfume had dissipated. The party was over. The band had gone home.

We talked about her work, where she lived. Her patients. "I don't go out very much anymore," she said. "This is a real treat."

"Are you happy here?" I asked. "Doing what you do?"

She nodded her head. "Very. Why? Don't I seem it?"

"I can't tell. You've changed so much."

"Yes, I suppose I have. I don't think that's a bad thing though, do you? It's not like I was happy before."

"Weren't you? You always seemed to be having a good time."

"Well, that's just it, isn't it? A good time and happiness are completely different. The one is a form of restlessness, a kind of fear of inadequacy. The other is its antithesis—peace. That's how I feel now. At peace."

I sat there comprehending while she sipped her tea. For some reason, her words made me think of the story of Ferdinand the bull. How he had this powerful body built for fighting, but all he wanted to do was smell the flowers. The paths we follow are not always the obvious ones.

"I'm glad for you," I said. "So does that mean you won't be coming back to New York? To Amagansett?"

"Oh, I don't know. I won't rule out anything. I don't miss the city, but I do miss Amagansett. It's my home more than any-where else, even if there are so few of us left now. Maybe I'll go back next year. For Christmas. We'll see."

"And you mean to stay in Barcelona and keep working at the hospice?"

She put down her cup. "That's another question. I feel that

I can do so much here, but there is great need elsewhere. It's no great hardship living in Barcelona. It's a beautiful city, safe, clean. I'd love to stay, but we'll see. Maybe there are other places in the world where I'm needed more." She shrugged and smiled. "Who knows?"

There is something daunting about encountering people more selfless than you are. It is why we show respect to priests, to the sick and crippled, to winners of the Medal of Honor; they have given up more than we ever will. While the rest of humanity tries to figure out how to make our lives easier and more comfortable, they know what it is to suffer; even greater, how to ease suffering. They have come through the refining fire and emerged on the other side, changed, purer.

I didn't know what to say to Cesca. She had chosen the greatest fight of all: to fight death knowing there was never any hope of victory. From me, though, any encouragement would have sounded hollow, false. I had no basis on which to form a judgment; her world of pain and open sores and daily mortality was far from my hyperbaric world of worrying about elevation heights, courting clients, and commuting to the office. I couldn't blurt out that her life would be nothing but an endless cycle of pain and suffering. Because, after all, was it? Her choice was the heroic one. There are those people for whom the arduous way is the only way.

I was ashamed that I found such a course unthinkable. But she had always been braver than me. She, like all her family, was a risk taker. Uncowed by second thoughts, willing to dive from the high board on a dare, or climb the tree and leap onto the roof. And I would always be the one wishing I was them.

It was time for her to go. She stood up, gathering her still-damp coat. I didn't want her to leave yet. There was still so much to discuss. "Wait, stay and have dinner with me," I said.

"I'd love to, but I can't. I need to return to the hospice. One of my patients needs me. Besides, I thought you said you had plans tonight."

"I do. But I can get out of them."

She shook her head. "No, but it would be nice to spend some more time." We were facing each other, and she took my hands in hers and said, "Tricky Wylie. It's so good to see you again. I see you still have the cuff links."

"Of course."

She smiled and rolled up the sleeve of her sweater to reveal the used Cartier watch I had given her years before. "It is the last little luxury I permit myself. It makes me think of you."

I blushed. "I don't know what to say."

"Don't say anything. Just be happy. You'll still write me? I enjoy your letters. I always have."

"I enjoy yours too. You write a wonderful letter. Too bad I didn't find that out until recently."

She giggled. "I know. I was shameful. But I've tried to mend my ways."

"I promise I'll write. Good luck."

"Thank you." She leaned forward and embraced me, and I held her tightly, feeling the warmth of her body, its lean but supple strength. She could live on locusts and rainwater. "Take care, Tricky Wylie," she whispered in my ear.

"No, you take care."

She looked at me for a second with the old mischievous flash of fire, the promise of sin in her eye, and released my hand. "I will. God bless you. *Adéu*."

I watched her walk away, stopping just before the revolving door, over which sat an ormolu clock and flanked by a brace of massive green marble columns. She turned and, with a smile, gave a final wave before disappearing into the street.

EPILOGUE

THE SKY OUTSIDE WAS TURNING ORANGE AND PURPLE. I had decided what to keep and what to throw out. What I did not want went into the Dumpster. The work was tiring, down four flights of stairs, out to the front yard, and back up again, two steps at a time, empty-handed. Despite the cool, I removed my coat. The exertion made it easier to act though. The only thing I felt when I threw a box over the side of the Dumpster and watched it spill open on impact was the desire to go up and bring back another. There is a strange satisfaction in smashing one's past. It was liberating even if it hurt. There is no point in being halfhearted about it. Don't just give them a little shove, take a hammer to them, burn them to the ground. Do the job good and proper.

By the time I was finished, the sun was almost down. It would be my last sunset here. The ghosts of summer lingered in the air.

With my few treasures in the back of my car, I walked out of the house for the last time. I got in my car and retreated down the driveway, abandoning it like a defeated fort. Its loss would take years to truly sink in. It was, after all, my home. Rooms I knew so well would appear unbidden in my dreams, come to mind in idle conversation, or be reflected in the morning light if it shone in a certain way. I was now unmoored, a ship without a port. I was prepared to be asked, "Didn't you used to have a place out there?" I would answer vaguely in the affirmative. We can only have one place of innocence, and this was mine.

There was one more visit to make, one more last good-bye. I drove farther east as darkness descended, down country roads that hinted at a disappearing rural past, adding time to my return trip to the city. Half an hour later, I stopped by a low split-rail fence and turned left.

I had only been there before in daytime. My headlights reflected off the gravestones. Fallen leaves lay on the ground. The air was still, silent. There was a smell of woodsmoke from someone's house to keep out the cold. A light in the distance. Otherwise it was black. From inside the car, I couldn't see stars, but I knew they were there.

Many artists and writers have been buried here. Pollock, Krasner, Liebling, his wife. More recently, Paolo and Esther. Also local families; working men and their wives; children who lived only a few years interred beneath humble, untended graves. In the corner was a large plot surrounding a dark marble monolith with a Star of David, and the name BAUM carved deeply in the midsection. Around it were several smaller stones. I stopped the engine but left the lights on so that they shone on the graves. I knew where I was going.

The biggest stone had the names Isidore Baum and Ruth Baum inscribed on it. Next to that was a smaller stone with Aurelio's name and the dates of his short life. It was hard to believe how many years had passed since his death. A brief epitaph: *AMB L'AMOR DE LA SEVA FAMÍLIA.* With love from his family.

There was one other grave, this one more recent. Cesca's.

SHE HAD BEEN AS GOOD AS HER WORD. SHE HAD GONE where the need was greatest. Several months after I saw her in Barcelona, she had volunteered to go to Rwanda. In one of her last letters, she had written:

> *The people here are desperate. Not only is AIDS running unchecked here but there's a terrible civil war too. Thousands of people are dying every day. Men, women, children. They have almost no one to help them. You wouldn't believe the conditions even if I told you. It's a nightmare and we live in a constant state of fear. But something needs to be done. There are only a few NGOs willing to help. If we don't do it, then the human misery will be even higher. The group I'm with is one of the best, though. We have a strong international reputation, a huge donor network, first-rate logistics, and dedicated doctors. Every day we manage to save lives, but there are so many we can't. It's heartbreaking but I wouldn't want to be anywhere else or doing anything else. I hope you don't think that sounds too crazy. Here I have a purpose. I don't know if you pray, Tricky Wylie, but if you do, don't pray for me. I already feel God's love. Pray for the souls of those who need His help more.*

I had heard about the slaughters there. Seen photographs in the *Times* of the hundreds of bloated bodies littering the shores of Lake Kivu. I couldn't imagine the horror of the place. But like a fireman, she was intent on running toward the conflagration, not away from it.

She had been killed two months after arriving in Rwanda.

There had been a mortar attack on the village where she worked and lived. It wasn't clear at first which side was responsible.

Kate had called me with the news. She had been at home, the television on in the background. She thought she'd heard a familiar name and ran into the room. A reporter in a flak jacket with a British accent was standing in front of a smoldering building. "The attack took place before dawn . . ." It had been a massacre, a dozen or so villagers killed, several Western aid workers. One of them American. Francesca Bonet. A blurry image from her wilder days appeared briefly on screen. Kate quickly dialed the phone.

It was all over the news for several days. The *Times* published several sober background pieces on the civil war, and the peril faced by doctors and aid workers in that part of the world. There was also a small obituary that focused mainly on Izzy and Cosmo, and Cesca's relationship to them. It was not enough that she had died. There had to be something notable about her. It was not enough simply to have been killed thousands of miles from one's home, helping people incapable of helping themselves. The black-and-white photograph they ran of her was perfect though. It had been taken in her twenties on the beach in Amagansett; a slight strand of loose hair blown across her cheek, she looked simple, natural, sweet as a girl. Kitty had given it to them. People were asked in lieu of flowers to send money to several different charities. A memorial would be held at an unspecified date in the future.

The tabloids, predictably, ran titillating headlines such as TRAGIC HEIRESS and MILLIONAIRE MARTYR. I could barely read the words. It was like a review of an opera that focused only on the first act. There were several photos of Cesca taken at various parties. One was at Studio 54 sitting between Andy Warhol and Truman Capote. In each she looked radiant, the cynosure of all eyes. Those articles too mentioned Izzy, Cosmo, the family's wealth and support of the arts, and, briefly, referred to Aurelio's death. Several people were cited in the story, claiming to be "old friends" and saying how Cesca was trying to "turn her life around," but I had never heard of any of them.

Even more irritating was how inaccurately they depicted Cesca, as though she was not a real woman but a stereotypical poor little rich girl. Someone with more money than sense, whose self-destruction was brought about by self-indulgence. What they missed was her humor, her intelligence, her sensitivity, her appetite for life, her humanity, her nobility. She had ceased being a person and become a cautionary tale. Of all that was unfair about her death, this might have been the most unfair of all.

There was, finally, a more moving tribute, thoughtfully written several months after her death, appearing in a small Catholic magazine. It paid homage to the sacrifice Cesca had made, recognizing the spirit of compassion that had driven her to reject her former life and embrace the suffering of unknown others. The author had obviously done her research and had spoken to a number of people who had known her. Kitty was quoted. Cosmo. A few of those she had worked with in Barcelona and, finally, in the little village outside Kigali where she had died. One of them, a Dutch nun, said: "When she first arrived, we had no idea who she was, or where she came from. It was obvious that she was extremely lovely, but she gave no indication whatsoever of vanity. She never complained. We only found out that she was rich after she died. She was there to work, to heal. I could see she was a tortured soul, though. She had found God in the end. There's great comfort in that, bless her."

During this time, I could barely function. I stumbled through my days, feeling sick to my stomach. The surreal shock of hearing Cesca's name mentioned on television, seeing her face stare up at me from the newsstand. Even though we had parted ways for what I had assumed was the last time, a part of me still died with her. Waking up in a cold sweat, feeling like an amputee, automatically reaching for a phantom limb, only to remember it is gone and will never be there again. For many nights, after Kate had gone to bed, I sat up in the living room, unable to sleep.

Kate and I attended the memorial held at a Catholic church downtown. It was crowded, drawing not only those mourners who knew Cesca or the family but also the ghoulishly curious. I saw a number of people I recognized but hung back, seeking to blend in with the crowd, and found a seat at the rear of the church.

Lio. Cesca. Death had come too early and too often to this family, as though they were forced to pay a grim levy for the excess of their gifts. I prayed for them all, adding an extra prayer that I would not have to mourn for this family again for a while. That they had given enough.

In the front pew I spotted Kitty, looking shattered. I could only imagine her grief, having to bury another of her children. And such children. Such beauty. Such unrealized promise. How could that happen? It was cruel. Shocking. What would she do? Roam from room to room in the darkness like a madwoman? Lock herself in Cesca's room, weeping over the detritus of her daughter's life? Curse God? Or would she have been sedated by a friendly doctor? The human brain can only absorb so much pain before it begins to shut itself down. I wanted to reach out to her. To offer myself as a vehicle on which she could pour out her tears, her anger, her agony. I felt I owed that much to Cesca, to the whole family.

But I also didn't want to intrude, to disturb them in their bereavement, the minor family friend unwelcomely breaking the silence with a finger on the doorbell or a call on the phone.

And, in their eyes, who was I to share their pain, after all? Did I even have the right? The privilege to mourn Cesca as they did? It would be like commiserating with the thief who burgled you.

Cesca would have laughed at my situation, would have felt no such compunction. She was never afraid to show her emotions. She would have marched right up and said what she had to say, always finding the right words, the right tone. She was like an animal who ate when she was hungry and slept when she was tired. Her needs and wants were straightforward, vital, uncomplicated. Come on, *hombre,* she would say to me. I need to fuck now. And we would.

Several weeks after the memorial, I received a letter from a law firm. It informed me that their client Ms. Francesca Bonet had left me a small bequest. A painting. If I would contact them and give my address they would send it to me. I replied, asking that it be delivered to my office. The painting arrived via registered mail rolled in a large cardboard tube. I signed the receipt and closed the door. There were no instructions, no note.

But I had a suspicion of what the painting might be. Was there any other canvas she would leave me? Among her many talents, painting was not one of them, so I doubted it would be anything of her own creation. Nor was it likely to be something random. A simple objet d'art or memento. No, there could be only one explanation. I tore off the tape that sealed the tube and eagerly shook the canvas out, tantalized by the rough, unpainted surface of the verso side. A few glimpses of color daubed at the edges. But I knew immediately I had been right.

It was Aurelio's nude. *Cesca en la llum de la lluna.* I had not seen it for years, but it had always stayed with me, since that first time in his studio on the Barrio Chino, years before. How proud of it he had been. How dazzled I had been. There she lay, Cesca in the glory of her youth, bold, provocative, as stirring as an ode, as desirable as love. I remembered those breasts, those thighs, they were as familiar to me as my own body. I felt my breath catch, my pulse tremble. The memories it brought back. The emotions. The never-ending sadness at her loss.

And then I had to laugh. Admiring her playfulness, her sense of humor. It was just the sort of thing she would do. She had hit me an unreturnable shot. Who's tricky now, Tricky Wylie? I could almost hear her say. The crooked smile, the wink that was as inclusive as a shared secret, the sweep of her life. Do not forget me, she was saying. I won't let you forget me.

As if I ever could. She was still always in my mind, my default daydream. I would see her on street corners, in crowds, the head that just turned, the person who had just left the room. She was still everywhere to me. If I closed my eyes, I could still hear her voice, feel her touch.

But it was too much. I knew I couldn't keep the painting in my office, and my apartment was out of the question. I felt like a bank robber who was sitting on a fortune but couldn't spend a nickel of it for fear of being caught. The thought of it hanging anywhere else, where it might be seen by strangers, was abhorrent. I had a horror of it winding up over a bar or in the den of some aging playboy or even in the hands of one of my descendants. *What was Uncle Wylie thinking? He must have been quite a dog in his day.*

No, Cesca had given it to me for a reason: It was to be a reminder, but I was also supposed to protect it. So I had placed it in the attic of my father's house, burying it like a pot of gold, placing it like an ark behind a curtain, never thinking I would need to move it until long after it had ceased to matter. Knowing that one day I might destroy it, but not yet. Maybe, when I was old and the memory of my youth had begun to fade, I would take out the portrait and look at it, and remind myself that some loves are not meant to be, no matter how badly you might want them.

I PLACED MY HAND ON THE COLD STONE. I WAS DRAINED from saying good-bye. Lio, Paolo, Esther, my father, my house, Cesca. The ones whom I loved most, who had shaped me for good or ill, were gone. A new man stood there beside her grave. The last lines had been cut. The barque was moving out into the open water in search of an unknown shore. I wasn't too old, not yet. There would be new shoals, new hazards, new lands to explore, but the old ones were gone forever.

Silently, I offered up a prayer for Cesca, thanking her for all she had given me and all I had taken from her. Remembering her as a child, a girl, a woman. The swell of her. The sounds she made when she slept. Laughter. The unprovoked kindnesses. The knot in my stomach whenever I saw her. The shock of her beauty. The first time I had gazed upon her naked body. On the beach. That summer many years ago now. In the moonlight. She was never mine, but I would always be hers.

In the end she achieved greatness, the only kind that really matters.

When I returned home late that night, Kate was waiting. Our son asleep in his room. "Are you all right?" she asked.

"Yes," I said, kissing her on the cheek, thankful for her presence. "Never better."

All that remains is a sacred memory.

ACKNOWLEDGMENTS

I AM FORTUNATE THAT SO MANY OF THE PEOPLE WHO SUP-
ported and encouraged the writing of my first novel, *Indiscretion,*
were there for this book too. First and foremost was my editor
Henry Ferris. Like all great editors, he combined the traits of
an indulgent parent, a skeptical teacher, a boon companion, a
skilled boxer, and a learned physician. He knew when to coax,
when to question, when to laugh, when to knock me to the mat,
and, most important, when to make things better. I have now
had the privilege of writing two books for him and know always
to trust him because he is always right. Thank you, Henry.

I am very grateful not only to work with Henry but also with
the rest of the team at William Morrow/HarperCollins, in particular Sharyn Rosenblum, public relations diva extraordinaire.

I also want to single out a few people who read the various
versions of the manuscript and thank them for their patience
and enthusiasm. Chief among them is Liz Warner, who loved
every version and actually took the time to read each one. My

old boss at Forbes.com, David Churbuck, was, as always, generous with his time and overgenerous with his praise.

Further, I want to thank my new agent, Jennifer Joel at ICM, for her shrewd insight and refusal to settle for anything but the best.

Last, I would like to thank my family for their love and support. My children, William and Lally; my mother, Isabella; my stepmother, Barbara; and my beautiful wife, Melinda.